AFRICA, LOVE

Volume 3 of the New Africa Chronicles

John Hatch

Story consultant, the poet Angela Jackson

Cover art by Harold Beaulieu, The Art Department

Design and composition by Archetype Typography, Berkeley, California

Manufactured in U.S.A.

Published by 2ndsightbooks.com
P.O. Box 5277
Berkeley, CA 94705

ISBN #0-9706854-1-6
Library of Congress Catalogue #2002092597

 The chapter header in this book is a swamp cypress needle cluster.

To loving and dreaming

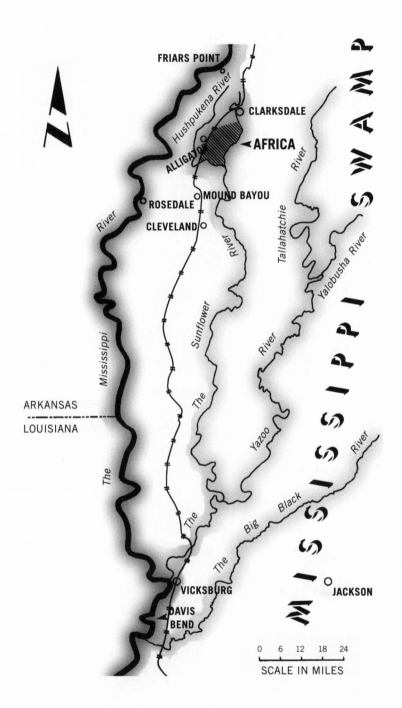

FRIARS POINT

Hushpukena River

CLARKSDALE

◄AFRICA

ALLIGATOR

River

MOUND BAYOU

ROSEDALE

CLEVELAND

River

Sunflower

River

Tallahatchie

Yalobusha River

River

The

Yazoo

Mississippi

ARKANSAS

LOUISIANA

The

Big

Black

River

The

The

VICKSBURG

JACKSON

DAVIS
BEND

M I S S I S S I P P I   S W A M P

0   6   12   18   24

SCALE IN MILES

Inside of a blackness touched by light from a minor star, this earth and all that will be simply is or it isn't. Cycles of dark followed by light have their way. Elements degrade into common dirt, and into all dirt some life must fall. An ancient wind chants this mystery through the swamp followed always by the rain. It drums the usually tranquil black water into a million tiny sounding craters. Close upon this deluge of noise, as if to fulfill its ominous promise, comes the flood.

As the grip of winter loosens and far away ice and snow melt, all of the great rivers grow large and rush into the Mississippi River. This Father of Rivers swells up moving south, and it throws an impossible burden against its banks, until so much sediment is knocked loose that the bottom rises, and a torrent of water and mud is unleashed across the land. When it recedes, the ridges defining streams and bayous begin again to hem in swimming and crawling life.

Come summer, a soggy firmament emerges, and seasonal life finds soil upon which to battle for sunlight beneath the ancient cypress, gum, willow, cedar and oak on the high ground. By autumn, all water has returned to land-locked streams and bayous darkening beneath a film of rotting leaves and spores. Everything above water begins to parch and to crack like an aging human face. Then will come again the time of sharp things, thorns and cutting cane leaves, weapons of winter.

Such was The Great Mississippi Swamp, a hot and steamy matrix of inland rivers and sloughs so rich, so teaming with life and towering ancient trees that darkness prevailed at noon. A chief named Chocsas guided his own into these lands. They migrated from camp to camp and grew and prospered until a yet newer group piled out of boats that arrived on Gulf currents. These newer people took over the Gulf coast. They cut trees for houses, gouged furrows into the land. New laws announced that no one before them had owned anything, and the most sacred of the old memories became sacrilege. They who would become the new keepers of recall judged the before-people vagrant for moving off and returning to land from which by custom they had always hunted and fished. Under threat of being killed like varmints, the before-people were forced away with only such history as their singers could hold on their tongues.

Even so, the Great Swamp remained a place so full of shadow and magic that once the water wet a man's feet and he heard the spirit hawk sing never would he choose to leave. In the time between the land-taking and the new people going to war among themselves, an uprooted white swarm rushed in to exploit this land, to plunder its force of life to make a new one for themselves.

For those snatched from Africa and abused into slavery, as minds cleared and hearts opened full tide with freedom, the swamp offered many a take-what-you-need life as an alternative to turning their fresh lives over to another. Tasting freedom, they rejoiced too madly to allow a frontier economy of exploit and prosper to again make them victim. Nor did the taking of wealth out of another's life seem right, memory of slavery being so close. So, into a wild new world they moved, claimed sanctuary to live apart.

Recall of these who picked up pieces of their lives and lived ad lib is fragmentary, but that is the chronicle being pieced together. In their shadowy new home of meandering water, communities traded with each other, but a prevailing fear of strangers kept them isolated. Even so, like so many grains of sand sharing the slope of a bayou, individuals dislodged by life-giving rain would sooner or later be observed to rub up against and nudge his/her neighbor to tumble into some more intimate connection. As the seasons changed, an infinite green morphed in a thousand leaf and spore colors in fall, much like the trials and errors of a people imposing passed-down shards of Africa memory onto each and every day.

ONCE SANCTUARY FOR OUTLAWS who preyed on steamboats, a narrow strip of land along the Mississippi River was now being farmed. It had been clean-cut for wood to fuel steam boats. There were a few settlements further inland but only on bayous that could provide transportation in and out because the interior of The Great Swamp was said to be full of fever lurking to fell the foolhardy. Not many of the Before-people remained either because so many who'd refused to be marched away in the 1830's had died or fallen victim to hostility. Most who now clung to the sanctuary of the swamp traced their blood back to Africa, as did Jasper and Verlean.

The rangy young man had broad shoulders from a lifetime of paddling and portaging boats between streams, and yet his face was as smooth as black velvet. Lying beside him on a pile of quilts was a young woman with her own well-fed proportion in limbs that were sensually dark as water at night. Beautiful, he had just called her and said that she looked like his mother. A thigh damp from exertion slid like silk across his lean naked torso as the woman raised up to speak.

"We could bring so much progress to this old swamp, Jasper—"

She closed her mouth and smiled as Jasper raised his beardless chin up close, but instead of a kiss, his callused hand seized her leg.

"Verlean, I ain't buildin' *nothin'*!"

"Why you use that tone o' voice?"

Jasper's response was to sigh. He closed his eyes and lay back down. Tenderly, his broad rough working hands began caressing Verlean's perspired skin, pulling her thigh back across his own.

"I swear," Verlean said, "you'n your momma musta had some real hard times."

"Why you talkin' about my momma?"

"Say I look like her—do you jump salty like this with her? It's time you built me a new cabin."

"I wish you'd ask 'steadda tellin' me what to do."

"So, what's your answer?"

"Non."

When Jasper first met Verlean, she had been a jolly girl of sixteen who was always laughing, laughing at him, at birds, at her old mother and aunt, at the green world around them. Their piece of that world stretched twenty miles from the Mississippi River on the west to the Sunflower River on the east, hundreds of square miles, much more than Verlean had ever explored while a girl child whose mother felt trapped in the swamp. Verlean lived on the Bogue Phalia, a sometime fierce flow of water a few mile inland from the big river beyond its ribbon of cleared land. As a girl, she once paddled to the headwaters of the Bogue and spent all day swimming and fishing until darkness sneaked up on her. To avoid an outburst of her mother's wrath, she slept alone in the swamp for a week and every evening left game she trapped on her mother's porch, until the woman could cool off and yell for her to come home.

Dirt poor, perhaps, and yet poverty is a relative concept and not very useful to those inside the swamp who owned a boat or two, and a place to sleep. Not to say that how people lived did not reflect differences of mind. Verlean's mother called Jasper a no-count even before she recognized his interest in her daughter. "Hard-livin' whiskey nigga" was the phrase, she used, and it took the young people more than a year to fight through her hostility. Jasper's mind never registered the slight, just that the woman didn't like him. To him, the old woman was different in a most basic way: she still thought like an outsider to the swamp.

Tragedy had brought a lot of people into the swamp who would not have planned it. With the death of her first husband at the hands of a vengeful overseer, Verlean's mother and her younger sister and sister's husband had been thrown off sharecrop land along the big river. A kindly old black man with the manners of a true gentleman had shown them pity, offered to allow the woman who would become Verlean's mother and her relatives to share his home. The need was so great, it had not mattered that the cabin was located more than a day's walk inside the swamp, not at first.

The odd-featured house consisted of logs stacked horizontally and stabilized at the corners by still-living trees, a more organic shape than square, and because the old man built the house way back while some of the Before-people remained, they had helped him. They went along with him using trees to build like the whites, but they warned him that the lowest logs should be left with gaps and space for the water to percolate through during flood. The floor was jerry-rigged upon a base of extended stumps—trees cut all at a comparable height—on top of which split logs had been notched into the walls as runners, floor boards on top of that. From that point up it was rough log walls and a roof like any cabin. Nearby stood abandoned older shelters, cane floors suspended on top of hacked away cypress knees in the edges of a bayou, window coverings woven from cane fronds attached to poles. Bent saplings tied together defined what had been walls and ceilings, now covered with decaying leaves and cane that had not been replaced for many seasons.

As Verlean's mother's temporary sojourn in the swamp stretched out, she became involved with her host and found herself with child. One of her ravings against lack of ambition led to a great bonfire into which she and everyone except Verlean's father helped drag the remnants of all of the "heathen" dwellings nearby, beginning with one the old man had shared with a woman who had chosen to relocate with her tribe to Indian Territory.

And so Verlean was born. A childhood later, after meeting Jasper and with him as her guide, adult Verlean visited for the first time the river of the flowers in summer. The banks of that river studded with huge yellow blossoms filled her eyes with tears. The Sunflower River had gouged its way for centuries thru layers of silt. Monumental banks grew higher by inches with each flood that would fill the river's cavern and then pour over its banks to deposit more sediment on top. After the water retreated, the gorge would fill up with quick-growing brush and cane—giant sunflowers, here in point, flaunting beauty as if oblivious to winter.

To show Verlean all that beauty, Jasper had paddled them in on the east-west branch of another swamp stream, the Huspuckena. Like a weakling's arm, it came down from the north but bent easterly to flow into the Sunflower. Waters in the Huspuckena retreated so low by late summer that its ridges were looming twenty feet over Jasper's head as he stood up to paddle the canoe. He lost his balance when Verlean screamed and jumped as if to avoid a surfacing gar fish. Her teeth bared in laughter were reflected through the water overboard as Jasper closed his own mouth before surfacing. Verlean's wager, that if Jasper could paddle a canoe standing up he could have her, was not collected that night. He slept in a separate bedroll as he had been doing for what seemed much too long, since Verlean first smiled toward him more than a year before.

"If I cain't whup him, I'll shoot the man put his hand on me," she'd warned.

Time alone is almost as deadly as a moccasin. It poisons social sense, can encourage violence and odd behavior, and while to avoid becoming odd was not at all why Jasper and Verlean spent time together, each had reason to celebrate finding a companionable person born to the swamp. Acting big and bad was Verlean's brand of beautiful, late dividend child that she was, and born to a mother given to raging against her fate because she'd thought herself beyond childbearing. Verlean's father died of old age the year Verlean met Jasper. Verlean's aunt at the time, the youngest adult she lived with, was forty-some years older. By reckoning, Jasper was a mere six.

Plying his trade had brought Jasper to Verlean's family camp, and his returning every three or four months after that proved just enough of a demonstration of interest not to ruffle Verlean's feathers, or her mother's. Jasper had been roaming around for almost a month before he met Verlean. All because Cicero Morgan, the man who would become his stepfather, had finally arrived to join Jasper's mother and to make the swamp his home. Jasper had stayed away because going back home meant he'd have to build a new cabin for himself, and he hated doing anything to disturb the face of the swamp.

When he finally did return home, Bill Williams, the little man who was half Choctaw, intercepted him near the area they all used in common. Bill took him by the hand and led him away to haul whiskey and, for the first time, to meet Verlean. In the coming years, her family on the Bogue Phalia came to celebrate Old Bill's visits. Verlean, however, had not yet been taken home to meet Jasper's mother, Rose. Actually, Rose was eager to meet Verlean because Rose wanted grandchildren. Jasper's not bringing Verlean home had been noted by all.

Stubborn grains of sand, both young people, it would take years after noticing each other for them finally to tumble. Now, some years following that first time, smiles and languid touches were stretching an intimate moment from afternoon into dusk. They had been making love on a pallet inside Verlean's tiny cabin. Its rough logs nestled on a ridge knee-high above a bayou off the Bogue that had been damned with soil and hacked away woody burl from cypress trees against washing out the cabin in a big flow. It was a sturdy small room that Jasper had helped Verlean to build in order for them to escape her autocratic mother. He had damned the nearby waters to make it more secure.

"Verlean, your stuff is too good to leave alone."

"You ought to come live with me."

"Non."

"Why not?"

"You was born in this swamp, but your ma's people came from outside, and you all think different."

"What's wrong with us havin' some pride?"

"Your folks cut more logs'n anybody I ever known for buildin', and you cut real close to where you live. Tell the whole world you here. Your momma got a trail cleared from her front door down to the Bogue and on around to her outhouse. She burnt a clearin' around it for all to see 'cause she scared o' snakes . . . You two fight so much I'm surprised you takin' up for her. "

"She still my momma."

"Alright . . . I love my momma, and I didn't have a daddy—not to my acquaintance, that is. One man who wanted to be my daddy, momma wouldn't have him. He was the brother of the man name, Mack, who headed the family what raised me. Mack spent a lotta time alone, and I'm same as him that way, people like me or they don't. So with your momma so set on changin' this swamp—and you think like her—make me see how much I think like old Mack about where I live.

"That man would whale the daylights outta me. Then he be laughin' his ass off, an' he'd say, A man cain't do no worse'n be wrong. He be lookin' at me laughin' 'cause he caught me doin' somethin' I wasn't supposed to. He be hittin' on me and sayin', A man cain't do no worse'n be wrong. Sometime I think I was wrong for somethin' I did. Next, I be thinkin' he sayin' somethin' like it don't matter what I done, and if I wasn't a fool child I would know it.

"Mack was a hellion. I'll always remember him sayin', A man cain't do no worse'n be wrong. What he really meant was, Nigga, when you big enough to beat me back, then I stop beatin' on you . . . That's what a man have to do. You a man, you got to stomp a snake, shoot a bear, break a fool's head open—no way you got time to worry about what's right ... Like if you was a slave runnin' for freedom an' worried about killin' white folks—Un unh! They catch your sorry ass 'cause worryin' waste time."

"Sound horrible, Jasper."

"Lemme finish . . . I done killed, see? And I ain't shame I had to do it. I'm like that. I do what I have to do. So I cain't be checkin' with somebody to see if *they* think I'm right. Got only the time o' threat to act—quick! Cain't discuss it."

"Momma say problem is, you swamp-backward."

Jasper licked his lips before replying.

"Verlean, if we was livin' in the same house, fightin' over difference wouldn't be no fun."

Verlean shoved her elbow up under Jasper's neck and began pushing as if to crawl out from under him.

"Aw, baby!" Jasper locked his arms and held on. "Keep your pretty brown eyes lookin' up at me."

From outside the cabin, came the sound of someone coughing. Jasper leapt up and began jerking on his pants as a disheveled looking man eased the door open.

"Do a Miz Verlean live heah?"

"Who wants me?" Verlean asked.

"'Scuse me, mister," the man said to Jasper, jerking a

coonskin cap off a bald head shades lighter than his sun-blackened face. "Pa name me Vern. Me'n Verlean has de same pa, different ma's."

"Well, I'll be snookered. Vern? Sure is you. Jasper, this my old daddy's oldest boy. He was full-growed when I was born. Lord a mercy."

"My l'il bear woman sis. How you been?"

"Just fine, Vern. Is your people moved back?"

"Naw," Vern said, shy eyes unable to avoid naked Verlean, "jus useless me."

"Why you come here?" Verlean asked.

The man shifted on his feet until he came to a decision. The palm of one hand gestured toward Verlean.

"De government takin' back lan' in Injun Ter'tory dey give dem tribes . . ."

Then the man held his other hand toward Jasper.

". . . So some o' us dat went out dere wit 'em, we movin' on. Me, I come where I were raise up."

"You couldda been shot walkin' in like that," Jasper said, pulling on deerskin trousers.

"Guess so, but I snuck up to de window, seen what y'all was doin' 'fore I cough. A man ain't got but so much feelin', gi'en what you was at."

"You got any more name than Vern?"

"Naw."

"Me neither. I was born in the swamp, too. Over in Louisiana. My momma run away from bein' a slave when I was born."

Jasper sat cross-legged on the bedding.

"My pa run-away and come to dis camp," Vern said, dropping to sit beside Jasper. "A tribal woman become my ma, an' dat was 'round Big Treaty time goin' on fifty year now. Verlean dere, didn't come 'long 'till after de North-South war. Dat's what brung me back."

"How you mean?" Verlean asked.

There was a moment of silence as the two men watched Verlean begin dressing. Then, as if Verlean's question had just registered, Vern balled up his fist and shook a finger toward his half-sister.

"It was dem Injun agents! Dey got mos' Injuns to side with de Rebels . . . So now, de gov'ment is takin' back land to punish 'em. My momma's one piece cain't feed grandchillen on top o' chillen."

"You hungry?" Verlean asked.

"Been walkin' an' paddlin' for weeks."

"Well make yourself home 'cause Big Verlean gonna cook us a welcome home supper."

That night, Jasper's whiskey made the mood even more congenial.

"What you of a mind to do," he asked, "now that you're back?"

"I kin'a fancy dat ridge where de Bogue is deepest. I could raise a cabin dere. You ain't mindin', is you?"

"Take him days to come after you if he did mind," Verlean said

"I kin talk for myself," Jasper said. "Anybody help me guard this swamp is alright by me."

"This here is momma's camp," Verlean said. "Jasper ain't got no permission to give."

Vern chuckled, wiped his nose. Jasper said nothing, but he clapped the newcomer on the back.

"Thankee kin'ly, Jasper. Jus glad I got here before dem new white folks climbin' all over the Ter'tory. So many, I 'spect dey stumble down dis way soon."

"Non, I don't let nobody come thru. They used to beat me as a boy—man named Mack did. Wasn't a man 'till you learnt how to control where you live."

"Dem immigrants is so po, dey live anywhere."

"Won't be so easy," Verlean said, "findin' they way around in this evil swamp."

"Dat's why a railroad comin', to haul out timber an' clear de lan."

"I be damn!"

"So, young Jasper, you has seen 'em?"

"Well, yeah. Told my momma'n her man I seen 'em blastin' tree stumps outside Clarksdale up the Sunflower, and I knew it was more than farmin'."

"Shiiit!" Vern said. "You ain't seen nothin' yet."

"So, what is immigrants?"

"Jasper, like if somebody favored you steadda dem white folks was to say, You free! Go gitchu some land! Take it from an'body you please! . . . Tha's what immigrants is. Don't know wheah dey come from, but dey take over your land an' kill you fer complainin'."

"Sound like you, Jasper," Verlean said slyly. "Wanna kill me for complainin'. We ain't no Injuns, an' if progress is near I want more'n this teeny-tiny cabin."

"Verlean, my job is keeping this swamp the way it is. If new folk comin' in is progress, ain't gonna be none. This swamp is still big enough for me'n my momma's family to hide in— yours too. Buildin' you a big house ain't part o' my job."

"Neither is you sleepin' here."

There was a long silence. A lone wolf howled in the distance as Jasper reached for his shirt, stood up and headed for the door.

"Jasper! Where you goin'?"

Verlean made it to the door after it slammed, but by the time she had opened it and stepped outside, she could no longer see Jasper in the dark. His angry feet were crashing through the undergrowth toward the Huspuckena and what Verlean knew was his way home. Cursing came faintly to her ears, then a howl, as if Jasper had blundered into something painful.

AFTER FLOOD SEASON, WATER percolates into the ground or flows away along bayous and rivers south into the Yazoo River and on back into the Mississippi from which it comes. Of course, mud dries and flakes and becomes dirt again, and by the end of a dry, hot summer, land-locked veins of stagnant water nurture clouds of mosquitoes.

So many of them had bitten Chester Bolls, he drew his blanket over his reddening face and silently cursed. The man alongside him had left a lantern flickering on the seat of the wagon parked on a dirt trail just south of Clarksdale. This man was something of a mystery. Square jawed and sallow of skin, he had joined the crew in Clarksdale and told everyone to call him Banyak. He wore his straight black hair parted down the middle as if to match the gap between his front teeth.

"Is it true dey got bears and tigers in this swamp, Chester?

"No sir, Mr. Banyak. Ain't no tigers never been in here. They's plenty bears'n wildcats, though. Try to rest easy. You got important work, tomorrow."

"Sir, do not tell me my business."

"Oh yeah, pardon me . . . Who you actually work for?"

"De Illinois Central outta New York."

"What they got to do with the Yazoo & Mis'ssippi Valley Railroad?"

"Immigrant like me, Chester, dey don't pay me to talk."

Chester Bolls was in charge of a railroad survey party. A redhead with a club-foot, he was too small to prevail in a brawl, but everyone liked him. Besides, his sister was married to the Yazoo & Mississippi Valley construction boss, and blood is thicker than swamp water. All of the men would have called themselves white.

Since the Civil War, railroad track had been extended only a few miles below Memphis into what would in another century be known as the Mississippi Delta. Barges on the hundred-mile long Sunflower River and steamboats on the Mississippi remained the only way to ship cotton. Now, an immense new railroad was on the drawing board. It would slice through more than a hundred miles of swamp from Clarksdale to Vicksburg.

Two youngsters were curled up under the wagon.

"Psst, Tommy! That lamp is gittin' us ate alive."

"Cherokee Jr., you git me fired over a skeeter, I kick your Injun ass."

"I ain't no Injun."

Cherokee Jr. lurched up in protest, but the beefier Tommy slammed his fist into the smaller boy's chest. Cherokee Jr. fell back, then scrambled to his knees and spit his words into Tommy's face.

"Least my sister ain't pleasurin' no cripple."

Tommy kicked Cherokee Jr. They were fighting before Chester Bolls, the crew boss, could climb from the wagon and pull Tommy away.

"He started it!" Cherokee Jr. screamed.

"Ahem." Banyak placed his hand on Boll's shoulder. "Leave de young fools have at it, I goin' back under my blanket."

"Just lemme settle this." Bolls turned back to the young men. "Both o' you is fired if I don't git some answers."

"Tommy call me a Injun!" Cherokee Jr. said.

"He tellin' lies 'bout you'n my sis."

In the dark, Chester Bolls' suddenly troubled breathing was audible.

"No, he the one lyin'!" Cherokee Jr. screamed.

"Why," Banyak asked from the wagon bed, "would the fat boy lie?"

"'Cause his sister got to feed all them men, and Tommy shamed how they all talk about her."

"Is that all?" Banyak sat up.

"Well, she a eyefull," Cherokee Jr. said.

"Hey, Chester?"

"Yeah, Mr. Banyak."

"When we go back to Memphis I want to meet this cook woman."

"Ain't nothin' you got to worry over, sir."

"True. Come, leave de boys be. I got questions about the man who was your governor."

Chester Bolls climbed aboard the wagon and reclaimed his blanket.

"Don't reckon my opinion worth much."

"Tell me anyway," Banyak said.

"Mr. Alcorn ain't governor no more, but his people had the power to git free swamp land from the gov'ment. They ain't had 'nough money to build no railroad so the Yazoo and Mississippi Valley bought the rights."

"Let that be a lesson, Chester. Now your railroad bein' snapped up by Illinois Central. In this beautiful country, is strong who survive."

There were fewer panthers than wildcats, and wolves hardly ever announced themselves any more. Bobcats and small bears were still common inside the Great Mississippi Swamp, and some people told of seeing bears large enough to carry off cows. Those who lived on recently cleared farmland considered themselves lucky to lose only a little corn or a shoat pig to marauding bears, and by and large the scales were balanced. If young hogs destined to become lard and bacon fed bears, grease and bacon from bears fed the people.

Up with the sun, Banyak commenced instructing the young men how to carry a plumb line and red flag. Chester Bolls was asked to carry the tripod to leave Banyak's hands free to make notations. The first sighting was marred by Cherokee Jr. running his red flag so far he couldn't hear instructions yelled to him. By the second sighting, he and Tommy were learning hand signals to move left or right, another to return. Sightings had to be shortened in places because the railroad was to go through uncut swamp west of the road, and no axe men had been hired to clear a line of sight.

That afternoon, Chester Bolls closed the tripod and hefted it to his shoulder. The wagon on the road was a quarter-mile behind them, and Banyak squatted to scribble in a notebook. Bolls lay the tripod down and ran to retrieve the wagon. By the time he drove abreast, Banyak was scooping dirt into a small canvass bag.

"Don't move!"

Banyak straightened up with a frown. Bolls lifted his rifle from the buckboard seat and fired. A rattler flew into the air from atop a log at Banyak's feet.

"This here is real swamp, Mr. Banyak."

"I am in your debt."

The echoing gunshot brought Cherokee Jr. and Tommy running. Chester Bolls was proudly stroking his rifle.

"Didn't know I could shoot, hanh boys?"

"No suh," Cherokee Jr. said. "Right smart aim you got."

Tommy picked up the snake and licked his lips.

"Sure am partial to fried snake."

A rifle shot split the air, and the snake flew out of Tommy's hand. Bolls and Banyak ducked for cover. The two young men ran to pull rifles from the rear of the wagon. Then they dashed back into the edge of the rough and eased forward stalking whoever had fired. The older and more cautious men looked at one another.

"Are you sure we was shot at?" Bolls asked.

"In godforsaken place like this, only thing Banyak sure about is my name."

"You ain't told me all of it."

"Other surveyors don't like this god-forsaken Mississippi Swamp. So here is Irving Pilsen Urbaniak. This is all they would hire me to do."

"Ah, to do what?" Bolls asked.

"To make sure that before the Illinois Central buys this right of way there is nothing to make laying track impossible."

"That's why you taking ground samples?"

"And why I asked about your Mr. Alcorn."

"Like I say, I don't know anything."

"So tell me, Chester, about your woman in Memphis?"

"Old Tommy's sis?"

"Yes."

"She too pretty to be my woman, but she friendly."

At that moment, Tommy and Cherokee, Jr. ran back in.

"We didn't find no sign or nothin'," Tommy said.

"By the way," Banyak said to Tommy, "I hear your sis is nice woman."

"Why you all keep talkin' 'bout my sister? She ain't a nigger to buy."

All of a sudden, the wind carried a rank wild stink that left a taste like metal in the mouth. Across the road to the east, the rough extended back several yards before the tree wall of the swamp commenced. Out of it moved a gigantic bear. He raised up on his hind legs and growled, huge paws flailing in the air.

"Holy mother!" Banyak screamed.

Bolls raised his rifle to fire, but the beast turned and vanished. The men stood silent for several moments. Cherokee Jr. sniffed at the air.

"Sure wish," he said, "we'da brought a bear dog."

"What is a bear dog, Mr. Cherokee?"

"Hit's a big dog, Mr. Banyak. Got heart enough to jump a beast."

"Well," Chester Bolls said, "at least we got rifles."

"You a good shot'n all, but you'd have to hit him in the head before he even slow up," Cherokee said." A dog at his throat would hold him long enough for us to put four, five bullets in him."

"Oh, I don't like this," Banyak said. "I did not come here to die."

"That bear," Bolls said, "is more scared o' us than we scared o' him, ain't he, Tommy?"

"Could be, Mr. Bolls, but I ain't goin' after him."

Dismissing the young man's qualms with a wave of his hand, Bolls led the way across the road. The ground was moist and Bolls moved slowly, eyes cocked. He halted when he reached the thicket where the light became dim.

"Surely, Chester," Banyak said, "you not going in there."

Bravado spent by now, Chester Bolls hesitated, but to cover his indecision he bent over to search the ground. Cherokee Jr. joined him.

"Looky here!" Cherokee pointed.

"That can't be ..."

"What you see, Mr. Bolls?" Tommy asked pushing close.

"... That ain't no bear spore," Bolls said.

"Hit's a man!" Cherokee Jr. said. "Looky—foot print, weeds fresh-mashed."

"Son, that monstrous devil ain't got no soul."

"An' we could smell him," Tommy said.

"A swamp man," Cherokee Jr. said, "would know how to spread scent."

"Wrong direction," Bolls said. "Beast was here, and the wind was behind us outta the west."

"Sure wish we had some bear dogs," Cherokee, Jr. said.

Banyak had remained in the open outside the uncut thicket. He was the first to head back toward the road. The others lingered, still exploring the ground. As Banyak approached the survey wagon, another growl erupted. The bear stood not twenty yards away from Banyak. Somehow, it had crossed the road and was standing there roaring with a very strange and uneven cast to its mouth, as if to open wide and roar caused it pain. Banyak screamed, but for some reason the bear did not charge. Instead, it uttered a series of grunts and turned its head back and forth as if curious about the craven man. Meanwhile, the others came running. Bolls drew up at Banyak's side and aimed his rifle, but as he did so, the bear swung its bulk away and again disappeared into the thicket. The men of the survey party gathered around Banyak who had collapsed on the ground shaking.

"He'll be okay, Cherokee," Bolls said. "Let's me'n you go have a closer look."

Chester Bolls and the young men circled before closing. A scar on a tree trunk near the thicket the bear had vanished into was dripping sap almost ten feet above the ground. Again the mouth-curling stink of some savage and untamed essence crept over the men, more intense and awful than before. Tommy dropped to his knees to retch. Somehow, right then amongst them, the bear materialized, lethal paw raised.

WHEN CHESTER BOLLS finally opened his eyes, he was lying in the survey wagon moving back toward Clarksdale. Blood was dripping down his face, along with a tear. Banyak handed him a handerchief.

"Don't try to talk," Banyak said. "De blow was so fierce your eyes was rolled up."

Tommy was driving the wagon so fast that the rutted trail was bouncing everyone up and down, making it difficult for Bolls to speak. Again, Banyak silenced him.

"De boys run off, and I was facin' certain doom when the thing find a rifle from somewhere . . . Look at dis."

"The bear had a rifle?"

"Is what I said, Chester—look! Shoot de scope off my tripod."

"Damn!"

"And den de little old nigger pop up."

"What nigger?" Bolls asked.

"Couldda bit me," Tommy said to the men behind him. "I seen him, but I ain't seen where he come from."

"Where is he now?" Bolls asked.

"He vanish," Banyak said.

"Well, he was back there, or not?"

"I asked him," Cherokee Jr. said, "why a little nigger sneakin' up on white folks. He say, tryin not to git shot."

Banyak nodded in support.

"What is so funny, Cherokee Jr.?" Bolls asked.

"Mr. Banyak asked if he seen the bear shoot at us?"

"What the little nigger say?"

"Say he be plumb crazy he was to say that."

In the dismissive argot of the white man, the "little nigger" was Old Bill, and his story as much as that of the swamp itself went back a bit.

Bill was a wiry little brown man who had used so many names even he couldn't remember all of them. For his whimsical ways, as a child he was first given the name Pusillanimous Bill by a white storekeeper with whom Bill's Choctaw mother lived. Bill resented the white man treating her like a slave, but before Bill could emancipate himself and his mother, the old store man began to mock adolescent Bill as Pimple Bill, finally Pussy Bill. Which was about the time Bill talked his mother into moving away from the increasingly abusive man, back into the deep swamp.

A year later, the Treaty of Dancing Rabbit Creek ordered the remaining people of the Great Swamp across Arkansas into Indian Territory, and all of northern Mississippi was forfeited to the whites. Bill's mother decided to go along with her people, but Bill refused to present himself for relocation and began calling himself Bill Williams in order to have two names like the people of the father his mother had described as wearing the color of the night. Of course, Bill had no freedom paper, so that ruse didn't quite work. While the Police Board man who'd detained young Bill was laughing, the skinny youngster made his run for it and took care never to be trapped again. He began selling skins and whiskey to grateful farmers. One of his customers named him Musty Bill because swimming was the closest he ever came to bathing.

Years later, disaffirming his previous fondness for living all over, Bill attached himself to a small clan inhabiting a piece of swamp along the Sunflower River south of Clarksdale. They, like him, were wedded to the swamp, to living apart from so-called civilized people because civilized people had never done them any good. He first came seeking the woman known to hold secrets of herbs and root, but when he found her and announced that he wished to court her, she told him that she was already wed inside to another.

That was Rose. Even so, she and Bill became friends. Later, after the arrival of the woman's husband, Cicero Morgan, they formed themselves into a family against the world, as had many who did not share the same blood but came together to rebuild lives disrupted by either the white people's land-taking or their slavery. In those days, the giant bear became Bill's protégé, young Jasper.

FOURTEEN YEAR-OLD JASPER first entered the Great Mississippi Swamp during the Civil War. He sneaked out of a Union internment camp and traveled alone more than a hundred miles on the Sunflower River into northern Mississippi to search out a new home territory. He did so because Cicero Morgan seemed to be spending too much time with his mother at the camp where Cicero worked below Vicksburg, and Jasper was unwilling to have the man persuade his mother to join him living outside the swamp. So he ran off to find a place for her to make a new home, them having left The Family in Louisiana where he had been raised, only to find themselves in the path of the Union army marching through the Louisiana swamp to get around fortified Vicksburg. A few years after the war ended, during bloody Reconstruction politics when Cicero joined Rose for good, Jasper took to wandering, which was when he met Verlean.

Toward the end of the winter following ambush of the railroad crew, and whimsically exercising his sixty years of stealth, Old Bill sneaked back into camp one evening. Six-foot Jasper, Rose—in size and coloring sometimes mistaken for Jasper's sister—and Cicero with his slim, bookish look were seated outdoors. A clattering of the lid on the stew pot made them all turn toward the doorway. Jasper reached for his nearby gun and bumped Cicero, knocking his glasses off. Cicero slapped him on the knee.

"Sit back down and be at ease."

As Cicero retrieved and pocketed his glasses, Bill Williams shuffled outside with a broad metal plate loaded with stew.

"Too hungry to waste time talking," Bill said. "How you, Princess Rose?"

Rose waved dismissively and stood up as if ignoring Bill. Her walk over to dip water to drink, however, was erect and provocative.

"Hey Rose!" Cicero said. "Bring some whiskey to take your son's mind off guard duty. We're sitting here at ease, and he wants to pull a gun on Old Bill."

"Such a mystery, my big boy," Rose said. "Swamp owns him like a slave, an' who he got to leave it to?"

"There are lots of mysteries," Cicero said under his breath.

"Like, what?" Bill asked with his mouth full.

Cicero stood up and stretched, scratched his mane of coarse gray hair. He was a slim brown man as tall as Rose with a large head that looked even bigger covered, as it was, with graying hair. He intercepted Rose, took the whiskey from her.

"Well, Bill, freedom so empty I call these trees my home rather than live on the outside. Early on, I had absolutely no doubt that I was going to change that world."

"Don't talk like you was the baddest one out there," Jasper said." I seem to recall me bringin' you back in here with your tail 'tween your legs."

Cicero handed Bill the jug of whiskey. Before taking a drink, Bill spoke as if to no one in particular.

"These beautiful trees don't break your heart like women do."

"Non, cherie!" Rose said.

"I could," Bill said to Cicero, "tell you some stories about that one."

"Told you Cicero was my man," Rose said, "first time you showed up. I don't break hearts."

"Why you ain't never give mine back?" Bill said. "Woman let me show her all around this swamp like she was mine, then poof! She yours. Got a son think he know everything about the swamp. She tell me you know everything about her."

Bill finally passed the whiskey over to Jasper.

"Well," Rose said, "I 'spect you found enough women thought you was a big catch."

"All I got to love is my trees."

"Why is your mouth so frisky today?" Rose asked.

"'Cause I feel like it, an' I don't treat livin' like no job. When people live together, got to share, and my words is all I got. Now listen—Jasper."

"Why we got to listen to one of your stories again?" Jasper asked.

"No, young man, no stories. There is a big flood comin'. I read it in the water, smell it in the air."

"Yes," Cicero said, "not quite manure, not quite decay."

"Smell o' change," Bill said. "Flood always mean change."

"So what?" Jasper said. "Our cabins don't suffer from high water."

"Our whiskey pots will. You'n me ought to go lash down the still before the high water git to it."

The next morning, floating down river on the Sunflower took Bill and Jasper past the usually cavernous mouth of the Hushpuckena River that flowed in from the west. The still had been built by Old Bill before he joined the family, so it was located on Black Bayou, a tributary of the Sunflower midway between where Bill had lived alone and the family's camp where he now spent most of his time. Before Black Bayou came into view, a gunshot echoed through the swamp. Jasper reached for his rifle only to feel Bill's restraining hand.

"They was cuttin' miles north from here all last fall," Bill said. "Now, they usin' the Hushpuckena to move the logs down and across to the Sunflower."

"Immigrants, you think?"

"No, Jasper, just loggers."

"But if we don't run 'em out, they be back next year."

"This time, let the swamp teach 'em a lesson. It's a dumb thing to move logs with a flood comin'. Git the hawk outta your eyes. They ain't railroad men."

Grudgingly Jasper obeyed. By the time they reached the still, the rain had indeed begun. They moved all of their jugs and utensils not already safely inside a buried cage, and they secured them in the forks of trees.

"The mash be lost," Jasper said.

"Least we won't lose the damn pot an' haveta drag another in from somewhere."

The rain became a deluge, and they hunkered down inside a lean-to and ate a meal of dried meat and the puffed blooms of corn soaked in wood-ash lye. Soaking in lye water made the hard corn kernels swell and burst their tough capsules. The soft goodness hinting of ash would be washed and drained. Fresh, fermented, vinegared, sweetened or salted, it was called hominy.

The rest of that evening and the night passed in waiting for the rain to let-up. The two men couldn't even kindle a fire, and as the new day unfolded they became too miserable even to reach for sleep. Still smarting a bit from Bill's disagreement about going after the loggers, Jasper endured his hardships without complaint. He admired Bill in many ways, but he thought that he was tougher than the old man. Enduring a leaky shelter became for Jasper a contest. Bill asking when he was going to marry Verlean was met with silence.

At some time the second night, they heard a low rumble away in the distance, and the water started to rise. They did not see the dirty white foam of a breaker move across the land because they were so far inland from the shore of the big river, but they heard water sweep away a piece of some retaining shoreline and explode down into the flat land toward them. Millions of gallons of water were pouring inland by the hour. All night in the dark they listened to the sly rush of water lapping around them on the modest ridge of Black Bayou before they had to abandon the lean-to altogether. Rather than paddle home in the rain and uncertain water, they lashed their boat to a sturdy tree, climbed it and huddled under wet blankets. By the morning of the following day, chafing from wet clothes, hunger drove them down, and they climbed into their boat to return home.

By the time the ridge lines defining the mouth of the Hushpuckena River flowing in from the west came into view, Bill grabbed a tree branch to hold them in place while he rested. During winter, the banks of both the Hushpuckena and the Sunflower stood fifteen feet above water line. Now, for both rivers, flood water was lapping across the top.

"Got to rest good 'fore we cross where them two rivers come together," Bill said. "I sure hope Rose got that big fireplace goin'."

"Hush up, old man!"

Jasper cupped his hand around an ear. A low rumble grew into a racket of branches snapping and logs grinding against each other. The first logs in the distance on the Hushpuckena made Jasper bury his paddle in the water and turn the boat back downstream. Then he paddled with all his strength to swing the boat out of the main river channel. The first logs shot out of the Hushpuckena and into the Sunflower as the two men were pulling their boat up and over what remained of the Sunflower embankment. Without pausing to catch their breath, they hid themselves inside a not yet submerged thicket.

The current in the narrower and equally deep Hushpuckena was shooting out the first logs with velocity. Instead of being caught up in the Sunflower River's current, logs were being thrust onto the river bank across from the smaller river's mouth. Like so many battering rams, logs were smashing against each other and soon forcing a mass of timber ahead onto the land. As more and more logs pressed in at the rear, the mass erupted upward in a melee of splinters and flying logs, but the jam came together and held, moaning and creaking as the current from one river tore at it while current from the other locked it even more tightly in place.

"Ain't never seen a log jam that big," Jasper said.

"Lots you ain't seen, young man . . . Here come the white men boat."

"What they waiting for?"

A second boat joined the first, altogether five white men. With a wooden stave, one prodded the logs nearest him before all stepped out of their boats and walked lightly on their toes across the jam.

"Cut us some poles!" One dropped to his knees exploring with a long stick. "We'll pry 'em loose."

"Not me. I ain't tryin' to unlock this mess."

"If'n we don't," the man with stick said, "they'll push up on land and spread everywhere when the water rise a might more."

"We could buy dynamite from the railroad," the other man said. "Cost money, but we stay alive."

In hiding nearby, Bill whispered, "Same one you already been shootin' at. C'mon home. Fancy me a plate o' stew."

Cicero had raised an earthen dike around the cabin before Bill and Jasper returned, and Cicero had stripped the storage cellar of anything the water might ruin. The three of them added a foot more of soil against the rising water, but it was breached. The floor of the cabin got wet, but the wood furniture didn't suffer. Late that night, the flood crested. They could tell because the sound of water rushing ceased. Always at its moment of greatest dominion, tired flood waters become quiet.

That spring, the Mississippi River breached every little farm levee in the area as if fate were reminding all the little land-scalping entrepreneurs along the bayous and rivers that nothing could stand against the inevitable. There was no single levee confining the whole River, more a crazy quilt of dikes built by those who'd farmed cleared land along the big river since before the Civil War.

Meanwhile, the family remained at Rose and Cicero's cabin most of the time. The warm middle of the days were spent on the roof top where sunlight filtered down through the trees. There was a boat tethered to a ring in a log near the front door for convenience. Keeping the boat near maintained valuable dry comfort because it could be used for calls of nature. Whoever had the urge climbed off the roof, off the bed or off the furniture and paddled away from the cabin to do their business before returning with dry feet.

They did little cooking even though the bottom of the fireplace had been set on stones a foot above the cabin floor, and a fire could almost always be kindled. But the smoke from damp wood didn't all go up the chimney. So, because of the close quarters, occasions for stoking up the fire were limited. They ate what they had: cured strips of bear meat, smoked fish, hominy, and pickled root vegetables that had been stored in the space beneath the roof. On special bright mornings while they stretched out in sun on the roof, someone would boil corn mush or fry up a huge batch of hoe cake.

Conversation was about all they had to amuse themselves, even while sewing, sharpening tools. Almost a week would pass before the water rolled on off, and Bill wore out his welcome talking about everything under the sun including the log jam he and Jasper had witnessed. At no time did Rose or Cicero do more than share a chuckle to acknowledge their boredom, but Jasper tried without success to silence the old man. Finally, on the day they had decided to come down and take up normal life again, Bill started drinking heavily to celebrate getting back on level ground. With a pipe in one hand and whiskey in the other, he then started retelling how he and Jasper had ambushed railroad men the summer before and he kept referring to "the boy".

"Only done," Jasper said, "what any true swamp person would."

"A hot-headed swamp person," Cicero said. "Way you ran in here screaming about immigrants I didn't know what ailed you."

Already irritated, Jasper leapt to his feet.

"You supposed to be a swamp man yourself. Act like it!"

"This is my home, too," Cicero said. "Trouble is you act before you think."

"Them loggers," Jasper said, "was gonna buy dynamite from railroad men. That mean they back. Now, mister swamp man, what we supposed to do?"

"Well, son, " Rose said, "I'd say it's a little soon after high water for me to travel."

"They workin' along that little county road," Bill added, "and the road is between us and them, Jasper."

"Besides," Cicero said, "we don't want a damn posse hunting us. Wasn't but a few months back, we chased those squatters out. So let's not keep picking at the white people."

"You been cooped up too long, cherie," Rose said to her son. "Go visit your friend Verlean and bring her back with you this time. "

"Quit treatin' me like a fool. I'm the one know what it mean to have a railroad come through. These trees our sanctuary, and I aim to keep 'em that way."

Jasper grumped out of the main cabin and slogged a half mile to his own through ankle deep mud. Both he and his mother owned full-length pelts of giant bears. When needed against briars or cold, there were also leggings, and Jasper had mummified the head and paws of one of the largest bears ever to come within' his gun sight. As he put it all on, the rain resumed, so he paused for liquid fortification against the elements. He was growling at the top of his lungs by the time he headed out in the rain.

HOT HEADED, PERHAPS, BUT CLEAR-MINDED, young Jasper,
though he had never attended a day of school in his life. Trees
were all the protection he had. The wild-grown flood plain
was sanctuary, a cathedral of nature in which he and his family
were privileged against molestation by exploiters jealous to
maintain absolute control over black workers whose freedom
had recently been snatched away.

As it would turn out, the Illinois Central balked at taking
over the railroad project from the local promoters. At least
one reason was projected cost overruns associated with raising
an elevated right of way over too many marshes. The refusal
would, however, be only temporary, until the purchase price
between the corporations could be renegotiated downward,
along with an additional grant of land by the Mississippi legislature, for the welfare and benefit of landowners in the wilderness part of the state who complained that their economy
could not grow until those amassing land inland could ship
crops on something more reliable than the Sunflower River.
During the delay, the men with little red flags disappeared. A
second winter passed, and Jasper congratulated himself.

Verlean's half brother, Vern, trekked over to visit Jasper's
camp, paid his respects to Rose, Bill and Cicero, invited them
to visit his new home. Verlean did not accompany her brother,

but she sent a message that Vern delivered in his own ambiguous way.

"Say to visit soon or she git her stuff from somebody else."

Cicero heard Vern whispering, and when Jasper looked toward him, he held up his hands to beg off saying anything.

"My stuff is good as any," Jasper replied, "but I ain't changin' my recipe."

Whiskey had become the family business of sorts. Not that anyone living inside the swamp had need for a regular income, but whiskey was money, for a gun, lantern, knife, whatever. With the arrival of a new spring, the family rushed to deliver the season's first whiskey. The price was highest when thirsty customers who had depleted winter stocks looked up to see the whisky man, or woman standing in the edge of a clearing. But there was only so much time between the worst of the cold and the seasonal onslaught of rain. Not that getting wet was more than an inconvenience, but there was always the possibility of flood. In it lay loss of a load of whiskey, even worse, mortal risk.

Because an unknown black woman could pass unchallenged more easily than a man, Rose usually handled trade with wilderness stores where a constable intent on rooting out vagrants might be encountered. If a large enough quantity of whiskey had been ordered, one or more of the men would deliver the goods to a nearby place from which Rose could make final delivery.

Thus it was that Rose set off alone with a boat load of whiskey bound for a wilderness store. It was a couple miles up the Sunflower to where what was called Harris Bayou branched in from the west, which was the way she always took to what the white people called the Alligator Lake. Cicero had offered to go with Rose, but she rejected his offer and reminded him just who had taught whom about survival in the swamp.

The whiskey-laden boat was riding low in the water as Rose strained against her pole to turn it into Harris Bayou, and she rammed a submerged log and nearly fell in. Heart beating fast on account of the mishap, she was seized by a sense that something odd was yet about to happen, and in the exercise of some caution, she sat down and closed her eyes.

Black water
sister water
all your water
mine,

she had chanted as a girl at the slave depot on the Gulf where, sheltered by the favor of the cook, Songhai, who had raised her, she had been allowed rare times to go play in the black water and to stare off into the distance toward a home across a sea from which her real mother had come. A body tossed overboard like so much trash in the commerce of slavery had been her mother, and a squalling infant had been delivered ashore by the tide. Knowing that she had been born in such desperate circumstance predisposed Rose to hold herself apart from anyone and everything connected to the slave depot. Her earliest way of understanding had been the sense that she was walking around yet unborn, as close to dream as to waking.

But unlike then, no visitation of image or of knowing came upon her now. She honored the connection between her world inside and the external one she had to contend with every day that so often seemed just a reflection of something she had seen before. After escaping to live in the swamp with her first family, that basic faith had given Rose comfort, and to it she had added use of healing herbs and, especially, the ritual of snake venom to bring on a sacred bending and collapse of the boundaries between her inside and outside worlds. A Choctaw woman in the family that had helped her raise Jasper had shown Rose how.

When Rose opened her eyes, she was calm. She glanced up at the overcast sky in a final invitation to whatever was to be felt or known. Then in the distance, she glimpsed movement. As she eased the boat ahead with her pole, she made out a white man on a long-eared mule stopping every now and then to look down at a map. When he galloped ahead yelling, Rose knew that she had been seen, and she stood up with her pole as the man dismounted.

"Nigger woman, what you doin' out here?"

"I got business. Pass on by."

"You a big pretty thing."

As the man walked down to the water, Rose stuck her pole into the shallow slough bottom and launched ahead.

"Come back heah, big gal!"

The man ran into the bayou and began closing. Rose picked up her rifle, and the white man paused, but only for a moment.

A gunshot echoes in the swamp. Cicero was working with Bill placing hot stones inside the green core of a cypress log. Its ends had been shaved off and planed smooth. What remained was the work more delicate than a hatchet or mallet and chisel could accomplish. After the heart wood was chipped away, to avoid an errant stab that would puncture the hull, only burning could accomplish the final carving out into a shell light enough to carry. Had the wood been dry, it would have burst into flame, but being green wood, it sizzled as the red hot stones turned water to steam and flamed away an inch of new wood as the stone was rolled along the bottom of the cavity.

Jasper was not helping them. To mask sign of the chore, they'd decided to work on the banks of the Sunflower down at the water level where the new flood season would soon obliterate all sign of labor on a new boat. Jasper—on occasion still an irrepressible boy—was offshore standing in his favorite old canoe whimsically trying to coordinate stepping into the rear of the boat to raise its bow out of the water at the same time that he dug his paddle into the water to turn him and the canoe on a dime. When the shot rang out, he almost fell in. He recovered, paddled to shore, and they all headed out. Jasper launched first. Bill and Cicero followed in Bill's flat-bottom boat.

An hour later, the two of them came upon Rose talking heatedly to Jasper. Face down in the bayou was the white man.

"He from that railroad," Rose said to Cicero. "He got huntin' gear and a map show where this bayou join the Sun-flower, so his people been thru here before."

"Been scoutin' our territory," Jasper said.

"Are you alright?" Cicero asked Rose.

"Course I am, don'tcha fret."

"I was worried when I heard the gunshot, and I felt maybe I should have been in that boat with you."

"Mr. Cicero," Jasper said, "your face still look screwed up. Momma ain't helpless."

"Look, Jasper, this railroad means that our swamp wont hide us forever. Armed confrontation should be avoided when we're outgunned. I'm thinking ahead."

"You think too much!"

"Calm down, Jasper." Rose said.

"Someday," Cicero said, "we may have to move on."

"My gun say, non! This ain't nobody's home but mine, and there ain't nowhere else to go, so I ain't thinkin' about leavin'. Right now we need to do something about this here."

As Jasper pointed to the dead man, Cicero shook his head. Rose signaled her husband.

"We ain't got time to talk now, cherie."

Cicero's mouth opened and closed. With a grunt, he turned away and walked over to pull the dead man from the water.

"What did this man do?" he asked.

"He was of a mind to abuse me."

Jasper joined Cicero and began rummaging through a blanket roll across the dead man's shoulder. From it, Jasper pulled a rain slicker.

"Them railroad people didn't heed me. I'm takin' them another message, and this time they ain't gonna forgit."

"Here, son!" Rose said, passing a wide straw hat she had been wearing. "It's gonna rain."

"May I ask," Cicero said, "why you are taking the mule?"

"Cause if I didn't ride him outta here, the varmints would eat him."

Bill commenced laughing. Rose moved behind Cicero and put her hand on his back.

"See, husband, my boy ain't cold-blooded. He got a heart for all creatures even if he ain't found no woman yet. Such a mystery."

"The mystery," Jasper said, climbing onto the mule, "is why you keep pickin' at me. Now listen, you all follow me over to where this man come from. I'm gonna go right in like ain't nothin' special. Be on watch for anybody try to shoot me. If my left hand go up, all I want is for you to shoot to warn 'em that they surrounded. Y'all listen' to momma. She know what my signals mean."

Jasper rode off. Cicero looked at Rose, who shrugged. She stroked his cheek with an ashen hand.

"You and your politics," she said, "couldn't change the world, and I know that Jasper won't neither. Life is just you and me, now, cherie, us here in our little piece of swamp."

"I know, hon. Just that thinking about where to go next makes me wonder what happened to all the people I grew up with. Must have been rough out there among all the white people."

"Go find out and quit feelin' guilty. Right now, quit rubbin' on me in fronta Bill, and shake a leg so's we can give my boy his backup."

An hour later, Rose, Cicero and Bill were hunkered down inside the tree wall along the trail that was being called the county road. There was no bridge where it crossed Harris Bayou, only mud. In front of them, a train crew was at work unaware of the eyes and rifles trained on them.

"Stand clear!"

Axe men scattered like termites as an ancient oak shrieked and twisted, then settled motionless, upright despite being cut through. All because its massive base was nearly as wide as the railroad flatcar waiting to haul it away. A gust of wind blew sawdust into the faces of the crew standing downwind. There was the smell of rain.

"Ain't fair Harry wasn't here to help us," a trainman said.

"Shut up," the crew boss said. "Run git a pair of mules and pull that damn tree down."

A train whistle sounded, and all looked toward the locomotive ahead of the cars piled with fresh-cut timber.

"Steam for home!" the engineer yelled. "If you go huntin', we git stranded if this track wash out."

"Naw, shut her down!" the crew boss said. "Listen up, Homer ... There is nothin' more grand than killin' a mighty bear—bamm! You see 'im rollin' all over the ground slobberin' an' bleedin'." The crew boss pointed down the broad bayou fifty feet ahead of where they had stopped laying track. "That runs into the Sunflower River accordin' to the map. They got three, four hunnert pound bears over in there."

"So?"

"We'll eat the hams and sell the rest in Clarksdale."

A spray of warm rain ended the exchange, sending men scurrying past to shelter underneath the flatbed cars that hauled iron rails into the swamp, logs out on the return to base camp. The crew boss climbed into the locomotive with the engineer. Even as the men were still seeking shelter, the shower withdrew. The earthy smell that always preceded spring rain, winter dust up and riding the air in a final frolic before being washed to earth, ripened into wet. The work was already behind schedule, and all work would cease to wait out the danger of flood when heavy rain arrived. Which was why the track was being laid so far inland from the Mississippi River and on a raised bed of dirt and cinders. As the men emerged from shelter, the engineer up in the locomotive cab pointed off in the distance.

"There he is!"

From the cab where he had sheltered with the engineer, the crew boss jumped to the ground.

"Right on time, old Harry—."

A gust of wind took his breath away. With an agonizing screech the stubborn cut tree twisted and began to heel over in the wind. The momentum of falling caused it to slide on into the water as the men stared.

"Git your mules out here!" the boss yelled.

Grumbling, the mule skinner led the first protesting mule out of the stock car. The dirt-streaked crew began dragging out saws and axes.

"Git them mules to work, boys! Once that wood is completely soaked you won't be able to saw it."

"It's wet already," one man said.

"Hey, Red!" The engineer yelled from the cab. "That fella riding up—"

"Wave Harry on in, goddammit!"

For yards on each side of the rail bed the land had been hacked and shaven like a drunk man's chin. It was clear of trees but pocked with stumps, blackened fire sites and craters where dynamite had been used. Ahead, though, snaking through the uncut wilderness was the narrow dirt road. In it, a rider in a rain slicker wearing a huge straw hat sat motionless.

"That ain't Harry!" the engineer yelled.

The men turned and stared ahead. Then the crew boss cupped his hand around his mouth.

"Come on in, whoever you is, cowboy!"

There was no answer. The crew paused and fidgeted, whispered.

"Whatsamatter with him?" the crew boss yelled up to the engineer.

"Jesus, Red, look like a nigger—just pulled a rifle, too!"

The approaching figure had halted. The crew boss walked ahead of the locomotive down to the edge of the bayou. He planted his fists on his hips and pointed.

"You wearing skins, I see."

"And you ain't welcome here."

"Well now, who you work for?"

"Nobody but a man named, Jasper." Jasper pointed his rifle toward the crew boss and raised his voice. "I will kill this raggedy-assed white man if you others don't stay put!"

"We got guns, too."

"Non! Your guns up under that train in back."

"What are you up to, nigger?"

"My people don't allow no strangers in this swamp."

"You tellin' a nigger lie! What that road doin' here if ain't nobody come this way?"

"Trouble is, you ain't keepin' to it."

"Coon, you in a bunch o' trouble."

"Say, boss," the mule skinner had approached his boss, "he sittin' on a railroad mule."

Jasper raised his left hand, and a shot kicked up dirt at the two men's feet. The crew boss dropped his cigar, and the rest of the crew huddled together. Jasper waved his hand overhead and three more shots rang out, one striking fire as it ricocheted off the iron of the engine.

"My people got you surrounded."

"Don't shoot no more!" The engineer scrambled down out of the cab. "That thing could blow."

"Then git on board and back outta here!"

Without more, the milling crew headed toward the rail cars. The mule skinner ran to join them.

"You—mister boss man!" Jasper said. "Stay right where you is. If I git shot, you and that engine man dead."

"But, but," the engineer said, "you cain't stop the railroad."

"That there's what the white folks call Harris Bayou. From here on south 'til you come to a river sunk in deep banks, I don't want no man in the swamp 'tween this road and the Sunflower over east. If I see you—me, I'll kill you."

"Yeah, I hear you, cowboy."

"Believe what you want."

Jasper pulled off his hat and wiped the mist from his brow.

"Why you dressed like that?"

"Like what?"

"That big hat'n all, skins, rainslicker—niggers ain't usually wearin' that kind of get up."

"Ain't your kind o' nigga."

"That so?"

"Me'n my people been in that swamp since before the war." Jasper moved his arm in a wide arc. "Over there is ours. Now, back outta here."

The engineer climbed aboard, but the crew boss hesitated.

"What about our tree? We git paid by the wood we cut."

"Leave it!" Jasper leapt from his mule. "This critter belong to you, take him 'fore the varmints eat him."

Jasper lifted his right leg and slid down the mule's flank to the ground. The crew boss waded through the bayou to take the mule, then back toward the locomotive. As he climbed out of the water, he turned.

"Where is the white man who was ridin' this mule?"

"Last I seen, he was floatin' in the water."

"Goddamn you, nigger—"

The crew boss ran toward the locomotive cab. A fusillade of gunshots forced the trainmen to the ground.

"Be smart, and live!" Jasper shouted.

But the crew boss leapt up and sprinted to climb aboard the locomotive. He made it inside, then leapt down with a rifle. A single gunshot rang out, and the man buckled like a punctured sack of sand. As the echo died, came the distant roar of a bear, then the gentler sound of rain. In the distance along the big river, small trickles of sand were already tumbling to the inevitable.

IN THE MORE SETTLED PART OF the state below Vicksburg, below the Yazoo River that was the southern boundary of the Great Swamp, in what was left of Hurricane Plantation, young Buck Morgan was staring up at a rain spot on the ceiling. The brown stain was spreading in the dim light, and drops were gathering on a tear in the plaster.

Those whose eyes have been the focus of this chronicle, to this point, had mainly turned their backs on the controlling white society, but not the family of which Buck was a part. They worshipped the American Dream and worked long hours laboring toward an elusive success. The good fortune was that they remained one of the few black plantations still operating in the state of Mississippi, the other of note owned by Senator Blanche K. Bruce whom the white folks loved enough to keep in minor office after taking over his political organization.

Buck lived in a building modeled after a Greek temple that had been the library of Joseph Davis whose brother became president of the Confederacy. It was a small, now going into disrepair building, but it sported twelve-foot marble pillars supporting porticoes on all sides. A crystal chandelier hung in the main room. Isaiah Montgomery and his father had carved all of the furniture with the help of others no longer slaves who had stuck together after freedom and now owned their old plantation in common.

"Get up, Buck!" Isaiah called from another room. "Put on your good clothes today."

A small dark man with a deeply receded hairline loomed in the doorway. Slowly, Buck turned out of bed and stretched before dashing on water from a nightstand basin. In a scrap of mirror, his coarse dark hair looked like a cap of dusty elderberries moist with dew.

"Who comin' to visit, uncle?"

"You hush up screamin'," his uncle's wife Martha said. "Your uncle got a lot on his mind."

Buck finished washing, dressed with haste because he was hungry. When he presented himself, Martha Montgomery silently pointed him to a chair, and he began eating ravenously. Martha's oldest daughter tried to keep pace with Buck eating until her mother slapped her wrist. Buck giggled and stuck out his tongue at the girl as some men arrived talking about repairing a plow. Isaiah left with them, and Buck followed, on his way out snatching the uneaten bacon from his uncle's plate just ahead of Isaiah's daughter.

"Orphan boy!"

"Watch your tone," Martha Montgomery said to her daughter. "Buck is your brother for all you got to say."

Hurricane Plantation sat on a peninsula that turned the Mississippi River west for several miles. The end of the peninsula was two hundred yards from the once showplace library. The plantation's smithy, its sawmill, and several other utility houses were all spread along the river bank in this area. All that remained of the Hurricane big house were foundation stones overgrown by weeds. During the Civil War, it had been mistaken for the Confederate President's house less than two miles away. With great ceremony, the Union navy burned Hurricane to the ground.

And yet, it was with as much pride as might be expected to swell Jasper's heart for controlling his territory that Isaiah Montgomery bragged of owning the first black-operated Mississippi plantation, and Hurricane was still operated by ex-slaves despite the terror that had broken out fifteen years back. Union troops no longer insured rights. White carpetbaggers from the North who'd bought Mississippi land now agreed that ex-slaves should remain vassal and powerless on the land. Like the word, poverty, the racism of their stand was obvious, but also less noteworthy than how subtly it was publicly defended and accepted. Those who had dared to propose dividing up the swamp among freedmen had been labeled crazy, intent on destroying the American way, and it was a judgment that almost everyone accepted with a healthy dose of righteous indignation against the reformers. Even black voters lusted after the opportunity to exploit some one.

Hurricane Plantation was the first of the showpiece experiments in what in a later century would be called black capitalism. Even though waning at the time, antislavery liberalism had led a Naval Admiral planning the Battle of Vicksburg to reward, a few years later, old Benjamin Montgomery's contribution to the War effort in managing Davis Bend as an internment camp for black people, for those who'd fled plantations seeking freedom with Union forces prior to the end of hostilities. To keep those slaves from hindering Union troop movements, all had been involuntarily interned on Davis Bend. Benjamin Montgomery's knowledge of the land and of crops made that internment work, along with the friendly black faces of his sons and other Davis family slaves carrying out Union directives. After the camp was closed, the elder Montgomery became a justice of the peace. Some time later, the Department of the Navy petitioned Treasury to authorize sale of the confiscated Davis property to the Montgomery group.

All morning, Buck dogged his uncle's side. The men who would have been working spent much of the morning sheltering from the rain and talking. As a child, Buck's sense of himself had flourished under the tutelage of these hardened blacksmiths and master carpenters who had once served the Davis family and now remained behind after freedom. They treated him as the princeling that he was, all in deference to Isaiah Montgomery in whose care Buck resided. He was now old enough to understand that there was an awesome frightening power called white people whose abuses of ex slaves like those around his uncle were legion. Somehow, his uncle had kept all that at bay. Master of white folk-ology, the men would brag.

Toward afternoon, a flat bottom boat with a canopy against the rain pulled into the dock.

"Steady as she goes," the pilot called to two burly oarsmen.

As the boat quit rocking, two white men carrying briefcases leaped ashore, and Isaiah snarled and threw aside a wood planing tool. Isaiah muttered something about easy-living white folks and, showing no concern for his good shoes and store-bought wool trousers, splashed out to greet the white men.

"You gentlemens come right in," Isaiah said, pointing them all toward the library. "Miz Montgomery! Miz Montgomery!"

They all hurried to be out of the rain, and as soon as they entered the building, Isaiah directed everyone into the showplace main room of the small building.

"You can see we work hard and keep things up here at Davis Bend," Isaiah said. "Y'all gentlemen have a seat."

"Thank you, Isaiah," the taller of the two said. "Let's get on with the business at hand."

He laid his briefcase on a knee-high tea table and hunkered down to search for papers. The other white man walked around touching things. When Isaiah nodded toward him, he smiled, then returned to examining the chandelier.

"Look at that, Frank. Mr. Davis brought it in from Italy. Must have been salvaged from the original plantation house."

The tall man paused to glance up, grunted, hung a pair of wire rimmed spectacles over his ears and returned to his papers before speaking.

"Yes, you done a fine job, Isaiah. Too bad you had to take advantage of your old master—aha!"

He extracted a document from among several spread on the hospitality table, then sat back on the couch.

"Isaiah, we 'preciates your bein' reasonable. Else, we be down in Vicksburg placin' a writ with the sheriff."

"I try, mister. I'm ready to talk this thing out."

"I am Mr. Frank Williams. That's my associate, Mr. Burt Whooper over there—say, gal!"

"Yessuh," Martha Montgomery said.

"Bring us a little toddy."

Martha rushed off, pushing her eldest daughter aside while mumbling about young ladies underfoot.

"Damn this weather—go on sit down, Burt. Nigger ain't gonna bite you. Joe Davis taught his darkies how to act."

"You got a proposal for me?" Isaiah asked.

"Ain't got nothin' to talk about because we just the lawyers represent the family."

Martha Montgomery returned.

"Mistuh," Martha said, "that water heatin' up now."

The man with the document showed it to Isaiah.

"You wasn't twenty when you signed this paper. That means, even if you wasn't a nigger, you was too young back in '67 to make a legal bindin' contract."

"Yessir, I 'spect you right . . . My daddy signed, too."

"He dead. That don't matter."

The sound of Martha Montgomery sobbing shocked Buck, and when Isaiah turned a fierce eye toward her, she walked back out toward the kitchen shack behind the building. The other white man placed a hand on Isaiah's shoulder.

"The legal heirs of Mr. Davis want to be fair because you are a nigger who keeps his place, and you rendered great personal assistance to Jefferson before he was elected president. Anyways, Isaiah, your signature on the original undertaking signed when the Yankees still had control wasn't binding, which makes the note you later signed to buy these plantations no good. Further, Mr. Joe Davis wasn't bound to sell, like he thought . . . Now, what we'll do, is offer you a sum of money for all the crops you have growing on the land. We don't have to, but you have a lot of sentiment on your side. Miz Varina, specially, can't talk enough of your pa—what the nigger's name, Burt?"

"Benjamin. It was Benjamin."

"Yes, Miz Varina remembers how much him and you helped her husband, Jefferson, as loyal as you was to your true owner. So now that Mr. Joe Davis is passed on, his kin have authorized us to pay a fair price for growing crops before we reclaim these lands."

"I 'preciate that, sir," Isaiah said.

"Your master didn't know what he was doing after the war, seein' his brother in one Yankee prison after another'n all. Had he waited, he could have reclaimed his land back from the government like some of the rest."

A whiskey aroma announced the arrival of steaming toddies on a tray. Martha served the white man seated, the one standing. Her husband waved her away. As the white men sucked at their whiskey, a cracking, high-pitched voice startled everyone.

"Y'all get outta here!"

The seated white man spilled his toddy. The other reached inside his briefcase.

"Please, mister," Isaiah said, touching the man's arm. "The boy here ain't knowed we was leavin' until right now."

"Git him out of here, uncle!"

Isaiah slapped Buck, whose eyes flashed angry before glistening over with tears. As he ran outside, the white men smiled toward each other. A briefcase fell to the floor as one man pocketed a pistol inside his coat.

Buck ran over to his mother's house. He said nothing as he made his way to the food. He swept a meal into a sack and left the house. It was late that night before he returned and eased himself inside where he would spend the next several days. He refused to return to where he usually slept with the Montgomery family, and he didn't want to talk.

"You cain't keep playing bedbug," his mother said, stripping the blanket off of him one morning.

"Aw momma, I'm just resting."

"Rest, you got. Lazy is another thing."

"Git him out heah!"

The voice was that of Buck's stepfather.

"Boy up, husband! He be out directly."

Buck's stepfather stuck his head inside.

"Damned, if he be ruled by his daddy's lazy blood in my house. Straighten up boy, or I bust your butt again."

"What I do wrong?"

"You lazy like your daddy, that's what. The world don't owe you no livin'."

"Why you got to talk about my daddy?"

"'Cause no-count Cicero Morgan ain't kept a decent job in his life."

Isaiah showed up the next day. The grown-ups whispered together, and then Isaiah walked over to Buck.

"C'mon, nephew, time for us to talk."

"Don't wanna talk."

"Well, the world go on with or without you. Your choice if you want to sit back an' pout."

"How could you, Uncle? How could you let 'em take everything from us?"

"Ain't let them white men do nothin'. Did you ever ask yourself how come we still doin' so good when there's many another had to fold-up here recent? . . . Heah on Davis Bend, we was the first, and now we almost the last black plantation in Mis'ssippi. Rest all gone. White folks got the money, they got the seed, they got the law. Hell, boy, you want me to go fight 'em all with my hoe? Hanh! I'm just supposed to march up'n say, 'Boo, Mr. Whiteman, ain't you scared of me'? Well, the world don't work that way. I'm makin' it possible for you'n all these others still left from the old days to have a livin'. Now, come on outta there'n take a walk. You need to hear what I got planned if you want to grow up and be a businessman like me an' Ben Green."

Ben Green was known to have a head for business, and Buck knew that Isaiah trusted him to deal with white people.

"We gotta do this, Ben," Isaiah had said a year earlier.

"We got one sawmill. What we need another for?"

"Ben, a sawmill up in Vicksburg would let us cut wood to order. Nobody up there gonna order from all the way down here. That's why it make sense for you to go up there and set up. We cut the timber and ship to you on barges."

"My wife want to know how long you think we'll have to live in Vicksburg."

"I'm sending my brother with you."

"Well, another good man be fine."

"Ben, I'm tellin' you something, but you ain't listenin' . . . One day, we going to need a business away from here."

So after the Davis family re-took possession of the land, Isaiah moved everyone into Vicksburg who agreed to stay to-gether—his brothers and their families and several others. With part of the crop settlement money, he opened a store, and the group worked both it and the existing sawmill.

To Buck, moving into Vicksburg was both exciting and frightening. He knew nothing of cities, and the everyday close-ness of white people frightened him, more than it might have a year before. White people had such power, and he felt so helpless, not worth as much as he had assumed. Isaiah's older daughter became jealous of the increasing time her father devoted to Buck. Like her father, she didn't bite her tongue. Just as often, her father threatened her for having no manners.

"Your father," Isaiah's wife would counter, "don't know nothing about being well-raised. Find you a rich man, long's he good to you. And 'till you find him, keep right on being headstrong. Just that . . . You got to behave well-raised."

Buck, too, had been lectured on being well-raised, but now in the big city he was impatient to grow up. He stayed away from home as much as he could. He learned how to fight, often enough with town boys who coveted his good clothes and comfortable living. In spite of everything, he still dreamed of living as his uncle had on the plantation, of being important in the eyes of the people around him. The problem was that he was no longer convinced that hard work and worrying about things ordinary folks didn't concern themselves with was the only way. Being well-raised certainly didn't cut it with the boys in the city, and a growing interest in girls encouraged him to enjoy the present more. Being too serious made the more forward girls laugh and turn to others, those willing to steal whiskey and hidden fun.

Isaiah's daughter, who secretly liked Buck, was the first to notice him sneaking whiskey out of the store. She lay awake until Buck sneaked upstairs.

"You a no-count!" she said.

Buck ignored her and tip-toed past the room where the girls slept, but she followed.

"They putcha in jail for stealin'."

"Keep outta my business!"

"You messin' up, Buck. Daddy say boys these days is actin' crazy'n he ever seen, what with no more slavery and things so easy."

A whole new crowd was helping Buck to break out of the old rut, and by sixteen, he thought of himself as a city boy. He understood about whiskey mills and fast women. When he could persuade both his natural mother and Uncle Isaiah into believing he was in the home of the other, he hung around the night-life places and the crap games down at the docks along the river below the city. Already, he'd recognized a tolerance for liquor, and growing rapidly—developing the solid physique of his mother, her smooth brown skin and curling black hair like wet wool—earned him all the attention he wanted from girls. That and being his "rich" uncle's nephew.

Despite Buck's lapses into what in another day might be called minor delinquency, Isaiah seemed satisfied for Buck to work the store every day, learn seasonal bargains, special sales, bulk merchandise, anything to be bought for less than usual and sold for average or better prices. Actually, Buck hated that store. He preferred more physical sawmill work, but Isaiah, always the mentor looking toward the bigger picture, insisted that Buck learn to work with his mind.

A young woman who wore a too-short dress because she hadn't finished saving for another worked one of the waterfront vegetable stalls from before dawn to mid-afternoon. To his friends, Buck called her his candy cane, his licking stick, like the candy he'd given away upon her first visit to his uncle's store to demonstrate how important he was. Her thank you had been her smile, sweet and shamelessly real to Buck, and it encouraged him to talk about himself and to move closer just to see if the girl would allow him to touch her. What she allowed was an hour of kissing interrupted only by customers. Nor did she object to anything that he did as the darkening afternoon settled around them like permission. Buck was too full of sap to consummate anything before his passion blossomed. He didn't have time to start over because the young woman pleaded that she had chores at home.

In the weeks that followed, his companion's circumstances were convenient for messing around when she got off work. The young woman was older than Buck, and she appeared to run the ramshackle house she lived in, caring for a blind grandmother and two smaller brothers. Their mother was away struggling to clear land upstate in the Mississippi Swamp with her husband, the same place Buck's own father, Cicero, was reputed to be. The relationship came to a sudden end when Buck decided to stay out all night and knocked on her door. A partially clothed older man answered the door, and the startled woman pretended not to know him.

In February, the year 1887, Isaiah made Buck dress carefully and accompany him.

"Where we goin', uncle?"

"What you know about railroads?"

"They got tracks."

"Got lots of stuff. They a big business, so big even gov'nors and presidents do what they tell them. Railroads got the gov'ment just givin' them land right and left. Got so much don't know what to do with it."

"Why, uncle?"

"'Cause men in the gov'ment get favors and such for doin' right by the railroads."

As a huge gray stone building loomed beside them, Isaiah paused and put his hand on Buck's arm.

"In here! Mind you, keep quiet."

"Yessir, but what we doin' here?"

"Gonna see about some land. Land is life. It ain't about some little room in a city. You got to own your own home, or you don't own your life. All this work I been doin' is to build enough of a stake to git back to some land, like on the plantation."

"How you get land?"

"Ain't nothin' free. Freedom wasn't worth shit neither— not hardly. Your own pa couldn't see that."

"Tell me about him, uncle."

"He never could see the need to work a business. He up there in them swamp bottoms along the Miss'sippi doin' God knows what."

"But sometime sound like he was like, a hero."

"Naw, naw, boy. He was more like a fool, trying to change the world. One man cain't do that, especially one our complexion. What we got to do is *trick* the world, make like we goin' along with it. Make the big people feel so good they let us step up'n join 'em, in a small sorta way."

"My daddy was in politics, wasn't he?"

"Yeah, but people like that just make it rough for folks like me. That's enough, now . . . We're gonna speak with a Mr. Jones Hamilton. He sent us them convicts to build levees back at the Bend. Remember them?"

Buck nodded.

"He also got influence with the railroads . . . By the way, I ain't lost all that much when the white folks took back our plantation. Another couple floods and that place be a island."

"Is that true?"

"Course it is. Didn't Ben Green say as much that year he moved away, when we began shipping timber?"

"Yeah, but couldn't you have sold out or something?"

"Well, that's a good thought, but you do what's possible. Everybody knew them Davis people was after my land title. Who you think wouldda bought from me?"

Talk of recent floods at the Bend where the Mississippi River had gouged a permanent channel along the mainland to turn what had been a peninsula into an island had reached Buck, but he had never considered that his uncle might have been thinking so far ahead in not disputing his ownership with the white men. That surprise, amplified by the size and grandeur of the marble-covered building Isaiah was marching inside, overwhelmed Buck.

"Is this the place, uncle?"

"Sure is. Mr. Hamilton gonna send me a letter to the Illinois Central Railroad. They built down from Memphis and hooked up here in Vicksburg a while back, and they own swamp land all the way. I'ma git us some of that land. Just remember, you got to keep powerful friends to git by, which is better than fightin' white folks about politics."

That next summer, a group of men including Buck and his stepfather took an overnight train ride into the low-lying bottom land alongside the Mississippi River and stepped off onto virgin swamp, 800 acres purchased through Isaiah's contacts with one of the railroad promoters. It was an awesome swampy world as far as the eye could see, stands of timber converging on the railroad in both directions. Water below the surface bubbled underfoot, and apart from the man-made ribbon of space set with iron rails, no human sign existed. Wolves, wild cats and bears—only childhood legends for Buck until that morning—howled and cried as the men chose the highest ground between two bayous that controlled surface water flow to make camp.

That first day, they cut all but the most dominant trees surrounding the camp and hacked away the thick underbrush. From sunup to sunset, they worked hard. Not all saw themselves as towering examples for the race, like Isaiah, they were men with families whose survival lay solely in their strong arms and hands. Toward evening, they erected a tent as mosquitoes descended in droves, and everybody rubbed down with coal oil before retiring exhausted. The second day, a tub of cornmeal mush was boiled because there hadn't been time for hunting yet. After breakfast, the big saws came out, and cypress, blackjack and gum trees kept falling. When the sun headed down and bathed every weary body with orange light, Isaiah walked among them with the orange glow burning in his heavy-lidded brown eyes.

"Y'all hear me! Some of you startin' to worry. Forgit it! Just go on to sleep, git up tomorrow and start at them axes again."

He raised his arms toward what had been a magnificent pastel sky. "We give thanks to the Lord, and we give thanks for *ourselves*. Have we not for centuries braved the miasma of slavery? What's a little swamp to us?"

"He givin' they tired asses what they need," Ben Green told Buck. "He know how to push folks. That's what bein' a leader all about."

"Go on preach, Isaiah!" someone yelled.

It was like that, thanking a generous God for the privilege of having some hand in their own fates, for these men were no strangers to the dire plight of the mass of black men and women on plantations like the one they had been slaves on. There was no freedom and little hope for most. Lives of grinning and crying and calling on Jesus, was how it was so often described. These men knew that they had lots to be thankful for.

That evening passed in uncommon camaraderie. As Buck tilted the whiskey jug for the last time before his uncle gave him a hard look, his thoughts about leadership vanished into the stars above his eyes. On the edge of sleep from the whiskey, he had no idea that he was the object of a loud burst of good-natured laughter.

It was months later in October, when Buck's mother Suzy led his two younger half-sisters off the train ahead of Isaiah and Ben Green's families. A leading woman in the community, Suzy hugged and kissed everybody. Buck held back thinking his mother's embrace marked him a child. Watching Suzy and his stepfather embrace, Buck started thinking again about his wayward father. All he knew was that Cicero lived somewhere nearby. That evening, Buck asked Isaiah if there were some way to locate Cicero. Isaiah advised him to wait until spring. There was too much work for him to traipse off on a frolic.

Land clearing slowed in winter, except for building dikes to encourage the next spring's flooding into the main bayous.

An area of built-up land under the camp turned out to be Indian burial mounds. Being least likely to flood, they were marked off for the first houses. Ben Green started calling the big bayou that ran north-south around them to the west Mound Bayou, and the name stuck for the settlement as well. For all of them those first days seemed a dream come true.

Before the spring rains and high water brought human activity to a stand-still, a handful of new families arrived, and Isaiah built a rough store. From the sale of timber to the railroad came cash, and some pressed to use every penny for down payments on more land. But Isaiah was cautious against going too far into debt and allowing the railroad to squeeze them by refusing to buy timber or to renew the land notes they'd all signed. Nor did everyone wish to remain a cooperative community any longer. They'd worked hard since slavery, and some wanted to hold title to their land in their own names. As a compromise, each family took title to its own home site and farmland, but a common fund was established into which half of all timber money was to be placed. Isaiah was granted charge of the fund from which all might seek credit.

Everything fascinated Buck. Isaiah used the common funds to stock his store, then repaid the money out of profits. When the people began trekking north to Alligator Lake and south to a new railroad town called Cleveland, they discovered lower prices, which cut into Isaiah's business.

"By god, you niggas think ev'ry li'l penny you spend with the white man make you smart. Hell! Support your own, and I'll support you. Spend your money with the white man, then go ask him for a buildin' loan. He'll laugh at you."

Isaiah made his point. There was a lot of complaining about his high prices, but the community generally accepted his logic. Isaiah then loaned Buck common fund money for a down payment on forty acres. He was so grateful that he never questioned the fairness of Isaiah's methods.

That land triggered a spurt of long hard hours to clear a portion. Like everyone else, Buck contributed a portion of his timber proceeds to the common fund, though he had to help his stepfather clear land four days a week. But now he could brag about being his own man. Isaiah suggested that Buck be put in charge of public improvement, and the people agreed. They also decided that everyone would give two days work a month to projects like dikes and roads, all of which Buck was told to organize. He was so proud of himself that he never questioned the motive of those allowing him to work on their behalf.

Spring brought water everywhere, and the people stayed inside except when they had to hunt. It was, however, a year of easy flooding off the big river. The water had slowly risen in the bayous and elsewhere, some of the low-lying land came under water, but there was no inland tidal bore that could be so destructive to houses and to people unprepared. To Buck's surprise, the men of the colony had been much more concerned than he had heard anyone let on.

When the high water receded, five new families presented themselves and were accepted into the colony. The railroad agreed to sell them land nearby because land toward the center of the settlement was now at a premium. Isaiah staked off building and garden lots of 100 by 100 feet and unsuccessfully offered them to two newcomers for a hundred dollars a lot, on land that had cost a few dollars an acre the year before, before partial clearing and before dikes had been built around the two principal bayous.

"Why you charge so much?" Buck asked.

"Got to build your value," Isaiah said. "Give it time. Enough people come here lookin' to settle next year, somebody will buy one. Then I'll raise the price a little more."

Value depended on improvement, but mostly on what people wanted. Slowly, it began to dawn on Buck why the other men had smiled and been so willing to award him forty acres

.

along what was called Little Mound Bayou furthest from the center of the things. His land was hard to drain and travelers claimed that the unexplored swamp to the east was hainted by a black Choctaw and an evil giant who looked like a bear. It was the middle of April, a few days before Cicero Morgan's birthday.

SPRING IS ALWAYS A NEW beginning, spirit increase Rose
called it, and she would demonstrate what she meant by lifting
her strong West African nose into the warm intimations of
flowers not yet fully realized, and she would breathe slowly,
and her bold mature face would take on the countenance of a
happy little girl, which would on occasion lead Cicero to
chuckle for he was a man with little left to believe in, and
though he, too, might stick his nose into that same warm
breeze, all it meant to him was scented air at the side of the
woman he loved.

Unlike some who might repose an unshakable faith in a
god or a system of philosophy or government or even in the
wisdom or kindness of people, Cicero did not. Like Rose, he
had seen people at their worse, both slave owners at the top
and those who'd do anything to earn the right to wield the
whip, black and white, their fermenting ambition barely leav-
ening the great mass of people who would never quite rise to
challenge anyone their bread and butter depended upon,
certainly not challenge the laws of heaven or hell.

Cicero never forgot the hard lessons, and he'd been
marked by them. The circumstance of his father earning his
freedom and then being forced back into slavery on Davis
Bend had left Cicero growing up at least as much at odds as
Rose with the people around him—the white ones whose

wealth was based upon him accepting his life as their property, as well as those like his mother, Nancy, and Benjamin Montgomery who did accept being slaves. Never a church-goer, because his father had not been, Cicero had lived for almost five years in Vicksburg with his father and not on Davis Bend. In his precocious early years, his father's gospel had been to grow up and make a better world.

Cicero's father, Morgan, had been bookkeeper for Hurricane Plantation before buying his and Cicero's freedom. Later, being arrested and jailed for being an unregistered freedman broke Morgan's health, and he agreed to return to the plantation to be near his wife and child. He succumbed to pneumonia weeks before he had planned an escape for his whole family. Torn up with grief, five year-old Cicero refused to perform the rituals of the master that were his mother's as well. The pain of the whipping Nancy administered permanently branded him with a child's guilt for maybe causing his father's demise, a nagging unease as to whether, had he prayed along with his mother in those final weeks before his father died, Morgan might have lived.

No longer unadulterated idealist, he was now modest, quiet perhaps to a fault, never picked a fight in cold blood. Since coming to live inside the swamp, he generally knew what Rose and Jasper or Bill were thinking. Their world had in some ways been simpler for him to learn—the commitment to die for each other—than it had been for him as a young man to come to grips with his larger world of what was supposed to be but which didn't exist except in his own dream of it.

Like termite trails etched into the smooth wood under an old tree's bark, Cicero's past seemed to him a twisting trail with less rhyme or reason than simply a story. Seeing things that way dampened the fire that had once burned inside a younger Cicero. He could see the connections between things and choices and people, but he lacked enough faith to confidently predict what was best or to preach to others as he had done helping the black sheriff, John Brown, organize a land boycott after the Civil War. A lot of people who joined them had died. One of Cicero's most painful memories was walking away from a field where election workers were being massacred by mounted white men.

Back into the swamp he'd fled, to Rose. The way it had happened, he could never put out of mind. Nor the outside world, and Rose knew as much. She was sensitive about that. Walk around like your fire out, she'd say of his distant way of being about the cabin, his mind off in another world that she did not feel part of.

While February frosts still smothered open spaces, Cicero was up with the dawn. New cedar shakes were wedged on the roof and tarred down. He hunted and filled up the space beneath the cabin roof with venison strips curing, stretched the hides on frames. With a salt brine, he pickled half of the flesh of a wild hog he shot. The other half, he roasted in a pit. Cicero's single-minded energy made Rose nervous, and she held off reminding him that there was little need to put away meat with good weather at hand.

It was the spring following settlement of Mound Bayou, a matter all over Cicero's mind, though he never simply opened up and talked to Rose about it. That spring, Bill Williams, who'd spent the winter away at an old camp of his own, arrived back in the camp they all shared. He walked inside Rose and Cicero's cabin to lay a sheaf of tobacco on the table.

"Didn't want to start the season empty-handed," Bill said to Rose. "Tobacco made you my friend once, so I brung you some more."

Cicero fingered the silken soft bundle tobacco and, with the energy that had ruled him lately, embraced Old Bill.

"So many presents for my wife," Cicero said. "What if I was off fishing when a home wrecker like you showed up?"

"Well, for one, quit huggin' me. I ain't a woman."

"He glad to see you," Rose said. "This rain kept me indoors a spell, but he been busy as a bee."

"A real swamp woman," Bill said, "ain't scared o' gittin' wet. You shouldda been helpin' your man work."

"Well, now, speakin' o' wet, who is it I never seen bathe?"

"Oops!" Cicero said. "Maybe I should go fishing."

"Let's smoke a peace pipe, Princess Rose," Bill said. "I a grown man come to honor my neighbor's wife."

"Well, honor is one thing," Rose said. "Your mouth is another."

"Good to have you back," Cicero said, walking to pull a tangle of fishing lines attached to ropes from beneath a door in the floor. "My dear Rose hasn't been laughing much of late."

"Don't pick at me, cherie."

"It's the truth," Cicero insisted. "Go on, talk to Bill, I have to work."

"Ain't about work. Truth is, you chasin' fool thoughts around in your big head again. Plain forgit I'm around when you do that."

"If you want something, ask me. Got to pull in some fish for you to have while I'm gone."

"Bein' gone, cherie, is our main problem. I wondered if you was plannin' to leave me alone again."

"What is the matter, woman? My chores are finished."

"Do you realize how much time we was apart on account of you gone away doin' your politics?"

"If you don't mind," Bill interrupted, "before you'n him git at it—I ain't ate all day."

"You sit down and cut me some tobacco," Rose said. "Got a choice o' pig or venison."

"Ahh, the pig, please—a foot if one got meat on it."

Rose went about selecting meat from a covered pan near the fireplace. Cicero sighed, tossed his rope set with fish hooks to the floor and, instead of leaving, sat at the table with Bill. Bill pulled out a pipe, offered it to Cicero who shook his head.

"Why you never smoke, Cicero?"

"Never started."

"I ain't got no wife, so when I'm alone I fix me a smoke and a drink and let the time pass."

"The drink part suits me."

"That," Rose said, setting food for Bill on the table, "and worryin' 'bout his politics. Can't be happy in this one little place. He fret about the whole damn world."

Bill dropped his head to bite off some tobacco, spit into his hand and rubbed the tobacco into a plug.

"Your man was in the government, Rose. Ain't that good?"

"All I know is it took him years before I laid eyes on him. We separated kinda sudden on account o' Abyssinia's trouble."

"A Union navy officer attacked my sister," Cicero said, "and Jasper killed the man. Rose sneaked Abby and Jasper out of Davis Bend and brought her up here."

"Here's yer pipe, Rose."

Rose snatched her newly filled pipe from Bill and sat apart. As she lit up, Cicero walked over and pulled a whiskey jug from beside the fireplace.

"Pour me some," Rose said. "Bill, too."

"People greetin' is time for celebratin'," Bill said. "Why else we live together, hanh?"

"Tell you what," Rose said, "pull out the good whiskey, Cicero. We ain't seen Bill for two months. A little socializin' make me feel better."

"I rather not drink too much right before I go visit my sister. I'll be away a month."

"A whole month? Figured there was a reason for all this work."

"First, Abby, my dear, then I have young Dick's lesson."

"Yes, Abyssinia's boy again."

"They pay me for his lessons, Rose. You encouraged me to do it. Why are you so prickly?"

"It don't take a whole month to visit Abby and go teach her boy. What's going on?"

"Abyssinia wants to move out of Clarksdale."

"Move?! She ain't got people nowhere else."

"She got it in her head to go take a look at this new town."

"Abby wouldn't last a week in a hardship town."

"It's not so bad."

"How you know, Cicero? They got log cabins and what? . . . Nothin' like your fancy sister used to."

Rose stuck her pipe in her mouth and began puffing away. Bill cleared his throat.

"I 'spect I oughtta go find Jasper 'fore it git dark."

"You can go to hell, Bill Williams!"

"Yes, my princess."

"And take Cicero with you."

A WEEK LATER, THE SKY WAS a cauldron of dirty wash as Cicero and his sister, Abyssinia, drummed their feet on the depot platform in Clarksdale awaiting the train from Memphis. As usual when outside the swamp, Cicero had left his skins and leather behind. He was wearing denim pants and jacket, a rain slicker on his arm against the inevitable.

"I am so thrilled," Abyssinia said, "to be going down to see Isaiah."

"You and your little boyfriend oughtta have big fun."

"Shucks, we were babies, then. You know I never liked any of those boys at the plantation. Something I'll tell you about one day."

"Hard to believe the whole Montgomery clan moving up here."

"Everybody uses that name, Cicero. I thought you was gonna come with me."

Cicero cleared his throat, shook his head.

"Twenty miles would be a long walk back home."

"Cicero . . . you are afraid to face your son."

"No, no! What I want is to take Rose down there with me."

"Ahaaa, so you never told her about Buck?"

"I told her when I moved up here."

"You oughtta leave that swamp woman and join the civilized world again."

"I am as civilized as I choose to be . . . Listen!"

A soft but insistent sound became a roar and then softened as the locomotive dropped steam on the long approach to the depot.

"Boy!" Abyssinia said. "Be careful. My good clothes are in that trunk."

"Yes ma'm, you must got a rich husband. That him with you?"

"No, this is—"

"A friend," Cicero said. "I'm a friend of the lady from olden days."

Dragging the huge trunk close to the train preoccupied the boy before he replied to Cicero.

"I'd'a said y'all be brother'n sister 'cept you bein' right brown'n all, her so light-skinned with that long hair."

There were a passenger car and three freight cars behind the locomotive. Four passengers boarded in Clarksdale, along with a mail pouch. Cicero ushered Abyssinia into the passenger car, and all eyes were immediately upon them. Abyssinia was tall, handsome of face and carefully groomed in an expensive dress. Though nearing forty, her hair was barely touched with gray. No separate car for black and white passengers. Few had the money to ride the train, and when they did, like Cicero and Abby, they made for empty seats. It would not have been unthinkable to sit beside a white passenger, but then, a passenger coach on a train through the swamp was seldom full. Cicero stopped at a seat near the rear of the car. He took the window seat.

"Unless I miss my guess," Cicero said, "the two men up near the front facing us . . . One of them is the sheriff of Bolivar County. Do you know how many stories Jasper and old Bill have spawned? God forbid they should learn I'm a political Radical from years back."

"It's been a long time since you was trying to take over government."

"Keep your facts straight: it was the white people who took over the government. *We* were elected."

"What so ever."

"I have made no peace with your world."

"It ain't the world out here, it's Rose keeping you in that swamp."

Abyssinia's leg bumped the barrel of Cicero's pistol, and she flinched.

"Are you gonna hold that in your hand all the way?"

Cicero placed his pistol under the edge of his sister's skirt and she covered it. He moved across her knees into the aisle, then toward the front of the car and through the door to the locomotive. Standing there talking to the men in the locomotive was the conductor.

"Excuse me for disturbing you," Cicero said, "but would you stop the train at Mr. Bobo's plantation."

The white man snarled at Cicero. "You pay up first."

"Yessir. How much?"

"You'n that pretty one both gettin' off at Bobo?"

"No, sir, she's going on down to Mr. Isaiah Montgomery's new town."

"What business she got in that nigger place? She best go back to whoever she work for in Clarksdale."

"Yessir, I'll tell her that."

Cicero paid and glanced at the sheriff whose eyes were closed as Cicero returned to his seat.

"Tell Isaiah I'll come visit soon as I can," Cicero whispered to his sister.

"Come on, go with me, now! We never been anywhere together."

"I have business with your son, darling."

"You can tutor my boy anytime, so that ain't in the way."

"I don't like being away so much."

"Rose again. She know if you stay out here long enough a man like you could find another woman."

Cicero looked away to stare silently through the window, and Abyssinia let the conversation drop. As the train slowed for the Bobo Plantation, Cicero slipped his pistol back into his pocket. He tapped his sister's thigh and eased into the aisle again.

"You take care of yourself," he said.

Cicero left the train a half mile from where he and the family had ambushed the track-laying crew a couple years earlier. Abyssinia, like a lot of ex-slaves, just would not accept the reality that black people were at war with white people, and so they did not take up arms in time. Race war was a bogeyman concept that scared too many into letting the bad times roll. Wilderness people like Rose and Jasper understood. Like guerilla fighters of a later century, they lived apart.

From where the train let Cicero off, he walked south to Harris Bayou and located the tiny hidden boat. As he launched into the flow, his argument with Rose about being away so much grew in significance. He reached the Sunflower and turned downstream toward home. He saw the two cypress trees marked by lightning, massive multiple trunks rising out of the water like so many stalagmites. He put ashore inside a shaded cavern carved by fire. It had been chosen to hide sign of the many landings all of them made. It was only after poling between the outer and inner tree—pivoting first down stream and then toward shore to wedge in beside another boat—that a person became aware that it was frequently used.

By now a fine mist was in the air. Distant voices came above the emerging patter of raindrops on the leaves. A rifle shot startled Cicero, and he halted, ear to the wind.

". . . some white boy out for a lark. Put a scare on his ass!" Bill William's voice.

"Ain't no such," Jasper's voice. "See, you ain't always right. I told you who it is comin'. Hey, momma, I'm right, non?"

"I got no time for squabble," Rose said. "Got to clean this fish."

"If your ma had married me," Bill's voice said. "I would'a teached her how to be a good squaw."

"And why, cherie," Rose said, "do you think you'n me didn't get together before my Cicero come up here?"

They were still laughing as Cicero neared the clearing around the cabin. Raindrops hung like jewels in a moist thicket of gray-flecked hair framing Rose's face.

"Mr. Cicero home, momma."

"We talkin' old times," Bill said to Cicero. "Times before you come live out here."

Bill stood up too fast and clutched at his side.

"Sit back down," Cicero said. "I'll join you soon as I put my slicker inside."

Bill's recently toothless mouth spread open more in pain than mirth as he eased back to the ground. He was wearing his usual beaded deerskin shirt, non-descript pants. Rose waved in Cicero's direction and doing so caused an indolent-eyed buffalo fish she'd been scaling to slip from her grasp. Watching it lodge pouting in the mud made all of them laugh as Cicero walked into the cabin.

"Always a pleasure to be home," Cicero mumbled.

"If you really mean that," Rose said. "How come you away so much?"

"You got," Cicero said, sticking his head back outside, "your family here all around."

"Don't you say that to me!" Rose waggled her long-bladed knife toward Cicero who raised his hands in apology. "If you hadn't been so block-headed a while back, we'd have a real family here now."

"I'll give you a baby," Bill said, "if you ain't too old. I coulda done it twenty years ago but you wouldn't have me."

"Don't, don't even start that again," Rose said to him.

"You the one talkin' fam'ly," Bill said. "I only come up here 'cause a friend o mine told me 'bout this woman sellin' herbs."

Jasper had said nothing. Rose pointed to Bill but spoke to her son.

"His woman friend was tyin' to git ridda nuisance."

Bill's head snapped around.

"Wasn't no such. The man sent me was Borgus Willin', the only other swamp trader 'sides me who was born in these parts."

"'I do remember him," Rose said. "Big old galoot with real soft ways. Maybe the strangest man I ever met."

"Borgus told me you was tradin' every thing but your own big self."

"Borgus! Nothin' on his mind but women. The man made me laugh, but he was fulla mess. He would say, Why a man gotta look down at the same star evuh night, when they's so many sparkling' all aroun'." Rose touched her breasts. "That's what women was to him, stars to touch once or twice . . . Wasn't enough for me!"

Rose picked up her fish, slapped it atop a tree stump and went back to scaling it. Bill jerked at Jasper's sleeve.

"Ain't no fam'ly here," Bill said. "Folks you can count on one hand ain't no fam'ly. Fam'ly big—mothers and children, cousins an' uncles and grandfathers, especially grandfathers. They tell everyone how a thing is done, how a marriage supposed to be made, how to bury a old man with respect."

"Here recent," Rose said, "you got so much misery, you oughtta go on off'n die."

"I'm gonna live to bury you, woman. If you should bury me, do it on the high ground. Don't want no water on my bones, or I come back an' shut your mouth for good."

"Be right nice to have you as a haint, you so full of fun and other stuff."

Cicero emerged at that moment to join them.

"Welcome home for real, cherie," Rose said.

Cicero smiled ambiguously as Rose opened her arms. His answer was a token caress as he moved past her and sat down.

The sound of Rose's knife thunking into a tree stump beside him startled everyone.

"Look at you, Rose!" Bill said. "My spirit come back and help Cicero beat you."

"You keep outta this, mister old man. Didn't I open my arms to him?"

Cicero stood up and belatedly embraced his wife.

"Mr. Bill Williams," Rose said, "ain't had no fam'ly life. Wouldn't none of them women from his ma's people have no skinny little runt with five names."

"Runt! I was married two times. First time I had a fam'ly."

"Well, where is they?"

Rose snatched up her fish and attacked the remaining scales.

"Goes to show you ain't listened much," Bill said. "Fam'ly important, it's why we live in a village. Man rather run with the panther, sleep under sky, play on the wind. You make a home, which ain't nothin for a man to do. We live in a village to help you women raise children."

"Hear that, cherie?" Rose said.

"You talkin' to me?" Jasper asked.

"Tell him again, Bill," Rose said, a forearm smoothing back her thick hair.

"Tell him what, Rose?"

"About fam'ly—my gran'babies. Else, why am I shootin' at folks to hold onto this land?"

"Aw, momma, don't start that."

"*You* ain't never started, not since you broke up with that Maidy gal years ago. She spoil you for marryin'?"

"Ain't time yet. 'Sides, momma, you got Mr. Cicero for company, me'n Bill, too."

"But, cherie," Rose said, "it's just us, non? No children at all, and I don't want memory o' all we had here to die out. There's folk here'n there live like we do—I don't count them neither. They hidin' out, lettin life pass. Non, we need young folks. It's too late for me. All I got left is you. Hey, Bill?"

"What?"

"You ain't never before said you had children."

"Their momma took then to Injun Terr'tory. She didn't want to live apart."

"Too bad they ain't close. I'd bring 'em in to visit. I want fam'ly around me—fam'ly! Like the white folks got. We good as them, and I wouldn't be no woman atall if I didn't want new life around me."

"We maroon, momma," Jasper said. "Too many in camp make too much sign. Was only four of us when I was growin' up."

"We was runnin' from slavery, cherie. Ain't the same now."

"Cain't keep white folks outta this swamp," Jasper said, "if you got beaucoup folks comin' and goin'."

"Look up at the sky," Rose said.

"Why?"

"Just look at it!"

"So?"

"What you see?

"Nothin' . . . clouds."

"And every one different from the next, non?"

Jasper nodded.

"That's life. Every minute, every woman different—depend on how the wind blow. So don't tell me about what was. You change! That's what you do, boy."

Jasper hopped up, but a big rabbit-skin covered foot slipped and he sprawled in the mud. Bill Williams cackled louder than anyone. He tapped Jasper with the barrel of his rifle.

"Git up'n listen to your ma. Gitchu a woman like Verlean! You be old one day, too. Remember what I say 'bout a old man cain't hardly teach nothin' in a new world. If you make a village, then you got a world where you be respected, an' the young mens listen to you."

Jasper sat where he'd landed.

"I wasn't raised," he said, "to turn my life over to no woman. Verlean, kinda rough."

"The boy," Bill Williams said, now holding his side in mirth, "is tellin' the truth."

"Are all of the young women like her?" Rose asked.

"They tell you one thing, mean another," Jasper said. "They fight about anything."

"Do you mean," Rose asked, "they're like you?"

"He means," Cicero said, "that getting together can't be forced. It happens."

"And now, you cain't remember where you live. Up with your sister, or teachin' her boy by that Alligator white man. If you had come join me when we first met . . ."

"Rose, look, I am truly sorry we missed having children."

"Easy to say."

"That's all I can say!"

Bill dug the butt of his rifle into the ground, pulled himself to his feet.

"Me'n Jasper ain't finished our work at the still. 'Spect we oughtta leave you have the rest o' this nice talk alone."

Rose grabbed up her fish and marched toward the cabin. The silence held until Cicero followed her inside, and she looked up from her work.

"Bill been tellin' me," Rose said, "about the new railroad town. The people come from Vicksburg."

Cicero nodded stiffly and turned to go back outside. Rose put aside her fish.

"Are you hiding something?"

Cicero shook his head but avoided Rose's eyes.

"Don't start lying—what is it?"

"Why you gotta call me a liar? I never lie! You tell me one time I've lied to you."

"Then, answer me."

"What do you know about the new place?"

"A few days after you left, Bill come in here and told me it was some of our people tryin' to build a town like the white folks. They come up from Vicksburg."

"The people are my old family from Hurricane Plantation, Isaiah Montgomery and all of those I left behind when I decided to come here and join you."

Rose returned to her fish. Doggedly, she finished cutting it into strips and swung the pot containing it onto the iron hook over the fireplace. As she added water to the pot, Cicero came up behind her.

"Remember I told you about a son of mine."

"Um hunh."

"Abby heard that everybody who stayed on the plantation moved up here."

Rose turned to face Cicero.

"Does that mean your boy in this new town?"

Cicero nodded, and Rose turned her face for a moment. It wasn't clear if what she was brushing away from her cheek was a fish scale.

"You know, Cicero, it ain't like you broke some rule with the boy's momma. Both o' you wanted some love, and for all you knew I was long gone, never to be seen."

"Rose, I was—"

"Hush! You was a man, her a woman, and we was apart. People got to take each other as we come. Even here after slavery, the white folks' rules don't work."

Cicero reached for Rose, but she avoided him and moved away into a chore. He sat down, cleared his throat before continuing.

"When this rainy spell ends, I'll finish putting Abyssinia's house up for sale. Then it's over to Alligator for young Dick's school time. After that, you and I can take our first train ride to visit my son."

"Your stuck-up friends still want me outta your life."

"No, no."

"Quit lyin'. Like Bill say, the only thing that folks like you'n me gonna have soon is young folks to look to. You, Jasper, Bill—all go off for one thing or another. Me, I just do a little trading."

"Fine! I came in here and gave up everything—everything I ever cared about—to be with you. You think that was easy?"

"Your choice, wasn't it? Ready to change your mind again?"

A surge of new rain unsettled an old hen brooding over some eggs in a hanging cage, and she began clucking away. Rose ran to move her to shelter. Cicero walked to the door and stood watching. Jasper and Bill had departed for Jasper's cabin. Despite the rain, Cicero was feeling so angry, he snatched up his slicker and walked down to the river to think.

That night, Rose put on her nightgown and pulled a rocking chair close to the fireplace to stare at the fire. After awhile, in a ritual that dated back to her first maroon family, she fetched a vial of rattlesnake venom and a knife of carved deer antler. Cicero sat on the bed nearest her with his bare legs sticking out below his nightshirt.

"I feel so empty," Rose said, "and my words are spiteful. I need to find my spirit."

"Are you sure this is still safe?"

"Don't be like my boy, cherie. You and me was raised different. Your dream was about makin' some new world where people ain't hateful. Which one of us got the more right to what we believe?"

"I cannot answer that. I tried my way and failed. I don't know your dream world."

"My dream world ain't no more than everyday but, like, stripped down and more intense. What I'm worried about or thinking on when I enter the dream kind of guides me through all the confusion."

"Confusion . . . I probably never confessed how guilty I felt letting Jasper bring me back here after our workers got shot up at Friars Point. The white vigilantes were mounted and armed, and most of us weren't. They outnumbered us, too . . . Just that I grew up wanting to be a hero like I'd read about in books. Fight to the last, to the death. Instead, Jasper and I arrived at the scene, took one look . . . So, much for heroics."

"Well, it was a lot more people than you fightin' them white folks. They was grown and made they own choice. You didn't make it for 'em."

"No."

"Past is past. Come back out of it and join me here."

Cicero stood and embraced Rose. When they stepped back from each other, he sat down on the bed beside her chair. She reached for the vial of venom and picked up the knife before sitting. She was humming again when she pricked her arm and smeared on a film of venom. As she closed her eyes and settled back to wait, Cicero leaned close.

"All I want out of life now is a little time like what I had as a child. Maybe that was my heaven. I had no needs because my father was there. I had a space in which to appreciate life."

Rose opened her eyes, a smile softened wrinkles in her forehead.

". . . I need to think, cherie. Takes a while for my thoughts to set . . . Right now, all I want is less fear that this little time we got now is over. It's better than ever. I'm gittin older'n I'm scared o' what come next. 'Cause I don't know. I never been old before. Jasper ain't the only one worry 'bout things changing. Got nothin' to do with the land, just me'n you on my mind, cherie."

Cicero reached over and cupped his hands around Rose's face. She chuckled, pointed to his lap.

"If I sit there, I be a girl in dream that I never was, but you wouldn't git no sleep."

"And I am too young to object, until you got up."

"Africa love, cherie . . ." Rose stood up and let her gown drop. ". . . A whole village in my past is tellin' me go-ahead an' be a woman."

He opened his mouth only to feel hers. There was heat, more intense than what was radiating from the fire nearby. Then her fingers, surprising cool, replaced her mouth and played all over his face. His eyes were closed and he thought to share how he felt, but he was being pushed backward, and her legs were opening around him. Trying to find words for feelings too huge to contain, all he could do was to shout.

By morning, the rain had moved off, and the sky was clear. It was as if Cicero and Rose, both, had returned from a voyage. She had slept deeply. At some point late that morning, she commenced cleaning out the cabin of its accumulation from winter, a chore she had delayed in some protest over his being away. The incandescence of the night had left her full of energy. She could hardly sit down without jumping up. Cicero had remained awake all night in one of his overnight thinking session that Rose usually complained about, but he had wrestled no demons.

He surprised her with breakfast: crawfish with slivers of salt-encrusted ham scrambled that she had taught Cicero to prepare. Sparkles of warm light from a large cantaloupe sun were filling her eyes and caressing her skin through the trees by that time. Not long after she and Cicero met, they swam the Mississippi to camp on the other side awaiting the huge mid-year morning sun like the one now full upon her. All morning, Rose's happy smile was an indulgence to Cicero, though he was deliciously fatigued from lack of sleep and the exertion of making love. Knowing that if he wished for more he could have it, he lacked the will.

While Rose was still eating beside him in the bed, he walked over to pull his skin-wrapped memoirs out of the storage cellar. Time to knit up memories of the past with the present. He had not in all of the years living in the swamp, before now, felt so guilty for not continuing his saga of the lives that had touched his own. His time with Rose had been part of all that back at Davis Bend, but he had written very little following the first years in the swamp. He would not have said that his lingering guilt about the massacre had anything to do with bleeding him of the focus his writing required, but this morning his only focus was love.

He noticed that the skins in which he had wrapped his writings were muddy, the wooden box they'd been in having swelled with moisture enough for cracks to open. Suddenly, he had a sense of what Rose would have called a time meant to be. Had he not just rescued his writings, the coming months would have reduced them to a blur of mildew. Anxiety at the thought of the destruction of his life's work flashed inside and lingered. He realized that a part of him was just as anxious about time passing as Rose had confessed. Time. Seasons of his own wintry birth during slavery, the spring of freedom and voting as a Radical, his fall into confusion from which only the swamp had provided refuge.

He did not wish to trouble Rose with his empty anxiety, so he stoked up the fire and spread his pages to dry. Then, he poked through to find what he had written years before about Abyssinia's son and, earlier, about his own son, Buck. Rose continued to smile as she began to pull up some of the whiskey made two seasons earlier that she would soon trade when she made her spring run. As she worked, pouring whiskey into smaller containers for sale, it seemed to her that Cicero was troubled, and she offered her smile as a talisman that refused to acknowledge anxiety.

But he kept sighing deeply, pursing his lips. So she came forward and parked herself on his lap whispering, "Even I cain't re-live what's past. Love teaches that." And Cicero's sorrow opened into a fierce embrace. Rose had had to carve her own lean existence out of a wilderness, and—Cicero suddenly realized—Jasper, too, had had a father, captured trying to escape and sold away. Rose had never laid eyes on that loving part of her self again. Wound to wound, the lovers shared a teary kiss, and a kind of healing was soon again passion as Cicero whispered, "Show me some more Africa, love."

"**G**ENTLEMEN, MY FATHER NAMED me Irving Urbaniak. You may call me Banyak. I am local railroad land salesman. I know that you are eager for hospitality car, and it is being provisioned as we speak . . . Yes, Mr. Hopson?"

"We might add more of that swamp to our plantation now that your railroad is hauling crops. Shippin' on the Sunflower River was a caution because the Corp' Engineers haven't dredged it in ten years."

"No they haven't . . . You, sir, please, I don't know your name."

"Not to turn this into wrestling match, but I wonder how young Hopson over there and several others I see can make common cause about the same land."

"Still too much swamp land around to fight about it," Hopson said.

Cleveland was also a new settlement along the rail line, though not the same type as Mound Bayou and others that had begun with someone buying and reselling railroad land. Cleveland was the site of a railroad supply depot on a spur track leading off the main. On that spur, three upholstered and brass-appointed luxury coaches were parked. Inside of one car, ten men sat on chairs angled toward the speaker in their midst. A door at the end of the car opened. A red-haired man walked in and shuffled forward.

"My name is Chester Bolls. I ain't—aren't—a landowner."

"Just what," the man from Hopson Plantation asked, "is your business?"

"I was working this area for near on three years. I got near-personal knowledge of four times when a giant bear-thing was seen at various places."

"Gentlemen, Mr. Bolls is my most trusted assistant. He introduced me to my good wife." Banyak placed his hand on Chester Bolls' shoulder, "He has information about all these strange things."

"Why," Hopson asked, "are you talking about all that stuff?"

"Mr. Banyak ask me to come in here," Bolls said.

"No offense," Hopson said, "but it's a waste talking about old shootings."

"But that's why nobody bought that swamp near the Sunflower," Chester Bolls insisted. "You don't need to be scared. It was somebody dressed up like a bear doing the shooting. I was in the first group got shot at."

"What we know," an unknown man said, "is that a clan of in-bred colored people are running wild over there. Don't make me feel no better if it was them shootin' ."

"That just mean," Bolls said, "you all got to hire some men to go in there."

"Do you really think," Hopson said, "that a little swamp land is worth so much trouble?"

Abruptly, as if presiding over a simmering pot that he did not wish to boil over, the man named Banyak stepped in front of Chester Bolls.

"Now, now. We all born white men, and we know that savages born to be controlled. Our job is to sell this land, and gentlemen, here is even more exciting information, truly exciting . . . In years after slavery, when the colored was working for themselves, they had to work hard to survive. Well, production went almost double what slaves produced on de same land during slavery. That tells you how rich that swamp land is."

"Are you sure about them numbers?" Hopson asked.

"Absolutely," Banyak said. "Official tax records show how many tons of cotton shipped south to Vicksburg usin' river barges. We compare that time to records for the same handful of plantations from before the war."

"So?"

"Listen, the numbers have doubled again. Mississippi Valley plantations is paying tax on more than double today the crop that was shipped in 1884 when this railroad commenced operation. The savage races have no vision. They only grow food crops and a little cotton for spending money. Sharecropping is making you rich, and the railroad give you easy transportation. Think how much that land will be worth in ten years."

"Hold on, Banyak!"

"Yes, Mr. Otto?"

The man named Otto came to his feet.

"If that land is so valuable, why are you selling?"

"As they say in my old country, idea is a raw egg you got to do something with. Railroad can't exploit the land. Besides, if you gentlemen buy land, that is good for me as salesman and for you."

"I suggest," Otto said, "that you have the sheriff extend the law over into that swamp. Is anybody here from Coahoma County? I don't see 'em—'cept for young Hopson, over there."

"Before the law will do anything," Banyak said, "you gentlemen here must first make a plan."

"Seems to me," Otto said, "you the one doing the planning."

Laughter rippled through the room.

"I represent the Mississippi Delta Plantation." The voice was that of a well dressed man sporting an immense jeweled ring on his right hand. All heads turned toward him. "You gentleman are deluded if you think people who risked their lives in this Miss'ippi Valley for two generations will allow you to bring in a horde of ne'er-do-wells. We do not favor more white trash or niggers flocking in without a plan for the stability of government and services along the River."

"Before you respond, Mr. Otto," Banyak said, "My employer anticipated such objection. First off, the railroad has already sold enough land to pay off building the rail line. None of you bought this land then. It is because you did not buy that we have a string of new towns rising along our right of way. We prefer you add it to your plantations because our railroad depends on freight revenues. You gentlemen are better equipped to develop the land for commercial use. So, you see, we on your side."

The coach erupted in side conversations, and Banyak ushered Chester Bolls to the door of the car.

"You did well, Chester. You told that old bear story and reminded them why they was scared in the first place."

"So they don't buy up too much land right now."

"Correct . . . I like the way you talk now—me'n you both. I don't say de an' dis too much no more."

Both men chuckled.

"The greedy bastards will fight with each other if anybody serious about buying land, but I think they here to have fun."

"Hope you right"

"Leave it to me, Chester. This is last time railroad gonna try to sell this land. Too hard to sell. Nothing gonna prevent me and you from taking over selling railroad land. Our bosses won't have no where else to turn."

"But if none of the people in there wants to buy, I don't un'erstand how we gonna do better?"

"Unlike the railroad, Chester, we will sell to railroad employees. Railroad bring them in to harvest timber, and we show them how to become landowners."

"There won't be any of that." The man from the Mississippi Delta had approached Banyak and Bolls unnoticed. "White trash or niggers would turn our government upside down."

"That," Banyak said, clapping the man on the back before addressing everyone in the room, "is why we come to you. If you buy this land won't be whole bunch of trash nowhere. Now, gentlemen, is time for entertainment. When you go to de other coach, you will be directed to the parlor car for refreshment and female companion. Make your selection and withdraw to your private bunk."

Inside the middle car, booths of leather studded with brass hugged both sides of the aisle. At one end, a wall of glasses and a countertop covered with beverages waited behind a beaming black man outfitted in a short white coat. He bowed as each guest entered, extended one white-gloved hand then another toward an open booth. Before all of the male guests were seated, the door at the other end of the parlor car opened, and the women entered. They were well scrubbed and fragrant, though a mixed bunch of wildflowers. Outside, Chester Bolls was busy ushering the last woman inside.

"Make your man happy, you take ten more dollars back to the house."

"Mister, I ain't no house girl, I do laundry."

"Chester?"

"Mr. Banyak? Thought you'd be enjoying yourself inside."

"Did you bring our charter papers from Memphis?"

"All taken care of," Bolls said, pulling a legal paper out of his pocket. "Lawyer got the company organized in Mississippi. But I just don't see why the railroad would let us take the land off they hands and re-sell it when they could sell it theyself?"

"Today is all for show, Chester. None of the men in there taking a poke at the pig will invest hard money in swamp land. Oh, they'd buy it on time, or if a bank loaned them the money. So today, am just an employee doing what I'm told. We will wait for the railroad higher ups to agree that their leftover land is impossible to sell."

"I cain't hardly believe that."

"The Illinois Central runs trains," Banyak said. "They can't manage selling land on credit from up in New York. That's where you and me come in—Illinois Central Land Associates. The name will have people believe it's still the railroad selling."

"And we make a lotta money?"

"Is the way to progress. People in my old country beat down like the people here, but they never talk about progress. This Mississippi got lot of people need that swamp land to survive, so we going to talk progress and get rich from doing it."

Howls and laughter, cigar smoke and body odors escaping the parlor car through the open door grew. Banyak and Bolls walked a distance away. Bolls leaned to whisper in Banyak's ear.

"What we do about them swamp people we run into?"

"We put a bear dog on de bear."

JAMES ALOYSIUS DOLAN WAS ONCE a penniless young Irish-man hustled out of New York City to work on what was called the Mississippi Frontier. He served his time before the Civil War erecting levees to protect the wilderness farm of James Alcorn, the man later to become a Reconstruction governor. Alcorn himself had arrived on a flat-bottom boat with his sister, two waifs of fortune seeking lives for themselves from the swamp. His sister married John Clark a few years after Clark organized a lumber camp on the Sunflower. Dolan had been part of the wave to follow them, and Dolan had to acknowledge and bow to the established trees.

Known as JD, after his levee work was cut short, he became a wagon merchant, then an outlaw after being fired for organizing a brothel inside Friars Point and by so doing scandalizing Eliza Alcorn Clark. As the Civil War came on, and unwilling to fight on anybody's side, JD wandered off to hide in Texas. Always ever onward in the pursuit of opportunity, he had again become a storekeeper when he met and took up with Abyssinia Morgan. Now, years later, he owned a farm southwest of Alligator Lake and a general store in the settlement on its shore. Ignoring threats of fever and flood, he had lived there since the year he settled into a log cabin with an infant son and hired a succession of wet nurses.

The boy was four when his father completed a plantation house, a two-story affair showing a front porch with the roof sloping down over it supported by a row of square planked posts dressed to look like columns in copy of grand antebellum design. Over time, the uncured wood columns warped. JD's son called it "snaggle-tooth house." Richard Cicero Dolan had been five—two years older than Cicero Morgan's own son—when Cicero arrived in northern Mississippi, and Abyssinia forced the well-dressed Honorable Cicero Morgan to go remind JD of his promise to have the boy educated.

Being once indentured to a levee gang and clawing his way up in the world had left JD coveting everything he had missed out on, including an education. So he readily hired Cicero to tutor his son. Occasionally over the years, the boy would ask Cicero questions that the child's father refused to answer.

"All I know of your mother," Cicero had said, "is that she was a fine up-standing woman who wanted you to grow up and make her proud."

"What's 'proud,'" Dick asked.

"Quit yer silliness," JD said from a nearby chair. "Mr. Cicero ain't got the time for such."

"That's all right. You see, Richard—"

"My name is Richard, but everybody call me Dick."

"Dick, you will make me proud if you grow up feeling as good about yourself as you do right now."

"Course I feel good. I ain't sick."

JD paused in his whiskey drinking to laugh.

"No, you're a very healthy lad," Cicero said. "Now, do you know what a lesson is?"

"No, but you going to tell me."

"Are you having fun talking to me?"

"If I didn't talk to you I have to go out in the barn by myself."

"A trifle too active, the lad." JD threw down a drink. "I make him take his play time into the barn so he won't be breaking the finer things I've bought for the house."

"And what," Cicero said to Dick, "have you got to say?"

"I like mules and horseys. I can talk to them when Pa don't want me around, and I don't like the women he bring here anyway—except for Sadie."

"Sadie's my housekeeper," JD said.

"And you like her?" Cicero asked.

"She cook what I like to eat, and she rock me to sleep."

"As you can see," JD said, "I try to give the lad what he needs, and Sadie is a very nice colored woman. No one I'm involved with mind you. Just a woman for the lad to know some of what havin' a mother is like."

"Did you," Dick asked Cicero, "know my ma?"

"You already," JD said, coming to his feet, "been answered in that regard. Your ma's dead, but she was a fine lady. Now quit askin' or it's back to the barn with you."

Dick shut his mouth, and, with a twist of his finger, locked it. JD left the room, but before he did, Cicero watched the child begin to pout.

"Not to disagree with your father, Dick, but a good thing about having a teacher is that I am not so busy as your father. You may ask me anything."

The little boy's eyes were glued to the stairs as the sound of his father's boots ascended. When the sound paused on the upper landing and then led off toward the back of the house, the child looked into Cicero's eyes.

"Pa say if I was a hound dog I be spoilt."

"And why is that?"

"I bark too much."

Once a month, Cicero would visit the Dolan house and remain overnight. The arrangement allowed for two sessions with the child. Young Dick was likely enough and, with the help of Sadie, the housekeeper, learned eventually to read and to write. It had, however, been like trying to keep a bird from flying to keep Dick from running, tumbling or singing during study time. Cicero told no one, but his job was a link to teaching school back on Davis Bend before going off to the legislature.

Cicero never heard the whole story, certainly no confession from JD of the circumstance in his white world that turned him suddenly fearful of continuing to raise Dick inside his home, but one day Cicero arrived to learn that Dick had been told that the barn would become his permanent home. Dick understood something of the emotional implication of that act, and afterwards, being called inside the house troubled Dick. Shortly afterwards, Dick blurted out his rage, and Cicero gave advice.

"The world isn't always what we want it to be. I was your age when I learned that."

"Somebody made you live in a barn?"

"In a slave shed, packed in with about twenty other children. It was awful."

"My barn ain't bad. 'Least I got mule to talk to."

"C'mon, I'll take you for a wagon ride."

It did not take more than a week for the irrepressible child to return to form, eager to talk about everything to an adult who would listen. He had a mass of blankets, a knife and a few toys hidden away. Inside the barn, Dick would do anything he was asked, even read lessons aloud. Also he formed a habit of walking up to a certain mule and turning his head to and fro while explaining what he had learned to the beast. Questioning Dick as to whether he understood enough to go teach his mule became Cicero's method of last resort.

Over the years, Cicero's delight in their sessions grew. He told no one of his growing fondness for Dick, not even Rose, though she sensed it and began sending the boy presents. Dick came to know her as the medicine woman who would appear out of the swamp and sell his father whiskey and herbs, sometimes skins or dried meats. By the time Dick was old enough to care for his father's store he quite predictably found himself with the job. That was when Rose began accompanying Cicero to the store, and after a fashion, she would tell Dick fanciful stories of magic in the swamp, or her dreamtime, of good and bad. And because Rose never required Dick to read one of the stories she told, he begged Cicero to bring her along

Young Dick's father would leave him alone for days at a time with only the cooking and light discipline of Sadie, the housekeeper. That time alone led Dick into fanciful conversations with his pet mule, to whom he would confide in detail the strange exploits of JD. Behaving like a pet dog at sight of the boy, the mule would whinny and trot along toward him, even bray and kick his hooves in what might be called mule frustration if Dick ignored him, or gave more attention to a certain horse. To JD, who had asked why Dick held his head to the side silent with a vacant look in his eyes, Dick said, "'Tis listenin' to Mule, I am."

One afternoon JD stepped into his front room only to be greeted by none other than Dick's favorite mule, his horse and two sons of Sadie.

"Jesus, Mary and Joseph! Git 'em all outta here!"

"Calm down, Mr. JD," Sadie said. "The boy and me ain't know'd you was comin' home."

"Damn what the little bastard knew. You know better!"

Sadie bowed her head in meek supplication, and in the momentary silence, she turned to young Dick.

"C'mon, Mr. Dick, help git these critter back in the barn."

Sadie began flailing her arms around the room, and the livestock spooked. The housekeeper's sons ran for the back door cramming their mouths from a platter of biscuits on the dining room table. The animals balked at running through the front door, so Sadie snatched up her broom and struck one. It bolted into a drunken JD, who staggered up and teetered inside the door as the second animal bolted past, knocking JD into the door jamb. He bounced off of it rubbing his forehead, snatched Sadie's broom and turned to charge outside to beat the mule, but he never made it. The broomstick caught on the door frame and nearly strangled the drunken man. Dick and Sadie were leaning over JD giggling when he recovered enough to breathe. He pushed them away, ran outside and attacked the mule with his fists.

"Don't beat on Mule!" Dick screamed.

Not accustomed to being ordered around, certainly not by his son, JD roared and stumbled after Dick.

"Oh, please, Mr. JD, it was my fault." The housekeeper tried to grab JD's arm. "The horse got loose'n I was the one let the boy go bring it in."

"Leave go . . . I'll bust his tail!"

Sadie stepped between JD and his son.

"It was just a joke him bringin' the horse inside, Mr. JD. "

"Git outta my way, Sadie!"

"The boy's pet mule started havin' a jealous conniption . . . "

JD finally lurched past Sadie, and Dick scampered out of range laughing.

". . . The mule wanted to be with the horse," Sadie pleaded. "So when he broke out—"

"What'n hell are ye sayin'?"

"Yessuh, Dick brung him inside, too, but . . . side o' your barn been kicked out."

JD gave chase too late to prevent Dick from running upstairs for a heavy coat. The boy then leapt past his father to the ground floor and came up limping. Despite his injury, Dick ran or walked more than a mile to the store where he rested briefly before picking up provisions under the allowance of a curious storekeeper who worked for Dick's father. Dick refused to say where he was going, whether north to Clarksdale, or south.

Dick ran out to where the trail paralleling the southern shore of cigar-shaped Alligator Lake intersected the county road. Off to the side, in the rough so as to remain hidden from travelers, Dick rested for an hour. He didn't want to travel the county road where his father might find him, but he had no idea where to go next. To the east, the distant big trees along the Sunflower River rose in mysterious splendor above the rest of the swamp. Because it was the only direction away from home without a marked road, Dick finally headed toward them along a path atop the flood ridge bordering Harris Bayou.

It never entered his young mind that he might be within less than a days travel of where his tutor, Cicero, lived. Furthermore, rumors of the swamp that had already come to young Dick's attention were of the wrong kind in so far as a young white man being welcome to frolic through. Soon, the gathering night made Dick halt and rethink the wisdom of walking that way. So he turned back toward the place he was running away from. It would be an understatement to say that he was startled by the sudden voice of a man he could not see:

> *Borgus ah willinnn*
> *What you ne-eed*
> *For whatchu you got!*

Dick immediately crouched low and waited. Then he heard it again, a man's mellow voice growling a peddler's ditty. It was muted and yet strangely powerful, also playful.

> *Borgus be willin'!*
> *What you need*
> *For whatchu you got.*

"Who is that?" Dick called out.

"Jes lettin' you know I'm heah so's yo' don't git scaird."

It was near dark. All along the trail were stands of brush and trees grown up since the original trees were harvested along a stretch of the ridge top. From out of the brush stepped a true giant of a man, oily brown skin with a shine burnt into his face by the sun and matted coarse reddish hair of a style whose exaggeration would one day be called dreadlock.

"Don't be feahful, young masta. Evuhbody borned in these parts knows Borgus Willin."

"Not to be disputin' with you, but I don't know you."

"What a gen'lman like you doin' in the edge o' my swamp?"

"I was . . . travellin'."

"I loves travellin' myself," the man said. "This crease in my forehead you keeps lookin' at, hit ain't nothing but a harness scar from when I goes peddlin'."

"Jesus! You pull a cart with your head?"

"That I do young masta. Every summer, I comes outta my swamp and sets up camp down where the two rivers come together—the Sunflower and the Hushpuckena in that 'er direction."

"Ain't many to trade with over there."

"Right again, young masta, but there's them has hid in the swamp an' doesn' like to be noticed."

"Who are they?"

"Whyn't you join me down below. Be nice to have young ears listen. Like my song says, 'Borgus is willinnnn . . . got words you need, for all the time you got'."

Dick followed the man several heads taller than himself down through a stand of cane into a tiny clearing surrounded by brush. From the number of old fire sites, Dick could tell it had been used more than once.

"I calls 'em the hidin' folk. This time evuh year I comes along the county road singin' my name."

"Was you born with the name Borgus?"

"Sit'n listen." The man tossed a skin of what smelled like whiskey to Dick. "Go'n drank. Hit's mainly water . . . I carrys pots and pans, knives, skins, whiskey and salves—I trades with a few little farmers, mainly the hidin' folk. Twice a year, they kin find me in summer where the two rivers cross, along this here road in fall. Ev'body know I out for help me, but always willin' to trade. Thas how I come by this name. A smart li'l woman call me som'n like Borgus when I quit her. She so sweet to me, I made her name mine. So I says to all, especially women, Borgus willin'. Gi' me some'a what you got, I gi' you a little o' what I got."

"And what," Dick asked, "would your Christian name be?"

"The swamp born me. Lives by seasons. Flood run me up a tree, summer find me workin' two rivers, fall I'm here. Winter time is for rest. I'm the only frien' a poor woman got, 'cause I willin' to talk where ain't no money."

"Why ain't you never traded at my father's store in Alligator?"

Borgus sat and crossed his legs.

"Siddown, young masta. Las time I live with a buncha folk, they got sent on a Long March . . . Live alone, a li'l sleep together is my way." A smile touched his shadowed face. "May as well go'n tell you, I usually stays away from your peoples, but you welcome to sleep here tonight."

"I ain't scared."

"Well, now . . . I once seen a giant of a man close by," Borgus made a great upsweep of his hands. "He had the head of a bear."

"I ain't a child for bogeyman stories."

"Well, if you do happens to run into that bear, Borgus sends his regards to the swamp rose."

Dick spent that night there, and no one saw Dick for a week. There was a mysterious break-in at the store in which only tin pans and ten knives were stolen. By the time Cicero returned to the Dolan house, Dick's face was bruised.

"Me'n the lad had a disagreement," JD said. "If he ever wants to run away again, I've given him the road."

Cicero cleared his throat, went back outside on the excuse of relieving himself. He beckoned to Dick who followed him and blurted out what had happened. When Cicero heard that Dick had slept in a thicket past the county road east of Alligator Lake, Cicero smiled.

"Grow up before you take off on your own."

"I ain't stayin' with him permanent, Cicero. Just 'til I make my plans."

JD walked out onto the porch.

"You heard where he run to. You'll be warning the little imp about that wild clan live over in the swamp."

Dick's eyes smoldered with anger.

"They kill people, and steal little white boys," JD said. "You been warned."

Years later, during the spring when Abyssinia took the train to go visit Isaiah Montgomery's new settlement, Dick was nineteen. He was of only average height but broad build. On top of his massive shoulders, he had shaggy black hair sheltering the green eyes of his father. It was two days after the night Rose shared her dreamtime with Cicero that he appeared in the back room of the Dolan store for Dick's monthly lesson. Distracted, Cicero spent long periods staring absentmindedly through the open door.

"Why is this lesson important, Mr. Cicero?"

"Just learn how to use the damn book, Dick."

"But the sun ain't been out in a month."

Dick buried his nose in the book for the time it took Cicero to go out and water his horse in the trough. He took his time and let the bright sunlight play all over his shirt. The heat felt good after a long spell of rain. When Cicero returned inside, Dick was fidgety. Cicero turned to him.

"After you show me that you can balance accounts, this lesson will be over."

"Writin' everything down ain't nec'ssary. Pa buys, I sell, there's money left after we pay the bills . . . What good is all this?"

Cicero consulted his instruction book. He looked up and smiled.

"I am not unwilling to shorten the day's lesson, Mr. Dolan."

"Aye, Cicero—Mr. Cicero."

"It's late already, and there are people in the new town expecting me."

"I heard talk of it."

"Did you now? I wonder what landowners like your father say."

"Not the good kinda talk."

Cicero lowered his book.

"There's this Alex, the Greek fella. Him'n pa are like cat'n dog. I guess pa used to know him in the old days, and they didn't get along. Alex says he's goin' to hurrah the new town."

"Are you serious?"

"Wouldn't lie to you, Mr. Cicero."

"My sister is down in that town."

"If it was my sister, I'd get ready to kill Alex Chicoupapoulis."

"You can't kill a man for talking."

"Oh it ain't that. Alex is a Klansman, and I hear he been in more'n one lynchin'."

Cicero picked up his instruction book, then tossed it away.

"Listen, Dick, would you agree to read two lessons for our next session?"

"Aye, and today's lesson is over?"

"I'll come through here one week plus one day. You read both lessons—or I'll go to your father."

"Jesus Christ!" Dick slammed closed the ledger book atop the crate that served as his desk. "That ain't enough time. I got people to see."

"Watch your mouth, or I'll let James Aloysius sort things out."

Full red lips in a pout, Dick kicked a clod of mud to pieces from where he stood. The violence of it disarmed Cicero.

"Go, get your father!"

"All I did was kick a little mud off my shoes."

Cicero walked out into the sun behind the storage room leaving Dick talking to himself. Separating out his anxiety about the town from the minor irritation of Dick's boyish challenge was impossible, especially given the immense emotional hurdle of re-entering his son's life. Cicero returned inside, picked up both his instruction manual and a slim bound volume.

"Take a look at this."

"Says here, it does, the 'Narrative of the Life of Frederick Douglass, an American . . . Slave?'"

"You asked me what being a slave was like."

Dick look away from the book, avoided Cicero's angry eyes.

"We've talked about black people and white people before. You *ought* to know what it was like. If more white folks had read something like this at your age, the world might be different."

Dick began running his finger over a page of text as Cicero walked into the deserted store, over to a shelf of tinned sardines he'd grown fond of over the years. Dick walked in holding his gift book.

"How is your lady friend, Mr. Cicero?"

"How the hell is your own?"

"You been keepin' us apart," Dick said. "Got something for Miz Rose."

Ignoring whatever Dick was bent-over doing behind the counter, Cicero ambled toward his wagon. At that moment, two dragonflies mating set down near the wagon, and Cicero almost stepped on them. As they flew away, their end-to-end configuration was awkward and somewhat comical, not unlike—Cicero whimsically thought—his own coming together with Suzy or even, in a sense, with Rose. Fleeing slavery, later an empty freedom, every man and woman had strained toward what he or she could make of love, seldom what the other expected and always in some configuration neither had experience with, all while fleeing oppression and dodging hunger. The dragonflies were nearby clinging to the underside of a leaf and each other. Falling into love, or into companionship, had been without much pattern. Young Dick Dolan, Cicero mused, was but another generation of dragonfly who'd soon have to create his own way.

Conscious suddenly, of staring, Cicero chuckled and climbed aboard his wagon as Dick ran outside holding a small bundle.

"This bright leaf come in from the Carolinas. Miz Rose, is partial to it."

Dick placed his tobacco in the wagon, and Cicero pulled on a droopy felt hat against the sun. He strapped his horse into a trot. As the store receded in the distance, he tried to empty his mind, but the tide of memory kept rising, of his father being arrested and forced back into slavery, of growing up unable to make his peace with either bondage or an empty freedom. He took a sip of water without stopping. Memories kept surfacing, of *Mr. Cicero's Book*, the collected records the Navy had paid him to keep of thousands who'd found themselves suddenly interned on Davis Bend with no prospect for the future, no way to reach out to loved ones separated by slavery.

By MID-AFTERNOON, THE DAY HAD become a full-grown scorcher. Cicero had sweated through his clothes, and it was a struggle to keep his eyes open. He mopped his brow with his hat and turned off-road, into a grove of trees. In the shade there, he gobbled up all of his sardines, followed by a sweet potato he'd brought from home. With his stomach full, not even the hard wagon seat under him could discourage a nap.

A wet amber sky was graying toward dusk as Cicero awakened and hastened underway. His stomach was in spasm, and every comforting posture concerning Buck that his mind sought gave way to its opposite argument, mainly that, despite those threats of lynching that had forced him to leave Davis Bend, he had not seen his infant son again. He and Buck's mother had fought, and because he would not join the Montgomery business and become a safe and well-connected husband, they'd separated. What Cicero admitted to himself now was that he hadn't tried to make arrangements to see Buck during any of the years since he'd settled in with Rose.

Despite the lingering heat, he whipped his horse into a canter before common sense took over, and he slowed. As hoof beats quieted, a muffled echo of axes led Cicero on in toward the new settlement. Logs were piled in tangles beside the road, and indistinct black dots turned into men working. One froze, ran toward him.

"Oh lordy, look what the bayou throwed up here."

Tears in his eyes, Isaiah Montgomery pulled Cicero off his wagon and hugged him.

"Old big-head boy!" Isaiah said, " Didn't know if I'd ever see you again."

"It was a rough time, but you knew I would make it if I could."

The two men embraced again, drawing others to watch.

"So you came up for the land," Cicero said.

"Aw man, yeah. Too much to tell standin' here. By the way, did you see Buck back up north of town?"

"No."

"Don't look so pained. He a fine young man now." Isaiah ran his fingers over his nearly bald head. "He bought some land in his own name near where you rode in."

Fifteen years had wrought changes in Isaiah. Cicero noted the loss of hair, a wispy mustache and goatee, and his frame looked almost emaciated compared to the chubby youngster he'd been so many years before. Out of the corner of his eye, Cicero glimpsed another familiar face.

"Goodness, Ben Green! It sure is a pleasure seeing you again. How is your wife?"

"She's fine as ever, Mr. Cicero. Always askin' about you. She be pleased you come to supper, tonight."

"Naw, naw, Ben Green," Isaiah said, "tonight is spoken for."

Isaiah led the way toward the center of the settlement, felled trees everywhere, tents, a few log shanties.

"Where is Abby staying?" Cicero asked.

"Oh what a sweetness she is."

"I thought you were married, Isaiah."

"Oh yeah, but it was still sweet seeing beautiful Abby."

"So where is she?"

"Gone back to Clarksdale."

"Is something wrong?"

"Oh no, she be back. I sold her a garden lot in the middle of town, and I can't wait for her to come on back and let me show her how to turn her money into land. When she sell her house in Clarksdale, be crazy not to join the rest of us in buying a little land for the future. You sure do look distinguished with so much gray hair on that big block-head o' yours."

As they walked, layers of darkness began to thicken and to smother toil. Men and boys with axes streamed in. Isaiah's wife Martha rushed into Cicero's arms and cried until they started laughing, and all three sat on stumps holding hands in what would later become the Montgomery yard. Martha was the one who told of Isaiah's father—Mr. Ben's—death, of them being evicted from Davis Bend, of the years in Vicksburg. Some women had quietly appeared while they were talking, each leaving food. Cicero was wiping at a tear as Martha led them to a table full of dandelion greens, corn breads, sweet potatoes, a roasted wild turkey and fried slabs of bacon.

"Here!" Martha said. "Look at these."

There were letters from several who'd been enslaved with them at Hurricane Plantation, one from Old George the Butler's widow, another from one of Isaiah's absent brothers.

"We even had word of a friend of yours," Isaiah said. "Remember Annye Mae?"

"I do, my first love. She got sold away just before the Union Navy took over."

"God only know what she been up to, but she was in Mobile."

Isaiah's oldest daughter, Mary, appeared leading her toddling sister.

"This big one was born," her mother said, "just before you left Davis Bend, Cicero. In fact, me'n Isaiah hadn't been married too long before you left, had we?"

"Seems right, but I don't keep marriage details too well."

"Little Mary, haven't I told you to be home before dark?"

"Yes sir. I was at Buck's house, daddy."

"I don't care, this place is growin'. You cain't be sure there ain't strangers around."

"Now, Isaiah," his wife said. "My daughter is as well-raised as any. Cicero, it's these white folks got him jumpy."

"What's the problem?" Cicero asked.

"Nothin'," Isaiah said. "Soon's a black man buy land, somebody else wish they had it. Ain't nothing."

"Daddy, when you gonna send for old crazy Buck?"

"Don't rush on my account," Cicero said. "I'll be around tomorrow."

"No such thing, Mr. Cicero," Martha said, then to her oldest. "Take your little sister and go fetch Buck right now."

"May I," Cicero said, "have a glass of whiskey?"

Isaiah patted Cicero's arm as Martha hurried toward the cook shack behind the cabin.

"This here," Martha yelled back, "is only make-do, 'till a proper house is raised."

"Look, Cicero," Isaiah said after his wife left. "I understand how you feel, but Buck all growed up. Just go'n act yourself."

"Act myself—how do I explain loosing an election by a whisker because a colored man bankrolled by racists split my people's vote and let Alcorn's man win? How do I explain that? Then there was that job thing you tried to set up, and the white man from the North starts off calling me insubordinate, because I wouldn't pretend he, and others like him, were our friends in the legislature."

"Aw shucks, man you ain't never had nothing to say. Just tell your boy how a man feels the need to move on like you did."

"Yeah, I moved on, and I had encouragement if I recall."

"So what was I supposed to do? I was in business, and you wasn't ready to compromise."

Martha reappeared and held a jar of clear liquor toward Cicero. There was only time for a single round of the jar before the sound of feet running riveted everyone's attention.

Cicero was draining the jar as Buck ran in panting ahead of Isaiah's oldest girl. Buck was Cicero's height but more robust with the full lips and vigor of Suzy, his mother.

"I am your father, son—Cicero. How are you?"

"Fine, thank you."

For a moment, neither moved. Isaiah's daughter started giggling when the silence became strained.

"Cat got your tongue, old crazy boy?"

"You—girl!" Martha Montgomery said. "Clear outta here and take your sister."

As the girls walked away grumbling, Cicero offered his hand to Buck, who refused it, leaving Cicero rubbing his hands together nervously.

"How come," Buck said, "you waited so long? You could've come find me anytime, couldn't he, Uncle?"

"Now, Buck," Isaiah said.

"I didn't run away from you. I had to go away."

"That's true, Buck," Isaiah said.

"But you didn't have to leave."

"After Isaiah and the people on Davis Bend elected me," Cicero said, "white people labeled me a Radical for demanding swamp land for the people. Think about it, Buck . . . four million acres of swamp land could have given every single slave family a living. The old landowners didn't want that. So the game was to call us the radicals while they courted black voters with promises of schools and such. When the Northern army pulled out, the nice words disappeared and the shooting started. That was when my being around Davis Bend put everyone in danger."

"It wasn't like your poppa knew all that," Martha Montgomery said, "when he first got into politics."

"Nawsuh!" Isaiah said. "None of us did."

Cicero ground his teeth, his jaws were shut so tight. But he finally smiled, and sighed. On some nights, the stars reflect the incandescence of those watching from earth, and on that sultry evening, an estranged father and a son stared at each other without speaking, barely able to communicate. Facial ticks masked their nerves and the questions too numerous to ask. Some time after the meal, Isaiah insisted that Buck show his father around, and Buck at first refused. Said he was tired. But Isaiah insisted, and Buck finally got up with a put upon air and walked outside. When Cicero followed him, Buck headed toward the quiet of the still uncut wilderness, following trails past the clutter of fallen trees and mounds of ash from burned-off brush. Buck said little until they approached the home Buck's mother and her new husband shared.

"Why you leave momma? Uncle say you could have been part of what we all been doin'."

Everything about Buck's mother that Cicero had ever disliked rose up and demanded to be spoken, but he swallowed the urge. Getting Buck involved in the battle between his mother and father would not be the way to understanding.

"What do you know about our government?"

Hostility touched Buck's face in the moonlight, and he looked away.

"Your uncle was trying to feed you and everyone. That was what the Montgomerys always did, they were business people. Back when you were a baby, slavery had just ended."

"I know all about that."

"How could you? You were only a baby."

"I listen to what people say."

"Well, we black people had too few guns. All the voting stopped after the Union army—you know about the Northern army?"

Buck nodded.

"It went away, as if the people in the North had better things to worry about. Local white people took over again. Even white folks from the North began changing, and when certain people threatened me, that left people around me in danger, like your uncle and you and your mother. They couldn't keep fighting the people they wanted to do business with, the so-called good white folks."

"Why you keep talkin' about all that stuff. It ain't no excuse for folks not workin' and living like you do."

Cicero fought to control his anger.

"What do you remember of slavery and the War?" Cicero asked.

"That's old-timey stuff."

Cicero grabbed Buck's arm.

"I wasn't much older than you right now. How can you call it old timey? Barely twenty years ago."

"You don't have to shout. Ain't my fault you couldn't do what you tried. Me, I'm gonna be a race leader like Uncle. Shoots, we gonna make that money. Trying to vote is crazy."

Buck crossed his arms, looked away. Cicero leaned against a tree, looked up at the sky and began talking as if to himself.

"I was in love with a beautiful woman named Rose. She moved up here with your Aunt Abyssinia."

"My aunt?"

"Um hunh. My sister—the lady named Abyssinia Morgan who just rode down here from Clarksdale. She had some trouble during the War, and Rose brought her into the swamp for protection."

"Really?"

Cicero nodded.

"They had to live out in the swamp an' all, for real?"

"We still do. Did your aunt tell you where Clarksdale is?"

"You sure you talking about the lady uncle invited down here—a pretty lady?"

"That's the one."

"She don't—I haven't ever talked to her but once. She a important lady, got land even without a husband, and Uncle say she got money, too."

"Perhaps."

"So you had to come up here to take care of her?"

"Are you jealous?"

"No! I'm beginning to understand. I just never knew it was something like that why you left."

Buck's evident hostility dissipated in more questioning, of all things how his Aunt Abyssinia had become a business woman without a husband. Cicero took the easiest course and answered. A sad clarity blossomed in his mind. The political struggle of his generation had been wiped out. No school teacher would have taught it, cautious ex-freed man or woman that he or she might have been, and even more aware of the hostile world than would have been the parents of his or her pupils. Just to keep a teaching job meant one had to maintain an unthreatening face to the white folks. Which was why remaining a school teacher had not satisfied Cicero. All that a teacher on the outside of the swamp could do on top of reading, writing and numbers would have been to give family support to children—food, a little money, a good word with the white folks to excuse some breach of racial etiquette—for as many as possible of the headstrong young people, those like Buck who didn't yet have a clue about the world. Cicero knew that teachers would not have yet begun to tell a true history of their people, who themselves had yet to recover from being terrorized out of trying to take part in their own government. And if the teachers hadn't yet agreed on a word to pass, white terrorists salving their consciences because it had happened so long ago would continue to tell the story their way.

It saddened Cicero to his core that all Buck understood was having to care for a pretty lady. The fight for civil rights, like the clothes Cicero had worn in the legislature, had become old-timey, something at which the young folks Buck's age spit their nervy ridicule. Working in that world had taught Buck to make money, and little else, apart from eating and sleeping, and girls.

Near the tip of a bayou a mile to the north, Buck led Cicero to a half-finished cabin. Inside, several blankets lay in a jumble on the floor. A second lantern hung on a railroad spike driven into the timbered wall. The lamp they had been carrying for hours was fading.

"I built this cabin, daddy. Uncle Isaiah loaned me the money."

Cicero wanted to say something about alternatives life goals. Instead, he said, "Congratulations, you're a grown man."

"You think so?"

After a night of talking and walking, Cicero was exhausted, but a sudden eagerness to get Buck off to himself and into his part of the swamp surged.

"Come home with me tomorrow and meet Rose."

"Who is the woman you call, Rose?"

"My wife."

"I'd have to take off from work."

"So?"

"You got to get Uncle Isaiah and stepfather's permission."

Buck spread a blanket for his father, one for himself before turning the lantern down to a flicker.

They slept through morning. When they awakened toward midday, studied politeness eased the time as they washed in the nearby bayou before stepping back into the clothes marking them for who they were, the father into some threadbare gray wool pants he'd acquired while a member of the state legislature, topped by a deerskin shirt, Buck into his overhauls and work shoes, their newness marking him as a young man of prospect. And then came a succession of the people shaking hands and embracing. When one admiring lady called Cicero, the Honorable Mr. Cicero, Buck turned to his father.

"Why she call you that?"

"My official title was the Honorable Cicero Morgan, State Representative from Warren County."

"For real?"

"I have no reason to lie."

"How come Uncle Isaiah never told me all this?"

"Did you ever ask?"

As the two of them wandered about that day, more people came up to Cicero and Buck. In the small talk that accompanied greeting, they detailed more of what had happened after the war.

"Daddy, everybody know white people in control of everything. What were you trying to do?"

"I was trying to put slavery to rest. There is no freedom without a way to earn a living."

"Okay, then what?"

"White people didn't want us to have anything that would free us from working their land. Even some of the black people who got elected with me became convinced that giving all of the people access to their own land would destroy what they called the labor market."

"But what did you do to be in so much trouble?"

"I insisted that the government treat people equal, not just black and white, but all people—rich and poor. The trap was that we handful of blacks who were leaders began to feel special because we were the first of our people elected, to own a plantation, whatever. We found ourselves talking like the rich white people, arguing among ourselves about the labor market and how worthy we were and silly things like that."

Buck said no more but his mouth twitched, as if he couldn't believe what he was hearing. As that first day ended, Cicero decided to postpone going home until he and Buck got better acquainted.

Abyssinia arrived back in the settlement the following day driven by a man named Eugene Woods with more of her belongings. Mr. Woods immediately set about erecting a tent on the home site Abby had purchased.

"Kinda roughing it, aren't you, kid?" Cicero said.

"Not at all," Abyssinia said. "This garden lot will be the center of town. Isaiah threw in the tent for me to use whenever I come down until my house is built. Over there, that's the start of the foundation."

"There is talk that white folks are out to cripple this town."

"What else is new?"

"It was your son warned me."

"How is he, Cicero?"

"Dick is fine."

They were leaning against a wagon. Abyssinia hugged Cicero and began crying.

"I'm sorry ," she said. "It's a shock every time you mention Dick. Your son, Buck, is a fine young man, too."

"Dick was in great spirits a couple of days ago."

"I should have cut his father's throat. I gave up too much letting him go."

Cicero took Abby's hands in his.

"Little sister, neither of us seems to appreciate family enough. You and I have things in common."

"You want to do something for your boy, but what can we? Somebody else raised him. Us odd-acting Morgans got to cheer each other up . . . You ever wonder why neither of us got hitched the regular way?'

"What do you mean by 'regular'?"

"You and your swamp involvement."

"Rose is my wife! Why can't you say that?"

"Now, now. Just that it wasn't marriage with a preacher and all. And my thing with JD is such old news that all I can remember is that he was good looking, and I thought I needed a man to support me."

"Well, you're surrounded by family now."

"Why don't you and Rose buy some land? I got money."

"No, thank you. I won't live where white folks play god. For me to do that would be the ultimate disrespect for the memory of all the men I knew who died fighting."

"Ain't so bad nowadays, Cicero, especially living where practically everybody around you is colored."

"Look, it may not stay calm here. Black people building anything will become a target."

"Yeah, I guess."

"Believe me, Abby, and think about it hard before you move down here. I'm taking Buck in to visit Rose, and I really hope that one day he may come live with me. It's the one thing that would make Rose and me supremely happy."

Abyssinia caressed her brother's cheek.

"I know what I want now, too. I'll teach school, and I may let Mr. Woods propose . . ." With her head, Abby indicated the man working in the distance." . . . Come visit. I'll be set up in a house by the winter."

"Is this love at last?"

"Hell, no! I have never loved a man. I know that now. At first I was exploring my own power to make a man treat me like a fine lady. Eugene is kind, and living with him will make both of our lives easier."

"Have you announced the marriage?"

"Oh no! I haven't even told Eugene yet."

THE FOLLOWING DAY, CICERO WAS still in bed on the floor of Isaiah's cabin. He was wondering whether JD would allow him to park Abyssinia's wagon at the store in Alligator and have Dick care for the horse until they were picked up. That way, he'd save a half day travel up to Clarksdale and then another half back down the Sunflower into the swamp. He had no boat in Clarksdale like the one hidden along Harris Bayou where the Alligator trail branched off the county road. Before he came to a decision, Buck was knocking at the door.

"Momma outside. She got some food for your trip."

"Bring her in."

"I heard him!" Suzy's voice came from outside. "Is he dressed yet?"

"No, momma!"

"Well, tell him to come out here. Your stepfather wouldn't understand me going in there."

Suzy was standing beside the porch holding a skin of rainwater when the door opened. She was larger and moved more slowly than Cicero remembered, beautiful eyes and skin, though there were lines around the mouth, across the forehead.

"Hello, Suzy."

"Hello, yourself," she said, smiling. "Damn if it ain't you. I thought maybe a snake would kill you, but you look good."

"So do you." Cicero turned to Buck staring from inside the screen door. "You raised a fine man."

"Come on out here, Buck," Suzy said. "He ain't never been shy."

"Shy like me," Cicero said, "when I met you."

"What y'all talking about?" Buck asked.

"Things ain't your business," Suzy said, then to Cicero. "Well, got to get on back. Brought you this here in case you and the boy get thirsty. Some food, too."

"A whole fried chicken, daddy."

"Why, thank you," Cicero said, reaching for the skin of water and Suzy's hand, but she pulled away.

"Goodbye, Cicero. You mind your daddy, Buck."

"I'm grown. I don't mind nobody."

Instead of remaining at his father's side, Buck started after his mother.

"Hold on, Buck. You're going with me."

"Oh, I forgot."

"You forgot!?"

"Why I got to go into some swamp?"

"You live in a swamp here, you arrogant little fool! What's the difference you coming with me? Harness the damn horse!"

As a sullen Buck moved to harness the horse to the wagon, Cicero began trembling with a rage that was more bitter because he sensed he deserved it. Cicero went back inside to finish dressing. As he gathered his odds and ends, he could hear Buck telling young Mary Montgomery that his father was forcing him to go see his old swamp.

Buck was already seated with downcast eyes when Cicero walked out and stepped aboard. As they drove, there was no conversation until Buck got hungry. The fried chicken then disappeared along with some bread pudding from Martha Montgomery. Hours of awkward silence later, the trees bordering Alligator Lake came into view. Everywhere, rows of trees on ridge tops that had year-round access to water grew taller than those in lowlands that drained and sometimes dried out in summer.

"I have to return the wagon and horse to Clarksdale," Cicero said.

"Why you telling me?"

Cicero's mouth was too tight to speak right away.

"One of your Aunt Abyssinia's neighbors cares for it until it's picked up."

"My aunt got a servant?"

"No, Buck, just a neighbor paid to tend the horse. The animal belongs to the man who drove your aunt this last time. He wants to marry her."

"So that's why he loan you the wagon?"

Cicero nodded.

"Don't you have the money to buy your own?"

"A wagon would have no use inside the swamp. There are no roads, so, yes! I do have money. I do not own a horse or a wagon."

"Just askin'."

"Tonight, I suppose we may as well sleep in Clarksdale. Tomorrow evening, you meet my Rose."

"Why you stop liking my momma?"

"I still like her."

It was such a half-truth, Cicero was amazed when Buck started whistling. His best mood all day turned Cicero impulsive as they neared the dirt trail that led west off the main toward the Alligator settlement.

"By golly—turn here!"

"What's the matter?"

"Just follow the trail," Cicero said.

Off the main road, they curved along the southern shore toward the settlement. It was near where the railroad trestle came across the narrow lake to continue past the Dolan Store. A rowdy crew of white men walked down off the rail embankment as Cicero's wagon approached. Buck pulled the wagon to a halt as the three white men reached the store. Two began tossing a jug of whiskey back and forth on the porch. The third man grabbed for it screaming, "Y'all gimme some!"

"Look straight ahead, Buck. Drive behind the store."

The men paid the wagon scant attention as it pulled around to the back. Cicero tried the storeroom door, but it was locked. Instead of rattling it to get Dick's attention, he led Buck around front. A man drinking was blocking the steps.

"Excuse me," Cicero said.

"Excuse hell, boy! Git your ass on way from heah."

"I need to go inside."

"I'm a white man, or is you blind?"

The white men snickered and waited for Cicero to slink off, but Buck stepped forward, and one of the men roughly grabbed the boy's shoulder. Anger burned all thought of backing down from Cicero's soul, that and the weight of his old friend Senator Charles Caldwell's pistol and its painful memory of the man he'd known as Blacksmith sprawled dead on a street during yet another of the massacres of black politicians all over Mississippi. Cicero whipped the gun out of the hidden pocket Rose had sewn into his coat, and he fired.

"Move!"

"Ah been shot! Oh lordy, nigger done shot me."

"Shut up, Frank!" another said. "Nothin' but splinters up your ass."

Cicero moved the pistol from one to the other. Two rifles were leaning against the porch. The man who'd spoken was holding his by the barrel.

"Drop it, white man! I'm mad at the whole damn world."

"Awright, boy. You ain't gotta shoot nobody. Hey Jim Bob, Luther, y'all be still."

Dick eased out of the dark inside the store, a pistol in his hand, and Buck yelled, "Look out, daddy!" Dick whirled toward Buck. Cicero leveled his pistol on Dick.

"Put down that gun!" Cicero said.

"What's going on here?" Dick asked.

"Folks trying to run me off," Cicero said. "I think you ought to put your gun down, too."

After a moment's looking back and forth between Buck and Cicero, Dick obeyed.

"That's fine—Buck!"

"Yes, daddy?"

"Pick up every gun and take them inside the store."

Dick cocked his head to the side when Buck called Cicero, daddy, but in the frenzy of Buck and he collecting all the guns, he said nothing.

"Where you men from?" Cicero demanded as Buck disappeared inside.

"From down by Cleveland, fella. We was goin' home."

"I can't return your guns. So git!"

"Damn you, nigger, just wait—"

"Be smart, and live awhile! . . . Go on down the railroad for a mile, then come back for your guns."

"Where you work, nigger?"

The man gave ground as Cicero walked toward him.

"I live in that swamp over there, and you best leave off with that nigga talk or you will be buried behind that store. Now, on your way!"

The men started off toward the track.

"Daddy, I'm scared," Buck whispered.

"No reason to be," Dick said. "The fights out of 'em."

"Richard Dolan, meet Buck Morgan—my son."

"Your son? . . . Damned to hell, I'll be."

The two young men regarded each other. Dick walked over and stuck out his hand. Buck hesitated, looked to his father perplexed. Belatedly, he took Dick's hand.

"Pleased to meet you, sir," Buck said.

"Same here. But what was that all about?"

"Redneck fun," Cicero said. "I wasn't in the mood."

"You better git away from here," Dick said.

Cicero looked off down the track.

"Come into the store a minute," he said.

Dick led the way inside. Buck grabbed his father's sleeve.

"Who is this, daddy."

"A pupil of mine, he's a fine young man."

"You teach *him?*"

"Aye!" Dick said. "Mr. Cicero is smarter than everybody—like my second daddy, he is, only he ain't white."

"I'm taking Buck into the swamp. I haven't seen him in fourteen years."

"You was out of sorts when you left here."

"What do you know about me'n my daddy?" Buck asked.

"Givin' me hell for no reason, your pa was."

Buck frowned.

"Well, he was." Dick turned to Cicero. "You was worried about meetin' him, wasn't you?"

"Family matters in general."

"He family, ain't he?" Dick said, scurrying outside to take a look down the track. When he returned he started putting together a pile of Cicero's customary sardines.

"What's this," Buck said, "about family? I'm your family."

"Family includes my wife, Rose," Cicero said. "She's never met you. I had hoped you'd have more enthusiasm for meeting her."

"Oh. I don't care."

Meanwhile, Dick cut a hunk of cheese from the cheddar round kept up on the high counter to thwart rats. As he threw a handful of crackers into the wrapping paper, he stared at Buck who walked over to the gun rack and begun fingering the Winchester Company's popular new rifles.

"'Tis a pity that you got to be off," Dick said. "Could your boy stay with me a little while?"

"Stay where?" Buck asked. "I don't work for nobody but Mr. Isaiah Montgomery."

"Before them white fellas be back, I could ride you to my house. Pa gone off visitin' a woman for two, three days."

Footsteps on the porch outside drew attention.

"Can I git some service?"

A young female was standing in the door, sun making a nest of red light of her hair and streaming through her worn cotton dress.

"Yes ma'am!" Dick preened his shoulders like a rooster. "What might I do for you?"

Buck started giggling as the girl spoke.

"I need five jawbreakers."

Her legs flashed unnaturally white in the sun behind her as she raised her dress to keep it out of the oil-soaked sawdust on the floor. The glory of female form in silhouette, tiny red hairs all over her legs, held the men's eyes as she paraded in to pocket her candy. Dick shoved his elbow into Buck's stomach as the girl sauntered back to the door without paying.

"Now, she is somethin', ain't she?" Dick said. "Name is Pamela Sue Harkins, and 'tis a fact she is something."

"I used to run a store, too, for my uncle . . . What we gonna do, daddy?"

"I need to get you out of here," Cicero said.

"You ever go hunting?" Dick asked Buck.

"Not much, but we gonna do a lot more now that I'm living down the railroad."

"I been huntin' all my life, and I can show how to kill more game than anybody."

"Maybe, later," Cicero said. "Buck, we should go."

"Daddy, I know where we goin', but . . . if I got to stay in Clarksdale tonight, couldn't I stay here? Then you could pick me up tomorrow."

"Nay, nay," Dick said. "Tomorrow's for huntin'. It take a whole day at least."

"No, Buck, come along. Dick, I just drove here to leave the wagon and horse, but now I don't think that's such a good idea with those rednecks headed back this way."

"Either way," Buck said, "you gotta come back this way. Why can't I stay?"

"Don't start that again, Buck."

"Start what? All I want is one day to go huntin'."

"Yeah, Mr. Cicero. Let him stay. I take care of him."

"Well, I could walk back in a couple days . . . Take you on home then."

Cicero took a deep breath, shrugged, which brought smiles from the young men.

"I know good huntin', Buck, and I know all the pretty girls. Some black ones live on pa's land, too."

"We goin' to your house?" Buck asked.

"Right you are."

"Daddy, I reckon I stay here then."

Cicero nodded. Neither of the young men had an inkling of the pain inside that Buck's preference for hunting was causing.

"Mr. Cicero, when are you comin' back?" Dick asked.

"Look for me in late morning day after tomorrow, right here."

Cicero drove away without looking back. He was still feeling the residual anger of his encounter with the white men, and he heard a door slam. Looking back, he saw Dick jump off the porch and swing up onto his horse behind Buck.

Sоме miles on, Buck switched places to ride bareback behind Dick, but he was afraid to wrap his arms around the white boy seated ahead of him. Meanwhile, Dick continued to fret about leaving the store untended, as he'd done the week before in order to spend the afternoon with Pamela Sue.

"Quit fritterin' away me business on a little tart," JD had said.

"'Twas only the afternoon, pa. Pammy was needin' a ride home."

"Aye! Needin' a ride, she was, and I'm bettin' you give it to her. Her pa's my old friend, and I don't fancy you givin' him offense."

"Harkins likes me, pa."

"Wants to hook his little wench up with you."

"Why don't you like her?"

"Lower your voice or I'll break your mouth! You keep your tail in that store or I'll be knowin' the reason why."

"Ouch!"

Buck crying out and then grabbing Dick brought Dick out of his reverie.

"Aye, what is it?"

"Your horse is mashin' my privates."

"Jesus, Mary and Joseph! Use your thigh muscles, Buck. Keep up off him."

"Easy for you. I ain't in a saddle."

"Whoa, Lightning!" Dick kicked free a stirrup to climb down.

"No, thank you. I'll walk, you ride."

"Why don't I ride a piece, then you."

Buck climbed down, and immediately Dick had to rein in his mount to remain at Buck's side. Lightning snorted and pranced, disappointed that he couldn't run. Then Buck dashed ahead playfully, and the horse followed his lead, cantering when Buck ran, slowing when he walked. Soon Buck was winded by the game, and he walked alone a few paces behind Dick, his usual talkativeness silenced by Dick's white skin.

"The Mississippi River," Dick said, "is straight across that marsh. Pa says the trees around here have all grown up since he come to the bottoms."

"Who's that ahead?" Buck asked.

"Old boy name o' Joe Bob used to mess around with the girl in the store. Nothin' but rednecks, his people."

"You mean—"

"Oh, it ain't that I'm sayin' one's better'n another. Just that my pa says a white man who ain't gittin' rich in this land is a fool." Dick halted Lightning, whipped his leg over the saddle and sat looking down at Buck. "Whatta you think?"

"You want me to say what I really think—cause you white, and that make a difference."

"Don't to me, not 'tween me'n you."

"Well, we call everybody white trash except rich folks because they sometimes ain't so evil."

Buck shoved his hands in his trousers and walked ahead, disconcerted by how easy the confession of how he really felt had been. Dick galloped past him.

"Hey up, Joe Bob!"

A lanky youth reached his hand up to Dick. Buck hurried to where Dick was talking from the saddle.

"This here's Joe Bob . . . This here's Buck."

"Pleased to meet you," Buck said.

"We goin' hunting," Dick said.

"Jesus creepers! Kin I go?"

"If you take off from the fields," Dick said, "your pa'll tell mine."

"I do what I please." Joe Bob said.

"Aye, 'till your old man whomps on your tail and you say it was me putcha up to it."

"Shouldn't we," Buck said to Dick, "go on where we going?"

"He givin' you orders like your nigger teacher."

"Damn you to hell, Joe Bob." Dick leapt from his horse. "I'll whip your tail."

The two young men stood face to face until Lightning whinnied and thrust his muzzle into Dick's back, propelling him into Joe Bob who gave ground but spat in the dirt between them. Buck had already started off before Joe Bob walked away. Dick, then, leapt into the saddle.

"Wait up, Buck!"

Some minutes later, a two-story white house inside a grove of trees loomed in the distance. Buck was now riding, Dick walking.

"You don't care if I call you, Dick?"

"And why would I be mindin'?"

"You white, that's why."

"Color ain't supposed to matter now is it?"

"To me neither."

"You ever killed a bear?"

"I been huntin' a little since movin' up to our new town."

"Take me down there. I work mules grading roads . . . What is it that's troublin' you?"

"I can't take you home with me," Buck said.

"We oughtta stay away from a lotta white folks, too."

A day and a half later, Cicero whistled through most of the morning, and he couldn't wait to pick up his son and head for the boat. He was tired from walking six miles down from

Clarksdale, but in an excellent mood. Over the day and a half, he had rested and taken stock. Like another instance of obeying some power beyond sight, Dick and Buck taking up with each other seemed a blessed event. Even more, Buck's whole demeanor after the shooting incident had changed a little .

Dick was sitting on the porch of the store alone.

"Got your lesson done, Mr. Cicero."

"So where's Buck?"

"Oh, he went home."

"Home!? Whatta you mean?"

"He left this morning and told me to say he had some work to do."

When Cicero heard Dick say that Buck had gone back to Mound Bayou, Cicero's skin suffused with so much blood that Dick lowered his face back into his book. Actually, Buck was hiding back along the trail from the Alligator settlement watching for his father to depart. Dick was saying what they had agreed upon. Cicero said not a word as he headed away.

Full of youth and energy, neither Buck nor Dick gave the least thought to what Cicero was feeling, for in fact Dick had spent his whole life making up lies to avoid JD's interference. Buck, on the other hand, had no such comfort. He was in uncharted territory, still angry about his father's years apart and not yet convinced that Cicero was an upright hard-working citizen. Besides, Cicero had introduced him to Dick, and neither he nor Dick had ever had a best friend before.

Several days later, Buck did finally go back home, but not for long. Summer into fall, he and Dick spent weeks together at a time, given that one or the other had to sneak off and waste a day traveling just to hook up with his partner. Buck decided that he'd done his share of helping clear the new town, and he'd get to his own land when there was nothing better to do. Dick played a more coy game, often telling his father he was working his mules in the county to the north when actually he and Buck would be riding them. Joe Bob or his father was always willing to work the store in return for a little whiskey that Dick replaced with water.

Cicero didn't mention anything about his displeasure the first time he returned to Mound Bayou because he was a little ashamed to open up his pain to others. He didn't realize the amount of time the youths were spending together until his second visit to Mound Bayou when Isaiah pulled him aside.

"He ain't here, Cicero, and he was gone almost three weeks, time before. I thought he'd finally gone on to visit you and your wife so I didn't go ask Suzy . . . He up with that white boy."

"He's experiencing new things, new people."

"You ain't never took him home yet, have you?"

"No, but don't fret. The young white man is my pupil. Buck is quite safe."

"But it ain't seemly, Cicero. A boy like Buck can lose sight of how he got to act 'round other white folks."

"Leave him alone, Isaiah. You sound like your poppa did back on the plantation, always worried about what the white folks want. Let me be the one worry."

"Well, look here," Isaiah said, "ain't much work been done on your sister's house yet, and that's 'cause Buck was the main one I had planned to work on it."

"Tell you what. I'm going up to Alligator tomorrow. I will cool Mr. Buck down and send him home. That, I promise you."

Buck was sleeping in the back of the store when Cicero arrived.

"Wake up! We got to talk."

"Hello, Cicero."

"You've been neglecting your work. Isaiah says he'd planned to have you help build your Aunt Abyssinia's house."

"He ain't never told me that, and you said I could stay with Dick."

"I introduced you, Buck, but there's work to be done. You don't have a rich father."

"Well, uncle ain't payin' me to work."

"Everyone does a little work for the community."

"You wouldn't work for him."

Cicero sighed.

"I was in politics. That was my work."

"What about now, you ain't in politics no more?"

"Take that look off your face! You obey your uncle."

Dick, who'd been lurking out of sight, walked into the open.

"Hello, Mr. Cicero. What's going on?"

"Leave us alone, Dick—family business."

Cicero motioned Buck to follow him outside.

"I am a maroon, son. For years before slavery ended, people like my family lived in the wilderness where no white man could find us. We are not lazy, but work doesn't mean the same thing to me it does for your uncle. I hunt, fish, provide wood and do what's needed at home to have food and clothes and such other things as I desire, like supplies for my work."

"What work?"

"Forget that for now, just listen . . . If where you live requires money, you aren't a real man until you can take care of yourself. Living with your momma one day, Isaiah the next, then running off up here is child's play."

"If uncle tells me what he want and I do it, can't I have my time free after that?"

"Sounds fair. Give your uncle two days a week on your mother's land—"

"But you'n me won't have no time together, daddy. Don't you want me to see where you live?."

"Don't give me that! I was taking you home when you and Dick started running around. You can come visit when your work is done."

Back in Mound Bayou every day, Buck was distressed to find the people ignoring him as if he had done something wrong by being away. Turned out, the somber mood had nothing to do with him. A couple of fights had broken out between men in the town and white men from a nearby settlement. A cross was burned followed by a week of isolated sniping. Mound Bayou's residents paid two of their own to keep watch.

The population had quadrupled. Mound Bayou represented the first effort to organize a town where the people and their law enforcement would both be African in origin. Isaiah's leadership of the group that hacked the town out of the wilderness had been just as extraordinary. He had encouraged, directed, badgered, and preached—each in its time, as his people had needed—and Isaiah was still fond of reminding the people of all that they had accomplished. The story of the Montgomery family began with old Benjamin Montgomery's work for the Navy. It had been described in national journals, and so had Isaiah's founding of Mound Bayou. Even Booker T. Washington had visited Isaiah. All that publicity accounted for an extraordinary run-up in the value of the land within those first two years. The town fathers daily received inquiries from families all over Mississippi seeking to move into town. As a business and social proposition, Mound Bayou had so much success that the brother of a black political hack who remained County Clerk of Bolivar County bought some land for a second black town. Big land money along the Mississippi controlled black intermediaries like the County Clerk who helped them control the Republican organization. The man, Ousley, would fail to clear all of the land. It would become Renova.

Frederick Douglas rode the train into Mound Bayou. Isaiah invited him because of an article of Douglas titled, "Fighting For Our Liberty." Douglas was a man of some perspective, though, not nearly the firebrand orator Isaiah had expected to come in and give his people a pep talk. After hearing of the local hostility, he told Isaiah that he was in a war without an army, and he warned Isaiah not to stay in Mississippi. What he suggested was that Isaiah's people cash in as they could and relocate to Indian Territory where the hostility of the various separate tribes could hardly exceed the likely violence of Mississippi white people, all of whose hostility was focused on Africans. But Isaiah buried the proposal in his handful of advisors and would forever afterwards curse when anyone mention Douglas' name. No town meeting was ever held about moving. Isaiah's faith in his own ability to play Brer Rabbit was supreme.

Meanwhile, two daily trains carried a lively traffic through the center of town. Most of the passengers were white and gave curious if not downright hostile looks from their train windows. The two black men authorized to keep order demanded the right to wear their pistols. Isaiah convinced the rest, no, but then the town agreed that no unarmed man should have to put up with abuse more that two days a week. When two unruly white men stepped off the train and began shooting in the air, the guards for that day went and got their weapons and disarmed the passengers. That night, another cross was burned on the train tracks, which sent Isaiah scurrying north to Alligator and Ben Green south to Cleveland to assure the nearby white settlements that, if only those town's constables would hold themselves available when requested, Mound Bayou's citizens would arrest no white person.

By the end of January, when parts for a cotton gin arrived by train to be unloaded amidst gawking passengers and train crew, a third cross was burned. An anonymous telegraph message warned against erecting the gin and putting white men out of work. Isaiah told Buck to put aside his hammer and to make ready for a trip. Buck had no idea what was going on when he presented himself at Isaiah's house and heard Ben Green's raised voice.

"We can't keep on pretending we don't have a problem. The Franklins is moving to where there's less white folks. They rather live inside the deep swamp than put up with this."

"Ain't that some foolish shit!" Isaiah said.

"Maybe. The men want you to come talk to everybody about things in general."

"Who arrange that behind my back?"

"I had a part in it," Ben Green said, "but some was gonna talk or they was gonna walk. Folks got eyes."

"What are you sayin'?"

"Isaiah, Daddy Montgomery always let people think they was doin' what they wanted. You got to let people git together and talk. You can't just run things."

"Then, have your meeting tonight."

So it was that men and women of the settlement gathered outside of Isaiah's store. Isaiah raised his hands for quiet.

"We will buy anybody's land," Isaiah said, "who thinks I led them astray."

Isaiah shrugged, turned and walked into his store without saying more. A murmuring commenced, then subsided as Isaiah reappeared.

"I went to get the books so people who want to move can settle up."

"How much you pay me for my land?" Franklin asked.

"Same as you paid," Isaiah said.

"That ain't right!"

"Say, Isaiah!"

"Yes, Ben Greene."

"You cain't expect folks to sell for less'n the land's worth."

"I don't expect nothin'," Isaiah said. "Just tellin' y'all what the town will pay you—by that I mean, me, as the custodian of all your money. It's your money I be payin' with."

A more friendly comment ensued as the smell of blood spread among the budding speculators.

"I see, now," Isaiah said. "You understand it ain't me tryin' to make no money. I'm just doin' my level best to speak for all you hard workin' folks stayin' the course."

Franklin stepped up close.

"Then I keep my land. Sell it in my own time."

"Fine with me," Isaiah said. "I cain't stop you from doin' nothin', and if you got the money to go git settled without what you put into your land, god bless you."

"What about," Franklin asked, "my part of the common fund? That's all I need to pay down on new land."

Isaiah turned to the crowd.

"What say y'all? We gonna let anybody get they money when they want? We agreed it take three months to pull out any money. If I got it invested in land, I can't snap my fingers and make it jump back into cash whenever you all come to me."

"What about loaning me the money?"

"Now look here, George Franklin. You want to move, you move, but the loan fund—that's only for folks livin' in town. Ain't that right, y'all."

"Isaiah, I got a question."

"Okay, Ben, what now?"

"This meetin' ain't only about Franklin's money. We got other problems, too. Folks worried about bein' in the gunsight of too many crazy white folks."

"Before we get into that," Isaiah said, "all in favor of giving Franklin a loan raise your hand."

No hands other than Franklin and his wife went up.

"What about," Isaiah asked, "giving him a profit on his land even though it's us all made it grow?"

One additional hand went up, the rest showed silent support for Isaiah.

"Shit on you!" Franklin screamed. "I ain't a slave for nobody, especially not for you, Isaiah Montgomery."

A group of families moved together near Franklin quiet, staring.

"You folks over there," Isaiah said, "I hear you all of a mind to go squat on land in the swamp, too?"

"That's right, we thinkin'," one of two other men said. "We ain't made up our mind. Depend on what you gonna do about these white folks."

"Goddamnit! You folks with children got to excuse me," Isaiah said. "How you standin' over theah blame me for what the white folks doin'?"

"Ain't blamin' you, just ain't willin' to go around turnin' the other cheek. Po-assed red-necks tryin' to run us off, and the law don't come this way."

"Is all this about the law?" Isaiah asked.

"Somewhat."

"We been putting out the watch day and night," Isaiah said. "That's the same as a constable. I say let's make it official right now. In fact, if you want to stay with us, you kin be the first constable."

"Why ain't the sheriff done nothin' for us?" the man near the Franklins asked.

"You know why," Isaiah said. "It's cause you a African. Now, we got us a constable. That satisfy everybody?"

"One more question."

"Yeah, Ben?"

"There's been talk about the white folks holding another constitutional convention. We know they gonna take away our vote. Maybe they take away our right to own land."

"They don't want us," an unknown woman said, "to do nothin' but sharecrop."

"Ben, you know the answer already, but I'm grateful you asked me this question . . . Folks, I can't read the future, but like Mr. Booker T. Washington says, we don't have to be equal to the white man on things social or political . . . But they got to have some of us for show if nothin' else. Me'n my daddy didn't just happen to buy Hurricane Plantation. It was because some Northern Navy people wanted to prove they were being fair to the race . . . This town got as much good reputation as my daddy did. So, I tell you, don't none o' y'all fret about losing the fruits of your work. If you own land now, you will still own land when that convention over. One thing the big white people ain't gonna do is mess with the god-given right to own land."

Rosedale was the county seat of Bolivar County. Formerly called Floreyville in the brief time when black people voted in numbers and controlled that community, it was in many ways an outgrowth of the Scott family plantation. They were the wealthiest family in Bolivar County. Though Republican, the family's sense of propriety had led the town to slough off the name Floreyville because Mr. Florey had voted to enfranchise ex-slaves. Also like Cicero Morgan, Florey had gone a further step and dared to assemble black votes toward control of local government. Buck had no idea how Isaiah had learned all that he was explaining. Further, according to Buck's uncle, the Scotts were the only local family that had the power to do just about whatever they chose to do.

Four days they walked, first down to Cleveland and then west across the Bogue Phalia through nearly twenty miles of swamp to the Mississippi. There along the river, the old white family presided over the Mississippi Delta Plantation. Jim

Dolan's acreage in the interior—part still uncleared—wasn't in its league. Charles Scott, the owner, ushered Isaiah and Buck into the parlor as soon as Isaiah was introduced.

"This here's twice the size of the Hurricane mansion when it was standing," Isaiah said to Buck.

"I never had the pleasure," Charles Scott said.

"The Union burned it down, Mr. Scott. Sad day for all of us."

"You don't say? . . . In there, please. We can talk."

"This is my nephew, Mr. Scott. I brought him along to see how the very big people like yourself live."

"You flatter me."

"Beg pardon, but the boy never had a chance to know Mr. Joseph Davis, who was the finest white man I ever met."

"Well, that is a very fine sentiment, Isaiah. How may I help you?"

"Folks threatening my new town, Mr. Scott. Not that we actin' outta place or nothin'. White men over along the railroad scared we take their jobs, which as you can see I wouldn't be of a mind to do. No sir."

"I am aware of your town and of those who worry that you will bring too many nigras in behind you."

"Won't do that, sir. All our people good'n upstanding. We wouldn't allow no flood of trash to come in behind us either. Wouldn't tolerate that for a minute."

"I don't fear that, Isaiah, but there are those who do. Those in Cleveland and settling all along your railroad are Democrats. I am a Republican. Your people are Republican, too, and though I have allegiance to my race, we are closer than I am to many Democrats."

"Thank you, sir," Isaiah said. "It is good to hear that."

"But I can't take a nigra's part against a white man."

Neither Buck nor Isaiah said a word.

"That doesn't mean," Scott said, "we don't have common cause."

"Hope so, sir," Isaiah said.

"My associates here along the river don't wish to see county government pushed out of shape by the Democrats or to have it moved from here as they did up in Coahoma County. Else we end up with all the new roads and bridges built off in the wilderness. We would like to depend on your peoples' votes for preventing that."

"Votin', sir?"

"Yes, voting. You have a reputation for not meddling in where you shouldn't, Isaiah. What I want is your commitment for a solid Republican front whenever it may be needed."

"But, sir—"

"Don't worry. When that is required, we shall make it possible for your people to cast their ballots in safety."

"But, Mr. Scott, I'm just a colored man know his place. I can't fight white folks about voting."

"Ah . . . I did not mean that you should fight anyone, Isaiah. I am simply seeking an arrangement. If your vote is needed, you will be told. All of you in that town and anyone else you know will be instructed to vote Republican."

"Ain't gonna be nobody shootin' at us while we votin'?" Isaiah asked.

"There will be no reprisal."

"Glory be!"

As if possessed by a righteous energy, Isaiah stuck out his hand. The old white man shook it.

"I must return to my work, Isaiah, but perhaps your nephew would like a tour of the plantation?"

"Yes, sir, he sure would, wouldn't you Buck?"

During a brief tour, the white man talked only of furniture and draperies, until he paused underneath his father and grandfather's paintings.

"Only through cooperation among the races," Scott said, "will our rich land be exploited, Isaiah. Which leads me to a final matter . . . You will be asked to run for a convention seat. You've heard of the convention to write a new constitution?"

"No, sir—well, yes."

"Yes, curse that infernal document forced on us by the Union army after the war. We have finally moved toward adopting a new one. And yet there are those who argue that the present constitution was adopted while the national government was exercising its War Powers, that it would be immoderate if not illegal to change it."

"I ain't a lawyer, sir," Isaiah said.

"Just agree to run as a delegate. Having one of your race participate will quiet some critics in Washington."

"I always do my part."

"Then I shall be happy speak to Joe Stafford in Cleveland on your town's behalf."

"Thank you, thank you!" Isaiah said, pumping the man's hand.

"Yes, Isaiah. We cannot overrate the importance in the national picture that a prominent man like you will have. Radical sympathizers still exist in the Congress who would re-impose Washington's control over our state's rights."

"Right your are, sir."

"The most radical concept of all is free land."

"Yessuh! We got folks in my town gone off to squat land they hope to git free."

"You will be our shining example against them."

"I appreciate your help, Mr. Scott, but folks say the Democrats in Cleveland don't always listen."

"You're an example to your people of the virtue of hard work. You will be protected."

"Even from the rabble?" Isaiah asked.

"We—that is, we who consider ourselves above that sort— we shall act in the interest of all the people. I would suggest, Isaiah, that you stop in Cleveland and talk to Joe Stafford. It is only because your people tried to take-over government after the War that ruffians of his kind have come into some influence."

After that peculiar meeting, there came another three days trudging back through the swamp, having to ford again the widest bayou Buck had ever encountered, the Bogue. As ordered, Isaiah stopped in Cleveland.

"Look boy," Joe Stafford said, "y'all outnumber us three, four to one. Your town pullin' in too many new niggers."

"Like Mr. Booker T. Washington say, the black man don't have to vote to live. My town is for livin', not votin'."

Isaiah's words creased Joe Stafford's face.

"Why," Isaiah continued, "would good colored people too smart to own a gun go up against you, Mr. Stafford. You come to Mound Bayou, you be welcome. No more'n a handful even own a rifle. These good people just like me tryin' to raise they kids. We ain't ask to be born here, suh."

"What if I pick a white man to run the votin' in your town?"

"Just gimme his name. Good as done. I'll keep my people from even tryin to vote except for offices in our own town. Won't that suit you, sir?"

"Well, it's a start, Isaiah. I heard tell you was a good'un, and I guess it was true. Lemme think about what you sayin'."

On the final leg of the journey home, Isaiah's bargain troubled Buck, though he had no real understanding of politics. Fighting about voting seemed old timey, he'd told his father. Yet, both of the white men to whom he'd just listened had considered voting at least as important as his father, Cicero, had urged on him, and Isaiah was giving it up. No sooner had they returned, however, than Isaiah again became the center of all attention, and Buck's small doubts evaporated because he had no experience with any alternative to Isaiah's always pressing ahead, praying as he could and conniving supremely where white folks were concerned.

Soon after they returned to Mound Bayou, Cicero showed up in Eugene Wood's wagon with a load of building supplies for Abyssinia's new house.

"Cicero," Buck whispered.

"Would you mind calling me, father or daddy—as you will?" Cicero asked

"I got a question."

"What is it, Buck?"

"Is there any way to keep from us losin' the right to vote?"

"Where did you get that question?"

"Uncle took me to the Scott Plantation. All the white man talked about was politics."

"So?"

"Well, he asked uncle to do something I wouldn't agree to do, I don't think."

"He wants your uncle to be a delegate to the new convention."

"How'd you know?"

"I was a member of the last one, and I follow these things. I even have two newspapers mailed to a box in Alligator."

"You do?"

"All the time . . . It's up to your generation to do something about the current situation. Isaiah is tied up in his land deals. Know what I mean?"

"I think so."

"He can't afford to defy the people who protect his town. So, there is no leader out here leading any protest. What about you?"

"Me?! No, no, no . . . I just, I was curious. Un unh, I'm gonna be a businessman. I don't wanna end up like . . . You know."

Not a word from Cicero, he turned away and snatched up a crow bar.

Hard work that afternoon pushed politics out of mind. Work intensified the next morning when Eugene Woods arrived. He made estimates of supplies and labor, drew up a plan. Buck and his father worked on the house every day to get the roof finished before the rains.

Gunshots rang out one morning. Up on the roof at the time, Cicero peered down the railroad tracks to see a horse staggering under a man whose jaunty hat marked him as Ben Green.

"Yo Ben!" Cicero yelled, struggling down a ladder for his pistol. "Go get your uncle, Buck!"

Instead, Buck ran up onto the tracks and toward Ben who was running now, dodging right and left, dropping to his stomach each time a new shot rang out.

"Stay down!" Buck yelled. "Help is coming!"

Ben Green made it in, and by the time he reached safety, Isaiah and some other men showed up with guns. Ben's horse staggered in covered with blood.

"Lucky them bastards didn't want to kill nobody," Ben said. "Hoss is done for."

"Calm down, now, Ben," Isaiah said.

"You ain't been shot at!"

"Hate to say this, Isaiah," Cicero said, "but you are going to get somebody killed in this new town of yours."

"You think it's me out there shootin' at my friends?" Isaiah said.

"Of course not! But these white folks are doing what they did fifteen years ago."

"What happened, daddy?"

"Shut up!" Isaiah said, then to Cicero. "I have succeeded in all I have done since we was boys. I will not fail this town. Look around you . . . Where will these men find another chance like this. Already, the price of land more'n double what we paid, an' town land is runnin' way 'headda that."

"I don't care about the price of land," Cicero said. "At the Bend, you had the army to keep the rednecks off you. When it left, you lost the plantation."

"I didn't lose nothin'. I simply made the best deal I could with what I was workin' under, and it didn't come out so bad. They got a island down where the Bend used to be. You don't understand the black man's position like me. What we supposed to do?"

"You tell me, Mr. Isaiah. I don't pretend to be a businessman."

"Gonna build my town an' let nothin' stand in my way. Scott in Rosedale least keep some of the white folks from gangin' up on us. For the rest, I'm going to a goddamn convention. I know they'll make me look like a fool, but a nigga gonna git used one way or another—you been in gov'ment! I'm just hopin' my people here don't have to fight 'cause soon as we kill a white man that's all she wrote. White folks get together quick and wipe us out. So, I hope them meddlin' crackers keep makin' noise at night and leave it at that."

"But if you don't shoot back," Cicero said, "they'll come on in and hurt somebody, bad. You could sell this land and move out west."

"Damn that!" Isaiah said. "You talkin' like that Fred Douglas nigga come in here tryin' to convince my people to *leave me* and move West. Where he got in mind? Some place in Injun Ter'tory, he say. Goddamn Injuns killin' niggas just like the white folks, and Injuns catchin' hell, too. I'm stayin' put, mister."

"I live in the swamp," Cicero said, turning to the group assembled around him. All axe work had ceased. "Some of you could move close by."

"How so, Mr. Cicero?" Ben Green asked.

"Why, come find you a homestead, like the people who moved a few months ago. We don't clear land, and we don't go buying it. Right now, we're still lucky there's enough of the swamp left there's no big rush into where we live. Shooting at people from time to time takes a lot of eagerness out of entrepreneurs."

"See how crazy that is?" Isaiah said. "Ain't no tellin' where them scamps at who run off and abandoned they land here."

"Refusing to trust the white man," Cicero said, "does not make them scamps."

"They was lazy," Isaiah said. "They was cowards."

"All of us know," Ben Green said, "the plan we put together with Isaiah to build us a black town is the right one. We ain't just another bushel o' niggas with nothin'."

"We got land!" Isaiah said, slapping his fist in his palm.

"Some of your people asked me," Cicero said, "about coming to live in the swamp last year. They knew that out here along the railroad it would come to this."

"Aw, Cicero," Ben Green said. "We know the risk."

"Well, I'm taking my butt home," Cicero said. "Is there anyone who wants to come stay with us, temporarily?"

"You askin'," Isaiah laughed derisively, "if these agricultural experts and business people want to move where *you* live?"

"Yes."

"My people," Isaiah said, "got too much pride to go hide in your swamp."

"Cicero right about one thing," Ben Green said. "Not everybody wants to sit'n take it."

"Shut up, Ben," Isaiah said. "We had a coupla folks left us last fall and moved down east of Cleveland. So what if they wanted more space 'tween them and the white folks. But ain't no more like them cowards. You people know that the world we gotta face is right here."

"Then make sure," Cicero said, "you all have guns. You have cover at the heads of both bayous where a small group of men could hide the next several nights. They'd be able to hold off Klansmen for the time it took the rest of your people to hear the shooting and go north to join them. That, is a plan!"

Isaiah walked close, put his arm around Cicero.

"We ain't never had the same view of the world. More guns just guarantee some white man git kilt. What we gotta do is keep our heads down, watch out for night prowlers. Ain't gonna be nothin' big against us. The white folks who want me for this convention will see to that."

"I can think of three places along the railroad," Cicero said, "with settlements of two or three black families. Do you think the white folks won't try to turn that around?"

"I can't control what they do."

"They will run you out. That's how terror works."

"And I know," Isaiah said, "that the men behind them sheets at night ain't the bravest in the world. We get by."

As the silence stretched out, Cicero opened his arms to heaven in resignation. The erection of Abyssinia's house was coming along, and Ben Green and Gene Woods would help Buck finish it. That evening, Cicero dined with his sister. She refused his advice to return to Clarksdale. Buck was eating at his mother's house when Cicero arrived to say farewell. After small talk with Suzy and her husband and toying with a plate of greens, Cicero pulled Buck outside.

"I'm going home, and you should come along."

"No, not now. I got work to do."

"Work to do? Would your work have anything to do with Mr. Richard Dolan?"

"No, I got to help finish Aunt Abyssinia's house. I cain't go runnin' off like you."

Cicero nodded brusquely and walked away. Explaining Buck's continued absence to Rose had not been easy. By now, a whole year had passed since they first discussed bringing Buck into the swamp for a visit.

Even before his father departed, something was shifting inside Buck. To begin with, a real pride had surged in Buck's heart when his father pulled a gun on three white men. All his life he had been taught to fear white people. And by now, there was no doubt that his father had been some kind of politician, not just a slacker unwilling to work. More recently, Isaiah's deal-making with the white people had become distasteful, too. Even more, Buck had belittled his father to the point he was feeling guilty. Making excuses for not visiting Cicero's home had been mostly lies. All of which translated into Buck deciding that perhaps Cicero did deserve at least one visit.

Because of that decision, Buck labored as never before in order to have the time free when Cicero came for him next. Not that he had any notion of making the swamp home, but he would visit. So he cleared a couple more acres of his land, and he finished building his cabin. Once again Isaiah and Ben Green smiled when Buck came around. Ben—at Isaiah's suggestion that they not burn the young man out—had hired another man to speed along completing Abyssinia's house.

At the same time, though, in the winter confines of a farming settlement, Buck felt for the first time like a penned-up young rooster. He bragged about his free run with Dick the summer before, until he discovered that there were few to brag to who wouldn't criticize his too easy ways. He talked a young woman into visiting his cabin. A rumor of it reached Isaiah, and the second time Buck disappeared during work hours, Isaiah came pounding on his door.

"Get your sense on straight, nephew. I don't know who in there with you, but if it's somebody got a poppa in this town, you get that gal home."

After the rains began, Buck found that scrub he had cleared once around his cabin was up and growing again, and all prospect of him hacking it away a second time seemed too infinitely frustrating to think about. Still, he did what the community would expect. He went at it, worked up such a sweat he had to throw off his winter coat two days in a row.

Spring soon triggered a bursting of buds throughout the swamp, and the earthy smell of it oozed into the air, into Buck's blood, too. Watching young women peeling out of their drab winter cover-up tuned-up his own adolescent impulses. Before dawn one morning, he put on his black suit and matching flat-brimmed hat and headed for Alligator Lake. There was a revolver in his waistband, carried just inside his carefully buttoned broadcloth coat, the way Dick carried his gun.

By mid-morning, the sun had forced Buck out of his coat. Before noon, he removed his tie. As he approached the Dolan store that afternoon, wagons and horses were parked in front. A group of young Africanamerican men were sharing good-natured banter on the porch of the store. Buck approached slowly, pulling on his coat and replacing his tie.

"Afternoon gentlemen," he said, swaggering up onto the porch.

The oldest smiled casually. All except him were broadly built with oddly small faces marked by high cheek bones and slanting eyes under ruddy black expanses of forehead fringed by straight black hair. Dick was behind the counter listening to an old woman with coarse gray hair meticulously pressed back from her forehead.

"I need camphor and Jaynes Expectorant," she said.

"How much?" Dick asked.

"A big bottle!"

"You don't need that much, momma," a woman said—a daughter-in-law, Buck guessed, because her yellow-touched skin was so different from the ebony men outside.

"Need enough for y'all, too," the old woman said. "Gimme a big bottle like I ast for."

"Dick!"

"Jesus, Mary and Joseph!" Dick vaulted the low counter and rushed to wrap his arms around Buck. "Been awhile, lad. Hold a spell . . . Aye now, ladies! Tell me agin, what you'll be havin', and take your time. The lad yonder needs to rest a spell before him and me'll be off."

Over in a corner, giggling until Buck's eyes flashed toward them, stood two bright-eyed young women in starched gingham dresses that crackled when they moved to whisper. Buck bowed politely, smoothed at his hair. He tried to think of something to say that wouldn't seem too obvious, what with the older women around, but he didn't want to sound too sappy either. The old woman broke the silence.

"Young man! . . . You theah."

"Yes'm," Buck said.

"I was watchin' you'n this bright boy run the store—y'all any relation?"

"Now Momma Lou," the older woman's companion said, "you cain't go messin' in other folk's business. You apologize to Mr. Dick."

"Quit, quit!" the old woman said, slapping away a hand before addressing Buck again. "Ast if you was related to that bright-colored one behind me."

"No ma'am. We good friends."

"Friends, you say! Ain't he white?"

"Why do you ask ma'am—meanin' no disrespect?

"Don't haveta say no more." The woman leaned forward and patted Buck's chest. "Had a feelin' about this store boy.

He ain't no more white man'n I is. All us got a mixup somewhere."

"Mommaaa! Excuse her, she talk too much, Mr. Dick."

"Aye, she can talk all she want." Dick said.

"Come here, you girls," the old woman said. "Don't git to
town but once a season. Make use of your time. Here's two
fine lookin' young men. Talk to 'em."

"Hush up, momma!" a young man outside said. "Ain't nobody want to know what you thinkin'."

"You hush yourself up, William. Fact your daddy was a
Chinaman ain't no reason you got to act like one . . . Now,
store man, I need some plasters for aches'n pains."

"Jew David's or De Lacounte's?" Dick asked.

An hour later, Dick and Buck were headed toward the
Dolan house leading Dick's horse.

"You could of talked them folks into takin' us home with
'em," Dick said. "They live over near the old swamp where
they sometime have the trouble."

"I ain't, " Buck said, "interested in no chaperoned
courting."

"You was lily-livered with them gals."

"I ain't goin' into some swamp no way. I decided to visit my
pa, though, but I'm not sure when."

"Your pa lives over there. Nobody would cause you trouble."

"What trouble?" Buck asked.

"Shootin's and such . . . " Dick looked at the back of his
hands. ". . . Do I really look colored?"

"Aw, folks embarrass me talkin' about Chinese and white in
the family."

"But I've seen colored people my color."

"Dick, it just ain't polite to mention white folks in the
family."

"Look, I respect whatever's botherin' you, but I ain't never
done nothin' against you, have I?"

Buck shook his head.

"Then talk straight."

"I am."

"We can have some larks if we was to go over on the river. There's some pretty girls—I mean colored girls. We could be cousins."

On no more than that, the two young men traveled half way to the Mississippi Delta Plantation where Buck pretended kinship with Dick. It wasn't all the wild time either hoped for, but they spent several days courting, sleeping outdoors at night. On the way back inland, a rivalry developed over who was better looking. They demanded that two sisters choose between them, the most handsome to have his pick of the girls. In the weeks that followed, Dick ceased being white whenever they ranged away from Alligator, which allowed for a more intimate fun. Buck slept in Dick's house whenever JD went away, in the store when JD was home.

Which was why Buck had not yet returned to Mound Bayou by Cicero's next visit, and both Suzie and Isaiah were in uproar. Cicero was so disappointed at being foiled again that he departed without spending a single night in town. A few weeks later, though, he decided to return, but instead of walking into Clarksdale to borrow a wagon, Cicero took a boat down the Sunflower, then west on the Hushpuckena River to near the county road where he spread his sleeping blankets. The morning of the following day, he walked to Mound Bayou. His idea was to buy himself and Buck a ride on the train back up to Clarksdale, an extravagance calculated to appeal to the young man. But when Cicero arrived in Mound Bayou, he learned that Buck had appeared briefly the previous day and disappeared again.

Instead of taking the train or his boat, Cicero began a daylong walk. He stopped in Alligator to rest. Dick claimed that Buck had just left for home. Cicero knew Dick was lying because Buck did not know enough about the area to travel on any but the main road along which Cicero had just himself walked.

"You tell Mr. Buck that I desire his presence. I'll be in Clarksdale for the next two days. If I don't see him, you and he are both in for it. Dick, I mean it, too!"

It was on the Friday night before the week of Independence Day that Buck appeared. Dick rode him into Clarksdale but sneaked away without speaking to Cicero or having any idea that his mother had once lived in the house where Cicero now rented an attic room.

"Ah, such a busy young man," Cicero said.

"Yep," Buck said, "I been busy."

"Working with Dick, I suppose."

"Why you pickin' on me?"

"I introduced you and Dick, but I didn't intend the two of you to gallivant all over creation."

"My land almost all clear, and—"

"Since March, how much work have you done?"

There was silence.

"Say no more," Cicero said. "In the morning, we talk. Now go to bed over in the corner."

"Where I'm gonna sleep?"

"On the floor," Cicero said.

Cicero listened to Buck fidgeting all night on the floor beside him, and he didn't fall asleep until late, which was why Buck had to wake him up the next morning.

"Can I drive your wagon? I want to see the town, and I'll buy us some food. You can sleep."

It was a Saturday, and Buck winked at the girls and ignored all of the boys. Driving along beside the Sunflower River toward the center of town, he allowed his coat to fall away in front of a group of boys so they could see the pistol tucked in his waist. Around noon, he pulled up at the Morrison Tavern, a white establishment that was covered with signs advertising sundries and supplies. As Buck leapt from the moving wagon, one of a group of white boys spit his way, but Buck hurried inside. A long bar made up one whole wall, and men were drinking at tables in front of it. A white man behind the bar gruffly beckoned Buck toward the back where food and merchandise were laid out.

Buck bought bread and, recalling his father's fondness, sardines. After paying, he walked back through the bar, noting for the first time that there were no black faces in the place. As Buck shoved through the swinging door outside, he pulled out a piece of beef jerky. A white boy slammed into him, and Buck's sack of food scattered. The boy made no effort to pretend an accident. Buck gathered up his food and hurried to his wagon. The word "nigger" reached his back along with a clod of dried mud. The troublemakers were closing as Buck turned. Frightened, he pulled his revolver and fired into the air, kept firing until the firing pin clicked against an empty cartridge. Then he leapt into his wagon and whipped the horse into a gallop.

"Daddy, daddy!" he yelled, running upstairs.

"Oh, so now I'm daddy?"

"I had to shoot at some white boys."

"You did what!?"

"They come pushin' . . . I didn't want to be rousted no more'n you."

At once, Cicero alerted the neighborhood. No one blamed Buck. In fact, he had considerable sentiment on his side. A woman who worked for a white family was sent off to find out if the incident had aroused more than the tavern trade. All afternoon, Abyssinia's neighbors and Cicero kept watch, and on through the night. Before dawn, Cicero roused Buck.

"Come on, boy, get up. I've had enough of you, so I'm driving you home. You come visit me when you like. I'm going into the swamp for a spell."

Buck drove for the first couple hours while Cicero napped. Afterward, as they neared Mound Bayou, Cicero awakened after a brief nod.

"What's it like inside the swamp?"

"My friends live there, and the woman I love—you know that—and her grown son, too, and a few other people who drift through from time to time. No white folks."

"None?"

"That's right."

"But how can that be?"

"We'd kill any white man who tried to come in. People like us—and there are others up and down the swamp, biggest group over east of Cleveland—were given the name 'maroon' way back."

"You jokin', daddy. No reason to kill somebody just because they walk into the woods. Besides, where y'all make money?"

"Here on the outside, you live by money," Cicero said. "The people I'm talking about are at war. White folks don't treat us like human beings, and what makes it so bad is that they control everything. In the swamp, we won't let it be that way. So we live off the land and keep our distance. We don't need much money."

"Why don't people in the swamp sell timber or something?"

"What for? Damn! You don't listen, do you. You can't do business with people you shoot at. They put you in jail . . . Jump down. Here's your momma's house."

Before Buck could stand down, Suzy walked outside. The left side of her face was swollen and discolored.

"Momma! What happened?"

Cicero climbed down and rushed toward Suzy and Buck.

"Nothin' much," Suzy said, hugging Buck and thrusting out her palm behind his back to discourage questions from Cicero. "Damn cow! Bent over milkin' it and 'whomp!'—she lemme have it with her big foot."

"Got something to eat?" Buck asked.

"You know where," Suzy pointed.

Buck dashed inside.

"So, what happened?" Cicero asked.

"Boys outsida town, Cicero. Anybody go too far out by his-self somethin' likely to happen now. Big ole foreign-soundin' white man north of town told Ben Green any nigga alone was fair game, and if we wasn't gone by the Fourth of July, Ku Klux Klan be comin' to burn us out. Me, I was lucky. Couple boys tried to drag me off. I ain't no lightweight fighter, you know? Me yellin' like crazy, couple men from town showed up, an' we run 'em off."

"Catch any of them?"

"You kiddin'? Isaiah be mad as hell, we hurt a white man round here. He hopin' they keep away, and the constable ain't worth shit. Rest of us been told to hold back on the gunplay."

Cicero went straight to Isaiah Montgomery. They argued into the night about how best to protect the town. The next morning, Cicero departed for Alligator, straight to the Dolan plantation. Taking his cue from Isaiah, he hoped that his years of service as Dick's tutor might persuade JD to intervene on the town's behalf.

"Come in, Cicero," the housekeeper said. "Mr. Dolan is at his Grange meetin'. You make yourself comfortable, though."

"In a white man's house, Sadie?"

"I hear it ain't too comfortable down where your friends come settle neither."

"From Dolan, you heard this?"

"Naw, naw. There's a old white boy work the land for us used to be in some kinda way-back mess with Mr. JD. I think maybe they was outlaws together. Anyway, this man was tellin' Mr. JD he got enemies same as them causin' Mound Bayou folks trouble. If you ask me, they ready to kill somebody."

* * *

Before dawn that morning, out in the partially cut country-side near Aaron Shelby's farm north of Mound Bayou, smoke had mixed with the gray rumors of dawn. The night before, a bonfire had been lit on top of a pile of trash raked to fill-in a low-lying area, and it had burned all night. Now, three men took turns stamping out the dying embers.

Most of those who had been present had departed shortly after midnight. Those now walking toward their horses had sat drinking into the morning. One was a rumple-suited Alex Chicoupapoulis, a middling tall, totally grayed Greek man whose bulk was almost obscene.

"Crummy bastards!"

"Ain't so bad, Alex. Them men had work. We'll have 'em with us when we need 'em."

"I hope you are right about thees."

"Too bad our deputy won't come with us."

"Sheriff ain't shit neither. Thees convention the last straw. I should be the delegate, not thees new town neegger."

"Can't wait to burn that cotton gin," said the third man. "Niggers think they can work a white man's job."

"For sure, we burn it to de ground," Alex said. "Democrats and Republicans both ain't nothin' but old men from anod-der time. I ain't goin' to kiss Joe Stafford's feet, and if you boys with me, we show the rich politicians there's some like you'n me bound to run thees Isaiah Montgomery back to where he come from."

"When the niggers git run out, we be the first there to take over that town."

Twenty-five years earlier, Alex Chicoupapoulis and his four brothers immigrated from Greece to New York and immedi-ately set out for a tiny river town in Mississippi. It was planned that the men would provide labor for a store. Problem was, the Civil War erupted and shut down commerce leaving the family scrabbling for survival. It was right after the war ended, that James Aloysius Dolan returned from Texas and proceeded to put together a new store himself. Rather than compete with Dolan who already knew the area and had some good will among the rough waterfront crowd, Alex Chicoupapoulis—on behalf of his brothers—bought JD's tent store to get rid of him, along with the right to run store wagons to the interior, something JD had mentioned, though he and Alex never quite settled on what that meant.

Alex was a big man with a small brain. JD soon met Stephen Levy from New York and, ignoring his venture with Alex, entered into partnership with Levy. It was a sharp deal on JD's part, but there was no written agreement, and JD never actually used the word partner when discussing the venture with Alex. All JD would allow was that he would pay the Chicoupapoulis brothers to truck his freight from Friar's Point inland.

Alex also had a temper. Back after the War, the Friars Point newspaper announced that a train through the hill town of Oxford would carry the wife of Jefferson Davis back into Mississippi. Alex and one of his cronys rode all the way up to the depot to pay their respects to the memory of the Confederate President. Mrs. Davis—Miz Varina—had a reputation for extraordinary beauty. Alex spent so much time fawning over the woman that the train conductor had to throw him off. Alex's companion shot the trainman, which was tragic enough, but Alex jumped on the wounded man and tried to choke him to death. His friend escaped. Alex was hauled to jail.

From the late 1860's when Alex made his bad deal with JD, no kind word was ever spoken between them. After the Chicoupapoulis brothers split up, Alex moved inland and south with his small grubstake where he braved the tales of fever and snakes and invested in a piece of swamp land in Bolivar county not far from land JD had purchased a few years before him.

JD and Alex both joined the local Grange Organization, a chapter formed like many in Mississippi less for the betterment of the condition of white laborers and farmers than to provide cover for some of the violence that snatched local government in Mississippi counties away from black elected officials. It was Alex's first brush with politics, and though it would not be his last, he was never a likeable person, and no one ever suggested he should run for anything. Out of which came his frustration with Isaiah Montgomery being chosen for one of two delegate slots from Bolivar County for the new constitutional convention.

A thing of long-rooted hostility, this feud of Alex Chicoupapoulis and James Aloysius Dolan, and it was about to boil over.

Toward noon that Sunday, just before Cicero Morgan would arrive at JD's house seeking JD's intercession on Mound Bayou's behalf, JD was on his way to a Grange meeting. Wrens scratching for grubs along a trail erupted in flight as JD rode toward the flock. Their noise, and a sudden darkness against the sun overhead, startled him. For the briefest moment he was aware only of his heart beating too fast. A second later, bird droppings peppered his head.

"Damn your souls!"

The flaccid, sun-spotted skin below JD's chin trembled as he shook his fist toward the ascending wave. He watched it bend in half and move away before wiping at his face with a sleeve.

"'Tis Alex the Greek, you should be damnin," the voice inside his head said.

JD yelled toward the departing birds as if the pulsing pattern were preaching at him, but he knew better. A specter of a long-ago deceased father still seized his brain from time to time, even had him yelling at Dick who seemed so ignorant of the hard truths of life. At fifty-five, JD seldom felt good any more. Blood pressure gave him headaches, and it blurred the vision in his discolored eyes, when they weren't already blurred from whiskey. His gouty left leg ached so much on most days he couldn't ride his horse. Today, though, he had forced himself to ride the horse and leave his comfortable wagon at home.

The Greek named Chicoupapoulis had descended on Bolivar County like a plague and immediately contested with JD for leadership of the Grange organization, a position that JD had used to the fullest in recruiting men to help clear his land. JD was president of the Grange, a member of Mt. Faith Church of the Redeemer for appearance sake, and by now engaged to marry, though few knew of it. He had been convinced for some time that a wife would give his old age more comfort, especially with Dick nearing the age to leave home.

Up ahead, a cloud of dust was billowing. A barefooted youth JD didn't recognize was approaching on a floppy-eared mule. Another poor-assed, white critter, JD thought, which brought to mind what he considered the little breeder trying to get herself a baby from Dick. A man named Harkins—in JD's mind a never-amount-to-anything sort with whom JD had spent a winter in the swamp after robbing a steamboat—had become his overseer. Harkins was loyal, but his daughter had her eye on Dick's inheritance. To avoid insulting his old friend, JD had tried without success to keep Dick away from the girl.

Pamela Sue Harkins was her name, and it didn't matter that she was good looking. JD had approached a family on the river about a certain daughter coming of age, which was an unthinkably wealthy prospect for Dick. Once married into the Scott family, no one would dare challenge Dick's race.

A rabbit flushed out of the scrub along the trail, and JD's horse reared.

"Whoa now! Steady down, fella."

The pain in JD's left leg was a reminder of just how strong Dick had become. A month before, JD had surprised him curled up with Pamela Sue in front of the fireplace. Several days' whiskey had burnt away whatever understanding JD might have exercised, so he'd cursed the two of them awake. A tongue of white-faced hellfire, the girl screaming "You whoreson, I'm a lady!" and other words that would have started a fight in a whorehouse. When JD grabbed her, Dick grabbed him and wrestled his father to the floor, wrenching his knee.

Amused now, by the recollection, JD turned his ear into the wind to a faint hint of music from the church on the edge of town. As he passed the burial mounds where church picnics were held, he was reminded of the sour-faced old church hags who had begrudged him his freedom over the years and spread so much gossip about his night life. Nevertheless, to help along Dick's cause with Charles Scott's niece, he was giving them a marriage to appear more respectable.

Now, his mare turned along the trail toward town, and the roof of Grange Hall appeared above the railroad embankment ahead. The sun was suddenly hot on his head, and he rubbed it. Remembering the hat on the wagon seat at home, he shook his head at his forgetfulness, also at the vanity that had him riding in a saddle rather than perched comfortably aboard a cushion-seated wagon. And for what? He already had his success, and marriage would ease his old age. Not even the Grange thing meant that much anymore. Back when he'd arrived in the county, when the first real estate tax was threatened after the war, the Grange had been the only way he knew in which respectable white folks could help take back the state from ex-slaves and carpetbaggers. He had done his part, and after being elected head of the organization, he had gotten lots of help in the early days of clearing roads into his swampy land. But that time was over and done, both clearing the land and fighting the black people, who now kept to their place.

The choir music ceased as JD entered town. He hated Sundays, the eerie silences and the sadness of so much singing. Songs about death and God and another world didn't sit well with him, reminded him of an old black man who once gave him whiskey and a curse for breaking a vow. That frozen memory was a dagger inside his soul.

A couple hundred yards away, Alex Chicoupapoulis stepped outside Grange Hall and yawned.

"Goddamn, you!" JD said, knowing he couldn't be heard as

he returned Alex's salute and headed for the hitching post beside him.

"Isaiah Montgomery is a pompous neegger. I warned the coon not to run for our conveention."

"'Tis enough of all that," JD said. "Mr. Scott and Mr. Stafford both want him. So what the hell are you sayin', Alex?"

"Come Fourth of July, thees boy, Isaiah, got a surprise coming."

"Not at the Grange's expense, Alex, but *you* don't give a damn. You don't own enough land to care."

Alex chuckled as if the insult had not landed, and he cavorted away rubbing the lapels of his extravagant white suit, back into the hall. JD glanced toward the people streaming out of the nearby church and rubbed the pain in his leg. One ailment after another had him drinking himself to sleep, and he hadn't heard Dick come home for two nights.

"Mornin', JD," the man named Harkins said, coming out of Grange Hall to greet his boss.

"Aye, lad. Have you whiskey?"

"Follow me."

Behind the hall, underneath a large willow, a grassy expanse gave way toward the Alligator Lake. Dismounting carefully on account of his leg, JD eased himself to the ground and walked to sit on the grass.

"'Tis a misery gittin' old."

"I'm older'n you boss. Have a sip o' this."

Harkins remained standing as JD drank. Harkins kept glancing back toward the building.

"What ails you?" JD asked.

"There's mischief afoot. Alex and his gang got a banner inside to spring on you."

"So what else is new?"

"You ought to know," Harkins said, "that they want to hurrah the new town come Fourth of July."

"Jesus, Mary'n Joseph," JD said, struggling up only to stumble.

"Just be easy for awhile, boss. I want to talk about your boy, Dick, and my Pammy."

"'Tisn't a subject for now, Harkins. Wait for a more congenial time."

"JD, you promised me a favor back when I saved your life."

"Aye."

"I was just a Good Samaritan haulin' you off that boat'n back into the swamp. Now, I'm askin—ain't much mind you, 'cause I know your Dick got his own mind. I been helpin' raise him since he was so high. Taught him to work the animals, and since sixteen, he been in charge of all your mules."

"Fine job, Harkins, truly, but today my mind is on pullin' that damn Greek's fangs."

"Yessir, but when a young man's got a disposition to care for animals, he alright in my book. You know what I mean?"

JD nodded.

"Yessir, your boy got a way with them mules. Kin sit on a fence and talk to 'em."

Harkins chuckled.

"To the point, Harkins."

"Well, sir, some folks would think Dick a little strange, but not me. I just want you to know it's alright him showin' my Pammy some attention."

"Well'n done, then," JD said, allowing Harkins to help him to his feet. "'Tis a matter I'll leave to the young folks."

A tolling bell announced the end of service at the Church of the Redeemer. Men like JD who seldom worshiped were already inside Grange Hall laughing, spitting tobacco and fiddling with cigars as JD approached the door with Harkins. A red, white and blue banner was provoking laughter in the back. Two men quickly folded it and went to their seats in a group apart. JD recognized them as Alex's cronies, one a tenant farmer, the other a laborer from Aaron Shelby's new white settlement.

A handslap exploded across the near-empty room. A skinny little man leapt up to uproarious laughter waving a squashed mosquito so big its legs were hanging off the palm of his hand.

"Goddamn gallon-nipper!"

"What say, Frank?"

"It's a goddamn gallon-nipper. Dranks least a gallon o' blood every time it bites you."

JD smiled, too. That season when the watercourses began to drop was upon them, and the quieter and often stagnant water brought on a plague of mosquitoes. JD didn't notice Alex enter behind him.

"Meester Dolan!"

"Aye, Alex? . . . Git the hell from behind me!"

"We got some business ain't been planned on."

"No, ye don't! You, rednecks, go siddown!"

"Some of thees boys mighty upset 'bout the new cotton gin down in nigger town. They doin' work for white folks, and thees ain't right."

Amidst applause, men holding the banner jumped to their feet. It read: Nigger Roast, July 4th!

"I said, siddown! Be quiet! This ain't no Klavern hall."

"Niggers in they own towns actin' outta place," one said." We got to do somethin'."

Under JD's steady scowl, Alex's henchmen quieted, but not Alex.

"Thees nigger who run Mound Bayou, he act polite as hell when it suit his purpose. What you say, meester president?"

"You be out of order, Alex."

JD took up his gavel and toyed with it while staring down the trouble-maker. Judging from the sympathy with Alex, feeling was widespread, so JD decided to let the talk run its course. As he turned to walk behind his desk and sit down, the two men jumped up and waved their banner. Again, the men applauded.

"Thees men are from down by the Shelby plantation. We gonna hoorrah some neegger on de Fourth of July. Is a holiday anyhow an' we all be off from work, hanh, boys?"

The general agreement put JD off form. He had not expected anything to come from all the grousing, and now he felt compelled to take control again. Lynching unsettled sharecroppers everywhere, and that usually meant the disappearance of valuable workers. JD banged his gavel.

"Tis out of order, you be, Alex. Use the hall later, but now, on to holiday planning for the Grange people. No more about niggers."

So little grumbling confronted JD's decision, it surprised him, as if the men around Alex harbored some secret. Nevertheless, he turned the meeting over to some of the good people who'd arrived from the church who were scheduled to talk about children and games and punch, all of which were a part of the Grange JD didn't care for, but it came with the position he held. So after a polite spell sitting silent behind his desk and smiling as if intent on what was being said, he stood up and walked out behind the hall to relieve himself. On impulse, he stretched out on the grass. The sun on his gouty leg felt good, and he dozed off.

Raised voices from inside the hall startled JD awake, and he returned back inside. He sat down heavily as nondescript details of the coming week filtered through his boredom along with Alex's white suit.

"Meester president, it come to my attention that you are hidin' something important from these good men."

JD flushed and jumped to his feet behind the front table.

"What's the matter, meester president?"

"'Tis dammed in hell I'll see your soul, Alex! The meetin's closed ... Sit down!"

Alex Chicoupapoulis turned toward the room.

"JD, here, got a *neegger* woman living in Mound Bayou!"

JD slammed his gavel on the table.

"Tis a fact, gentlemen, the meetin's closed!"

"Is you wantin' to protect your special seetuation?"

A man sitting behind Alex fairly hissed to the men behind him, "Mother o' his boy's a nigger!"

The swell of ribald laughter turned JD's face blood red. He knocked his chair over, stomped to the front of his table, and the crowd hushed.

"Tis a helluva fight you just bought!"

JD rushed the larger Alex, and the two grappled before Harkins leapt in and tried to separate them. One of Alex's friends put a pistol to Harkin's head. Men dived to the floor. Others ran out. Harkins raised his hands as Alex drew his own pistol and held JD at gunpoint while telling the whole story, about JD owning a store in Shufordsville right after the War, about the black woman he'd lived with, and about Dick—the woman's son—whom JD had been palming off as white, more recently on an innocent and unsuspecting white girl.

"Say somethin', JD!" Harkins demanded. "Is it true?"

When JD nodded, Harkins grabbed his head and screamed, "I ain't never done you a wrong, and you do me this way."

"Wasn't me put your gal to my boy. Don't blame me."

The scorn of the assembled men now leapt at Harkins, fiery tongues of ribaldry, contempt. He spat into JD's face and ran out of the hall to mount a shave-tail mule that looked like a huge rat with ears.

"Don't blame yer boss!" Alex yelled after Harkins. "Yer gal did choose the nigger buck!"

Harkins paused in the distance and turned back.

"Damn your soul!"

"Ain't my fault, Meester Harkins."

Harkins rode off leaving JD alone.

"Tis all lies," JD announced to the men around him.

"So tell us the truth."

"You ain't worth the truth!"

EARLIER THAT MORNING, DICK had awakened before his father. With Buck delivered to Cicero, Dick had spent Friday working a six-mule drag loosening a section of earth to be scooped out for an irrigation ditch on the edge of his father's land. The next day, a Saturday, he toiled into evening and rode home dead tired, neglecting a promised stopover at the Harkins house to see Pamela Sue. So, that Sunday, he ate a hearty breakfast of spoon bread and plum preserves washed down by a whole quart of clabbered milk sprinkled with pork cracklin. After a visit in the outhouse and a quick dip in the pond, he pulled on a freshly laundered shirt and twill pants, creases starched in by the housekeeper.

Pamela Sue saw him leading his horse down the dusty road from the Dolan house, and she dashed indoors to comb her hair and change clothes.

"Take care of my dress, Pammy," her stepmother said. "You got to remember me'n the rest when you git Dick to marry."

"Yes'm, I will. What about these shoes?"

"Oh, child . . . Don't walk in 'em no more'n you got to. Your big feet break my little shoes all down."

Pamela Sue walked out to greet Dick, slowly, to show displeasure for his unexplained absence. Her four younger sisters and brother had no such hesitation. They rushed past her like a mob once they glimpsed Dick, begging and pulling on him until he hopped astride his horse.

"I got no candy on me! Leave us be and tomorrow, I'll bring you jawbreakers."

Squeals of childish pleasure beat about Dick's ears as he pulled Pamela Sue up behind. The flash of her bare legs under the white dress lined with a grenadine muslin made his groin even warmer in the sun. He turned as he felt Pamela Sue squirm.

"Just takin' my slippers off 'cause they tight. How you, Dick?"

"How about yourself?"

"Oh, I thought you was takin' me for a ride yestiddy, but you cain't be trusted."

"I was workin."

"Humph! Busy with them little nigger gals workin' for your pa over yonder."

"Ain't no different than you."

A loosening of Pamela Sue's arms told Dick he'd made an error.

"'Course, they ain't pretty as you by half."

"Don't you sweet talk me, Dick Dolan. I heard how you an' your pa is with colored women."

"Well sir, hear tell you was givin' it up to a Mister Joe Bob used to live where you moved from when your ma died."

Pamela Sue stiffened.

"You was doin' it when you wasn't but twelve."

"Ain't no such thing!"

"Joe Bob said you was naked in the river with him."

"Shut up, Dick Dolan! I ain't no girl like that."

"That's what he said."

They rode in silence onto a narrow trail atop the ridge north of Jones Bayou, which broadened into fields of sharp-bladed Johnson grass and stands of young cane rooted since the last big water flow. The trail ended at the Hushpuckena

River, and they had to dismount to descend its steep banks, braking themselves by grasping trees along the way down before leading the horse across the seasonally shallow water and up the other side.

Then they glimpsed the tiny clearing of grass and gone-to-seed flowers they sought. An old flood had uprooted and piled a tangle of trees below the ridge to alter the natural flow of a rill. Water seeping around the obstruction had built up a band of fresh sand. Sunlight erupted off the water and dazzled Dick as he headed down toward it. When Lightning slowed and began to graze, Dick gave Pamela Sue an arm down.

"Oh, Dick! I could be a bird and just fly away."

Pamela Sue stretched out her arms and whirled like a top down the slope to the water below. When her feet plunged into the wet sand, she squealed in delight and shuffled her toes in the crystal shallows. Sun underneath her raised skirt turned her freckled legs into columns of light. Dick sighed and started turning handsprings awaiting her signal to approach, but he tumbled onto a tree limb and screamed. Pamela Sue ran to him while he lay holding his side.

"Go on, leave me be."

"You ain't hurt bad?"

"Not on your life, girl."

Dick lay looking up at the liquid sky, until his eyes watered and he closed them, marveling at patterns of cloud etched on his eyelids. He took off his boots, then shirt, and remembering a saddle blanket, he came to his feet painfully and walked back to his horse. While he returned from the ridge top, Pamela Sue removed her dress and sprawled in the open water face to the sun. Under Dick's patient staring, her blue eyes opened, and she cupped handful after handful of water over her breasts, between her legs. Dick marveled at how white she was where the sun never touched.

He tossed aside his blanket and pulled off his clothes. They began playing like children in a gigantic tub, splashing water and giggling. They made love in the water, then pulled the blanket into some shade because her fair skin wasn't for sun. Lying with eyes closed, his hunger for her still raged as he watched breeze stir wisps of hair along her legs and in the red forest glistening between her thighs. So he pulled her to himself and started over again. Languorously, she welcomed him without opening her eyes. Afterward, they lay beside each other, moving ever so slightly to invite the breeze to touch them.

"When we gonna git married, Dick?"

"Hunh?"

"We in love, ain't we?"

"I guess so."

"Ain't you know? You ain't playin' with me, Dick?"

"Nay, nay! Waitin' 'till pa turns the business over to me."

"What?"

"Said he would, you know. So we got to wait."

"Sometime a body cain't wait, Dick. You so good-lookin'."

"Pa got a righteous willfulness. Disown me, was what he said, if I don't listen to him."

"Oh!"

"Yep . . . Lemme sleep. Worked hard all week."

Pamela Sue muttered and allowed her body to rub against Dick, but he would not respond. Soon, she, too, closed her eyes.

Some time later, as the afternoon spent itself, and the sun headed down toward the tree line bordering the Mississippi River, Dick awakened startled. He tried to remember whatever dream it was had made him so uneasy, but only the memory of being chased and hounded remained. Cooler now that the sun was waning, he dressed and walked to his saddle for a canteen. The water was warm, so he spat it out and walked down to the water pooled amidst the fallen trees. While attempting to drink, he heard the rustle of Pamela Sue's clothes. Then he stretched to find a deeper flow of water to keep the sand out of his mouth. After drinking, he returned to the blanket, flopped down and closed his eyes while Pamela Sue finished dressing.

"Oh, Dick, you got sand all over my new dress."

Dick's horse snorted then. Glancing up, he saw it turn toward the east. Sound of a twig snapping brought Dick to the crest of the ridge at a run. A solitary figure was approaching on foot. Anxious minutes later, Dick recognized Harkins.

"Pammy! Put your clothes in order, 'tis your pa."

Even as close to home as they were, wrongdoers sometimes waylaid unsuspecting people so Dick was actually relieved to recognize Pamela Sue's father, until sight of Pamela Sue fidgeting with her clothes made Dick wish his time alone with her was not about to end.

"Come up'n join me lass."

"I got sand all over my dress."

Dick paid no further attention to Harkins for running down to brush at sand crusted on the rear of Pamela Sue's dress. He took his time running his hand over the body underneath, and when he quit, the girl still looked indecently draped by the damp cloth. Then Pamela Sue looked off toward the ridge above, and Dick followed her gaze. Harkins was pointing a shotgun toward them. A wind gust plastered Dick's damp shirt to his chest, and Pamela Sue's nails dug into his palm. Heart thumping but outwardly calm, Dick snatched his hand from Pamela Sue and started backing up onto the ridge to place his horse between himself and Harkins.

"Stay put, boy!" Harkins said. "Doesn't want to do you in, but I will."

Harkins continued advancing, more quickly now that Dick was reacting.

"'Twas no disrespect meant, me bein' here with Pammy, Mr. Harkins."

"No tricks, boy, you best stay put."

"Pa, you put that gun down!" Pamela Sue walked between Dick and her father. "What's wrong with you?"

Harkins ran downhill off the ridge to keep Dick in line of fire, then shifted the shotgun to a single hand. He grabbed his daughter with the other.

"Git outta the way, gal!"

"No, pa . . . No!"

When Pamela Sue reached for her father's arm, he back-handed her, and she tripped on the hem of her dress and tore the bright-colored lining from the stitching at her waist as she stumbled downhill. While the girl was sprawling nearly naked, Dick made his move toward Harkins, then froze when Harkins thrust the double barreled shotgun barrel into Dick's stomach. Light erupted as the gun stock slammed into Dick's head, and he lost consciousness.

Slowly, he came to. In the distance, Pamela Sue was riding away on Lightning.

"Be still a spell, boy," Harkins said. "We got some talkin'."

"Don't like this one bit, Mr. Harkins, and my pa wont."

"You talkin' like a boy, and that ain't good seein' as how you got a hard row to hoe. Your pa an' me got things in common you ain't never heard of. Just . . . things ain't simple for a man with mouths to feed."

Harkins backed away and squatted.

"You in trouble, Dick, and I cain't have my girl hooked up with you."

"I don't understand."

"Um . . . Well, no reason you should yet." Harkins stood up. "I advise you to hightail it outta these parts. Your pa got enemies, an' they'll be your undoin' if you stay here."

"Something happen to my pa?"

"I just left a Grange meetin' that'll cause some changes around here. I'm a way-back, old boy, got no prospects an' ain't never expected to rise. JD been on the good track, and he done pretty good for hisself. Now there's others want to come forward, and they tellin' a lot of old stuff 'bout your—."

Dick leapt and bowled Harkins over. Dick found himself on top only to feel a sharp pain in his groin.

"Stop, boy!" Harkins said. "Don't move less'n you wants to be gelded. That there's a dirk shoved up your britches. Just ease off."

Dick followed instructions. For the first time, he saw fire and cunning in old Harkins.

"You got grit," Harkins said, putting his knife away as he retrieved his gun. "Don't waste it around here 'cause you cain't fight what's happenin'. I been more'n a dirt farmer in my day, back when I swore a solemn oath to help your pa. I'm doin' that right now. But you stay away from my girl, and things be quit 'tween you'n me. I see you agin, I got to do worse by you than I wants to. Just leave my Pammy be . . . Now, git!"

Dick was distracted by pain where the knife had drawn blood as he started walking. It took what seemed hours with Harkins' gun on his back, until Harkin's turned off home. When Dick arrived home, Cicero Morgan's buckboard was parked in front, but the house was dark. No porch lantern had been lit, which was usual when visitors were present. As Dick stepped onto the porch, his father's drunken voice boomed out.

"Tis for nothin', you've come. I'm not your guardian angel."

"But Mound Bayou is special for both of us. If I could protect it myself, I would."

"Dammit, Cicero, I got problems of my own!"

Dick sneaked inside. In the dark Cicero was outlined by the lingering dusk through the window. JD was hidden, but for his wheezing and coughing.

"Hello, pa," Dick said.

"Boy!"

"Yes, pa?"

"'Tis a good talkin' we need. Cicero, I am sad you've come this distance for nought, but truly 'tis not my brother's keeper I be. Good evenin' to you."

"Perhaps when you're not drinking—"

"Drinkin's my own business! Git your nigger self outta here!"

Cicero turned and stalked out. As he was climbing into his wagon, Dick stepped outside.

"Stay yer ass put, boy!" JD yelled from inside.

Dick halted just below the steps and turned to face his father who knocked the hallway lamp to the floor trying to light it. When JD finally got the lamp lit, Dick's bloodstained pants became visible to Cicero

"What happened?" Cicero asked.

"Be on your way," Dick said. "I'll explain later."

Belatedly, JD saw the blood.

"Oh! What have they done ye?"

"I'm still a man," Dick said, "if that's your question."

"I'll kill the bastard."

"No, pa, you won't. It was Harkins. What's goin' on?"

The sound of Cicero's wagon interrupted.

"To bed with you," JD said. "We'll talk in the mornin'."

"But pa—"

"Go to bed!"

In bed that night, JD was in crisis. He had come into the Mississippi frontier down-and-out but city slick. Only upon arriving had he learned that he was to spend the next two years of his life working inside the Great Mississippi Swamp to protect a little piece of some worthy person's cleared land with a new levee. To move from indentured levee builder to where he was now, he had done many unprincipled things. There were a string of victims who'd come to harm trusting in him, even loving him, and the only excuse he had ever had was a voice in his head egging him on toward success, the human cost be damned. Though he had forced Abyssinia to give up

Dick, raising the boy as his own had seemed his one good decision.

A pain in JD's left leg distracted him. He sat up and shrugged off his shirt, then stood to drop his trousers around his boots. The light had almost vanished but for the sheen of the moon glistening atop three sea trunks with metal studding the edges. Images softened as JD was overwhelmed by all of the guilt he had ever felt, and his guilt held him prisoner as three stud-scaled dragons came alive in front of him. They were guarding a window through which glistened a silver castle. Somehow, all of a sudden, he was mounted on a horse and galloping toward the treasure-filled palace, but every time he drew close a fiery exhalation threatened to engulf him. Out of the smoke emerged the face of a bruised woman he'd sold to Mr. Alcorn, and JD's mount trembled in response to his own regret, but as in life, JD charged ahead, across a field of accusing bones into a fiery exhalation that turned his every move into agony. He prayed to hold the pain away, but no use, and when it came to mind that it was not his time to die, all he could summon was an agonized scream. He felt the earth grow cold. He was an old man without zest for another day. "Fool!" the voice JD recognized as his long-lost father whispered. "See what a hard life, a soft heart'l earn ye."

DICK AWAKENED TO THE SMELL of smoke and voices raised in alarm. The pain of his wound struck when he sat up. Through the back window, he saw that the roof of the barn had burned away and the hay inside was still smoldering. As he snatched on his clothes, a sting from the turpentine his father had insisted on pouring into the wound struck again, but Dick was relieved to find that walking downstairs caused no great discomfort. Outside, JD was standing pale and disheveled watching a black share cropper, his two oldest boys and the white man who worked the store slosh water onto the smoking barn walls.

"Where's Harkins?" Dick asked his father.

"Shut your mouth!"

"Where are my mules?"

One of the sharecroppers pointed Dick to where several animals were milling around loose in front of the house. Dick walked back through the house to check on them. When he returned behind the house, shards of light from the new sun flashed above the trees.

"Nothin' left to be done, boy. Go on back inside."

"What's wrong, pa?"

"Jesus, Mary and Joseph, my goddamn barn is burnt! 'Tis inside, I want you!"

Men carrying water paused as Dick walked up the back stairs, and when he turned to watch them from inside the screen door they went back to work. The burning, events of the day before, and JD's temper continued to stand in the way of answers for Dick. Then, his stomach growled, and he remembered that he had missed supper the night before. So he went to the pantry and piled leftover fried fish and corn bread from Sunday onto a plate.

JD, meanwhile, continued to curse the malice that had burned his barn. He had hoped there might be some way to silence Alex Chicoupapoulis and to explain away the Grange incident, but even his sharecroppers had already heard the report about Dick, and there was no way to ignore the message of the fire, which even Alex wouldn't have dared without near unanimous sentiment on his side. He began the long climb up the back stairs. Dick was at the kitchen table eating.

"Do you know what this is all about?"

"It's Klan work."

"Aye, true."

"So how come?"

"Your ma, Dick . . . A colored woman, she was—got to tell you straight out."

Dick flushed. He staggered up and wiped his mouth while staring into his father's face.

"Don't be upset."

"She was . . . colored?"

"Yes, she was. Why are you getting so angry?"

"And why the hell not?"

"'Twasn't me or your ma's fault."

Inside Dick, a certain rage that had been simmering broadened into a quandary as Dick stared at his father. His mouth opened, but there was no sound.

"Sit down, lad. 'Tis a piece of news, I'll wager."

Dick crumpled into his chair, his mind playing back over his father's odd behavior with Cicero the evening before—a "nigger boy" sign outside the house a few weeks back.

"Does Harkins know?"

"Harkins knows, lad. Him and the good and righteous Grangers all know. To nigger hell, may the Good Lord damn their souls."

Dick kicked his chair away.

"Get on with it! What does Mr. Cicero have to do with it?"

"Nay, nay, lad, another matter entirely."

"What, then?"

"'Twas to help his people through the holiday that he sought help. 'Tis likely the same people did such a fine job of my barn, but under the circumstance, what could I do to help him?"

"Is it fightin' that scares you?"

"Don't you use that tone with me."

"You tell me my ma is a colored woman, and yet you'll let some son of a bitch murder my colored friends? Stop it, for Christ sake!"

"'Tain't the way o' the world to be helpin' all what asks. A man's arm is just so long. In this land, you got to take sides. You're white, or black. Now go upstairs, pack a bag while I figure out what to do with you."

"Do with me? . . . If ma was colored, you know she was just like—I mean what's the difference between her and us?"

"I'm sending you to Cincinnati, it's what I'd planned if something like this ever happened. A little money will buy you a situation."

"What about ma?"

"What about her, lad?"

"Did somebody make you get rid of her?"

As the words whistled out, flecks of spit struck JD in the face and hung like nasty teardrops, wet and accusing, and his fist struck out, knocking Dick sprawling into the table and his half-eaten breakfast.

"You half-breed son of a bitch! Don't you dare judge me!"

Dick sprang up snarling and charged. Grappling together, father and son tumbled through the screen door, down the back stairs to the ground outside locked in rage. Two young men pulled Dick away. Joe Bob's father stood and watched as they pushed Dick off through the barn. When they emerged behind it, Dick ripped an arm free and accidentally elbowed one boy.

"Watch yourself, Mistuh Dick. Your pa bein' a white man don't give you no cause to carry on like this."

Sunlight dazzled Dick's eyes after the brief walk through the dim barn. Early heat rode the brightness and now gentled his body like hands on a mule's flank. He climbed the fence at the rear of the corral and perched on it, paying no attention to the people talking in that other world out front. Lightning galloped up, and Dick recognized Harkins' voice returning the animal now nosing into Dick's face. He straightened to avoid being knocked over and clasped his hands on both sides of Lightning's head to steady himself. Gently, he blew into the flaring nostrils, and Lightning jerked and pranced away, then lowered his head and again extended his muzzle as the other animals were driven into the corral. Dick called to the mules, but they made no response this morning. A bump from Lightning toppled him backward over the fence.

Hitting the ground stunned him, and he lay there. He was still James Aloysius' son, but now just another bastard the likes of which years of coarseness came to mind. Every white man Dick had ever worked for had a bastard. The sharecropper's boys had already called him a nigger. He jumped up and hurried past everyone, up to his room. He did not think as he pulled off the clothes he had been wearing and dressed again. He threw things into a saddle bag and was out the door and saddling his horse before JD could find him. As JD's inquiring voice drew near, Dick hurried away, leading his horse along the road away from home, still undecided where he would go. He was wearing his Sunday best and had two changes of clothes, two rifles, cans of sardines, a handful of crackers and one hundred dollars that he'd taken from his father's safe-keeping. Cicero came into his mind. There being no one else he could trust, he headed for Clarksdale.

By MID-MORNING, DICK WAS walking as fast as he could to burn off energy, still leading his horse to avoid riding on his tender groin. Since leaving the house, the sound of Sadie's voice singing "Motherless Child" had been running in and out of his head. He had had no pattern of feeling sorry for himself as a child, so the music just seemed to fit his off-key mood, nothing like self-pity or despair. He tried to hum the melody, but singing had never been for him. Now, all he could do was hum snatches of the mournful song. The sun was bright and hot and he was beginning to sweat.

He glimpsed figures ahead moving in his direction, and he slowed his pace wanting no company. By the time he looked for them again, they were larger, and Dick realized that unless the two lived near Alligator Lake, they'd simply take him for white. If they were Africanamerican, he was now indeed a 'colored' person, too, so he picked up his stride.

"'Day to you, young mastuh," a slim brown man near Dick's own age said as Dick approached. The speaker's companion—shorter and blue-black under the noon sun—tipped his hat."

"You got it wrong," Dick said, "my ma's black as yours."

The dark-skinned man spurned Dick's hand.

"Free road, boy. We ain't gots to talk to nobody, has we, Bill, Jr.?"

Lightning nuzzled Dick in the back, pushing him into the feisty little man speaking.

"Goddammit, nigga!" He pushed Dick away and drew a knife from his boot. "Keep away, you yella son of a bitch!"

Dick watched the two men walk away casting glances over their shoulders.

"Fuck your momma!" the slim one turned and said, grabbing his private parts.

Dick followed, perplexed. The strangers were half way to Clarksdale before they sat to rest alongside the road. Dick walked up.

"If you're hungry, I got some sardines," he said.

The pair looked at each other. One shrugged, the other licked his lips and motioned Dick over. Dick reached two tins of sardines out of his saddlebags.

"Why you givin' away food?" the tall man asked. "Got a horse and two rifles—what's your name?"

"Name's Richard."

"My name's, Jason," the shorter of the two said. "This here's Bill Jr. We from Cleveland. What about you?"

"Outside of Alligator. My name's Richard Dolan."

"You talk like a white man, Richard. Bein' light complexioned as you is, me'n him don't appreciate you cappin' on us. You know your momma ain't black."

"Whatcha mean by that?" Bill Jr. asked. "Callin' your momma black."

"My momma is black." Dick said.

"You somethin!" Bill Jr. said, mouth full of sardine.

"Look here, Dick," Jason said. "Your momma is colored. Ain't no possible way she be dark, and you light as you is."

"Yeah, Dick, they ever tell you that your momma was a alligator?"

"And your daddy," Jason said, "must swim damn good."

"Whatta you mean?" Dick demanded.

"Must of had a real powerful stroke, your poppa," Jason said.

Dick frowned.

"Oh look at his face, Bill Jr." Jason jumped to his feet. "Where your momma live, Dick?

"Do she," Bill Jr. demanded, "give up greasy sardines, like you?"

Dick turned red.

"What about the Fourth of July?" Jason asked. "Will your momma climb my flagpole?"

"He don't," Bill Jr. said, "celebrate that. He red, but he ain't white, and he sho ain't blue."

As the others roared, Dick reached for Lightning's reins.

"Fuck you and your Fourth o' July!" he said. "I'm one-fourth black, one-fourth white, one-fourth me and one-fourth gone—assholes!"

It was late afternoon before Dick reached Clarksdale, located the house he wanted and climbed the side stairs to Cicero's attic room. No one was there. So he waited. The accumulated heat in the roof and walls was fierce. Dick pulled off his clothes, lay on the bed and fell asleep.

Footsteps on the stairs awakened Dick. Sound of a woman humming was drifting through the window on the cooler evening air. Then Dick remembered that he left had Lightning untended in the yard below. He ran for the door and straight into Cicero.

"Whoa, there, boy! Where are you off to in your drawers?"

"My horse! You seen my horse?"

"Yep. The woman downstairs took Lightning out of the sun. She wants us to have supper with her, too, but I rather not—to keep things business-like between her and me. But, follow me. There's a house nearby where a meal costs only ten cents."

"Haven't eaten since this mornin'."

"By the way . . . what are you doing here?"

There was a moment of silence before Dick picked his eyes up off the floor and looked straight at Cicero.

"Kinda of a long story, Mr. Cicero. Can we go eat first?"

It was in the middle of supper that Dick explained what his father had told him, and it was Cicero's turn to remain silent and to seem merely sympathetic. "Well, isn't that something," he kept saying, until Dick had emptied himself of words.

"Come spend the holidays with Buck and me in Mound Bayou. I hadn't planned on being down there, but what you told me changes everything."

"It does?"

"It'll be good for you down there with your own people."

"What do I do, Mr. Cicero?"

"Just be yourself."

"But I ain't never . . . Tell me what to do."

"Dick, you have your whole life ahead of you, and you can live white or black. It'll be up to you."

That night, Dick asked more about Mound Bayou, and Cicero explained as best he could about the people who had built it, his history with them during and after slavery. That conversation stretched out for hours. As Cicero described the threats against the town and JD's refusal to help, Dick grew red in the face.

"Jesus, Mary and Joseph! If it's the folks I'm thinkin' behind this trouble, there's only one solution, and I've two of 'em in my saddle holster."

Cicero hid his grin. What a memorable holiday for Abyssinia. In but a single day, Dick would learn they were all family, and not only would Dick come visit in the swamp, he'd bring Buck along. That night, after turning in, Cicero turned onto his back and kicked his legs for joy, part of something bigger than himself. Shit happened, an unpredictable chain of events, life, eating and eliminating, extraordinary events like a beautiful sunset, terrible events, too, like a father arrested for trying to be free. Love had to exist before the word was ever used to describe it. Abstractions always came after the fact, like attitudes birthed by slavery. Africans had been enslaved long before the word, abolitionist, came on the scene, and they, the white people who fought for principle, were no longer much honored by Africans running from the past like the Americans around them. The thought gave way to a convulsive cackle, and Cicero stuffed the edge of his pillow into his mouth.

Cicero allowed Dick to continue sleeping while he dressed, harnessed the horse to his borrowed wagon and drove into nearby Shufordsville where Eugene Woods lived. Abyssinia had asked Cicero to invite Mr. Woods down to Mound Bayou for the Fourth of July. Unfortunately, neither Eugene nor his brother, Joe, were to be found, and Cicero left the invitation with Joe's wife. He also got permission to hold onto the wagon. By late morning, when Cicero returned to Clarksdale, Dick stood in the yard grooming Lightning.

"Had me wondering if you left without me," Dick said.

"Of course not, boy."

"Couldn't you be callin' me somethin' else? I'll be twenty-one this December."

"Of course—*son*. You may use my first name, as well."

Despite eyeing Cicero oddly, Dick made no comment on the word, son. He tucked away his brush and began saddling the horse as Cicero walked chuckling upstairs for his travel bag. Dick was in the saddle when Cicero walked back down.

"Tie Lightning behind the wagon, Dick, and ride with me."

"Lightnin' needs a long ride. A mite frisky, he is."

"We can switch horses and put him in harness midway."

"Aye, run him a bit. It would be more comfortable in the wagon."

"You weren't seriously wounded, were you?" Cicero asked.

"All parts in workin' order far's I can tell."

Dick asked nothing about his mother. He was still under the impression that she had died, the convenient fiction JD had used. As the hours passed on the long drive down to Mound Bayou, Dick kept inquiring about black people, why black people didn't like being black, and why more white men didn't get shot.

"We are no more violent than anybody else," Cicero told him. "How many white farmers carry guns?"

Dick thought for a moment, then shrugged.

"That's the point. The people of Mound Bayou are not soldiers. They're not vagabonds, nor gunfighters. Family people don't carry the weight of weapons, and we black people are no more nor less willing to fight than anyone else. The people who threaten us, catch us most often unawares. Many don't have the price of a weapon. But I put my money to good use. I do carry a gun."

They changed horses then, put the frisky stallion into harness and tied the spent horse behind the wagon. Dick took over the driving, and set a fast pace. After that, the conversation lagged for several miles, until Cicero lifted his pistol from underneath the wagon seat and shoved it into his waistband as they neared the little settlement around Aaron Shelby's farm between Alligator and Mound Bayou

"Speaking of our good citizens around this area," Cicero said, "What do you know of Alex Chicoupapoulis, why would he attack your father?"

"Pa never said. Just that he was tellin' about my ma."

"Is there anyone I can reach to get Alex called off?"

"I don't think so . . . What you call good white folks?"

Cicero nodded.

"There ain't none," Dick said.

Cicero made no reply as Dick veered off road suddenly, toward a nearby stream to water the horses. After they had drunk, Dick drove back onto the road, and the rest of the trip was unexceptional, until the land clearing that was Mound Bayou appeared in the distance.

"Now tell me again," Dick said, "why these people don't use their guns?"

"In this case, the people know of the threat, but they have decided not to confront it head on. Fear of reprisal. Ever since the fight over voting after the war, white men have been teaching my people not to fight back on pain of worse."

"Buck didn't say so, but they sounded kinda weak-kneed."

"Not that I disagree," Cicero said, "but it would be wise to hold your opinions until you have more experience among us."

"But ain't no reason to let a man get away with what some white people do."

"That's for each to decide, don't you think? You, Mr. Dolan, must get along with all kinds. Keep your mouth shut until you learn more."

An armed figure neither of them first recognized as Buck came running.

"Hey, Dick!"

Dick vaulted from the wagon as Buck approached.

"Whatta you doin' here?" Buck asked.

"I have a surprise," Cicero said, "for the both of you."

"What now?" Buck asked.

"Something I never thought I would have the chance to say."

Two hawks fighting over a fish in the nearby bayou startled them and allowed Cicero to choke back tears without being noticed. Buck cocked his Winchester.

"No, Buck!" Dick said. "You ain't that good. I'll show you some shootin'."

"Don't you two run off! . . . Buck, Dick is your cousin."

As the squawking of the hawks faded, only the crunch of wagon wheels on a gravelly stretch of ground punctuated the silence. Buck and Dick looked toward each other, both frowned, then turned in confusion toward Cicero.

"Dick, your mother is my sister."

Buck was holding his rifle in one hand. He threw his free arm around Dick and started shouting as Dick dropped his eyes. When Dick looked back toward Cicero, Buck threw his gun down and hugged with both arms. Only then did Dick smile, a tiny flicker, and tears welled up.

"This good news, Dick. You don't haveta cry." Buck started yelping like a puppy dog. "We can have all the fun together."

Slowly, turning his head every few seconds toward his tutor-now-uncle as if to be sure what he had heard wasn't a joke, Dick seemed caught up between laughing and crying, until Buck's enthusiasm finally drew him in. A rider from the town interrupted the boys. Isaiah had gotten word of Cicero's arrival and wanted to see him right away.

Cicero unharnessed Dick's horse from the wagon and drove away using the other. Aside from talking with Isaiah, he was anxious to reach Abyssinia and to tell her of events before Dick walked up and announced himself. He heard Buck repeating to himself, "I do declare! I do declare . . . I do declare!"

The evening came on quickly, but the shadows held the heat of the day. When night finally draped its black crepe around Buck and Dick, it smothered none of their excitement. Sprawled outside Buck's cabin, they held one wrestling match after another, until Dick began to get the upper hand. Then they lay silent for awhile.

"How do you feel about me?" Dick asked.

"It ain't nothin'," Buck said.

"It ain't nothin'? What does that mean?"

"I like you."

"Your pa likes me, too. Now I know why he taught me all the things he did."

"You was carryin' on some when we first met."

"Aye! He's like my father."

"Why you keep sayin' that? He ain't your daddy."

"Don't be so jealous. How come you never went to visit him?"

Buck dawdled.

"See!" Dick said.

"You want to git whipped again."

"Never on your life, Bucko."

"Anyway, ain't you curious about your momma?"

"Why?"

"She live right here in town."

"Are you sure?"

"You ain't asked about her either?"

"Cicero didn't say."

"I bet he's getting her ready to see you."

"Maybe I should wait here. Got to learn how to act around our people."

"You ain't got nothin' to learn, just be like me."

Buck held forth on many subjects, especially women. He assured Dick that both of them were as good-looking as they came. When talk turned to threats against the town, Buck explained that Isaiah had been persuaded to buy rifles and ammunition in Memphis for his store. Each family had been warned to turn in early on the holiday, and those who didn't own a gun had been offered a rifle on a time-pay plan. Those who didn't buy would be loaned a weapon that following day, which was the Fourth of July.

"'Tain't a proper way to handle trouble," Dick said.

"Whatcha know 'bout fightin' with guns?"

"Soldiers say surprise is the thing, and firin' all your guns at once is all the rest, so's to kill up a bunch. Put's a fright into the enemy when they hear all that noise. That's why people hidin' inside, an' being all spread out ain't right."

"Maybe me'n you oughtta get our hands on a bunch o' guns and do somethin'," Buck said.

"Your uncle's store, hey?"

"Yeah, we could shoot hell outta some Klansmen, an' the girls—wouldn't they talk about us. You be the 'Winchester Man', and I'd be 'Cowboy Buck' . . . Except, what about afterwards? You got to think ahead."

"Ahead to what? Protect yourself today, tomorrow will come in due time."

"You really mean what you was sayin'?"

"Serious as stroke, I am, Buck. Wasn't to git killed, that I came here, and I know them boys won't be lookin' for ambush. They expect your—I mean, our people—to lock up inside an' act scared."

"We ambush 'em, hanh?"

"That simple," Dick said.

"Well, I'm with you!"

"Then how is it we get the guns?"

Buck rubbed his lower lip.

"Uncle *is* bettin' on a hope and a prayer."

"Of course!" Dick said. "Tell me about the guns."

They decided to borrow as many guns as hadn't been sold and bring them north of town. To seal the undertaking, Buck pulled his private whiskey from under a plank of his porch. After winning a contest to determine which could drink longest without pause, Dick was swinging around a post waving the jug in the air.

"Quit yellin'," Buck said.

"But didn't you yourself offer me a drink?" Dick said.

"Yeah, but we ain't supposed to git drunk in public."

"Then shut your face'n drink up before you hear a complaint."

Less than a quarter mile away, Cicero was sitting on a stump in Isaiah's yard.

"Can't have it both ways, Cicero. You works with the good white people or not. Just like when I got you a job after you lost your election. You up and told the man he was wrong for supporting Alcorn's people, and you knew that man didn't want to hear that."

"Truth is truth, and if not, it's time our people made up our own lies. Point is, it's *our* lives. We live them as we see fit. How could I work for a man willing to argue to my face that good white people should take over as if we were still slaves."

"Well, Mound Bayou ain't your fight. Somebody saw you up north o' town with that white boy, and I don't know what's in your mind."

"Richard Dolan knows the men threatening your town. They're Klansmen."

"Klan, whoever, just a mangy bunch o' no-counts. We git by."

"No you won't! Not if they ride on this town in mass."

"What you talkin' about? We inside our own homes, doors locked. I give my people rifles."

"But then what? What's your defense plan? Are you posting look-outs?"

"Cicero, I ain't plannin' for a war. Just trying to take steps ne'ssary to keep us alive."

"Hoping is not a plan."

"Damn it aint', if you a nigga in this land!"

"Damned is what you may be, 'cause you could be dead come the Fourth. Isaiah, my sister lives in this town, my son— do something!"

"We may as well stop talkin'. You too hot-headed."

"No . . . You're confused. I'm not even trying to be some great American hero. I wanted to be one when I was younger. You wouldn't know, but we had a massacre up in Coahoma County during the 1875 election. Black sheriff was John—"

"A what?"

"Black sheriff, a little over ten years ago, and you don't even know about this . . . Well, we had a real thing going on, a land boycott, in fact. Landowners had begun to cut the wages they paid freedman, and this sharecrop thing was starting. So, most of our election workers were folks who'd already been pushed off the land or were afraid to return home. We started working with them and visited all the plantations to tell the people who to vote for and about the land withdrawal. We were hoping to pull at least half of the trained workers off the fields to force landowners to pay a good wage. And we had the votes to control the county board. Well . . . I was inside the sheriff's office when the vigilantes attacked us. My stepson and I had to run out of town only to hear this chanting. Our election workers had been camped near Clarksdale. They headed toward us when they heard the shooting. By the time Jasper and I got up on the Sunflower River ridge to look, all we could see was this army of white men shooting from their horses, and our people running every way . . . I have *never* felt so bad as on that day, and I don't want to feel that way again here in Mound Bayou."

"That is a sad story . . . Well, I know how evil white folks is, but just proves I'm right. Ain't no sense in us goin' up against no armed white men."

"Damn you, Isaiah! We have guns here! My election workers didn't . . . and you have time to prepare!"

When Cicero finally left Isaiah and returned north of town, he was grouchy and short-tempered. Cicero hadn't yet visited Abyssinia. Buck and Dick were near drunk by the time Cicero reached them, but sensing his mood, they calmed down and behaved more soberly. Cicero motioned them aboard his wagon.

"Tell me about my ma," Dick asked, as the cousins boarded the wagon.

Cicero strapped his horses ahead.

"All I could say wouldn't be worth two minutes of being with her. Wait."

They all saw her standing in the rear of her new house with a hoe, chopping weeds from a crop of summer vegetables. Perched atop her head was a wide-brimmed straw hat circled by a yellow ribbon. An over-large man's shirt over a faded dress made her look forlorn and slight standing in the dark working alone.

Dick eased to the ground. His mother was faced away from the road and did not see him. He approached her in cadence with the scuffing of her hoe until a twig snapped underfoot. When Abyssinia turned, she raised her hoe as a weapon, until she noticed Buck and Cicero.

"What do you want here?"

Her eyes flashed up to Dick's black hair, the green eyes crinkling in the corners as she remembered another. The hoe dropped from her hands.

"Who are you!?"

"I'm Richard Dolan."

"Oh my . . ."

Abyssinia rushed for Dick, but she stumbled over the hoe. His hands kept her from falling. She snatched off her hat only to crush it between them as they embraced. When Cicero reached them, Abyssinia pulled away and fought to gain control of herself.

"Come inside you all," Abyssinia said. Then suddenly, she sniffed the air. "Who gave you that whiskey?"

"That was me, Aunt Abyssinia," Buck said.

"Take my hand, son, I've got something to show you."

Abyssinia led them on into the unfinished, unscreened porch, through the big barn-like room in which she would teach her classes—as she explained to Dick that it was her intention to become the town's first school teacher—and on to the doorway of a spacious bedroom. It was crammed with furniture from Clarksdale awaiting installation of a hardwood floor in the rest of the new house. She pulled Dick alone into her cramped bedroom and closed the door.

"Come here and squeeze your momma. I wondered if I would ever see you."

Abyssinia moved out of Dick's arms to rummage in the drawer of a massive wooden bureau intricately carved with flowers. She drew out a lacquered chest and placed it on the bed.

"Go on, you sit too."

She unlatched the chest and turned it toward Dick, only to bounce up and go fumble with a lamp. By its flame, Dick looked inside the box to find the first graded reader he'd used. Below it lay a wooden bird without a head, the one he had carved with the first knife he'd owned. There were marbles and tiny little gloves, also a folded piece of paper dated 1883—the Clarksdale Grange organization's announcement for a turkey shoot—and a prize ribbon bearing his name: "Master R. C. Dolan of Alligator Lake."

Abyssinia wiped her eyes.

"I thought you would never, never find me, you bein' a white man in your mind and all. I just tried to keep a little piece of you where I could."

"Quit your cryin', ma. I'm here now."

Dick's words only loosened more tears.

"Other women kept their children, but I . . . let you go. Told myself it was for your own good, so you could grow up white and free . . ."

Her voice trailed off plaintively, and Dick pushed aside the mementos and reached for his mother, but she moved away, pleading almost like a child.

". . . You got to believe I felt so bad lettin' your pa have you. My old mistress knew a white woman had to raise a slave woman's child. Don't you see? This slavery thing made a lot of women live strange."

Abyssinia pulled off her shirt and dabbed her eyes, covering her face inside of it for what seemed an eternity to Dick. As her sobbing subsided, Abyssinia uttered a shuddering sigh and turned toward the mirror on the bureau. With a downward glance at the shirt, then her dirty hands, she continued.

"I'll never let you go again, baby."

Dick draped his arms around his mother's shoulders, and he looked into her moist eyes, drank in the open loving apology for a sin that had never wounded him before that day, and then, in a most curious way, he felt the recent wound to his own sense of himself begin to heal. The affection of a new but intimate parent was so much more than the snatched-away familiarity of JD who, despite his life-long presence, Dick could never recall embracing. Nor had Dick ever held a woman in his arms except where lust prevailed. So different with his mother. He loved her, would give his life for her, and it triggered an almost painful feeling of tenderness and wishing good things. One day, he promised himself, he would find a woman like his mother, someone with whom the simple act of looking gave birth to feelings. Right then, because of all those enchanting new feelings, Dick vowed that no nightriders would come swooping down on Mound Bayou, not while he drew breath.

"Are you hungry?"

"Aye, ma."

Abyssinia led her son into what she explained would become her parlor, pointed to covered platters along a sideboard.

"For the Fourth of July, I like to bake."

Dick crammed his mouth with a whole biscuit.

"Only thing I've eaten all day," he mumbled.

"Bring whatever you want into the bedroom."

Dick reached a plate and piled on the food. For several minutes after returning to the bedroom, he ate silently while Abyssinia watched.

"Did you'n him," Dick said, "ever live together?"

"Your father owned a store, and we lived on top of it. Have you ever been to Shufordsville?"

"No."

"Well across the river in the colored part, the store's still there. I think a Chinese fella owns it now."

"How did you meet?"

Abyssinia paused to sweep up a growing accumulation of crumbs from her coverlet. She and Dick were still sitting on the bed.

"He thought I was John Clark's wife because I was cooking in Mr. Clark's kitchen. I thought he was a colored man hustling up a free meal."

"So, you liked each other."

"That doesn't quite fit . . . Back then, a woman alone had to look for her opportunity. My brother and I got separated during the war."

"Mr. Cicero fought in the war?"

"No, no, child. I got into a situation with a Union officer . . . You ever meet a man named Jasper?"

"I don't think so, but he lives in the swamp with my Uncle Cicero, doesn't he?"

Abyssinia nodded.

"He had a crush on me and got carried away while I was walking one evening with a Union officer. I had to leave because the stupid man got a little forward, and Jasper killed him. No way for me to explain I had nothing to do with it."

"And you've lived up here in the bottoms ever since?"

"Yes."

Abyssinia picked up a fragment of meat that Dick had dropped on the bed. Someone knocked on the door.

"That would be Cicero," Abyssinia said. "You wait here."

"Evenin', Miz Abyssinia," Buck said as Abyssinia emerged. "Dick ready to leave?"

"Leave for where, pray tell?"

"Me and Dick got to prepare for the trouble."

"What trouble . . . Oh, you mean pass out guns'n stuff?"

"Dick and me promised we'd help."

Dick emerged from his mother's bedroom and joined them.

"Aye, ma. We have to go."

"Not tonight, you don't. Both of you, just sit down. Now, Buck?"

"Yes'm?"

"Why don't you have a piece of my cake?"

Buck grinned. Out of Abyssinia's view, Dick signaled frantically, no.

"I would but me'n Dick got lots to do."

Following Buck's eyes to her son, Abyssinia crossed her arms.

"I don't know what you two are planning, but save it for another time."

"Yes ma'am," Dick said.

"You can visit with your cousin here, Buck. Overnight, if you wish. I have to clean up for bed after working the garden."

Dick and Buck wandered through the unfinished house while Abyssinia pumped water. She brought the water bucket inside and disappeared into her bedroom.

"Why can't I," Buck whispered to Dick, "have some cake?"

"She said it was for tomorrow."

"Oh! I see."

"Have one piece," Dick offered, "like me."

An hour later, Abyssinia had put on a colorful hostess gown, but after watching the young men giggle and sit what she considered unnaturally still, she could no longer pretend that her son and Buck were interested in her talk of the new house and school.

"What is bothering you two?" she asked.

"Nothing, ma'am," Buck said, giggling uncontrollably.

"You don't have to sit right under me. Just don't wander off."

"Could it be," Dick said, "you'd let us come back later?"

All of the breath went out of Abyssinia. A sob punctuated her sigh.

"Beggin' your pardon, ma."

Nevertheless, Buck was soon giggling again, and his "but she's the prettiest one" came to Abyssinia's ears.

"Oh, now, I see!" Abyssinia said. "It's girls, is it?"

"No ma'am," Buck said.

"But I sat right here and heard you, young man. I was young once myself, and I understand." She took a deep breath. "You and Dick have an interest in one of the town girls?"

Neither young man spoke.

"You're almost a man, Dick, and even more handsome than your daddy was. If I was a girl, I don't know."

"I haven't met any yet," Dick said.

"Is he telling the truth, Buck?"

Abyssinia made no further protest, and Buck again suggested he ought to keep his word to the other men. As the boys walked out of Abyssinia's house, Cicero emerged from the shadows.

"Come on in, brother," Abyssinia said. "Spend some time."

"Wanted to allow you time with your son. That's the only reason I disappeared."

Abyssinia kissed Cicero and led him inside.

"You never know what will happen," Abby said.

"I'll put a dollar on that bet, myself."

"So . . . whatta you think—"

"You want to know where Dick is sleeping tonight?"

"Don't grin so much, Mister Mind-Reader. Course I'm curious."

"I haven't asked, but for sure somewhere in town. He'll never go back to his father. JD's enemies have seen to that."

Abyssinia moved forward smiling and draped her arms around her brother's neck.

"You have made me happier than any man I've ever known."

"Oh, now! Don't start lying."

"I'm not. You cannot imagine . . . I couldn't even *pray* for Dick to walk into my house like he just did and love me. So, yes, I am happy!"

"How is Mr. Woods?"

"Eugene is super. He'll be down tomorrow evening. He's a hard working man, you know."

"Working to keep you happy?"

"Like I said, Cicero, he's a good, good man." Abyssinia moved away from standing in her brother's embrace and took a seat. "But you're the one who's made me the happiest I have ever been."

Thank you, Abby. Your grattitude is sweet, but I'm worried about all this Klan stuff."

"Don't be. We'll be alright."

"I wasn't there for my son as he grew up. You know what that feels like, and I sure don't want to go home and leave you and Buck with this Klan threat hanging over you."

"Let me be the big sister for a change. It's like right after freedom. You don't know what to do with it."

Cicero smiled and walked to sit beside his sister on a narrow settee.

"There's a part of me that knows I didn't do everything for Buck."

"Cicero, shut up!" Abby took his hand. "No reason for you to feel guilty about anything."

"Riggght!"

"I mean it. Look, why don't you stay the night here. I want to share something with you, and now's the time."

"Okay."

"I'm bein' your big sister, now, okay?"

"Okay, okay."

Abby smiled.

"I have a secret. Everybody thought I wanted to be a plantation belle like my mistress . . . Oh, Lord, I had such a bad experience with our master. He never quite raped me, just would touch me and make me touch him. Momma Nancy had already scared me about what men would do to girls coming of age. Meanwhile, I went ahead pretending I was the grand Belle of Hurricane Plantation for my own little family, for the mistress . . . Your friend, Annye Mae—that child was truly in love with . . . She got me to join in her little play for grown men's attention. Master Jefferson entertained a lot. First time Annye Mae took me over to Brierfield to serve one of Jefferson's little meetings, the men groped all over us, laughed and called me the queen of England. Didn't do more than that because Miz Varina was liable to drop in, and if they really wanted sex, they had the usual choices. Momma and my mistress had scared me so much about men having their way, the more attention I got that evening the more scared I was . . . Annye Mae just grinned through it all, and later she explained that handsome men excited her. I know you remember her almost causing Mr. Ben's oldest son to break up with his wife."

"Yes, but I don't follow where you're leading."

"Seemed awful to me her getting so worked up about men."

"Whatta you mean?"

"Love-making—I didn't see what all the shouting was about. Until one day, Annye Mae came and took me to spy on Old George and his young wife in one of the cabins. Now, watching them got me really excited, for the first time in my life, and you know what?"

"No."

"I let Annye Mae pull up my dress. I was startled at first, but I let her go on touching me because it felt so good . . . and I touched her back."

"You don't have to tell me this."

"Hush!"

"There's nothing to feel guilty about, Abby."

"It didn't stop there. For a couple years after that, until Annye Mae was sold away, she and I would sleep together when we could. My mistress didn't know what was going on. She just thought I was growing up and wanted my own room to myself instead of sleeping on the floor of her bed chamber. That pretty boy I met—the coach man? By that time, I was just wondering what it was like with a man. He was young and inexperienced. Remember Commander Grey?"

"Yes, hired me to keep records."

"I didn't feel much better with him. I only gave way to really feeling something after he gave me this trinket to pledge his love. I was feeling so successful having him fawning over me, that made me happy. He thought I was excited for what he was doing to me . . . So, that's your sister."

"What now?"

"I'll be married." It's the easiest way."

"Oh, Abby, wipe your eyes."

"Hush! Reason I'm telling you this is I'm so happy tonight, and I could hear you and Isaiah yelling all the way over here. I've known for years that walking away from that shootin' up near Friar's Point made you guilty. Well, forget it! Tonight I got enough good feelin' for the both of us. And don't feel so bad on account Buck won't come visit Rose. Now that Dick is in the fold, won't be long before he'll bring your son to his sense."

Back some minutes earlier, as Dick was climbing into a wagon Buck had borrowed, Buck whispered to his cousin,

"You come meet my momma, now."

"Tomorrow," Dick said. "I'm tired."

"But we spent all this time at your momma's."

"I'd never seen her before, Buck."

Sullenly, Buck drove the remaining distance to his cabin. The young men were climbing from the wagon before either spoke.

"Might I have a taste of your jug?" Dick asked.

Buck pulled out his whiskey, and Dick took the jug outside to sit alone. When Dick began to wander alone about the dimly lit clearing, Buck yelled through an unfinished window.

"C'mon back in, Dick."

"I just want to be alone."

"Why?"

"You wouldn't understand."

"Hell I wouldn't. Tell me."

"I can't stop thinking of things like if I was still white. I try, but I can't. How do you think black?"

"What do you mean, 'think black?'"

"Ain't tryin' to make you mad, but all I think of when I think black is sufferin'. You know—ma havin' to give me up, Mr. Cicero livin' in the swamp, the town here. Lotta other things, too."

"Hell, nigga, ain't nothin' strange about that. Just quit worrying . . . Pleeease, come go home with me. Have a drink to perk yourself up."

Buck hurried them back into the settlement, but what was to have been a quick visit to Suzy's house was complicated by the presence of Isaiah Montgomery's oldest daughter, accompanied by her little sister much to the older girl's mortification. She played at courting Dick on the porch outside where they all sat despite the mosquitoes to be away from the old folks. When Dick told the daughter, Mary, that she was pretty, Buck pulled him out into the yard.

"Uncle's daughter take a serious interest if you keep that up."

"And what's the harm?"

"Town girls are looking for husbands, they ain't for play. That's the rule here."

When they finally drove back north, hanging out a lantern against the thick darkness away from the settlement, it was after midnight.

"What now, Buck? I don't feel like sleepin'."

"Me neither. Lordy, what a picnic we gonna have tomorrow."

As they reached the cabin, Buck jumped out of the wagon and ran inside.

"You cain't leave the poor critter in harness."

"Leave 'im for a minute."

"Why?"

Buck lighted a candle in the doorway and used it to light his porch lantern.

"Looky here, Mr. Winchester Man."

Eight Winchester rifles were stacked on the porch.

"From your uncle's store?"

"Yep, while you was with your momma. Lets go look around like you said. Catch them Ku Klux between us, tomorrow."

"Riiight!"

Buck carried the lantern from the porch. Dick unhooked the one from the wagon. For the next hour, they tromped around between Little Mound Bayou and big Mound Bayou before selecting two clumps of trees within sight of lanterns held aloft. Buck chose the small bayou side, Dick the big one. Then they loaded and stashed their guns among the trees before returning home in high spirits, firing make-believe guns at each other, falling on the ground like little boys.

By now, it was the balmy fore-dawn of a holiday eve. Crickets and bullfrogs drowned the occasional human sound from the town, until a bottle breaking pricked up the cousins' ears. Thinking a couple from town out for a lark, they doused their lanterns hoping to sneak up on an unwary couple making love. Dick tripped in the darkness.

"Your white folks feet too big."

"Almost broke my peter."

Choking back snorts of laughter, they fell into each other's arms.

"Forrrnication is evil!" Buck said in mockery of a preacher as they inched slowly toward Buck's cabin and town.

"Forrrnication is heaven," Dick replied.

Then suddenly, behind them came the sound of twigs snapping and of a horse snorting. Buck and Dick grabbed each other because the only noise should have been coming from town in the opposite direction. They ran toward the sound until Dick grabbed Buck's arm and pointed. A light flickered over toward the big bayou, the sound of a horse, then another tiny light.

"Klan comin', Buck! Goddamnit, they comin' a day early!"

"Aw shit!"

"We're ready."

"Well, yeah . . . Whatta we do?"

"Damned to hell or dead I'm not gonna run! Go sit with your guns, and don't you shoot until I do. Empty a rifle at a time. Don't worry about hittin' nothin' till you emptied at least two of 'em."

"But Dick—"

"Run, fool! You ain't got time to talk."

They ran as quietly as possible. As they approached Buck's outpost trees, Dick whispered,

"Shoot for all you worth, Buck. Got to scare 'em 'till help come!"

"Maybe we should go get help?"

"Ain't got time!" Dick said, turning to sprint for his hideout.

The three-quarter moon emerged from behind a cloud in the western sky. Buck wedged himself between two trees where he could look northward awaiting the Klan's approach. Then he stole a glance across the tree-dotted field, but he was unable to pin-point where Dick was concealed. Fear riding the whinnying of a horse into Buck's ears dispelled all thought.

Across from Buck, Dick was more calculating. If the white men intended only to hurrah the town, there might be as few as fifteen or twenty, but if they intended to storm and to burn it, there would be many more. Suddenly, he felt rash and swore he would never again commit such a sin, if only he survived. Then, he heard the same loud whinny that had startled Buck. It was some comfort that if his father were correct in blaming Alex Chicoupapoulis for the trouble, the group would likely be small.

A hooting owl beat the air noisily as half a dozen shadows emerged into the open from the trees edging the railroad clearing. Buck saw the riders clearly as they moved, hugging the trees for cover, and he hoped Dick had them in sight. When the horsemen paused, he counted twenty, but as they donned white robes he re-counted, and there seemed to be more. Suddenly angry, as he remembered his mother's bruised face, he was delighted the moonlight marked her tormentors so well.

A raucous laugh broke the still, and a single white figure galloped forward, waving his white-clad arm as a signal to the rest. Then the man out front paused and turned to await the others. At that moment, Dick fired a volley that crumpled him like a rag. His horse bolted with the man or his white robe dragging along the ground.

"Goddamn you to hell!" Dick screamed, tossing aside his first empty rifle and grabbing the next.

Then Buck opened fire, cocking and firing from a crouch as quickly as he could. In front of him, horses reared and trampled on each other. Screaming filled the night. The Klansmen could only fire wildly because they had no target. Nor could they come to a firing position without offering themselves as a target, which led them to circle helplessly as the cousins poured round after round into the melee.

In town, the first shots brought men out of bed grabbing for rifles. The first three to come together near the center of the settlement dashed without thought along the railroad toward the noise.

"My Buck's out there!" Suzy yelled from her porch, then ran down carrying a shotgun.

Cicero found himself alongside Isaiah, both in their underwear.

"Git your asses goin'!" Isaiah said to those hanging back. "We got men out there!"

The more cautious stayed a little behind the leaders. Their numbers were swelled by hard-headed children armed with hoes and axes.

"Let our boys know we comin'," a man said.

All of them took up the cry. A handful of men on horses overtook the group and forced their way past.

Dick had emptied his fourth rifle and was starting to worry. He had only a loaded pistol remaining. A few white-sheeted riders had galloped off, but others had dismounted to help those fallen. Dick wasn't sure he'd have time to reload when he and Buck ceased firing. If the white sheets advanced, he and his cousin were done for.

When noise from town turned into a roar, Buck started cheering. The racket immobilized the Klansmen. Disoriented by the ambush and all the noise, the nightriders took to their horses in panic. White sheets disappeared into night as swiftly as foam from the crest of a spent wave. In the glare of fallen torches, Buck stood up to take careful aim at a straggler.

"Get down, Buck! Goddammit, get down!" Dick screamed, standing up himself.

A bullet struck the tree to Dick's right and kicked bark into his face. He grabbed his eyes, cursing, as men from the town rode up. A handful rode forward to reconnoiter as the first of those on foot reached the clearing. Someone cleared Dick's eye with water, and he dropped to the ground in relief. Men and women in various stages of undress smiled and trotted over to shake Dick's hand. Some of the more adventurous now ran along the railroad track yelling taunts after the vanished Klansmen. Buck wandered through the melee looking for Dick. He winced in the torchlight every time a man leaned down from a horse to clap him on the head.

No one slept that night. After the people returned to town, the holiday commenced as if it had been planned that way. Breakfast was cooked and served in front yards and along the railroad to people sitting on the track. When dawn finally came, a huge barbecue fire was gleaming brighter than the sun. The morning train had to stop before it reached the station because the people refused to be moved.

By midmorning, both cousins were drunk, toasted from one end of town to the other and granted liberty to kiss all the girls even in front of usually strict mothers. They stumbled along together, dragging rifles like badges of honor grown too heavy. Cicero found them dozing in Suzy's house. He demanded they get up and follow him.

Inside Isaiah's store, some like Isaiah were frowning and had refused to join the drinking. Some of those celebrating were now threatening to leave town and go build their own settlement, a place—they said—where men could be men and damn any white folks who showed up making trouble. Others kept returning to the point of contention: what to do about the dead white men north of town. A decision had already been made when Cicero arrived with the cousins.

"Boys," Isaiah said. "It ain't that I'm not grateful for all you did because I am . . ."

Voices along the wall agreed. Some nodded decorously, some cheered from wooden crates. A few remained silent.

". . . We got a problem! Last night ain't gonna be talked about—ain't never goin' into the record book. Constable here didn't see nothin' happen 'cause if he did he'd have to arrest somebody. White folks would come in and want to investigate. If that happened, we all know they'd hang you boys or send you to the penitentiary. This land cain't allow no black man to kill a white one. That's just the order of things."

"Lord know, he right, y'all," Ben Green said.

"Lord, my ass!" another said. "It's a shame you even think of turnin' these boys out."

"Ain't me!" Isaiah answered, one eye quivering. "Y'all know what these white folks like!"

"Got to live somewhere," Ben Green said. "We got to be men and face life like it is."

Fatigue in the cousins' faces turned to alarm.

"You boys," Isaiah said, "are goin' into the swamp with Cicero—just be quiet, Dick . . . Two white men dead, an' no tellin' how many got taken away or wounded. Be tomorrow before the sheriff git word an' start up from Cleveland. The hotheads might come back, but most'o us think, naw. Fact is, you embarrassed them Kluxers, and they may even be too embarrassed to say anything about last night. Hell, they could claim that whoever turn up dead, that they was last seen drinking, gambling, whatever . . . Point is, we cain't chance you two being arrested, and this town don't have the power to fight the law."

Buck and Dick looked like little boys not understanding a grown-up world. Their eyes circled the room. The men along the wall, lounging on the store counter—none of them returned the questioning look, except for Isaiah. He put his hand on Buck's shoulder.

"Remember, boy," Isaiah said, "you got two daddies. We can probably gitcha back outta that swamp when things cool down. Be suicide you stay here now."

Around noon, Suzy and Abyssinia were weeping and hugging each other standing on the bank of the little bayou as their sons departed pulling a boat behind Cicero. Anticipating that a posse with dogs might track them, Dick left his horse for safekeeping with his mother, and Cicero kept them walking in the shallow slough until they neared the east-west branch of the Hushpuckena River. They carried the boat the mile between, then moved down inside the river cavern and launched east into virgin swamp. Since the time Isaiah announced that the cousins would be going to live in the swamp, Buck had been silent.

The weight of three men made the boat ride low, and Buck fidgeted every time water lapped over the edge so close to the water. The cavernous river bank rising above them didn't make his peril seem any less, either. When the planked bottom grated on a submerged tree, Cicero eased clothes and all into the channel to lighten the load. He chuckled at the anxious eyes in the boat until they saw that the water barely reached his waist. Then he crawled back inside and let the current do the work again, pulling an occasional paddle stroke only to avoid bumping an obstruction and leaving more sign of their passage.

Ribbons of cloud had persisted from the morning, and they blocked the hot sun of recent days. Buck was lying in the bottom of the boat following a bird of prey riding the air over-head. Isaiah had purchased Buck's land and added a nice profit for the cabin and clearing.

"Git up, Buck!" Dick said, slapping him on the head. "My turn to lie down."

"You git killed doin' that, nigga!"

Buck refused to move at once, and Dick tried to climb over him.

"Be still!" Cicero said.

He grabbed an overhanging branch to steady the boat while the two changed places. Dick rested his feet on the prow of the boat as an old brown turtle eased off a mottled log on which he'd been dozing. His dark shadow lurked under the pea soup water until his head surfaced twenty feet away, stick-ing out motionless like the turret of a tiny iron-clad warship as he studied the boat through shifting, marble eyes.

"What happen if I call *you*, nigger?" Dick asked.

"You're one yourself." Cicero said.

"I'm gonna be a teetotal nigga," Buck said, straightening his legs alongside Dick. "No more work. Sleep long's I want everyday."

"White folks try to make you take it," Dick said. "'Nigger' is a game. They want to see if you'll take it."

"Uncle Isaiah say most niggas ain't no good 'cause only thing plantation taught 'em was how to get outta work. So if I'm gonna be a shiftless nigga I may as well get some rest out of it."

A splash up ahead drew everyone's attention. A gar fish nearly as long as the boat rose out of the water behind a dart-ing school of minnows that broke the surface again seconds later in a spray of sparkling light.

"Damned to hell that ain't the biggest gar I ever seen," Dick said.

"What did your uncle mean," Cicero asked, "about—I think you said—niggas learned to be lazy?"

"Niggas—"

A silver shimmer of minnows still eluding the gar sprayed the surface of the water again.

"Black people," Cicero cautioned, "like us."

"We don't work like we should," Buck said. "Got to go along behind us, make sure we doin' things right . . . Except for Ben Green and, you know, the people Daddy Montgomery trained."

"Why would one man work somebody else's land," Cicero said, "except for the pay?"

"If a man want to git somewhere in the world, he got to work hard."

"Who's world, Buck? How do you 'git somewhere' if its somebody else's land, or somebody else's store or you're a slave worried mainly about surviving?"

"You work hard and somebody notice you, they put you on top of some others. That's why they put me in charge of town improvements in Mound Bayou."

"You listen to me, Buck Morgan . . . You can work for somebody until you die, and that man will live longer than you because you are doing his work. If a boss respects your work, he should simply pay you for it, not call you lazy because you won't give him more effort than he is paying for . . ."

Cicero paused as Dick rose up from the bottom of the boat to hear better.

". . . Don't ever call a man a nigga because he won't work as hard as *you* think he ought. Is sharecropping worth hard work, if it won't let you move ahead and live better? Though I warrant, sharecroppers work harder than anybody. Besides, why do you want to 'get ahead?' Is it to join up with the handful near the top, to join the white folks who keep everybody else sharecropping and practically starving in the first place? Is that what you want to do with your life? . . . Life ought not be based on taking advantage of another—that is, if you claim to have principles. Otherwise, there really is no right or wrong, lazy or whatever."

By the time Cicero quit speaking and returned to paddling, Buck looked sullen. Dick had quit listening. He was thinking about Lightning and wondering if he'd ever see his horse again. In youthful exuberance, Dick cupped his hands around his mouth and let out a scream.

"Shut up!" Cicero said. "Never do that again, not in this swamp."

"Just yelling."

"Don't play. You'll be the first outsiders where we're going."

For a dozen strokes of Cicero's paddle, tension held them all quiet. Only the bumping of the bottom of the boat on logs was heard, sounds of the swamp.

"To answer your question another way," Cicero said to Dick, "nigga is just a word, no magic about it. One more thing . . . I have shared this little home we're headed to with the woman I love, her son and another man for several years. We don't have any rules or laws, as such. We pretty much know what each other expects. Jasper gets a little rambunctious sometimes, but he's the youngest. Older than you boys, but younger than the rest of us. So, I welcome you, and Rose will, too. Dick there's met her, knows she'll love to see you, but you have just recently become men. Don't hold it against us if we don't live like you think we should. How we are living may change, but . . ." Cicero wagged his finger in the direction of Buck. ". . . you don't know our world. Learn it, before you challenge anything."

Jasper was on his way home when he heard Dick scream, and it made him angry. Too many times that season, strangers had come ashore off the Hushpuckena during the season of cutting and rafting timber. None had cut near where he lived, but both the Sunflower and the Hushpuckena were still being used to float logs south toward Vicksburg for sale. One group had camped out for almost a week. Jasper had not molested them because Bill Williams pleaded they were measuring the land for the government.

The rule that Jasper had honored all of his forty-odd years was control, beginning with the parental command for self-control that he had first taken as adult interference, but as the boy began rushing toward manhood, his appreciation of the concept broadened: a man had to control his piece of swamp, and that began and ended with keeping strangers away.

He had sensed in the others a mellowing toward the outside world. Not that any of his family had said that he or she wanted to go back to where life was not within their own hands. To his way of thinking, age had brought a certain inwardness, thus a dropping away of cautions that seemed for Jasper something forever worth honing sharper. Even so, he didn't think of himself as some reckless youth. He was a man whom life had granted charge of keeping the community's vigilance.

He hunkered down and closed his eyes listening, mind focused on the blackbird, frog, cricket, dragonfly and other common noises. When they quieted, it was a sure sign of someone approaching, but now the cawing and ratcheting and buzzing resumed, which allowed him to relax while listening for another sound from whoever had screamed. What most bothered him was that no timid outsider would have walked in to arrive at dusk, when every peril—from poisonous snakes in the marshes to the occasional wildcat or bear that still prowled—would be cloaked in darkness. Hunters would be on their way home or toward a camp on the edge of the swamp by now. A swamp dweller would know better, too. Out of respect, he or she would travel openly during the day to suggest good intentions.

Somebody rafting on the Hushpuckena seemed the only answer. Jasper had run off so many it had become a chore. Standing up now, he headed toward the river, mindless of noise, figuring anyone willing to announce themselves with a scream would never hear him coming. Sure enough, as he neared the river, there was less critter noise. Nor would the swamp have quieted so on account of his own movement. He spotted the edge of the fifteen-foot drop-off down into the river cavern and crawled forward on his stomach to wait.

There wasn't much light left when Cicero's boat poked through the trash and spores coating the water and floated toward Jasper. It was too dark to see clearly, but Jasper made out a white man sleeping or wounded in front of a young black man, and then he recognized Cicero paddling. Instead of rushing down the slope as the boat came ashore, he waited in hiding, unsure why strangers were coming into his sanctuary. Only when the young men began stepping out of the boat, did he ease himself down the embankment.

Invisible surrounded by vines against the rough, lichen-spotted trunk of a massive tree, he lurked with his gun cradled until Dick and Buck were both ashore. He was prideful enough to feel satisfaction that he could stand within arms length of people and not be noticed. After Cicero had picked up all of the rifles, Jasper stepped out silently. He tapped Buck on the shoulder.

"My god!" Buck screamed.

Buck leapt downhill into Dick who fell into the boat and capsized it. Cicero went under with him.

"Who be you?" Dick said, coughing helplessly, hands raised.

"Mr. Cicero?" Jasper called out.

Even now, the young men couldn't see Jasper clearly because he had withdrawn back into the shadows.

"That you, Jasper?" Cicero asked.

"You safe, non?"

"Yes, yes!" Cicero said, fishing rifles out of the muck. "Come help me, Dick."

Dick turned and accepted the rifles. He didn't see Jasper walk into view until he turned back around. Before anyone could stop him Dick dropped all but one of the rifles and swung it at Jasper who half parried the blow, but the rifle butt glanced off Jasper's forehead.

"Damn your soul, white man!"

Jasper charged like a bear, and Dick had nowhere but the river to go. He splashed off into it screaming for help. Cicero grabbed and struggled with Jasper until he calmed down.

"C'mon back, Dick! It's only Jasper."

"Who, d'you say?"

"This is Jasper—my other son!"

"Your other son?" Buck said.

"Yes." Cicero released Jasper who was still snarling and rubbing his forehead. "These boys are with me. I brought them here."

"Why'n hell, you do that?" Jasper asked.

Jasper stepped into the river and blocked Dick's path.

"They need a hideout from the law," Cicero said.

"From the law?"

"We had a little trouble in Mound Bayou," Cicero explained.

"Nothin' out there ain't surprise me," Jasper said, backing out of the water and turning back into the trees growing out of the steep embankment.

"Who was that?" Buck whispered.

"That is Jasper. I've known him and his mother since before the War ended. His mother is my wife."

"Come on," Jasper's voice said, "before it get plumb dark and y'all be stumblin' into stuff."

Dick was cursing under his breath as he pulled himself up the embankment, rapidly moving ahead of Buck and Cicero.

"Walk quiet!" Jasper's voice yelled toward Dick.

Cicero couldn't be sure what was on Jasper's mind as his broad-shouldered outline, gun slung over his back, led them home. Nor did he take the easy way. He walked about as fast as a man could and seemed to barge into and through thickets of nettles everyone else had to ease around. By the time they reached the clearing in front of Cicero's cabin, there was no light.

"Wait here!" Jasper's voice said.

Unseen by the others, Jasper marched across to the edge of the clearing and sat on a chopping block. He planted his rifle like a staff to lean forward on and watch as Dick and Buck felt their way about the unlighted clearing bumping into the chicken coop and knocking the wood pile loose. Cicero was the last to arrive. He took the lantern from the cabin door and lit it.

"Sit down, boys," Cicero said, sitting on a block of wood himself, then holding the lantern toward Jasper's face. "You don't look happy."

"I ain't."

"What's bothering you? I don't read minds like your mother, and I am dead tired."

A hint of a smile softened Jasper's grizzled face. He wasn't wearing a beard as such. Wisps of coarse hair garnished his upper lip and lower chin.

"Why you bring them two in here?" Jasper asked.

"Be leavin' tomorrow, you don't want us," Dick said.

"That you will, white man."

"No, no," Cicero said, "he isn't a white man—not any longer, at least."

"'Course he is. Ain't got all night to argue."

"Buck is the dark one over there, he's my son. The other is—you remember my sister?"

Jasper's head snapped alert.

"You mean he work in that store near Alligator Lake?"

"He's the one I've been teaching all these years."

"Well, I b'damn, I b'damn! . . . This your Mr. Dick Dolan here."

"Shake hands with Jasper, Dick."

Cautiously, Dick stepped forward and reached across the small space separating them.

"My momma said she knew you."

"Um hunh," Jasper said, keeping his seat through the handshaking. "Long time ago, she lived with us one winter, but she wasn't our kind."

"'Tain't likely I am either."

"My name is Buck. I'm his son."

Buck lay his hand on Cicero's shoulder, then offered it to Jasper.

"I know that," Jasper said, disdaining the handshake, then to Cicero. "Why you bring 'em out here?"

"Because they ambushed a passle of Klansmen."

"They did *what?*"

"I said, they ambushed a bunch of Klan folk. Don't your ears work?"

"Course, they do," Jasper said, coming to his feet. "These two, here? They shot up a buncha white folks?"

Cicero nodded, and Jasper slapped his thigh in mirth.

"Wasn't our fault," Buck said. "They were attacking us."

"Where was they attackin' you at, young fella?"

"In Mound Bayou—I'm part of the Montgomery group. Dick was visiting me—"

"Dick was visiting his mother," Cicero said. "Old Man Dolan's enemies told all. Now the white folks know who Dick's momma is. They burned Dolan's barn. So Mr. Richard Dolan here is now officially one of us."

Jasper held out both hands, one toward Dick, the other toward Buck.

"Maybe I was wrong about y'all. That's a good piece a business, I'm hearin'. Them sorry-assed white folks won't come lookin' for trouble soon, non. How many you kill?"

"A bunch," Dick said. "Others took most away, but they left two bodies behind."

"You be the fighter, non?"

"He's the Winchester Man," Buck said. "Everybody been callin' him that."

"Bon!" Jasper said. "If I was you, I make it my new name. Help to keep niggas and peckawoods scaird. Like, when I get 'em scaird, they don't come through huntin' and such. Me'n ole Bill used to scare folk for fun, him with his evil lookin' face he paint all up, and me in my winter coat and a bear head hat."

"You are the giant bear my pa warned me about?"

"Spect so, boy. Like I say, pay to keep folk scared."

"Well, Mr. Winchester Man and . . . Mr. Cowboy," Cicero said. "You can sleep inside the cabin. Tomorrow I'll show you where things are set out in case you ever have to run and need a gun or some food."

"Non, non!" Jasper said.

"I was just explaining about finding stuff—"

"Ain't likely no posse comin' in my swamp, and in that case, what need they got to know about my food'n guns hid away?"

"They have to live here like the rest of us."

Jasper tossed his rifle aside.

"Siddown there, Cicero'n listen . . . Back durin' slavery, folks come escapin', we help 'em, but didn't none of 'em stay on. Too many folks get in one 'nother's way. Now, ain't like I'm worried about no patrollers—or even no posses 'cause I kin out fox 'em any day—but it ain't easy for a grown man to have no 'nother grown man livin' practically in his house. You know that. Took a long time for me'n you to learn one 'nother. Didn't it?"

"Not really."

"Ain't no 'not'!" Jasper said. "A man got to be a man. Got to do what he want to do. That's why I ain't never seen nothin' but small groups of maroon folks. We all got our own space to be in."

"Don't you be worryin', Mr. Jasper," Dick said. "I be outta here tomorrow mornin'."

"Peace, boy! Ain't no cause to act hound dog'n possum with me. You seem like a good man'n all."

"Aye, an' you can bet on it."

"I like the way you talk, son, but it ain't easy bein' a maroon. Know what that is?"

Buck looked toward Cicero. Dick shook his head.

"Me'n my momma'n Cicero over there—least since he come live with us—we maroon. Ain't but one idea: to survive, livin' where the white folks cain't go 'cause foolishness always follow 'em. Which mean them or us gotta die."

"What's that," Buck asked, "got to do with us?"

"Only way a maroon can live is to control where he livin'. Two grown men cain't always agree, and ain't every man can trust the next with his life. I give you boys a place for a few days, but you got to go find your own swamp if you set on livin' like me."

"What about," Cicero said, "your mother?"

"What about momma?"

"For a long time, she's been wanting more people in here."

"That's different. She talkin' babies."

"No, she craves family! And these young men are my family."

"She want me to marry, that's what she want."

"Wouldn't that mean bringing someone else in?"

"But a woman ain't the same as a man."

"What about Bill's opinion?"

Jasper hesitated.

"Tell you what," Cicero said. "We leave things just as they are now. Wait a few days, talk to Rose. Bill might even have an idea about this."

"Ain't no harm in that," Jasper said, smiling up toward the cousins. "What I just said don't mean I don't like you. I'm a fair man, but I been young, and I know young men got to do things they own way . . . So y'all rest here'n be safe. We decide what to do after momma come back."

"Where is she?" Cicero asked.

"Down with Bill. He cain't hardly eat."

"What's wrong with him?"

"Them pains in his side reached his stomach. He quit eatin', and I come got momma to make him well."

"What is she?" Buck asked. "Some kinda doctor?"

"She know roots," Jasper said.

"I used to buy 'em from her," Dick said.

"That you did," Jasper said. "Now it's gittin' late."

"We ain't sleepy," Buck said. "Let's build a fire."

Jasper chuckled, shook his head.

"We don't usually make fire after dark."

"Why not?" Buck asked.

"Cause that's my rule!" Jasper pointed toward the cabin. "Sleep in there. I take Cicero with me."

Some time after settling Buck and Dick into the cabin, Jasper led the way to his own.

"What about tomorrow?" Cicero asked. "Do you mind now if I show them around?"

"Don't worry 'bout the young men."

"Be patient, Jasper."

"I been wantin' to see a old friend o' mine, so I will take the long way around. Show 'em what they need to know."

"Like who's the boss?" Cicero said.

"I treat 'em kindly, and they fit in while they here."

THE FIRST HINT OF DAWN WAS just filtering through the trees
when Jasper awakened, picked up a handful of dried bear
meat and a raw sweet potato and headed over to where Dick
and Buck were sleeping. Eating along the way, and realizing
that he was about to march the cousins over near where
Verlean's brother, Vern, lived, Jasper considered that he had
never truly repaid Vern's invitation to Vern's new home. On
the other hand, with two outsiders like Buck and Dick tagging
along, Jasper doubted that he and Vern could enjoy themselves. So Jasper decided that, instead of a neighborly drop-in
visit while in the vicinity, he would send word and invite Vern
to come visit him.

"Move smartly! We got lots to do today."

Neither young man moved until Jasper stepped inside Cicero's cabin and yelled. Groans of aggravation answered
Jasper. The cousins then straggled outside and moved to perform their toilets in the edge of the rough.

"That there leave all kind of sign," Jasper said. "We got a
special place for doin' that. Follow me."

Jasper took Buck's arm and walked him to the edge of the
clearing. A path led the way to the outhouse.

"I'm through, now," Buck said. "What if it's cold?"

"Depend on how cold," Jasper said. "If I do my business
where I sleep, I got to clean up."

"We ain't children, you know," Dick said, returning inside the cabin for his shirt.

Into Jasper's mind came a bitter memory of his own trouble as a young man, how the old maroon named Mack had always insisted on being in charge, demanding obedience. Toilet training was the beginning. All the two in front of him knew was how to piss away from themselves.

"Get dressed, too," Jasper told Buck. "We're leavin'."

"What about breakfast?" Buck asked.

"Ask me again, after we move out."

He was not being totally arbitrary. It seemed necessary to get the boys away from Cicero who would tolerate whatever they did because he, like Rose, wanted family near. A foray around the edge of what Jasper considered his territory seemed the answer, just move the cousins out and force them to continue, and if they got tired or didn't like it, well . . . And if they dared to argue, when they came near Mound Bayou where the cousins had come from, he would send them on their way.

Jasper made no effort to be friendly. With hand signals to follow him, he started out. He led the boys through the swamp until full light when they paused at Harris Bayou. Only once had Jasper mentioned food in any way. Now, he showed the young men what could be eaten and how to find it without leaving more man sign than need be. The cousins declined the raw herbs, the land-crawling grubs and tubers fleshy and fat from growing out of the water. With no apology, Jasper ate his fill for the second time that day.

Afterward, they backtracked along the Sunflower where Jasper showed them the boats hidden inside their ring of cypress knees. He demonstrated how to launch into the river without scuffing tree bark. By the time they had finished and then walked back to Harris Bayou, it was getting dark, and they camped for the night back off the ridge of the Bayou where their sign would not be so obvious. Leaves raked over themselves was their cover. Aside from a handful of nuts, two stomachs remained empty.

The next morning, now anticipating no meal at the end of day, Buck and Dick picked pecans and black walnuts from the floor of the swamp as they moved along. Jasper confirmed for Dick that this was the extension of the trail that Dick had walked along while running away from home. Then he explained to Buck how, during flood season, the bayous crept up and sometimes over ridges like the one on which they were walking.

"I know all that," Buck said.

"I'm tellin' you because you only got boat travel then. It ain't good to go no long distance unless you have to."

"And why would that be," Dick asked.

"Because you cain't run in water. The boat can be a trap. And there's critters disturbed by the water, especially the snakes. Ain't that you got to stay inside," Jasper said, watching Buck's face contort, "but ain't no sense plannin' no big travel if you ain't got to. And it's hell to get rained on when it ain't safe to light a fire and dry out."

"Buy a rainslicker," Buck said.

Dick smiled before Jasper replied.

"Don't think money can buy you a life in this swamp, young fella. Sure, I got a rain slicker, but it don't help me unless I'm on the water or walking a road. Most trails around here, the thorns will rip it up, and it make noise when you tryin' to hunt or track. Just listen to what I say—it works . . . Now, time to move out again."

"Let me get more pecans," Buck said.

"Stay behind me. You leavin' sign."

"So what harm?" Dick said. "Folk's know you're in here livin'."

"But they don't know where, or how many. You understand?"

Dick nodded.

"And if anybody come along who been raised in the swamp," Jasper said, "he can look at a trail and tell a lot if you ain't careful. Now come on . . . we' turnin' back into the swamp a little."

"Why?" Dick asked.

"To get away from this south fork of Harris Bayou. Folks come floatin' by sometime. I likes to travel away from it a bit so they cain't see me. Keep the water in sight to give direction."

They moved back into the thickets where movement was slow because they cut no path. Jasper was wrapped in animal skins that blunted the thorns and sharp edges of cane leaves that had Buck and Dick cursing every five or six steps until the south fork became a marshy field. Here, they moved out of the rough and west toward the main county road. They reached it several miles south of Alligator Lake. It was late afternoon.

"Ain't we gonna walk along the highway?"

"No, Mr. Dick, I'm tryin' to show you how a wilderness man travel. Ain't no sense callin' yourself one if you cain't live like one."

"But, who would be lookin' for us?"

"Maybe a sheriff. Pick up all the nuts and fruit you want. Travelers come here scroungin' all the time so leavin' sign don't matter. But no shootin'. Just so you know, you can fish almost anytime, but you cain't build no fires even along here."

"How we gonna eat the fish?"

"Shut up, Buck! He knows we ain't eatin' it raw."

"One fish eat another raw, don't he? " Jasper said, stretching out against a pecan tree to rest. "We gonna camp here, I think. So find you a tree to climb or somewhere you feels safe."

"But what about a meal?" Buck asked.

"You want my fish hooks?" was Jasper's answer.

By the middle of the next day, fruit and nuts were all they had eaten, and two stomachs remained unsatisfied. They were skirting all contact with outside people, especially incursions by farms into the edge of the swamp. That day, however, Jasper relented. He allowed them all to walk in the road. When someone loomed ahead, he would head off inside the trees and emerge only after whoever it was had passed.

"People see and remember—how you look, what you wearin'. Over time they learn your patterns."

That night, after having crossed the Hushpuckena, they crept in near Mound Bayou to camp. To please Buck, they moved in close enough to recognize voices.

"You remember, Ben Green, Dick? . . . That's him talkin'."

"Let's pay him a visit and eat, aye?"

"They kicked you out," Jasper said. "Leave 'em be."

"No, no," Buck said. "They didn't have no choice."

"How come you say so?" Jasper asked.

"If the law come lookin' for us," Buck said, "how could they fight?"

Jasper made no reply beyond laughing, loud enough that neither Buck nor Dick remained unclear exactly how he felt. They moved away to whisper together.

"You don't haveta like what I say," Jasper said. "You kin go where you want. Both of y'all grown men, far's I can tell."

When neither of the two answered, Jasper came to his feet.

"I expect you fancy a change in food. I got supplies close."

"Oh yes, Mr. Jasper," Buck said. "Whatever you got."

Away from town apiece, Jasper located a solitary tree with broken limbs. From inside a stinking hollow, he pulled dried bear meat and a sack of hard corn.

"The skunk scent keep the varmints away. Save me some."

The next day, Jasper was awake before anyone. He led the cousins on below Cleveland, and then paused in mid afternoon.

"Where you off to?" Buck asked.

"You boys settle in. I got business a distance from here. Old friend, well he ain't such a old friend, but he fed me in his house, and I ain't invited him to mine in a while. I'm gon' send word for him to come visit."

"Who is it, ye be invitin'?" Dick asked.

"Brother of a lady I spent time with. She's outta my life, but her brother, Vern, is the main one I go see about what's happening in the swamp that's left 'tween here and the big river. There's people called immigrants—they'll kill you if you let 'em."

Jasper was away all afternoon, and Dick led Buck in a search. They located the cabin of a man clearing land off the railroad and traded a small skin of liquor Jasper had left with them for corn bread and preserves. Then they hurried to return where they would sleep before Jasper could return and discover that they had ignored his instruction to stay away from outsiders.

Jasper didn't return until the following morning.

"Git up!"

He was standing over the young men when they roused themselves.

"What is it now that we done wrong?" Dick asked.

Jasper blew out his nose and draped his hands over the barrel of his rifle.

"I asked why ye was angry?" Dick said.

"You ain't important enough to make me angry."

"So why is yer face so screwed up?"

"I don't want nobody lookin' in my face thinkin' I'm happy to see 'em. When they see me, my face tell 'em they got trouble."

Without more, Jasper waved for the young men to follow, and he headed out. That morning, he led then back toward the east. They traveled all the way to the Sunflower and across through more dense swamp, toward what Jasper called the Quiver River. Buck didn't like so much fat in Jasper's dried bear meat, but he spent much of the day chewing at the hard kernels of corn that had Dick's teeth aching. Late on the sixth day they reached the Quiver River and turned along it. Bill Williams' split-cane roofed cabin came into view at dusk. Rose was outside grinding corn and talking with Bill who was propped against the wall.

"Come hug me, cherie," Rose called from a distance. "Who them with you?"

"This is Cicero's boy, Buck."

"What is he doin' with you?"

"He brought 'em in, momma. They killed some white men."

"Well, well, pleased to greet you," Rose said.

Buck stepped in front of Dick and marched forward with his hand extended.

"Likewise, ma'am."

"And this one," Jasper said.

"Mr. Richard Dolan."

"How are you, Miz Rose?"

"Doin' well, Dick. How's your pa?"

"I don't want to talk about him."

"Oh?" Rose looked to Jasper, then back to Dick. "And why would that be, cherie?"

"Private business."

"His pa had it told that the boy's momma is Abyssinia," Jasper said, chuckling.

"It ain't no joke by a damn sight, Mr. Jasper."

"And you be right, Mr. Winchester Man, but this here's my momma. When she ask a question, answer it."

"Young men's got too much energy," Bill Williams said. "Put 'em to work, Rose."

Jasper grinned and waved toward Bill.

"That go for you, too," Bill said. "What you been doin' side's walkin' about?"

"Well, Mr. Bill, I brought you some comp'ny, so you'n your bad stomach don't get lonely."

"Got a swellin' in him," Rose said. "Ain't much to do, but he in good spirit, and I got him built up with my cookin'. . . . Would you boys be hungry?"

"Yes ma'am," Buck said.

"Rest'n have a drink, then" Rose said. "Some rainwater over in that barrel."

"Got any whiskey?" Dick asked.

"Eat first. I ain't your momma, and she ain't here."

"Did you know of her all these years, Miz Rose?"

"Sure did."

When Dick sat down nodding to himself, Rose rushed off and commenced pulling out bowls and pots.

"I think that I will like feedin' young men."

She gave them hominy to chew while waiting on supper, and they shoveled it in as Rose dragged a pot of stew out of the cabin.

"Didn't smell that there, momma," Jasper said.

"If you had a wife, she do this for you every day."

Bill's laughter startled the cousins.

"She been tryin' to git this manchild o' hers married since I known her. He scared."

"No such, old man, and if you ain't careful, I bury you in the river when you die."

Buck and Dick gorged themselves, and that night they regaled Rose and Bill with tales of the big shootout in Mound Bayou. Bill insisted they retell everything. Dick seemed rather eager, and he preened a little more as he talked. When he finished, Bill leaned over and tapped Buck on the wrist.

"Now your time."

"You just heard it again," Buck replied.

"He knows that," Rose said. "He is enjoying himself. He's hearing about our people winning, the white people losing. Think about what the whites have done to both of his people."

"Life in the tellin', young mens. Is the way you git passed down to them follows you. If you cain't sing your praise nobody—"

Bill grabbed his side.

"Are you alright, Bill?" Jasper asked.

"Ain't ready to be buried, that's for sure. Hey, Rose, tell us about goin' into dream and seein' us all come together here."

"Help him inside the cabin," Rose said. "He been up all day."

"Talk-Too-Much-Woman—that's your name! Leave the young mens tell me again 'bout the dead Klansmen."

"Now, Bill, you need rest—your mouth, too."

"I'm still grown. Go git the young men's some whiskey—the good stuff."

Jasper went and brought a flask outside. He passed it to Dick who drank and passed it on to Buck. They began retelling their tale with even greater embellishment, often to a merry clapping of Bill's weathered hands when they reached the part how they'd emptied eight rifles. Because of the whiskey, neither of the cousins would remember falling asleep that night.

Rose awakened before the sun and started home alone to rejoin her husband. Only Jasper got up to see her off, and it amazed him how excited she appeared to be, so full of a whimsical glee about going home too prepare for her family. Later, Jasper set bowls of water beside the cousins and kicked them awake. Showing no sympathy for their miseries, Jasper forced them to depart immediately through the thickest swamp they'd yet encountered. A short distance to the north, they came upon his still. He pointed out the hiding places for mash, the stone cistern covered with mud to look natural. When it came time to taste the last year's run, Buck and Dick declined.

After a languid afternoon of fishing in a nearby bayou, they all returned to Bill's house. He did all the talking that night.

He told them of a Choctaw mother and runaway slave father, of his father's recapture and of a hard life alone in the swamp after his mother was marched into Indian Territory by the soldiers. During all the telling, Jasper directed Buck and Dick in the cleaning and roasting of the fish they'd caught. Both listened with increasing interest to Bill's legends of the Choctaw and to the names and territories of the tribes to the north and south of what had been Choctaw land. Whenever Bill sensed their attention flagging, he would begin a new tale or begin to retell what had seemed a favorite of the young men. With each telling, whiskey was passed around.

Jasper felt Bill's hand on his shoulder. The others were asleep.

"Why you hard on the young mens?"

"They ain't nothin' but trouble."

"Wheah you learn this?"

"Cicero brought 'em in to keep 'em safe, which was rightly done, but I ain't happy to have them two crawlin' all everywhere like big dumb dogs."

"They blood kin to Mr. Cicero, ain't they?"

"So what?"

"They family—good strong boys, too—for your ma, for one. I told you a woman got to have village life. When you gittin' a woman?"

"Had plenty!"

"Brought any home?"

"Yeah!" Jasper sat up and threw off his sleeping blanket. "Gimme some whiskey."

Bill passed the jug.

"What happen when you brought a woman home?"

"Long time ago. Wasn't nothing but trouble."

"Give your momma's life another woman. If you don't want to do it, let these young men come in. They kin make the babies you ain't."

Procreation, the imperative of all life, was about to go forward whether the children were Jasper's or not. He didn't snarl at Bill this time, but his lips tightened. Two men younger than him had now appeared, and all Jasper had to do was to search his memories of his own explorations with his first girlfriend Maidy, with Verlean, in order to know that soon there would be other women to compound his problems. The only answer was, the two young men had to go. And yet, because Jasper recognized the wisdom of what Bill was saying about building a community, he decided that he would himself have to find a woman to marry. It was the least he could in the interest of that hated word, progress.

The next day, Jasper led the cousins back home, and Rose and Cicero welcomed the three with hearty handshakes and hugs, though it shocked Buck as much as Jasper when Cicero announced he'd located a site for another cabin to be built.

"Do I have to clear land, again?" Buck asked.

"Non!" Jasper said. "They can stay in my cabin while they here. Leave the trees alone."

"Come here, cherie!"

"It ain't funny, momma. Ain't no little boy."

Jasper moved away, and Rose darted after him. Dick laughed when Rose finally grabbed Jasper, and her strength was enough to keep him from escaping right away.

"Cicero told me whatcha feel about these young men," Rose said. "Well, I understand, but I got to say this . . . You had a hard head as a youngster. You had to do things your way. You know how hard it is for folks to agree on things. Me'n Mr. Cicero couldn't hardly agree on how to live until he'd done his piece out there in the world . . . But that don't mean a fam'ly cain't come together. These boys got his blood. You want him to just turn 'em away?"

A subdued "non" emerged from Jasper's mouth.

"Give us the winter," Cicero said. "Then let's talk about it again. Doesn't bind you to anything, but it gives these two a chance to get settled down and decide what they want."

"Whatever y'all say."

"It's *us* decidin'," Rose said. "We all livin' in this swamp."

"Not only that," Cicero said. "Forgive me, Jasper, if this sounds like I'm thinking too much, but consider . . . There is no tribe like the one we could build here. It would be neither isolated and temporary, nor open to the world, and not bowing to the white people, or run by people bent on owning everything. We have the extraordinary opportunity to build a tiny new world. All would be equal. No slave or master, no landowner or tenant, no government or law separate from us . . . We can realize the dream men and women have shared since the beginning of time, to live peacefully among family. We have little bits of the Choctaw, Africans, Irish, English, Arabian from my father, Morgan, and a lot I don't know about. We are people of the world, a tribe of the whole world. And that is our dream, our hope!"

A loud sigh escaped from Jasper.

"So," Rose said, "what's wrong, cherie?"

"What kinda talk is that?"

"Did you listen?" Cicero asked.

"I grew up one way—"

"I know you did, Jasper! That is past. You are no longer a boy. You are a man, and you have choice."

"Talk sense, Cicero."

"Ohhhh . . . I am most certainly talking sense. See, when I was a boy, I really didn't understand what my father meant telling me to build a better world. I thought he meant go out and change that world that made us slaves. Maybe he did . . ." Cicero shook his head. ". . . But lately, as the beauty of living in this swamp comes to me, I see another choice. Got nothing to do with other people. Just with us. We change the way we live right here. *This* is our world. There is no one or nothing standing in the way. Remember what old Bill says, only in a village can an old man be respected—or you, Jasper, pretty soon."

Rose walked over to her son, and lay her hand on his back.

"We still protect each other, and we reject the white people's ways as much now as we ever did. That's what Cicero talkin' about. But we don't have to run people off because we got too many in one place. Just have to live."

"What about them boys over there?" Jasper asked.

"Well," Rose said, "we said they stay for the winter. Then see if they fit. If not, they go on about they business. But if they join us. . ." Rose raised her hands beseechingly, ". . . Now, let me finish cookin'."

Jasper walked away shaking his head. Buck led Dick off to whisper. Cicero hunkered down beside Rose near the outdoor fire.

"Thank you."

"For what, cherie?"

"You know."

"Oh, looks like we both gonna have our wish. Jasper ain't no problem. Just don't push him. The real thing is what your boys want to do. People make a world. A world don't make the people no different."

"Well, would you mind spending some time talking to my boy."

"Cherie, I got to cook if you want fritters for the next few days."

"I'll finish frying them . . . Go talk to Buck. He has so much of Isaiah inside, I don't see room for me."

"As you wish . . . Tomorrow, we should send you and Jasper back to bring Bill up here. He ain't doin' so well. I want him to be part o' what's bein' born here."

"Let's make it a celebration, then. Jasper and I will go bring Bill. Day after tomorrow, we feast."

"Who gonna cook? Rose asked.

"Anything for you," Cicero said. "Leave it for us men after we come back."

That next morning, Jasper and Cicero set off paddling the largest of their boats, the one Rose used to transport liquor. They made good time on the Sunflower because the current was with them, and Jasper knew that stretch of river like the back of his hand. They encountered no obstacle, rested only once. By early afternoon, they had negotiated the river and walked a mile inland to where Bill was overjoyed to see them. Not only in good spirits, as soon as he heard there was a celebration afoot, he was up and ready to travel even before Cicero and Jasper could rest and eat.

Back on the river, with Bill sitting between them, though, the return took more than twice as much time. Cicero paddled and Jasper used a pole, but despite their best effort, the sun disappeared as Jasper estimated they were still a couple hours from home. Bill was drinking and singing to himself, had been for much of the trip. Without consulting Jasper, Bill just reached under bracing planks in the bow and pulled out a lantern. He lit it and set it in the bow of the boat to light the water ahead.

It was late when they put in.

"I had hoped you'd be back early," Rose said as she spread her a blanket and one for Cicero a distance from the others. "I was thinking you might not object to more dreamtime."

Cicero chuckled.

"I know you're tired, cherie. But with the cousins in the cabin, I put us out here a space so I could rub on your back."

With the morning sun, Jasper went hunting. Cicero had spent the morning digging a pit and lining it with wood to burn. He fired it and kept adding wood and then tossing in dirt to dampen it down. Jasper returned around noon pulling a wild hog on a travois behind him, and they added a final layer of wood, brought it to a red glow of coal, lined the whole cavity with wet grass, split the wild hog to cook evenly and buried it to roast.

"It's a big hog," Jasper said. "I wanted two, but this'n was huge."

"You got more pig," Rose said, "than we can eat in two, three meals. What was you thinkin'? . . . You don't do nothin' without a reason."

"When I was down near Cleveland with the two cousin's I sent word to a friend o' mine to come see me."

"So?"

"I mean, if them two boys stay here, then ain't no need bein' so cat'n dog with my old friend Verlean's people."

"Oh, cherie!"

"Naw, momma, I ain't gittin' married. Only one I invited was Verlean's brother. He fed me, so I figure I owed him a feed. Ain't have nothin' to do with today, but it's been over a week since I sent word, so he could show up. That's why I wanted a big hog."

"What about Verlean?" Rose asked.

"She married now. Some man come in from this mangy little settlement called Renova. Showed Verlean and her ma how to claim land from the state. Vern say they gone ahead and started cuttin' trees because that big white folk's plantation offered to buy cleared land for three times what they paid . . ." He leaned close to whisper. ". . . Them cousins could get ideas like that."

"Jasper," Rose said, "we made an agreement last night. Stick to it. Don't go spoiling today's fun."

Rose went inside the cabin and began stirring together corn meal, onions and oil to fry up more fritters, and she uncovered a finished plum stew—sweet, fruity and loaded with dumplings. She returned back outside to the open fire as dusk was nigh. Softly at first, there came a steady noise from the direction of the Sunflower. The cousins were busy listening to

Cicero talk about something, but the others lifted their heads. Then Cicero noticed.

"Who's that coming?"

Out of the shadows stepped a man in skins. He held a coonskin cap in one hand, both of which were raised to show good intentions.

"'Scuse me, my name, Vern," the man said.

"Hey, Vern," Jasper yelled and stepped vigorously toward him. "We got good food tonight. You come at the right time."

"Thankee for invitin'."

From the unseen dark, there issued a dramatic cough, and Verlean stepped out to stand beside her brother. No skins or common wear, she was dressed in a fancy skirt of shiny black material belted at the waist. Her blouse was bright red.

"I heard you was more civilized," Verlean said, "so I say, maybe I come see. . . ." A smile flitted onto the woman's face as her eyes locked on Rose. ". . . You must be Rose."

"That's me, cherie, and who might you be?"

"Why—ain't he told you, I'm Verlean."

Cicero chuckled and Dick cocked his eyes in curiosity. Rose opened her arms, and the two women embraced.

"Cicero!" Rose said.

"Yes, hon?"

"Come and meet Jasper's friend—you are his friend?"

"Well, I ain't his enemy, Rose. I been wantin' to meet you for years. Howdy, Jasper."

"He'lo."

"Well aintcha gonna welcome me. Gimme a hug."

Rose stepped back to allow Jasper close, but he crossed his arms and didn't move. Rose put her arms around Cicero and ended the strained silence.

"Verlean, this is my husband."

"Jasper said he had a step-father, but I ain't know you was so good lookin'."

Cicero swallowed, flat-out disarmed by the flattery.

"I'm pleased to meet you, young lady."

"Oh, I ain't so young no more, but then neither is Jasper. When I heard he sent for me—"

"I sent for Vern," Jasper said.

"Well, you don't have to lose your manners."

"Let me," Cicero said, "introduce the rest of our family."

"We just had these two young men join us," Rose said.

Dick and Buck walked forward as Rose beckoned.

"Richard Dolan," Rose indicated. "And that is, Mr. Buck Morgan, my husband's son from before."

"Before you landed him?" Verlean asked. "Or after?"

"Some things," Rose said, "are not so simple."

"Busy li'l handsome devil, weren't he."

"Why you come, Verlean?" Jasper asked.

"You two go on off and have a nice talk," Rose said.

"Naw," Jasper said, "I ain't seen her in years, and I ain't interested in nice talk." Jasper shifted to speak directly to Verlean. "Heard you took up with somebody."

"I sure did. Right civilized gentleman, too. He a frien' o' that big negro work for the white folks in the gov'ment, and we gonna make a lot of money."

"How is that?" Buck asked.

Everyone looked his way.

"All I know is," Verlean said, " we pay so much down to the state. Next, we git some men to clear the land nearest the outside. We sell the trees, and then, a white man named Scott offered to buy the land."

"Verlean, I would never come into your camp and brag about doin' something you'n your momma don't hold with," Jasper said. "But you come in here to my home an' brag about clearin' the swamp like you some immigrant . . . I don't want to see no more o' you."

And with that Jasper, turned, motioned to Vern, who looked to his sister, who flipped her hand as if flicking an insect away.

"I ain't really intend to stay here, Jasper. I got a boat waitin' on the river. I just come pay my respects. I'm a married lady now . . . Very nice to meet you, Miz Rose."

Verlean turned and walked away. As everyone waited listening to her steps recede, Bill Williams grunted as he came to his feet.

"Jasper, a woman you turn down is more deadly than a blue runner snake wit big teef."

Jasper and Vern halted and bent over laughing, as did everyone else.

"Sure glad you wasn't snake-bit," Rose said.

"Not even," Jasper said, "in your dreamtime."

Of a sudden, the happy mood of the afternoon returned.

"Git the hog outta the ground!" Bill commanded. "You young boys . . . bring us all some whiskey, and don't you git drunk until the food laid out."

"Why is that, Mr. Bill?" Buck asked.

"Goes to show," Bill said, "you ain't never depended on drunk folks for yo' food."

And so the drinking became more celebratory. Jasper sat apart with Vern matching drink for drink with Bill egging them on. Cicero and the young men pulled the pig out of the ground and mounted it atop the family's outdoor table covered with a tarpaulin and freshly picked grass run up from the river by a not too happy Buck. Dick took the whole event in good spirit. It was the first real family meal that he had ever attended. About the time second helpings commenced, Cicero stood up and opened his arms to Rose.

"In honor of our family being together, Rose wants me to give thanks to the Great God that the old Africans knew— even though I don't believe in religious things." He smiled toward the boys. Rose had her eyes closed. "That includes the Christian god, Old Bill's Great Spirit—all the same . . . Seems to me we live in-between all of these gods, between African gods and old Bill's and the white one. Pray to whomever you wish, but we make the rules down here on earth. Nothing fancy, but they're *our* rules. Pretty soon you'll raise families. Will you raise them in a world where you are not the equal of any man?"

"Damned if I will!" Jasper said, leaping up unsteadily.

Rose's eyes opened and fastened on her son.

"Will what, cherie?"

"Hunh?"

"You gonna have babies for your ma?"

"Aw phooo!" Jasper said, dropping on his bottom like a sack of corn, jostling Buck, to whom he turned. "What about you? . . . You tell her!"

"Me neither," Buck said.

"Neither what, cherie?" Rose asked.

"Ain't gonna live in no world I can't be equal."

Dick said nothing. Rose took a deep breath.

"This a Africa fam'ly, like where me'n your daddy come from, Jasper. Anybody move in here—woman or man—got to be told how things is 'fore they settle." She moved from Cicero's arms and knelt beside Jasper. "We cain't be fightin' among ourselves, if we gonna be one people against the rest."

"We owe it to ourselves," Cicero said, "to recapture the sense of being one that we had in our old country. Listen to me now, young people . . . My father's name was something Mahmoud. I don't recall now what the rest of his name was, but we all called him Morgan. Rose never knew her momma or poppa. What we have in common is our people being dragged from some place in Africa."

Jasper leapt up. "I name our swamp, Africa!"

Rose embraced her son, and Jasper submitted stiffly.

"Do you mean it, cherie?"

Jasper grinned.

"You ain't sayin' this just because you had too much to drink?" Rose asked.

"I ain't never drunk too much."

"Are you ready to think on marryin'?"

Jasper stiffened, and Rose rubbed his shoulder reassuringly.

"I understand about Verlean, but you must meant it be alright for other members of this fam'ly—these boys—to marry in your place?"

"I think," Cicero said, "that we need not push Jasper to do anything."

"Non, non! Hush up, Cicero! Jasper seein' things rightly tonight. Let's get this settled."

Jasper chuckled and gave himself over to his mother's arms.

"Momma like that 'Africa,' non? Look how she squeezin' me."

"I want you to have fam'ly," Rose said. "I would trade almost anything for that. Meanwhile, these boys will stay. They my fam'ly, too, through Cicero. We all fam'ly now, you hear?"

"Then, so be it," Cicero said. "We Africans are one family. One family to bind up the wounds the white man made."

Rose got up to embrace Cicero then, and they moved away from the others. Before they entered the cabin, Rose halted and turned to the others.

"Quit talkin' about 'the swamp' when somebody ask where we live. Tell 'em you live in Africa! . . . 'Cause if you gonna use the name, let folks know it."

"To Africa," the green-eyed son of Abyssinia Morgan and Jim Dolan said, raising his whiskey. "If I'm to live colored, I'll do it the right way."

"Whatta you mean, right way?" Buck asked.

"No white man'll treat me like a mule. They'll know better when I tell 'em I live in Africa."

That night, Buck lay back under the stars wondering what Isaiah Montgomery would say about a name like Africa. Not yet sleepy, he turned on his pallet to watch Dick oiling his gun by the embers of the fire Rose had insisted they leave burn through the night. Dick was engrossed with his weapon. It hadn't been cleaned since being dunked in the Hushpuckena. He smiled toward his cousin, the whiskey inside giving extra comfort to the thought of being surrounded by family for the first time in his life. Living inside of Africa seemed just right. His fear of not knowing how to live as a black man evaporated. A man from Africa would have to create himself anew in a hostile land.

THAT FALL, BUCK AND DICK agreed that building two new cabins was unnecessary. Sharing one seemed a lesser evil. Because fall was the whiskey season and Bill Williams remained ill, Jasper rendered no assistance. Aside from work on their new cabin, however, life was as free as Buck could have hoped. Jasper demanded only that the cousins make a twice weekly circuit along Harris Bayou from the Sunflower to Alligator Lake to make sure nobody hunted there or cut timber. Shooting a person for being in the wrong place worried Buck. Dick was curious about making whiskey.

"Be helpin' at your still, if you like," he told Jasper.

"That's business, Mr. Winchester Man. I ain't havin' you drink it up."

"Nay, nay! I want to help out."

"Are you willin' to travel outside the swamp?"

"Aye."

"I need to show you where me'n Bill go buy sugar'n corn."

"It ain't safe out there," Buck said.

"Course, it is," Jasper said. "Anybody look at Dick gonna think he a white man."

"I'll just keep away from Alligator," Dick said.

"But Dick got to help me finish the cabin."

"*You* can do that," Jasper said, "while Dick workin' for me."

"You got us goin' way up north o' where we buldin' to cut the logs," Buck said.

"So?"

"It take a long time for me to cut timber and haul it back."

"Like I said, you finish the buildin'. Mos' trees been cut. You need more logs, come git Dick."

The new cabin site was four hours spirited walk from the Alligator Lake once the cousins learned the connecting trails out of the swamp up to what they dubbed "road" to Alligator along the flood ridge bordering Harris Bayou. That ridge became well worn because neither Buck nor Dick liked taking a boat on Harris Bayou and having to walk once they put ashore. And here in a first small way, the swamp itself bowed to time, human time, for the road was soon wide enough for a wagon the cousins purchased to haul timber in, though following Jasper's admonition, they refrained from changing the surface of the dirt trail. Except for that one trail, they honored Jasper's rule never to use the same trail going and coming.

While Dick was away working with Jasper, Buck decided he, too, could leave the swamp. He had not lived down the feeling of being taken advantage of, so he ranged along Harris Bayou and up its north fork, across a mudflat. He cursed the sulfurous blue mud that fouled his only pair of boots. Then he glimpsed a cluster of cabins. Buck was surprised to find men, women and children all home, until a group of boys throwing rocks at a swarm of blackbirds informed him that it was a Sunday.

A girl's scream startled him. An attractive, petite girl was looking directly at him as she ran into a house. She had curling hair framing huge dark eyes in a pixie-pretty face. A bulky young woman who looked like the small one's sister—the same dark eyes and tiny full lips whose blackness seemed a ripening of the undertones in her mahogany skin—was holding what he didn't recognize as a hair-straightening iron. Being a fugitive of sorts, Buck's first impulse on hearing the scream was to run. Then he smelled burning-hair. An older man stuck his head outside.

"Whatcha want around here, young mister?"

"Just walking by," Buck said.

"He was watchin' us, pa!" the voice of the girl hidden inside the house said.

"Wiggins, is my name, son. I don't know your face."

"I was born down below Vicksburg, sir," Buck said.

"My fam'ly works on the Bobo Plantation. Me'n all my five boys was born there—my girls, too."

"Where is that?"

"Not a mile west o' here, toward the big river. I'm near'bout same as a overseer for the house people. Stayed on after the War 'cause I wasn't about to git in the road with all the rest of the shiftless niggas. Where your folks live?"

"My uncle is Mr. Isaiah Montgomery."

"That true? You be's a relation of Mr. Montgomery?"

"Yessir. I sold my land in Mound Bayou and put my money in a land venture over in the swamp."

"You don't say—Sara! Come back out here, Sara! This young man from down by Moun' Ba'ou."

To Sara Wiggins' father, Isaiah Montgomery was a great race man, more so because, All the white folks does respect him. Wiggins inquired if there might be room for his family in Mound Bayou, and Buck promised to make an introduction whenever Mr. Wiggins found time to travel.

"Be pleased you worship with us, Buck. Then you'n Sara have chance to talk."

Buck was so enchanted with Sara that time between the father's invitation and the family arriving at church seemed no time at all. Buck paid no attention to the preaching. He kept his eyes on Sara, who seemed a lovely little bird full of energy. Mrs. Wiggins startled Buck when he realized that she was whispering in his ear.

"This ain't nothin' but a shed, but we's all quality people. Just cain't afford to build a reg'lar church."

"Yes ma'am."

"People of quality will be the salvation of our race, and that is how we carry ourself."

Mrs. Wiggins whispered to her husband, who nodded his concurrence in something. She then walked to the front in the middle of a song by the choir and beckoned to the preacher.

"Mr. Buck Morgan?" the preacher intoned. "Will you come forward, Mr. Morgan. Introduce yourself to the church."

Buck spoke swiftly, with the barest flourish of information about being a trader in land. After he paraded back to his seat, Sara whispered.

"You a good speaker, Buck."

"Think so?"

"Yeah. Daddy say it take that to be a success."

After church, everyone pressed in to shake the hand of Isaiah Montgomery's nephew. It was evening before the Wiggins family returned to their simple rooms.

"Mr. Wiggins built my cookhouse hisself," Mrs. Wiggins said. "He gonna add to the house after our youngest boy get old enough to draw wages."

"You do good work, Mr. Wiggins," Buck said. "I built a house for my aunt just last year. I know a little about building."

"Don't say? Made your aunt proud o' you, I bet. What about your people, ma and pa?"

"My mother lives Mound Bayou. My daddy don't—or he didn't live with us."

"Well, he helped you out, I suppose."

"Nossir, he didn't. He ran away and lived up here in the swamp. I just met him recently."

Wiggins paused, cleared his throat.

"Well, young sir, I was born in the swamp myself. It was a time when men like myself—your poppa, too, most like—wasn't happy to bow down to the white folks."

Mr. Wiggins smiled and wandered off, and Buck felt only mildly reproved. So, he stayed for supper, and he reveled in the attention of father, mother and, above all, pretty Sara. Her big jet black eyes were surrounded by the purest white, not a hint of discoloration, and they stuck on him. After the meal, Buck led her out behind the house where she set up two chairs so they could talk, but her oldest brother insisted on joining them.

"He want to marry," Sara said, "but he ain't got no money, and I wish he'd leave you'n me alone."

"White folks don't pay nothin' for work," said the young man whose name was Jeff. "Daddy won't let me bring my new wife home cause I cain't support her, but I be happy to work for you."

"You would?"

"Yessir. What you said about Moun' Ba'ou sound like it's the place for me."

"Don't know about that, Jeff. My uncle won't let just anybody in. How can you buy land if you don't have any money?"

"You got to do that?" Jeff asked.

"Absolutely! Keeps Mound Bayou a family place."

"Well, I be happy whatever you can do, Buck. Pay you back however you say."

"As long as you're willing to work, Jeff, I can help. But you got to work hard, and no funny stuff about you bein' older'n me, OK?"

"Sure, Buck."

The short winter day was drawing to a close when Jeff walked back inside, and Buck sighed.

"Sure wish we could spend a lot more time."

"Me, too, Buck. How you gonna help my brother?"

"Haven't figured on that, yet, but there's trees to be cut and sold, and I think there's ways to latch onto land."

"You mean buy from the railroad?"

"That, too . . . I guess its time for me to go."

"Where you goin'?" Sara said. "Not all the way to Mound Bayou tonight?"

"No, no. I work out of a cabin over in the swamp."

"It's yours?"

"Yep. Me'n a friend built it."

"A woman friend?"

"I ain't married."

"Sara! Time to come inside."

"Yes momma. I'm sorry, Buck."

"Me, too."

"Sara!!!"

"Yes'm, I'm comin' fast as I can."

Mrs. Wiggins appeared smiling at the back door.

"Mr. Morgan, Sara got to come in, but we know you got a piece to travel. So you could spend the night with our boys."

"Oh!"

"Somethin' wrong?"

"No, ma'am. Thank you kindly."

Buck was given space on the floor on the boys' side of a side bedroom. Sara made her pallet across the room alongside her sister.

"Good night, Mr. Morgan."

"Good night, Miz Sara. I appreciate your hospitality."

"Oh, it ain't nothin' . . . Buck."

He sat up more than once pretending to turn over on his pallet, just to catch a glimpse of her outline on the floor. It was warm in that little packed room, and Sara soon pushed off her quilt. The brown skin of her leg below her nightgown seemed to glow in the dark. Never before had Buck felt so close and yet so far from heaven. He touched himself and grew embarrassed when one of the boys turned over against him. As he continued to stare at Sara's naked leg, he could do nothing to calm his wild breathing.

December brought icy frosts. At dusk, Buck and Dick were staring at lanterns mounted on lacquered iron poles standing thirty feet apart in the corners of a huge whitened tarpaulin stretched over the ground. Smaller lanterns, colorfully adorned with bright cloth skirts, hung on ropes stretched overhead near the Bobo Plantation house. Years before, the Clarksdale Bobo house had been sold. This was the country home. Five black musicians were seated up on a wagon. All of the dancers were white.

When the musicians quit playing, liveried servants criss-crossed the tightly stretched tarpaulin spreading cornmeal to keep the dance surface lively. Others carried trays of steaming punch among the crowd. To one side of the dance floor, smil-ing black faces were poised to carve several turkeys, a roast pig and a barrel-sized haunch of beef at the pleasure of the crowd.

"C'mon," Dick said, tugging at Buck's sleeve. "Feelin' a trifle uncomfortable so near these white folks. The Bobo's know my pa. They got to have heard about me."

"We miles from Alligator, Dick. This Coahoma County. Just follow me."

"Ain't so many miles, Bucko."

Buck circled the big dance floor, staying clear of the white couples as Sara had instructed. At the back of the house, an-other set of lanterns lighted a tightly packed group of black re-tainers dancing to a harmonica. The band from up front was walking back to join their own people to eat. Sara approached the cousins wearing a pink cotton gown with puffy long sleeves and high gathered waist.

"Ain'tcha glad you dressed up?" Buck said to Dick.

"Rather be undressed with her."

Buck feinted as if to strike. Dick scampered away laughing.

"Thought y'all wasn't comin'," Sara said, breathless from dancing, holding a heavy wool shawl around her shoulders.

"No sense comin' to a party before it get dark," Buck replied.

"What you gonna do in the dark, Mister Morgan?"

"Ahem!"

"Oh, Sara . . . this my cousin, Dick."

"Pleased to meet you." Sara curtsied. "I'm glad y'all didn't miss the dancin'."

"Ain't gonna miss no dancin'," Buck said. "You ain't seen nothin' 'till you see me strut."

"Do you have a sister?" Dick asked, head cocked like a dandy.

Sara frowned, looked away.

"Dick just jokin', Sara."

"You want to meet my sister?"

"Better than standin' here" Dick said, "playin' with myself."

"You have a very rude way of speaking, Mister . . ."

"Dolan."

"That name sound familiar. Do I know your people?"

"Nay, lass. Guess I'll be takin' leave of you two."

Buck chuckled, grabbed Sara's elbow and moved away. Dick was irritated that Sara had taken his small jest as rude. He watched the couple move past a surly young man who eyed Buck walking past him. Dick couldn't relax. White folks—some of whom might recognize him—were milling out in front and beside the house. On top of that, his skin made him easy to spot among the unknown black people. For several minutes, he hoped one of the girls who had noticed him would walk over and talk. He was too unsure of himself to approach them.

After the musicians had eaten, they started tuning up behind the house, and Sara pulled on Buck.

"C'mon dance."

"Why you want to dance right now? Show me around. I want to see what they got in the big house."

"But the music, Buck. Musicians gonna stop after they play one more round."

Buck spotted his cousin and yelled across the yard.

"Hey, Dick! . . . Sara, where they got the refreshments for us folks?"

Sara pointed to a small table near what appeared to be the cookhouse.

"Get us something to eat, Dick!"

As Buck led Sara to dance, Dick strode self-consciously toward the refreshment table, feeling all eyes on himself, trying to walk in a self-assured manner. As he pulled a flask from his jacket, an attractive, banana-hued woman with brown hair and freckles on her nose stared at him while serving punch. She was wearing a shiny red dress, and after she smiled, her tongue rolled provocatively over pink-brown rouge-less lips.

"You ain't from around heah, is you, pretty boy?"

Proudly, he held his flask toward the woman who glanced about, then nodded. Dick poured in a cup and passed it over the table between them. She tossed down the whiskey and licked the edge of her cup.

"I'm from Africa."

"Ha ha ha! From wheah?!"

"Africa."

"Lord God, pretty man, you ain't no Africa nigga. What you talkin' about?"

The woman moved from behind the serving table.

"Africa is what we call our camp over in the swamp."

Relishing the woman's sly glances, Dick said no more. When the music started up again, Dick's eyes searched the woman's body under its shimmery dress.

"So where is this Africa?" the woman asked.

"Exactly where I told you. Do you live closer by than that?"

"Could be, but I got to work. What's your name?"

"Richard."

"Come here, Richard."

The woman extended her hand, smiled, but Dick made no move to take it.

"Walk yourself on back behind your table," he said. "Ain't fair, a fine woman close by, and a man cain't touch nothin' but her hand."

"I like a man know how to put his lips around words." The wind gusted and blew a starched collar into her face. "Gittin' chilly, Richard. Where you goin' when they close up?"

The wind lifted the woman's skirt disclosing ankles encased in white. She wiggled a foot toward Dick.

"Come on, pretty man, you ain't give no answer, and it's gonna be cold tonight. I run a little social club."

While the music held the crowd in thrall, the two were left alone. Dick closed the distance between them, and when the woman refused to give ground, he stood with his manhood pressed as if casually against her hip. A scream shattered their tete-a-tete. Over in the light behind the house, the dancers parted as if watching somebody perform. Dick turned back toward the woman, but she frowned and pointed.

"Ain't that the boy you come with?"

"Hunh?"

"Lord, Richard, they fightin'!"

In the middle of the crowd, like gladiators, Buck was grappling with the insolent one. Dick ran toward the fight.

"Kill the son of a bitch!" someone in the crowd yelled.

Three men were urging on the young man struggling with Buck. Sara was holding her face between her hands.

"Stop it, Jim Hibbler!" Sara said. "You leave my friend alone."

Dick paused at the edge of the circle. Glancing around, he judged it a family crowd, older folks who'd threaten before attacking and young men who probably wouldn't be carrying weapons. He pushed through the ring of onlookers and pulled Hibbler away. Buck jumped up and slugged Hibbler while Dick was holding him.

"Stop, Buck!" Dick said. "Look about you."

Young and unfriendly faces were closing.

"Told you to leave my woman alone, nigga," Hibbler said, pulling away from Dick. "Now, I gonna beat you into next week—you and your snot-colored friend. Come on, boys!"

"Y'all leave that pretty man alone," the woman from the refreshment table said. But her words had the opposite effect. Two older men stepped alongside Jim Hibbler. Dick drew his pistol and fired.

"I'm damned to hell or dead I don't cripple next one of you sets one foot front of the other."

The music abruptly stopped. White folks who had been dancing in front came running back. Buck sprinted away. Dick bowed toward the woman in shimmering red and took off behind Buck.

They ran for all they were worth. Outside the circle of party lights, they had to slow down. It was completely dark, and neither had a lantern to light their way home.

"Jesus, Mary, and Joseph! Look what you got me into."

"I ain't got you into nothin'. Weren't my fault."

"Damn that! Gal you sweet on got a man ahead o' you."

"Shut up, Dick. You don't know what you talkin' about."

Walking through the night for the next half hour, neither said anything to the other. By then, two sets of teeth were chattering, not a single heavy coat between them.

"We cain't make it all the way home," Dick said.

"Don't you worry. I got it all planned out."

Buck explained that he had planned to spend the night at Sara's. Instead, to remain out of sight because, though he didn't say so to Dick, he felt marked as a trouble maker, he led Dick past the workers' quarters toward the cotton gin beside which stood several planked sheds for storing cotton. They broke into one and spent the night snuggled together for warmth under a layer of harvested cotton.

Several weeks passed. Buck remained embarrassed by Dick's gunplay, and because Jasper insisted he and Dick help lug a passle of corn down to the still, Buck didn't see Sara again for weeks.

"I never thought you was mixed up with gun-totin' folks."

"No, Sara, it ain't like that atall."

"I know what I saw."

"But it was that or us get whipped. You saw all them men after us."

"But why your cousin carry a gun?"

"See, he the Winchester Man—"

"The what?"

"Winchester Man. Him'n me ambushed this bunch of Klan folk one night."

"I ain't no fool, Buck Morgan. You talkin' nonsense."

"No, Sara, please, listen. Dick and me live in the swamp over east of here. My people in Mound Bayou thought it be safer."

"Why?"

"Because of the shootin'!"

"Musta been that Dick whatever-his-name. He the no count one."

"Wasn't his fault. He was visitin his momma in Mound Bayou last Fourth of July when him and me heard these Klansmen ride up. We ambushed 'em."

Sara stared open-mouthed.

"Why ain't I heard nothin' about it, Buck?"

"White folks don't want to own up to it."

Sara took Buck straight to her father and made Buck repeat about him and Dick.

"That's a monstrous story, young man, monstrous."

"But it happened," Buck insisted.

"Well, now, I ain't in a position to say I believes you, but sound like somethin' bad happened."

Mr. Wiggins walked away.

"Ain't nobody," Sara said to Buck, "heard about no Fourth of July mess. If you want to be my friend, you got to keep better company."

Dick accompanied Buck to the Quarters next time, but they separated. Dick walked around for an hour and soon found himself fascinated by how people treated him. Some with distance, others caution, yet always taking some note if not deference to his presence. He was invited to come talk by one young tough who had threatened him and Buck. An older woman whispered to her well-fed daughters to look away because he was common. None of which offended Dick. There seemed to be some good and bad in the reaction of all who remembered him pulling a gun at the Bobo plantation. Which was a fairly accurate gauge of how the community saw Richard Cicero Dolan. First of all, he was black, in the sense of being part of what exploitation had done to them all. He was pointedly called colored by some who found white skin attractive. Beyond that, he was a crazy nigga, possible lover, whiskey man, and—in the words of an older woman—Lord, I hope young son ain't trying to git kilt.

The diversity of opinion was fascinating, and Dick lingered, too engrossed in the chain of conversations to want it to break. As evening came on, the woman from the refreshment table made her appearance. With a clapping of her hands as she looked Dick up and down, she said, "New breed o' colored man, my Africa man." Then she took his arm and paraded him home. Along the way, Dick read admiration in other women's eyes, and that night, in bed with the woman, there were games to play he'd never considered. Her name was Matilda. Her home became Dick's home, and the Social Club beside her house became a regular customer for Jasper's whiskey.

As winter passed, Buck and Dick had their fill of drinking into morning and sleeping into afternoons. To the delight of

Cicero and Rose, they became like brothers. Most days, as Rose prepared supper, they would appear.

"Boys like good food," Rose said.

"Yesterday," Cicero said, not looking up from reading a newspaper he picked up at the post office every month, "your 'boys' ate my plum stew, and I never even tasted it."

Jasper started giggling.

"Bear got sense enough to run off a cub before it eat all the berries."

"You're right, son, they my babies."

Jasper slid off his chair laughing.

"Grown men," Cicero said, snatching off his reading glasses, "should provide for themselves. Look how they just come in here'n eat up everything."

"Well, I'm the first woman got two babies with no help from a man. That's a marvel, so you just bear up a little while. Boys git hooked up with women soon, won't they, Jasper?"

"Hunh?"

"I *say*, they get hooked up with somebody soon, non?"

A MILD WINTER PASSED. Early March rains dotted meadow edging the swamp with flowers. Before the big river overflowed even once that season, the bayous were already full enough to begin flowing just on account of the rain. Inside the swamp west of the Sunflower, streams of human time were also gathering, young men coming of age and bursting the buds of youth, an energy like never before. Everything was in ferment.

Rose divided her time between home and Bill Williams' cabin. He was little improved, but so restive despite his pain that he insisted on traveling downriver a piece to visit a couple who had more or less introduced him to Rose and with whom he and Rose had spent several companionable evenings in those early years. Every couple of weeks Bill would insist on walking to his and Jasper's still where he would poke around, and he insisted on mixing a new batch of mash.

Rose herself began leaving her cabin more, trading herbs and remedies with the families farming along the railroad on the edge of her swamp. Dick went along and put her up to trading directly with the people instead of selling to JD's store in Alligator, though Rose continued to trade with the store, too. The money was of little significance, but talking with the women, having children sit on her lap after they lost their fear of the woman from the swamp enthralled Rose.

During what was usually a time of ease, Cicero was writing on his memoirs. He spent most of a month hunched over in a corner near the window or leaning against a sunny outside wall of the cabin. Buck and Dick's arrival had given new impetus to what he had put aside. Rose encouraged him to update the stories concerning his sister Abby's confession, JD and Dick, the new black town and the young cousins coming to live with them.

Jasper, too, was pressed. Bill had become more of a hindrance than a help. There was an abandoned still site not far from Dick and Buck's cabin. Jasper had not used it since he and Bill began working together, but now that Bill was not available, Jasper hauled most of his cooking apparatus back to his old still. Doing so made it natural for Dick to help make whiskey as well as deliver it to families in the edge of the swamp.

Buck was as busy as every one else. He had used the money from selling his land and cabin in Mound Bayou to support his social life with Sara over the winter. Without telling her parents, Buck took Sara to Memphis on the train. They returned late that night. Sara's mother was so pleased with a lace table cloth that she quit complaining about Sara coming home late. Mr. Wiggins pulled Buck aside.

"Sara is special," he said. "I just want you to know I got equal parts love and hate inside, and I parcels out to them what deserves."

Spring brought Buck fantasies of harvesting the magnificent timber around him. From building their cabin, he and Dick remained in possession of tools Cicero had obtained from Isaiah. Buck was certain that his uncle would buy timber from him and resell it to the railroad if Dick would haul it to Mound Bayou. Dick told Buck to cut down near the town, so they would have to drag it a couple miles at most. He knew that cutting close to town would be on land already claimed, but any further east and they would be treading on Jasper's domain. Stung by Dick's clever avoidance of helping him cut timber, Buck turned his attention to Jeff Wiggins, and he asked the young man to find out if the railroad would buy timber at the Bobo train stop north of Alligator. Trouble was, they would have to cut trees nearer where Buck lived, and that would certainly cause Jasper to complain.

That summer, Dick and Buck cleared a space for a corral behind their cabin, and to arrange for mules to haul timber, Dick visited his father's plantation. As Dick walked up the back stairs, JD saw him.

"Look who's here."

"Aye. Is it safe?"

"Come on inside," JD said.

"How you, Mr. Dick," Sadie the housekeeper said.

Dick smiled toward the woman who had once been like mother to him. He followed JD through the house to the front and outside where JD looked carefully down the road Dick had ridden.

"You got to be off, right soon," JD said.

"Are they lookin' for me, pa?"

"'Tis taken care of, the incident in Mound Bayou. But 'twas at a cost and a promise. I told the good sheriff if he put my name on a wanted poster, I'd treat it as a matter o' honor."

"Then, I'm free to go where I will?"

"'Tisn't a fool, I raised, is it? There's men'll put a bullet 'tween your eyes if they catch sight of you. They know you for the mulatto stranger of the sheriff's report that I paid dearly to have filed away. Now what did you come for?"

"Mules, pa. I need a team of four to work timber."

"Where are you livin'?"

"Off in the swamp."

"Cicero and his people, aye? The old nigger finally got you in the family."

"Can you buy the mules for me?"

"There's somethin' I got to repeat," JD said.

"What?"

"Move away! Mr. Cicero won't be worth a damn when you're trapped."

Dick nodded, then walked back through the house and down the back stairs. His father stood in the door.

"Don't misunderstand my help, lad. I'm quit of you—me'n my new bride."

"New bride?"

"Aye, lad, I'm wedded'n bedded. If the woman was here now, I'd deny knowin' you on account o' protectin' her feelin's. So if you refuse to make your life away from here, I'll not be keepin' the watch. Someday, you'll have only yon gun to look to."

"So be it. Give me use of the mules when I come for 'em, and I'll be my own man."

For a week after the encounter, Dick loitered around his cabin. No matter he had chosen to live as a black man, he was tempted by the seeming simple life in Ohio where he imagined that he would be just another man, a white man. Then too, the swamp was becoming a lonely place. Buck was off on his own affairs, and though Dick looked forward to the whiskey work with Jasper, it was work. It was also disconcerting that, aside from sneaking into Mound Bayou to visit his mother, there was only Matilda's—one place in the whole world outside of Africa—where he could find a welcome. Buck changed the subject every time Dick wanted to talk about JD, angry one moment, embarrassed the next to hear Dick talk about the white man who had fathered him.

While Dick worked through his crisis, Buck was spending more and more time at Sara's. The house was an original front and back room, just 2 rooms, but room additions had been added on either side. At the rear, stood the cook shack, a most rudimentary construction of ten-foot timbers topped by a slanting roof, more a shed than a room with only three board walls and the front open. There was a huge wood-burning

stove in the middle with shelving for food and cooking utensils. The shed was at least fifteen feet deep, and the rear section was used by the Wiggins family for storage. Sara had
described playing house inside with her sister.

"We ain't supposed to be doin' this, Buck."

"You don't want me to stop."

"I know, but wait! . . . Do you know what my momma would
say if she walked in?"

"Your momma gone, you told me so. Daddy, too."

Sara's face dropped as Buck touched her cheek. He pulled
her close and again began running his hand along her flank.
He could feel her heart beating faster as he kissed her, until
her hand grabbed his.

"Come on, let me touch you good," Buck said.

"Naw, naw . . ."

"Sara, you know it feel good. If it didn't you wouldn't been
in here so long. C'mon!"

With a smile somewhere between shy and sly, Sara began to
unbutton the top of her dress. Buck grabbed for her, but Sara
held him off. When she finished partially disrobing, her
shoulders were bare. Covering her bosom was a much washed
chemise top. Buck reaching toward her bosom was much too
unceremonial, and Sara slapped his hand.

"Kiss me first, like we was doin'. Then you can touch me
while we kissin'."

And so they embraced, this time with so much enthusiasm,
they slid off the pile of stored clothing and family what-nots
they'd been perched on for two hours. When they picked
themselves up, Buck pressed against Sara, and when her arms
rose to encircle him, he pressed her back on top of the pile of
clothing.

"Oh, Sara, I love you so much."

"And I love you Buck."

Buck's hand eased underneath Sara's long undergarment,
and when he began probing, she clamped her legs together.

"What you plan, Mr. Morgan?"

"We grown. I want to make love to my woman."

Sara grabbed Buck's hand as it moved higher.

"You can do anything you want, but . . ."

"But what, woman!?"

All of a sudden, there was the sound of footsteps outside.

"My sweet Jesus! What y'all call yo'self doin'?"

"I know it look bad, Mr. Wiggins, but—"

"Git up fore I kill you, Buck! Sara git your dress down!"

The sound of Buck's bare feet hitting the loose floorboards over the ground was a drum beat behind Sara's soprano wail of anguish as she snatched at her long dress only to have it come down below her breasts because she had unbuttoned the top earlier. Her father scowled.

"I'm sorry," came to Sara's mouth because she knew that the water in her father's eyes were a reflection of the icicle in that warm father heart in which she had always been his favorite.

"It was my fault," Buck said, only to be silenced by an outstretched muscular arm pointing ominously.

"It ain't about fault, Buck Morgan. Maybe if you'd learned more from your father you wouldn't be so hung up on fault Your fault ain't shit! I'm lookin' at my baby here with her drawers near off, an' all you can say is it was your fault. Hell, little nigga, it ain't a matter for fault."

Sara wiped at her eyes, then scooted back on the pile of clothing to button her top. Her father looked away.

"Naw, little nigga, that ain't about fault. It's about I don't know you good enough to turn my baby over to you. And, Sara, you git that look outta your eyes too, cause I'm tellin truth, an yo momma ain't around. Love that woman too much to spoil her nice lady-view o' the world. She got it from her momma who used to be a lady's maid at Bobo. She was just about your age, Sara, when she let me do what you was doin' with Buck . . . She was so upset with herself—cryin' and tellin' me to stop, tryin' to kiss me at the same time—I had to stop . . . Hell, quiet is kept, I'm a slave for her'n all you children, every last one. So, I gotta be sure you two don't bring scandal on her."

"No sir," Buck said. "I understand."

"Naw, you don't. Personally, I ain't give a hoot about scandal . . . But my big baby do. And my li'l baby ain't a baby no more. So, git dressed Buck Morgan—Sara! Didn't I tell you git dressed 5 minutes ago!"

"Yes papa."

"I'm gonna go back outside like I ain' seen nothing. Sara, when I see you, be calm an' carry on. I got to leave now. Got a job servin' table at the big house in a little while. Sara!"

"Yes, papa?"

"When your momma git back, go tell her you'n Buck is serious. Say it's time your family met Buck's fam'ly. Cause that's what your momma gonna want."

"Thank you, sir," Buck said.

"Take my advice, Buck. You go make up to your daddy 'cause if that Isaiah Montgomery raised you a spoiled child an' you cain't see your way to makin' up to a old man like yours, well so much the worse. I was a swamp nigga myself. I come along and met Sara's momma before the War. She felt so good to me—and of course she didn't have no full parents, her'n her momma being bought slaves o' Mr. Bobbo—I had to do everything possible to keep her seeing me. First, I let her have Mr. Bobbo make me a slave and own me. All I wanted was to be with Sara's momma. *She* was my freedom! I learned them white folks manners lickety split. Mr. Bobo said I was the smartest bush monkey he ever see. Yep. I learned how to live like white people and made Sara's momma think I believed in all that stuff. We jumped the broom soon as freedom come, and I been a leader o this community ever since. Folks took note o' my ways, seen how I made Sara's momma love a swamp man . . . I got to go to work, children. Buck, you go make up to your daddy. We needs to meet."

If the Mona Lisa had been an African, that would have been the look on Sara's face as she turned to Buck. Her eyes had narrowed in a parody of something she had seen or heard a grown woman talk about, and her smile was beyond description, a honey-honed blade that cut away all of his self-control. It made Buck's stomach ache in longing, and he snatched at his clothes again as soon as Mr. Wiggins had departed.

"No, keep your clothes on, Buck. Don't mess up. Daddy told you what you need to do. We ain't got time for messin around now."

"How come you stop likin' what I was doin'?"

"Oh, Buck, I still like it, and I want to keep doin it, and Daddy say it's all right, too. But I got to go talk to momma. You got to talk to your daddy."

"I want you Sara, now!"

"Me, too, Buck. I'm so glad papa told me its right—long's you gonna marry me."

"My Uncle Isaiah say a man disrespect him and the girl he marry if he don't already have a house and some land."

"Oooee, Buck, you gone do that for me?"

"Yeah, me'n you. We own our own stuff, big house, too. All I got to do is figure out a way to start cuttin' some timber, and that let me hire some men."

"My brother Jeff?"

"Oh yeah! He can help me look around for some more men, too. I'll pay a little more than the white folks, good pay. Dick and I got a cabin down off Harris Bayou in the fork of what they call Dry Bayou this time o' year. Him'n me could clear a space for a new house a little piece away from us. No reason I have to . . . Hmmm."

"You worried about somethin'?"

"No. Just some backward folk o' mine down in the swamp. No disrespect to your daddy, but swamp people got old time notions like they don't want their trees cut. I'mma build us our house anyway."

"You mean it?"

"Cross my heart. Sara, you gonna be proud o' me."

"What about your daddy, Buck? You say he want Africa a even-steven place. Is he gonna let you be big boss man, workin people so we kin git rich?"

"Come to think of it, I ain't gonna tell him. Cicero don't like the idea of people getting' up in the world—can you believe that? He start telling me about fairness and shit. Forget that!"

"But, Buck—"

"Look, we'll be okay. Go on, talk to your momma. I'll figure out some way so your folks won't have to come meet mine because ain't no tellin' what your momma would think if we took her out there. You come meet 'em, though, see my cousin again, too."

"That no count!"

"He's not! Dick my best friend. He just don't give a damn about manners, but he a good guy. We cousins and, we different, but he's a good guy."

In the months that followed, Buck cared for little but his precious arrangements to enter the timber business. He spent the middle of most days walking along Harris Bayou, up it's flaring mud flat to the north, its branch forking south. Everywhere, were small clumps of trees that had matured long after the wholesale cutting of timber had ceased. The small stands on the outskirts of Africa were not numerous enough to attract commercial loggers, and Buck counted that a blessing. A few farmers along the west of Africa even paid Buck to clear portions of land they intended to farm, and it provided the first work for Sara's brother and a couple men he knew. Buck got his initial leads from Dick who sold whiskey in the area. And there was Sara. When Buck asked to introduce her to his family, Cicero asked if Sara were with child. The question angered Buck, and his irritation fed a suspicion that his father was not such an upstanding citizen despite all the talk about him once being part of the government.

"Good for a footloose nigga," Rose said, "to find somebody worry over you before nobody will have you."

Jasper walked away, but Rose kept after him.

"What you gonna do when you porely like ole Bill? Tell me now! Your ma cain't—an' won't—worry about that, cherie."

"I got friends."

"Oh, you do? Why don't I never see 'em?"

"'Cause I'm a man, and some things is private."

Jasper sat down and folded his arms.

"Get your privates off that choppin' block and bring a woman to have supper with Sara. We can feed her too."

"We invited Sara's folks," Buck said, "but the plantation got a big whing-ding they got to serve. Sure did want them to meet you, daddy."

"Well, at least we can entertain your young lady," Cicero said. "I'm sure she's very nice."

The meal was laid out on a grassy expanses high above the Hushpuckena River. Buck suggested the scenic expanse as a background for the meal. Rose did some of the cooking the week before and made sure, the day before, that Cicero hunted up and roasted a wild hog along with a couple of their chickens. Potatoes were roasted over the same pit the morning of the festive day, while Dick and Buck lugged a pot of boiled greens from the cabin to where all would dine. Corn bread, pickled vegetables, along with a sweet pudding of cornmeal and buttermilk rounded out the feast.

Jasper was absent the previous day, and when he showed up that morning, he was accompanied by a woman from a timber camp east of the Sunflower. She was an ample, plain-looking woman named Mabel Scroggins, carrying a toddler whose father had been killed in a logging mishap. Not quite but almost as tall as Rose, she wore her hair brushed back from her forehead and parted in the middle as was considered sensible with no effort toward style. Her face was a cup of sweet cocoa exuding friendliness. All afternoon, she moved about eager to talk or to help with the food. Dick took care of her boy, some game called 'hound dog' where Dick scurried around on all fours howling. The child screamed in joy.

Buck arrived in mid-afternoon with Sara. She was dressed with obvious concern for looking both grown and well-off. The spotless white dress belonged to her mother and was a trifle large. She removed her common boots after arriving and put on slippers. Buck wore his black suit. As everyone else rushed around doing last minute things, she and Buck sort of sat apart, smiling at each other, touching.

The eating and drinking commenced without ceremony. Cicero continued drinking until all had settled down to eat. Then he offered a toast.

"Here's to the woman who keeps our Jasper warm away from home."

"Thank you, Cicero," Rose said. "Now come sit down."

Cicero ignored the command and turned again toward the new comer.

"Tell me, Mabel, has our Jasper been visiting his still all the nights he's been away?"

Rose pulled Cicero by his shirt. Liquored up and unprepared as he was, he fell in a sprawl. When the young men began to chuckle, Cicero crawled up against his wife.

"Rose, let's me'n you celebrate, too."

"Man, I'm still eating!"

Cicero wouldn't stay quiet for long. He began a not very discrete poem about bottom country that had obviously to do with Rose's anatomy, and Sara turned away. Rose yanked on Cicero's arm.

"Cherie, listen to me . . . Some of the young folks won't accept the things you'n me do openly."

Rose nodded toward Sara, who averted her eyes.

"Cicero at home, Rose," Bill Williams said. He'd eaten very little but never stopped drinking. "Let him enjoy his fam'ly. It ain't only for women to enjoy."

"Where your gal, Dick?" Rose asked.

"Ain't got none."

"That's a lie," Buck said. "He got a friend, Momma Rose, but she workin' today."

This time, Sara blushed. In her understanding, polite folks didn't talk about the woman who ran the Social Club on the outskirts of the Quarters. Just how rough, she wondered, might these swamp dwellers around her be? The afternoon had brought one surprise after another, all of the wrong kind. No one, as she had hoped to meet, of the ilk of Mr. Isaiah Montgomery. Just backward negroes of the worse stripe, familiar with guns, whiskey and fallen women.

"Hush up, Buck Morgan," Sara said. "I am not the kind of person who talks about folks like Matilda . . ." Sara paused, aware of Rose watching her. ". . . Miz Rose, I apologize for my Buck losin' his sense in a bottle."

Sara stood and walked to help herself to more pudding leaving Buck sitting like a scared rabbit. Cicero's head swiveled all around sensing a rift but not understanding what was going on. Off to the side, Dick was nursing a grin, and old Bill was making incomprehensible sounds to himself. In the gathering dark, a hooting owl broke the silence. The omen made Rose close her eyes for a moment. Then she began to chuckle.

"Well," she said. "it's time we called the day quits. Sara, my own Mr. Morgan here needs to go to sleep, and I would assume that your Mr. Morgan wants to take you home . . . Would you spend a moment with me?"

"Yes'm."

While the men salvaged what they could of the food, Rose took Sara aside.

"You like this boy, Buck, cherie?"

"Yes'm."

"Well, here's my advice. Don't know if you belong together or not, but I 'spect you two pretty much alike. He a good boy. Mr. Cicero, his pa, was in government after the war."

"Buck told me, but I don't believe it."

"Well, things sometimes be true, and this be some times. Besides, I 'spect you know about his uncle down in Mound Bayou?"

Sara nodded.

"Only problem I see, Sara, is you still young—him too. And that mean y'all got lots of growin' up to do whether you together or not. Think you can make a home for your man?"

Sara blushed.

"Reason I ask is you got to be sure you can stand the company he gonna keep. In this world, it's more likely you keep his company than him keep yours, though I ain't sayin' that's the right way for things to be . . . Coming into this swamp can be upsettin'. You don't know nobody, and you meet a group of folks like us . . ."

Sara's face dropped in embarrassment.

". . . We all got to live, cherie. Me'n you an' all the rest of these people. Not all women raised to be the kinda woman I expect Buck want. You could be that woman, but you got to look to some changes in your thinkin'. There ain't no trash people in the world, not even white trash. Life hard. We cain't waste the people we lucky 'nough to come in friendly touch with 'cause they different from us. You make sure they got the right slant on life, that they respect theyself'n others and they generous, helpin' people."

Rose embraced Sara, who smiled tentatively as Rose led her back to the others.

"Bill? Where you, Bill? . . . Lookit! He ain't in no condition to walk nowhere tonight."

When Bill made no answer, Jasper left Mabel's side and poked Bill with his foot, but he still did not move. Frantic,

Jasper scurried over on his knees and grasped the old man's head. It rolled back lifeless.

Jasper screamed so loud every head in the vicinity snapped toward him. Cicero was startled awake and tried to kick away whatever had awakened him. Rose lay her hands on him until their eyes met, but she said nothing. Cicero then sat up in time for Jasper to groan out, "Don't goooo!" It was all he said, before giving way for the first time in his adult life to tears. Rose remained silent, as if she had suddenly become estranged from the world around her, as Mabel ran to Jasper's side and threw her arms around him. He did not resist, and he sat cradling Bill's lifeless body as sadness continued its sway.

"Would you help, me, Miz Mabel," Rose said.

"Don't have to ask," was the answer.

Mabel gently pried Jasper's arms from around the old man as Rose knelt beside the deceased. Her fingers caressed his forehead to smooth away a certain look of surprise on Old Bill's face.

Rose sent Dick to the Sunflower for a couple buckets of water. As was done, the front door of the cabin was unhinged and laid on the ground a distance from the cabin, but within the glowing light of the fire. Jasper, who had pulled Bill's body home, now placed it onto the door and out of the dirt so it could be prepared for burial. As soon as Dick returned with water, Rose immediately washed the body and left it uncovered to dry.

Buck departed with Sara, just before Dick left. Cicero had gone to sleep again. Mabel consented to stay the night because of the death, and Jasper walked her to his cabin. So Rose ended up sitting alone with the first death in her family, and she was full of equal parts sadness and apprehension. She thought of going into dreamtime but decided against doing anything that might disturb the thoughts coming as they were. Tired already from preparing the meal to celebrate Buck and Sara coming together, and then Bill's remains, she was soon dozing with her back against the cabin, and as her consciousness receded, the rest came forward. She dreamt of incomplete places and thoughts, until her mother, Songhai, emerged in a Louisiana fog that swirled over the rocky promontory of Land's End where Rose had been raised. Songhai's voice issued from the mist.

"You are the connection. Do not forget . . . "

Rose tried but could not speak.

". . . Songhai is my name, but you have forgotten my face. What will your children know and their children, if *you* forget."

That next morning, Rose could recall her dream vividly. Sadly though, she couldn't call Songhai's face to mind, and she remembered that Cicero had had the same experience of forgetting what his father looked like. She looked down at Bill's empty and lifeless face. Who would know of the trails he'd walked, of his life among so many including people of his mother, most especially of the treachery he had witnessed. Would the soldiers who had marched the Choctaw Nation into Indian Territory remember? Would they teach their children of their own greed? Bill's truth—like that of the slaves marched off ship at Land's End—wouldn't merit even a page in a hidden book touched by a feather duster such as Rose had wielded in her second master's library, in that house built by slaves so felicitously named Bon Place.

There must be children to build a community, came her answer. Only a community gives life to its past. She thought of her brief time with Cicero's child; she was almost certain of it, but at the time, Cicero was caught up in his land boycott outside the swamp as if that were his world of choice. So, with great sadness, she had eaten the bitter berries, and what might have been was no more. In the muddle of purpose surrounding that act of long ago, she sensed through a logic of her own that she had lost Songhai's face. Sore in conscience she resolved that she would lose no more of the past. Through her three grown boys, now, she would have children, and they would tell of what she told them, her truth, Bill's truth. Cicero would write it all down.

"I'm sorry," Cicero said crawling to her side. "I must have dozed off last night."

"Hush, cherie. Ain't nothin' deserve blame. He just gone."

"But I wanted to wait up out of respect. Bill told us so much. I hardly know where to begin his story."

Rose looked at the papers in Cicero's hand.

"Come on walk with me, Cicero."

"Where we going?"

"Oh," she said caressing his cheek, "I never realized how your truth and mine would become one. Your book, your memories—even a swamp woman deserves having her story told."

"Well—"

"Shhh, put them papers down'n take off your glasses. Let's go find us some new sun before we come back and pick up these old lives."

For the next weeks, Cicero would have one thing on his mind, his memoirs. Instead of venison and pork, he and Rose would roast turkeys as Cicero shot them for writing quills. Ink was made from lampblack and soot mixed with water and set open to evaporate to the proper consistency. Begun back during the occupation of Davis Bend by the Union, Cicero had started a personal journal to keep track of the many displaced slaves interned there who wanted to have a single place to which all could send others seeking to link up. This was before Cicero was hired to do essentially the same thing for the Navy. Afterward, however, it had seemed perfectly logical for Cicero to take each member of his extended family—including the Montgomery family, other slaves left from the days before freedom, even Rose and Jasper after they arrived at Davis Bend—and he began a family tree. Next had come the asides and comments noted in margins, and finally, as Cicero learned that his work for the Union Navy was being called Mr. Cicero's

Book, he decided that he would indeed write his own book, however many years it might take, and he would tell the stories of all of the human beings he had loved or who had loved him, no matter how intimate or distant the relation.

For the next week, Cicero poured over what he had written, and then he began to bring up to date the stories of Isaiah Montgomery and his people from the old plantation. There was more to be written about Buck and Dick, even about Dick's father JD, who already had merited his own page from the time Abyssinia had prevailed upon Cicero to go meet the man and become Dick's tutor. Finally, Old Bill—Cicero had never written about him. Strange, it seemed to him now, but it was an omission that leaked sadness for Bill was no longer around to answer all the questions Cicero had.

Like the season of flood, memories rose up and overwhelmed Cicero. He ignored chores around the cabin and served only his work, the human stories, giving very little attention to the political lessons that had seemed so important in the time right after coming into the swamp. Now, the political fight would have to be the focus of other, younger generations of dragonflies or whatever they might call themselves because even names for his people, he sensed, were works of art, creative expressions of origin, often humor or anger, sometimes affection. Cicero hoped that those of his son Buck's generation would honor their connections, though he had his doubts. To Cicero as a young man had come the high tide time of a people in action upon freedom, followed by a time of people as a group doing nothing, whether out of fear or, more damning, out of misunderstanding the world in which they lived, where a handful of tokens like the Montgomerys gave rise to the illusion that something like an integration of the races—if not rich and poor—was underway. Progress came to mean looking up at a handful of success stories, and in but one generation, youngsters like Buck had come to worship only the dollar. In the meandering trail of

Cicero's life, Rose had become the rock to which it was his privilege to cling, her sense of things, her rock hard certainty. Memory. Not to be owned but shared, all that a people could be, not the big houses or buildings of commerce or public monuments to small empires. The worth of life lay in memory. Those who would not keep the past sacred would soon think less of themselves. And that, Cicero suspected, would be the most bitter lesson that Buck and generations later would taste.

The morning after Old Bill's death, Dick had awakened as Buck threw open the door of their cabin with a demon of a smile on his face. He leapt onto his cane frame bed and yelled. "Love!" at the top of his lungs. Dick lurched up.

"Damnit, nigga! I'm tryin' to sleep!"

"Now you say nigga' like you supposed to."

Dick lay back grumbling. Buck jumped on top, pinning him underneath his blanket while rubbing hands all over Dick's face.

"Smell that, boy that's love! It's looooove!"

"'Tis what I figured when you didn't come home. Finally got some, eh?"

"Hey, I don't go to no old lady for nothin'.."

"And I say, if you ain't got it 'til now, you ain't no man atall."

"I'm man enough to get some from your woman. You want to wager?"

"Wager what?" Dick asked.

"Lets say, whatever we get from the timber we sell."

"You got a bet you gonna lose, cousin. A quick nature, like a rooster, ain't what a woman want."

"You think so, hunh? Well, Dickie boy, I got 'nough nature left to go out right now an' chop down a tree 'fore you can get half through."

"Like hell!"

Buck hopped up and released his cousin.

"Then get up off your ass and git your axe."

It was overcast when they set out, but that mattered little. The wager became a fever. Buck demanded spring-boarding on the Sunflower. No simple axe contest was good enough, and Dick agreed. Carrying a plank to stand on—the springboard—the cousins reached the river and pulled their boat out of hiding as thunderheads began mounding up in the sky.

"Look like rain," Dick said, sitting in the boat they'd tied off shore waiting for the current to take them to tether's end.

"You want out of this bet?" Buck said. "You know you gonna lose."

They floated past the chosen tree to cut. The rope on the boat was too long.

"Untie the rope!" Dick said. "Tie us to the damn tree we'll cut."

"A falling tree could break-up this boat."

"You the one scaird. You want out?"

"Hell, no!"

In the devil-may-care logger's game, two men perch on opposite ends of a long board wedged into a notch cut into a tree in the river while sawing instead of chopping down that very tree. Last one off the plank when the tree topples over, wins—if he survives. Like modern day Russian Roulette, the game could be deadly. The tree might fall in the wrong direction or a dive to escape it not be deep enough.

Within a half hour, the two had tied off their boat, notched the tree trunk with axes and wedged in their board with shims. Gingerly, after stripping to their underwear, they climbed out of the boat onto opposite ends of the plank. When it began slipping, they had to scramble back into their boat. They now wedged a short piece of another board under the first, and they pounded it in tight. Remounting the springboard, they eased the big, two-man ripsaw out of the boat and tried to make a first cut so that the saw would rest in the cut tree. But it was awkward going because the board was the same length as the saw, and neither man could get body leverage into his stroke.

After they finally nicked the tree bark and cut a niche for the saw blade to rest in, the contest began in earnest. Back and forth they struggled with the saw, but lack of leverage still foiled progress. Instead of facing each other at the end of the blade, they had to stand alongside the saw, which forced first one then the other into a balancing act when it was thrust in his direction. Back and forth, the saw moved, biting very little wood. A half hour later, they called a truce and rested their aching arms. From a jug in the boat, they took liquid fortification against both pain and the dismal day. As soon as the liquor struck Dick's brain, he leapt atop the springboard to dance.

"You cain't dance worth a damn," Buck said. "Watch this!"

He grasped the end of the board and eased himself out of the boat directly into a handstand. He then vaulted up with a spring of the board and, with a triumphant yell, dropped upside down into the river. A small barge was approaching. Its crew hooted at Dick's frantic efforts to stand on his hands.

"Goddammit! Lets get this over with," Dick said, pulling himself out of the river and back onto the springboard.

The contest started up again, but also rain. Pulling the saw back and forth as rain wet the cut turned each stroke into agony, and the cousins finally had to give up. Dog tired, they collapsed in their boat, and the contest ended, but not before they took turns pissing at each other.

Jasper was watching. He had been preparing to haul Bill William's shrouded body to a place in the low hills southwest of the swamp that Bill had selected. Because his destination was across the Yazoo River, Jasper had come seeking Dick's help. The sound of a saw had led him to where he now was, spying, waiting for the rain to slack off. When it did, he stepped forward, just as Dick tried to jump ashore.

"Break your goddamn neck!" he commanded, startling Dick, who fell into the river . "Both of you, get in here. I got somethin' to say."

The cousins struggled ashore and into wet clothes. Jasper towered over them, waiting.

"Buck . . . Dick, you be welcome to my home just like Mr. Cicero, but he older'n me and don't play round. Now, I was young as you once, too, so I ain't forgittin' how it is. But I wasn't plain stupid. Don't never cut on nothin' around here. Don't leave no mark less'n you doin' it for a good reason. These trees the walls o' my house. Cain't have no hideaway without trees. Y'all agree? . . . 'Cause it open for discussion. But if y'all don't agree, you got to move on somewhere's else. *That* ain't open to discussion."

Dick said nothing. From embarrassment, his feelings leapt the gulf of guilt into anger, but he feared Jasper. So he remained quiet, staring at the ground.

"Y'all got nothin' to say?"

"We sorry 'bout the tree," Buck said. "It was just a bet."

"Don't make no difference. You cut down one tree, pretty soon you cut down the rest, non? Then where my home be at?"

"Me'n Dick want to do some logging. I figure you want us to do something steadda hangin' around all the time."

"Non, non! I don't care 'bout hangin' aroun'. It ain't my food you eatin'. Keep your hands off these trees."

"Thinkin', we was, to cut over back of our cabin beyond Dry Bayou," Dick said. "Close to Alligator as possible . . . or north toward the Bobo place."

"Alright by me, but ain't much roun' there but leavin's, and most that land claimed by somebody or another."

"Below the Hushpuckena, then?" Buck said. "Over by Little Mound Bayou so's we can float it down to the town? How 'bout that?"

"That's your business. Long as you fellas keep off the trees north of that river."

Jasper then turned and disappeared. He'd been there one minute, then he was gone. Dick and Buck picked up their gear, pulled their boat ashore and secured it. Tired and dispirited they walked home dragging axes and the saw. They were lying in bed before they began talking again.

"Buck Morgan?"

"Yeah."

"We ain't been havin' no fun together. Why don't you come visit Matilda's like you been wantin'. Sara don't haveta know."

"I don't need one of them old ladies at her place. I got plenty."

"Don't haveta lie about Sara. I know she was holdin' out. Women work in Matilda's know what's what. That nature you got stored up gonna git me kilt fightin' big ole Jasper."

"You lyin', nigga. You ain't man enough for that."

"Well, maybe I let him slide 'cause o' Mr. Cicero," Dick said.

"You the one cock-strong. Stuff you gettin' ain't no good. That's why you near crazy 'nough to jump on Jasper."

Dick turned away, but Buck continued.

"Listen, Dick. If you change your manners a little, you could hook up with one of Sara's friends. They good lookin'."

"Them tryin-to-be-lady types ain't for me."

"Whatcha think if I was to git married?"

"Suit yourself."

"You sound mad about somethin'?" Buck said.

"I got my friends, too."

"That old lady-stuff got you messin' with Jasper. I hear you been pickin' at the white folks, too."

GARGOYLES IN BAS RELIEF HAD been carved into the green marble facing of the ground floor lobby, depictions of demons chosen for no clear reason but done richly and with intricate detail as if, if not in worship of inhuman powers, then some acknowledgment that the only ruling inspiration within the edifice was Mammon, man-made and born of greed, the nether divinity equally worshipped by the rich and by those having nothing. The bizarre figures were repeated above the elevators and on each and every floor of the tower of the building. Glimpses of brass cuspidors and a rich tobacco smell issued from hidden corridors as the open elevator cage ascended past doors creaking open and slamming. Glass and shiny red wood doors, metal fire doors, rough wood doors— all marked 'Illinois Central Railroad'. The name was even more conspicuous in gold across the double rosewood doors of the chairman's office as Irving Urbaniak stepped off at the top floor.

The Illinois Central office had always struck Banyak as pretentious, but then, everything about big business was. There were performances within performances for lesser or greater bosses, for the benefit of those who bought the train tickets to ride, to keep the shippers of wheat, bacon, steel, carriages, and newsprint from complaining about tariffs. Finally, there were staged readings for shareholders who applauded only profit. His own coming performance was thanks to a boss above him who didn't want failure to sell swamp land on his record, so he'd signed off on Banyak's suggestion that selling such land was an unsavory business that ought to be done by "those kinds of people."

Banyak had dressed in a new blue wool suit for this the biggest performance of his life. Coming to fruition were years of dreaming and planning while putting up with being treated like an unworthy immigrant, years of dropping hints followed by carefully thought-out propositions to bribable minions above him who had carried his ideas to higher ups. He had been cursed, challenged and dismissed scornfully until one man demanded a written proposal, and that had led to a contract drafted by lawyers. Illinois Central Land Associates had convinced the railroad, in principle, to grant exclusive rights to dispose of Mississippi swampland in Tunica, Coahoma, Bolivar and Washington Counties—though most of the land lay in the latter two. It was no sweetheart deal. A strict schedule of payments to the railroad had to be met or all rights to the land would revert to the railroad. The land company had one clear opportunity: to sell fast and to sell dear, plowing every penny of the initial year of selling into paying off loans and dividend rights of bondholders on top of scheduled payments to the railroad.

Nonetheless the concept had been considered do-able by the best financial minds Irving Urbaniak had been able to consult. From the beginning, the simple logic of his plan had led his advisors to point him in the direction of both the investors he needed to make the initial payment to the Illinois Central Railroad and to others who had explained how banks and insurance companies would figure in the equation.

The people backing Illinois Central Land Associates were betting that a new wave of immigrants even then being signed up by the Railroad to harvest timber on swamp land would mostly remain and make Mississippi home as had so many

Union soldiers following the end of the Civil War. During and after the timber harvesting, those people would be hungry for opportunity, and that meant buying swampland. The railroad wouldn't encourage its workers to quit, but Irving Urbaniak's real estate company wouldn't hesitate to do so. That much his bankers were betting on, but Banyak had admitted to no one other than Chester Bolls what his real view of the market for land in Mississippi was.

As of Friday the week past, he was no longer an employee of the railroad. He was now president of Illinois Central Land Associates, and Chester Bolls was his Special Assistant. Today's meeting with the chairman of the railroad was ceremonial, and Banyak was eager to have it over. He would smile and shake hands, pose for photographs and be introduced to officials of the railroad he had never met. His time was limited by a scheduled meeting with a major insurance company that had agreed to make loans to railroad employees desiring to buy land. Banyak had not explained that he was no longer a railroad employee or that Illinois Central Land Associates was not owned by the Illinois Central Railroad. This was a key piece of the puzzle: an insurance company keen on investing in high interest mortgages. That way, Banyak's venture wouldn't have to wait for time payment from penniless buyers to get its money out of the land.

"We're ready for you, Mr. Urbaniak," announced an unsmiling woman with white hair and pence nez.

Banyak paused for a deep breath.

"Come along, sir. The Chairman's schedule is tight. Immigrants mustn't be found unpunctual."

Irving Pilsen Urbaniak put on his best smile.

Later that same week, in Memphis, Irving Urbaniak stood in another more modest office, that of his own Illinois Central Land Associates.

"I went a little overboard, Chester. Brass fitting on the gas lighting, dark wood paneling and furniture—that was what made me choose this building. Around the walls I had those little cubicles built for our files. We'll keep a copy of every deed issued from here, send the original to the county recorders in Mississippi, another copy to New York."

Chester Bolls nodded toward his boss as a woman in starched blouse and tight little knotted tie smiled up from a desk for four identically dressed women busy making entries in ledger books. Chester took his boss' arm and led him a discrete distance away.

"They work for practically nothing," Chester Bolls said, "compared to what the men keeping books and such want."

"You've done well. Look for the people cain't git nowhere without you, and they think you a king for giving them a job. All of the people working here like you."

They were in downtown Memphis, Tennessee, on the second floor of a building built with a nod to Gothic style, but only four floors high and more of a warehouse than a soaring cathedral. Its exterior was gray stone block arrayed in arches over the central entry way and ground floor windows. On floors above ground, wooden-framed windows that could be pulled up for air admitted welcome light into the work space where everyone worked out in the open. Illinois Central Land Associates occupied the rear quarter of the second floor, around and behind a central core of stairways and arching roof skylight.

"Damn, boss, I'm nervous."

"Don't be. Everything is legal. You have a small piece, and I have fifteen percent of Illinois Central Land Associates. The bankers are holding rest of the stock to secure their measly little money. Our bondholders who put up rest of the money can buy the stock when we are a success."

"Lordy, but we git paid, don't we?"

"Yes, my friend. And handsomely. Bonuses when company meets sales targets. I am here to tell you that we will do it. We will make so much money, I don't care who own the stock, and you need to know, I don't give a damn who we have to run-over to peddle that land."

They entered an enclosed area Banyak considered his personal office, and he thumped his fist on a desk.

"I been practicing, Chester—pounding a desk and lighting up a cigar, things de capitalists do."

Both men smiled when Banyak planted a long cigar between his teeth and strutted over to the window while hooking his fingers behind his suspenders. As he stared out, Chester Bolls spoke to his back.

"Could I give a job to some people I know?"

"Sales jobs?"

"Yes."

"Now, Chester, like I told you, nobody local in sales. Not from Memphis, not Mississippi."

"But why not?"

"Because who would know their loyalty? They might talk to de railroad, local plantation people. Deal is still too delicate. We don't want nobody knowing our plans. After a year, we can hire your friends."

"Tell me agin' why we got to wait?"

"Men from Chicago will sell to who I tell them. They are smooth, experienced salesmen—including some colored ones. I don't know how we'd go about finding people with those skills down here, and even if we could, hiring local would give away our secret too soon. I want salespeople on every Illinois Central train busy selling land before I get my first complaint about us selling swamp land to the colored people."

"You sure that ain't gonna come back and bite us in the tail?"

"Nothing is certain, Chester, but, we make the money while we can. Immigrants and colored will pay top price. They buy from us, or they got to sharecrop. So if we dare to sell to them, they going to pay our price."

"How we git on this crusade to change the world?"

"No, no, we are not. It is the poor people who buy from us who will say we are crusaders. They hear about us selling to them, and they think we love them. They even going to tell their friends about us. All the little people trapped down in the Mississippi Valley, if they got a little gumption, they come to us . . . And they thank us for taking their money."

"Where their money gonna come from?"

"A good salesman can tell in a minute if a man been working hard all his life. Hard workers pay a little less than the whole down payment as long as we get enough from them or from the mortgage company to pay the railroad. All the installment payments is profit, plus big interest. Oh . . . I am so excited, Chester. You been good luck to me."

"I just hope we don't get lynched."

"If stupid minds don't like what we are doing we explain that de swamp land only going to last a few years. If de ones complaining offer to buy the land instead, fine. If not, I tell 'em leave us alone."

"They ain't gonna like that."

"They got their law and their Klan to push de colored around. We all gouging hell out of people."

Sara was holding her stomach against every jolting step of the old mule. It and the one Buck was riding were a team Dick now kept behind their cabin, and because the trail down into the swamp to Rose and Cicero's cabin had not been cut, there was almost a mile of cane break to pass through, and the winter-hardened leaves slashed at Sara's face. Nine months had passed since Bill Williams' death, and Sara was pregnant, hugely so, given her small stature.

Mrs. Wiggins had been embarrassed beyond belief after Sara could no long swaddle herself up and pretend that she was just dressing oddly. Someone mentioned the Wiggins' daughter's condition to Mr. Bobo, and he came with lascivious harassment, gloating and reminding Sara's mother that her daughter had now proven herself as eager a vixen as Mrs. Wiggins had been as a girl upon meeting her bush monkey man. The ribald scorn heaped upon one laboring to make something of herself, one whose very value as a person slavery had cast in doubt, lead Mrs. Wiggins to scream at Sara, who slapped her mother for yelling, only to prompt the older woman to shove her daughter outside and bar the door. Sara took shelter in the kitchen shack until her sister could go find the trail to Buck and Dick's cabin and return riding mules with Buck.

Cicero was transfixed as he watched Sara ride toward his cabin so full of life. He was not eager to say anything because Buck had reacted so angrily when Cicero asked about Sara's condition before Buck brought her in to meet them all. He stood silently as Rose stepped out of the cabin and joined him in front of a yard fire they'd kept burning on a whim, to avoid kindling a fire in the hearth so they could enjoy sleeping under Rose's huge quilts in a chill room.

"Take some fire inside, Cicero. We need to warm the place up."

"Hello, daddy."

"Hello, son."

"Uh . . . Me'n Sara didn't have nowhere to go."

Rose moved to help Sara dismount, and as soon as the young woman's feet touched ground she began weeping.

"Oh, Momma Rose, I'm sorry."

"About what, cherie? About what?"

"Oh, everything! This baby . . . I didn't mean no wrong."

"'Course not, cherie. Buck, you help Cicero build a fire inside."

"Yes'm."

"I think," Cicero said, "that baby can't be long from coming. Boy, why you wait so long?"

"Ignore him, Buck," Rose said. "He's more nervous than you. Soon as you finish making that fire, Cicero, I want you to haul all of our wood and leave it right outside the door where I can get at it."

"Why do you want—"

"Hush. Just do it. I'm gonna ask you to go stay a few days with Jasper while I tend Sara."

After the fire was built inside, and the cabin had become toasty, the wood stacked close, and water brought up from the river because the rainwater barrel was always low as winter came on, Cicero stuck his head in the door and saw Rose massaging Sara's swollen legs with camphor. The smell was like a talisman warning against male intrusion.

"Buck and I are off. Sure you don't need help?"

"No. I've done this more than a couple times. All these years, babies got born, and I was sometimes the oldest woman. So, no. You'n Buck be off—and don't worry, Buck."

"Yes'm"

"Don't be so scared."

"No'm."

"Cicero?" Rose asked with laughter in her voice. "What if this was you'n me?"

Cicero did not respond immediately.

"Think on that while you at Jasper's," Rose said. "When this is over, we go into dreamtime together."

Rose laughed so heartily that Buck was perplexed. He looked toward his father for some explanation.

"Nothing I could explain very well," Cicero said.

"Rose is kind of a healer, ain't she?"

"Yep. That she is."

"Well, I want to thank you and Rose for helpin'."

Cicero opened his arms. Buck hesitated until Cicero beckoned him close and put his arm around his son's shoulders.

"This is what family is all about," Cicero said to his son as they headed off leading the mules. "We may not always agree, but I will help you anyway I can."

Moments later, inside the cabin, Rose ended her massage. She had rubbed Sara's legs and her arms, and with some resistance, Sara had consented to but not yet taken off her clothes to wrap herself in a sheet warming before the fire. Rose regarded the young woman as she nervously disrobed.

"You got a nice spread behind you, Sara, but your hips ain't so wide."

"What you mean, Momma Rose?"

"I mean, sometimes women with small hips can have trouble letting their babies out. Now, don't worry. I will pull you through, but you need to get real comfortable with me. Don't worry about anything that happens. Women having babies lose control, and I want you to rest much as you can because it may take some time before it's all over."

"Well, I been havin' pains, but Buck said it was the mule bouncin' me up'n down."

"Oh, child, how could you or Buck know anything?"

"We grown, ain't we, Rose?"

"Got nothing to do with bein' grown. This your first baby, and the only kind o' bouncin' up an' down you know about is clear. You ever help one into this world?"

"No'm."

"So, you just relax and listen to me. Now, go on, git outta all them garments, else you ruin 'em."

The afternoon passed, and Sara's labor continued. By the next morning, Rose was nodding off in her rocking chair when Sara let out a wail. Before Rose could respond, Sara's water broke and she was trying to scoot back out of the wetness.

"No problem," Rose said. "We put you on a pallet 'till I can haul that bedding out to dry."

"I'm sorry—"

"Hush, concentrate on your body, what it's telling you."

Late that evening, the baby was born. Sara was exhausted and immediately fell asleep. Rose was frightened because the child never cried. It was alive, but it had a sickly gray pallor to its brownness, and it hardly moved. But he was a lovely child, in his face was all of Sara's pixie prettiness expressed in big pleading eyes and long eye lashes. Rose held the child to her bosom in front of the fire, and she prayed in her own way. It was not a petition; rather, she sat in reposeful openness looking into the child's huge sad eyes, trying to feel the energy of the infant that she sensed was so weak. A snow fall commenced outside, and it was the soft sound of ice crystals coming to earth that roused Rose out of her reverie that next morning.

By the time, Sara awakened, giant snowflakes were floating to earth outside the cabin in a rare and musical silence. For the first time, Sara noticed that each notched timber wall was covered by a new green, red, yellow, or brown patterned quilt that Rose had acquired in trade. The quilts blocked drafts between the logs and made inside cozy. Rose continued to cuddle the child in her rocking chair, though she now turned her back to the fire to allow Sara to watch her infant. Sara smiled and then dropped back off to sleep.

Sara made the cabin home for several months. There was no way to gauge how her mother's feelings might have changed. Rose was as unselfish as any woman young Sara had ever met, and through Rose's demeanor, Sara began to sense that there might be something to the value her own father placed in what he called "the worth o' good folks" that had nothing to do with table manners and a sense of dress. Not that Sara had not been raised to be polite. That she surely was, but she had her mother's sense that there were those who would be the salvation of the race, and then there were all the rest, those with whom people trying to get ahead were afflicted.

As far as the new baby was concerned, there continued to be a feeling of weakness about it. Rose held it and talked to it day and night to give it strength while Sara rested to increase her milk. Cicero—at Rose's suggestion—was having an extended visit down in Mound Bayou with Abyssinia. The infant was the answer to Rose's prayers, the beginning of a new generation beyond Buck and Sara. True to her vow upon Bill's death, she told the baby all sorts of things, some momentous, some not. Sometimes, it was of her mouth-pain from teeth Cicero wanted to pull, once of stringy sweet potatoes Jasper left at her door. She never tired of confessing her happiness that Little Buck listened so well without crying.

"Evenin', Sara. That was some nap. You been sleepin since you fed the boy at noon. Come on get him. He hungry."

Sara leaned forward and took the child into bed. She rested a small but burgeoning breast in its mouth, and when the sucking commenced, she grew enthusiastic.

"I was dreamin', Rose."

"You don't say."

"Yes'm, about my reward for that hard labor."

"Sure was hard, child. Too bad your momma wasn't with you."

"But we made up, her and me. Buck say she ain't mad no more about me havin' this baby. And this year gonna bring so many good things. My brother and Buck be finished with our house, and I'm gonna make him a home so wonderful he won't have no trouble giving up life with that wild Dick Dolan."

"I wonder about your Buck sometimes, why he puts so much effort where he does."

"He got ambition. We gonna have three bedrooms, a kitchen, living room and a dining room, and it be built with store-bought lumber."

"I'm glad you over your embarrassment. No reason you to feel ashamed cause Buck Jr. arrived so soon."

"Yes'm, and Buck say everybody at the Quarters now agree I done well by myself. I helped daddy'n Jeff out, too."

"You or Buck doin' that?"

"Buck, I guess."

"I'm makin' fun, child. After layin' your shame to rest, don't pick up another burden."

"What you mean?"

"Don't you nor Buck have a thing to prove."

"I ain't follow your meanin', Momma Rose."

"Just rest up, you doin' alright."

Sara relaxed. She was doing alright, indeed, not only herself, but her family, too, her wildest dreams for everyone coming true. In return for help building Buck and Sara's house,

Buck had loaned Sara's brother a down payment on land near Mound Bayou, and the agreement was that in the fall, Jeff, Buck and Mr. Wiggins would begin clearing it. Her father had plans to move the family down in the spring and to build a two-family house. Jeff was sharing Buck and Dick's cabin to be near Buck's home site on the west end of Dry Bayou. At Jeff's belated wedding, their father had cried.

"Worked like a fool, me. Didn't really think it amount to much, but it did. Y'all kids done good, an' I'm mighty proud. Folks in the Quarter proud, too. They happy y'all got away to somethin'."

"Whatcha thinkin' 'bout, cherie?" Rose said, watching the far-away expression on Sara's face.

"Hunh?"

"Your face like a baby with honey in her mouth."

"Just thinkin' about my new house, and my baby."

Rose walked over and stooped to stroke the infant's cheek as he clucked and smacked violently against his mother's breast.

"Lookit!" Rose said. "Got a willful streak in him."

"Yes'm. It's his big head, Buck think. Say he got a lot o' Mr. Cicero in him."

"Sure got his big head, alright. Listen, Sara, you a natch'aly good mother, but you need to make Buck help you raise this child."

"Whatcha mean, Rose?"

"You'n Buck got no reason to live like me and Mr. Cicero do. Generation 'tween us. But when folks get together so quick like y'all, it's blood talkin'."

"How many other girls got a man buildin' a house like Buck doin'?"

"You gonna sit home and let that man run like him and Dick been doin' last few years?"

"No'm, I ain't."

"How you gonna stop him? How he keep you from liftin' your dress to the first nigga come 'long when you mad at him? Tell me that."

Such openness put a frown on Sara's face. The obvious answer was that she and Buck were in love. He loved her and she him. What better proof than the baby she'd presented him with. What better proof of his love than seven-day work-weeks to finish their house and to help out her relatives?

"Ain't tryin' to be your momma," Rose said. "Just that I seen men'n women fight each other because neither one give much thought to what they really wanted outta life."

"I got everything I'm s'posed to have. Ain't nothing goin' wrong, God willin'."

"*God* willin? . . . Cherie, its things in *this* world—mainly white folks—you got to worry 'bout. They can make your man a cripple, lynch him or take his heart away. That's why we all out here. That god you talkin' 'bout bein' willin'—that's the white folk's god."

"You ain't a Christian woman, Momma Rose?"

"I a Africa woman—here, where my life is. Cain't tell you where my ma or my pa come from. Little I do know come from a woman named Songhai. That's a Africa name from 'cross the sea. They got a Great God, too, though I don't remember his name. I like to think of that one as my god . . ." She clasped Sara's face in her hands. ". . . One thing you ought to learn about me'n Cicero an' Jasper. Most of what we learned from white folks wasn't fit for nothin' but makin' good slaves. Here, I pray to the Africa god over all the people, even the white folks."

"Miz Mabel a Christian lady, ain't she?"

Rose nodded, but ambiguously.

"Somethin' wrong with her?"

"I hope she talk my boy into makin' a home be good for both of 'em." Rose pulled her shawl onto her shoulders against a chill. "She more Christian than you, and she older and she been through a lot. Lost her husband when a tree fell on him. Her religion took up more time and got stronger to carry her through. 'Spect now that she got holdta Jasper, she have somethin' to put that religion in its place."

The baby was blowing milk bubbles. His head had dropped away from Sara's breast in sleep. Rose stepped from the bed and stretched, then moved to the window to watch the snow.

"You got to fight that man of yours, if it come to that. Teach him 'bout home life if that's what you want. Buck be easier to deal with than that Winchesta Man. Whoeeeee, the women keep after him, an' he ain't never had no home life to speak of."

"Buck want to be a big man, Momma Rose, like his uncle in Mound Bayou. I want him to be one, too. That make him work hard and stay home lots."

"Just make sure you'n him agree. Forgit about what's right. It's you two got to be together, non? And that mean you better not forgit that talk we had first time I laid eyes on you."

Sara was grinning.

"You remember, now!"

"I will."

Rose took up her pipe, looked at the baby and lay the pipe back down. Instead, she reached the whiskey jug from under the table and grunted toward Sara who vigorously signaled, no.

"Still don't hold with ladies drinkin'?"

"Oh, no, Momma Rose. It's alright."

"You best get in the habit o' comin' clean about what you thinkin'. Right or wrong, you only got one life."

The infant fell asleep again, and as on most afternoons, Sara soon joined him. Rose hummed and rocked in her chair. The snow fell softly.

By SUMMER, BUCK HAD ALMOST finished the new house. It sat less than a mile west and a little north from the cabin he and Dick had shared. Buck had spent so little time with Sara that she began insisting on traveling, baby in a sling on her back, between Mound Bayou and her home whenever Buck did. The child became fretful, given to crying and small rages. Most times, a quick feeding was all that was needed, but Sara, who was nursing, refused to nurse along the road. Buck finally objected to bringing the baby along with them, but Sara insisted that she and her baby belonged at the side of her man. Unlike Sara who cared for the infant day in and out, the infant's fragility frightened Buck, especially when the baby screamed at the top of his lungs. He went and consulted Rose

"The child ain't sick, but he is weakly. Life is like that, different for all, valuable for every one."

"But isn't there something we could do?"

"I don't think so, cherie, aside from feedin' the boy on time, makin' sure he git rest. You'n Sara both seem real busy."

"We got so much we doin'. You know about my new house, Sara's family movin' to Mound Bayou?"

"I do know."

"Well, we keep pretty busy."

"Your father and I would love to keep our grandson with us."

"Hanh? Your grandson—oh, yeah."

"Well. What about it? You'n Sara only have one life."

"Let me talk to Sara first 'cause she is one fierce woman about this child."

Rose chuckled.

"So, what you recommend I do to make Little Buck well?"

Rose opened her hands and shrugged.

"Life keeps its own counsel."

Buck had no idea what Rose meant, and feeling somewhat ungrateful for refusing Rose's offer to board his son, Buck kept trying to understand what life keeping its own counsel meant. That led him to Cicero. Despite Sara and the baby spending months living in the cabin with Rose, the distance between Buck and his father had not closed, though they were polite on both sides.

"Can I ask you something?"

"Anytime, son."

"Umm, I asked Rose about Little Buck, and maybe I did something wrong."

"What did you do?"

"I didn't do nothing."

"So what is the problem?"

"She said something about life keeps its own counsel."

"She said that?"

"Yep. And you know Little Buck been weakly, so . . . I just wondered what she mean by that."

"Maybe you oughtta spend more time with my new grandson."

"When I can, but you know—"

"You're busy."

"Yeah, I got my house, the Wiggins' house, the lumber business—ain't but one of me."

"So, why don't you ease up a bit. Spend more time with Sara and your son."

"I do what I can, but I don't want to live like you. I want to get ahead in the world."

"Well, I was young once, and I did not spend as much time with you as I might have. You were born right when the conspiracy started to turn black folks away from voting. Lots of lynching and shootings . . . I thought I had too many important meetings and such."

"Oh, daddy, it ain't like that. People depend on me, the whole Wiggins family."

"Well, life keeps its own counsel . . . Bring Little Buck to his grandpa whenever you and Sara need us."

"Okay, he be through nursing soon."

Meanwhile, as Buck and Sara occupied the new house, Dick shifted his sights from a cooked meal at Momma Rose's to Buck and Sara's table, and Sara resisted. When the two men's drinking began encroaching on Buck's free time—now that his work was reduced to helping clear the timber on her brother's land—she and Buck had their first argument.

Afterward, smarting from the bruise to his boyish fantasy of Sara the perfect wife, Buck made the rounds with Dick of some of their old haunts and, for the first time, Miz Matilda's Social Club. Because the club was in the Quarters, which was a small community, a girlfriend of Sara's saw them enter, and she told. Sara stewed in silence, debating whether to go have another talk with Rose, whose predictions about married life seemed amazingly accurate. A week later, Buck announced he'd invited Dick and Matilda to supper.

"I'll not have a woman like that in this house. All people don't mix."

"What kinda talk is that? Some more of what Rose said?"

"I got my own mind, mister. If you want me, *Matilda* don't come in my house. What would your uncle say about a woman like her?"

Buck had no idea that his visit to the Social Club had been reported, that his own conduct was at issue. Instead, he concluded he'd simply never grasped the dimensions of his wife's hostility toward Matilda, and that all squared with what he would always fondly recall of the day Mr. Wiggins walked in on him and Sara. Mother and daughter were straight-laced people. In the wake of his anger, he turned acquiescent, concluding not unhappily that Sara was a snob.

That evening, he knocked at Dick's cabin. Dick, who was napping, reached automatically for his rifle as Buck walked in with his namesake squirming in his arms. It was a warm summer evening, and Buck left the door open.

"Good evenin', Mr. Dick . . . Say 'good evenin,' Little Buck."

Dick grinned as Buck waved the baby's hand toward him.

"First time, I seen you out with your own son. Sara must be gittin' careless."

"Ah, we got a problem, Dick."

Buck sat on the bed that had been his until recently. Dick reached for the writhing infant, and Buck surrendered him.

"Come here, li'l fella. Kiss your uncle."

"Sara don't feel up to cookin' supper Sunday, and she wants you to know she feel sorry and all."

As the words were spoken, the baby slammed a fist into Dick's lips, and he lowered him to the floor. Buck leapt to reclaim the crawling baby who started fretting as soon as he was denied his freedom.

"What's the matter?" Dick said. "Sara mad at me or something?"

"Oh, no."

"Matilda been plannin' on this all week. I mean . . . 'tisn't somethin' you shouldda known, but she didn't want to come anyway. You know how people at the Quarter look down on her business."

The baby screamed as Buck prevented him from reaching the floor again.

"Put the goddamn baby, down. Let him have some fun."

"Floor ain't clean, Dick. He puny kinda."

"Some more o' Sara's tellin' you how to do."

"I got to go right back, Dick."

"Look at yourself. Won't let a baby crawl natural on the floor. That high-hatty wife bring ideas from the Quarter in here'n cause a nice lady to git turned away from supper."

Dick hopped up off his bed and walked outside. Buck followed with the baby.

"Sorry you feel this way, Dick. Sara brought up a lady even though her daddy was a just a slave with no connection. He taught his children to try and be proper."

"Go on home, Buck. No reason for one man to think he better than another 'cause a white man say he scratch his head proper."

Buck sucked in his cheeks and exhaled wearily, then stepped off the porch toward home. Little Buck reached back over his shoulder toward Dick.

"You'n me raised different, Winchester Man. My uncle—"

"Damn your uncle, Buck! What little he got to do with anything ain't good in my mind."

"It ain't easy bein' black in a white man's world. You should know that, by now if not before you come out here. It may seem like Sara's people'n my uncle look down on everybody else, but it ain't so. They ain't lookin' down on nobody. They just holdin' on tight to the fact they ain't common like the white man say . . . Just because a man have to scratch his head for the white man don't mean he cain't live like a proper person. Uncle been raised to let people know he ain't trash."

"So he act high-hatty toward other folks?"

"Ain't no such. Just lettin' other niggas know he ain't trash and ain't gonna stand for no mess."

Dick shook his head and sat on the porch. Buck shifted the baby to his other arm and stepped closer.

"People like uncle are doin' good for a lotta people. They got a right to let folks know it. Niggas like you run out here and live alone and always got somethin' to criticize. Well, it just ain't fair. Some of us—yeah, me too! Some of us willin' to take on a little of the other fella's burden. Don't make it no less of a thing 'cause I make a little money on it. Hell! I deserve it."

"It's all double talk," Dick said. "Life is simple. Act natural, they like you or not. Actin' one way to white people and another to black don't make sense."

"*You* couldn't do that if it wasn't for Africa. You'd have to leave this state."

"May be, but I ain't tryin' to prove nothing to nobody like you and your uncle, and I don't call folks trash."

There was no precedent, no focus in Dick's life that would have led him to ask whether Buck might subtly believe the lies white folks—and a lot of black folks—had been telling all his life, if not about him then about more "common" or "trash" people. Raised to be special and apart, Buck assumed that most others weren't raised to be so special. People like him never questioned the rules of a world where a few became a success and all the rest remained common. To the few, success was a question of character. If Dick had been a student of human nature he might have marveled that a person so persuaded would work and strive endlessly to redeem himself. But for Dick, a man was face, arms, legs and body, and all of it deserved the same fair shake that he gave his mules. That Buck would never erase inside himself whatever spawns lies about people different from one's self, Dick might have agreed, if he'd considered the matter. Though he probably wouldn't have realized that driven people—the Buck Morgans and Isaiah Montgomerys of all nations and tribes—drive the world in various, sometimes predatory directions, as had James Aloysius and a generation of white men before him who had come into the swamp to prove something to those on the infant nation's east coast who were *their* betters, who'd themselves navigated an ocean to escape from their own nemeses a generation earlier. To have believed that, would have made Dick a cynic, and he was too uncomplicated for that.

In face of the distance growing between him and Buck,

Dick became lonely. That and curiosity about James Aloysius, took Dick out to the old plantation again.

"Know you're wonderin' why I popped up," Dick said, "but I sell whiskey now. I need sugar. I can buy it elsewhere, but nowhere convenient as here. And the whiskey you usually sell is pestilential."

"My whiskey's good as any."

"Taste this."

Dick handed his father a flask of Bill's special recipe.

"Liquid delight . . . and you'd be offering this in payment?"

"Delivered at a price of one dollar a gallon."

JD laughed, shook his head, no.

"But this is premium," Dick said, "and if you ain't satisfied I give it to you for seventy-five cents a gallon. Surely you see the beauty of it? You can sell my whisky for two dollars a gallon easy. Else, charge one twenty-five a gallon and still make decent profit."

"Leave the pricin' to me, but I'll accept your proposition. Would you be needin' corn?"

"How much a bushel?" Dick asked.

"Thirty cents is fair?"

"I can get corn for twenty cents and trade common whiskey. No, just sugar."

"Done! . . . Call for it after midnight to avoid trouble."

"What trouble would I cause you?"

"You got a reputation," JD said. "My sable-hued sharecroppers have been heard to brag about your bustin' up a certain fight in Bobo, and they say a white man called you "nigger" outside Cleveland, and you drew on him."

"Aye, the son of a bitch ordered me under a wagon to retrieve his goddamned wife's bonnet."

"You can't act like that, Dick. It ain't the way of a colored man."

"So damn me to hell for it."

"What really happened?" JD asked.

"This here," Dick pulled his pistol, "chased him'n his scrawny-assed wife on their way."

"I'll have no such from you around here."

"Just give me the sugar when I come, a month from today, after midnight."

Almost two months passed before Dick got around to collecting that sugar. Driving a wagon was tricky because if caught unawares he'd loose it and two mules—from the four he now kept in a corral behind his cabin. His father, who'd been sleeping on the porch of the store as he drove up, staggered to the ground.

"Jesus, Mary and Joseph, 'tis a full-grown man you are.

For the first time since leaving home, Dick felt his father's hand on his shoulder.

"Yes I am, pa," Dick said, the word feeling awkward in his mouth.

To avoid his father's touch, he moved away and looked around pretending to be cautious about trouble. He kept a calm face as he accepted the key to the store, but he was in turmoil. James Aloysius was another so-called good white man who would never challenge the evil that made him seem good by comparison. Dick lit the lantern and commenced hefting hundred pound bags of sugar onto his wagon. After the last sack of sugar slammed into place, Dick scrambled aboard and raised his rifle in the air.

"You can stop worryin'. I ain't called the Winchester Man for nothing."

During fall and winter, good and bad whiskey sold for two dollars a gallon as arguments raged over a law to dry up Bolivar County. Merchants—including JD—began stocking and pricing up.

"The people votin' dry claim to be for progress," JD said next time Dick came for sugar. "But the goddamn progress-talkers do their drinkin' like the rest."

"Why all the bitchin' now?"

"A way o' celebratin' the new levees, I'd wager. People at the top want to look good to all the churchy white souls who could settle nearby. There's many a such who'd applaud the Dry's on Sunday mornin'n stand me a drink at the whore house the same night. Business folk say the reputation of this place is in the balance. Land prices'll go up once the government fixes our levees—aye, believe me! 'Tis the politics of it. All's forgiven between North and South, lad—about the War, that is. We got a brand, spankin' new Mississippi Constitution in the makin'— Are you listenin' to me?"

"You're talkin' white folks' talk."

"And what would that be?"

"Politics—constitution. We're no part of it."

"Nay, nay. You've ought but the truth of it. What of the good Isaiah Montgomery? One of the delegates what drew up the new constitution, he was. Him standin' for election brought on your own ruin."

"Don't talk politics to me, 'tis a black man I've become."

"Remember this—white man's land an' free niggers workin' it. North'n South are one. You're not an outlaw on account o' the whiskey you sell. It's because you challenge the order of things. Come away from that Africa. There'll be no more nigger politics in this state."

"You could be wrong. You don't even know how to say 'nigga'."

That year, Bolivar County voted itself dry, and the Winchester Man doubled his customers because out-in-the-open distillers were put out of business. His Winchester Man reputation helped keep the grafters in line, and now that there was so much money in whiskey, he made his peace with the sheriff of Bolivar County as did the other "illegals" whose business was booming. Dick ignored local town constables who generally gave him no trouble. One was shot to death in Cleveland, mysteriously, and no one could prove how or why, but the man had bragged of going after the "white-lookin' whiskey nigger", which only added to the lore of the Winchester Man.

Dick began working double, hauling Buck's timber in between transporting liquor. He was still selling more than ever, taking orders on horseback one trip, filling them the next. Dick squirmed whenever someone would recall that his father was the planter outside of Alligator. Black people usually offered a silence that he learned was common when situations like his came up, and he remembered Buck's reluctance to talk about him looking colored back when they were masquerading, or so they'd thought. White people offered no such courtesy. If momentarily Dick were mistaken for white, faces later turned blank or eyes narrowed with suspicion. Those who recognized him right off drenched him with stares that overlooked any response he made, stares that meanly wounded without a word. To all such—those who acted as if Dick were carrying a secret and monumental sin—his response was anger.

All the wasted anger began to bother Dick. Even as a young man he'd paid little attention to people's opinions. Now that he was black there was a consistency to white folks' behavior, a constancy to their arrogance, and, slowly, Dick came to understand while not accepting, to live in the midst of but still not internalize the insanity and think less of himself. A change did occur, from the warmth not returned, the hate he couldn't ease, the weariness that attended always fighting. He didn't see or feel the change happen, but calluses formed on feelings too often bruised or bottled up. A constant wariness descended over him. To ease hostility inside and outside, he developed a coolness, not always surly but not friendly, ignoring but not ignoring. He dampened down his feelings. Seldom did his behavior betray true feelings anymore. Except where a white man refused to back away from confrontation. When that happened, it was everywhere soon known that the Winchester Man held no life sacred, not even his own

Jasper had not been blind or deaf to all of the sounds of
Buck clearing land and building. His rage was so great,
though—especially in light of his explicit warnings not to cut
trees south of Harris Bayou—that instead of confronting Buck
he complained to Cicero. Rose was at that time already aware
of Sara being pregnant, and she answered her son.

"You agreed the cousins was to build two cabins. Leave 'em
alone. It ain't so big a difference that Buck is buildin' a mansion for his child."

"But momma, it ain't that simple." Jasper turned to Cicero.
"Your boy don't listen, and I do not intend to have somebody
like Verlean in here tryin' to turn my trees into a business."

"I agree," Cicero said, "but this is not about business. It's a
place to live."

Right on the tail of this, Dick told Jasper about the government in Washington hiring men to build levees along the Mississippi River. He had a much greater apprehension than Dick
about what levees meant to his way of life, so he followed Dick
over to take a look. The engineering idea was to completely
pen up the Mississippi with walls of earth hundreds of miles
long from north of Memphis to below New Orleans, to allow
the water to rise but, in theory, to prevent its annual rampages
over the land. It was the early 1890's, and as JD had noted, all
was forgiven between North and South. An army of men was

swarming over places west of Alligator where Dick had played as a youth.

"Old Bill told it. They pen up the river like a fat snake, make the land go dry."

"What're you sayin'?" Dick asked.

"Swamp need water. Them levees'll dry it out. No more runnin' bayous in spring. Things be changin' over where we live."

"Would it make sense to maybe scare 'em a little?"

"Hell, yes! . . . But it got to be all of 'em." Jasper pointed toward hundreds of men working. "We cain't do that, Dick. Ain't enough of us."

"Don't talk that way."

"Progress-talkin' folk takin' water from the land an' whiskey from the people. Buncha goddamn white ants ain't got sense the first. Fuck 'em!"

To the north along the Mississippi, there stretched a scar of earth miles long, the soil in places brown, elsewhere red or gray. It was being dug thirty to forty feet inland from the river's natural shoreline ridge by men with 8 mules in a team. They were plowing the trench deeper and deeper after other men with teams of mules pulling scrapers had piled together the fresh earth for yet other teams of men to haul up and spread along the inland side of the trench. From a pit further inland, tons of gray earth were being hauled by lines of mule-drawn wagons to dump into the bottom of the trench. This was the least porous of soils, a clay that would be heaped into the ditch and mounded over like a seal of caulking at the bottom against a rising river undermining the finished levee with its incredible pressure from below, to make it leprous, to boil it out, make it spring to pieces. Where this work had already been accomplished, other men with steam driven machines were driving trunks of what looked like cypress and fir trees down through the clay seal into undisturbed soil below, to hold the clay in place. Off to the north, from which the men were working south, dirt first plowed up out of the trench was now being dumped on top of the bead of clay into a mound that rose what seemed a hundred feet high to Jasper. Once tamped down, this incredible, endless man-made hill would become the finished levee. Like white ants, Jasper had said, men with wheelbarrows were running everywhere. A tent city crouched barely visible beyond the work. What seemed hundreds of smoke trails rose into the sky from the hive where the antmen would rest, eat and sleep at night. And some of the ants were black.

More than four million acres had been wrestled from Choctaw and other native peoples before Mississippi became a state. Much of it remained pockets of wilderness. The new Mississippi River levees would make that rich land extraordinarily attractive. White people in Clarksdale and Alligator couldn't talk enough about the energy that would be provided by the new immigrants who were expected to be white like themselves and also potential voters who would erode the superior black to white population ratio. For the first time, mortgages were being offered. It had been more than ten years since the railroad first sold land to finance laying track, land often as not returning to the railroad when purchasers failed to pay off the inflated time-price. Forty acres had traded for as little as a rifle or a cow when a homesteader cashed in to move on.

With such matters on his mind, Jasper not only said nothing about Buck's new house, he said nothing about the sporadic timber cutting in the vicinity of Africa that never actually came into the heart of what Jasper considered his swamp. By this time, Jasper had looked upon Buck's new son in Rose's arms, she told Cicero the child so softened Jasper's heart that he'd actually tried to make the sad eyed infant smile, called him Li'l Fella.

Meanwhile, of course, Buck had no knowledge of Illinois Central plans for selling their swamp land, but he was the first to worry about remaining a squatter. Even inside the edge of the swamp, however unlikely, someone might buy his land from under him. While Dick had been busy selling so much whiskey the year before, Buck was in the early stages of executing his own new plan. He hired two men introduced to him by Sara's brother. They had no money or prospects until Buck lured them out toward Africa with wages and the promise of advancing each money for down payment on a piece of land. Both men marked off partially cleared land along the still dirt trail called the Alligator Road that ran parallel to Harris Bayou. Jasper now accepted this trail as the northern boundary of Africa, instead of Harris Bayou less than a hundred yards to the north. Buck steered the newcomers to settle there where technically he didn't have to seek Jasper's permission.

Thus, into Africa came Lemuel Huntwell and Arthur Canada. Ruddy-cheeked, rangy and good-natured, Lem had a face dominated by a spreading nose that seemed twice as large as it should be. A friendly and out-going sort, by the spring of 1893, Sara would invite Lem to visit even when Buck was away from home. Art Canada was in his forties with a bend in his spine from falling off a horse. He was the shy and nervous sparrow he resembled, pointed nose and all with a black birthmark smudge under the right eye. He worked such long hours for Buck on top of clearing his new land that he never socialized. His wife and three children joined him soon after he settled in, an event marked by Rose walking up out of the deep swamp to visit the new woman even though she said nothing to Jasper.

That winter, after a summer of clean-up timbering, Buck, Lem and Art all traveled to the Coahoma County deed recorder in Friar's Point to ask about buying the land they lived on. Unfortunately, the trail outside Buck's house was roughly the north-south line between Bolivar and Coahoma counties. Only the part of Africa to the east was in Coahoma

County. The rest lay in Bolivar County. There never had been a full survey of the swamp thanks to Jasper and Bill scaring people, and the metes and bounds county line descriptions were vague in application.

"Damn it all," Buck said.

"No choice but Rosedale," Lem said. "Me'n Art's land in Bolivar County."

The white man with the eyeshade and neatly buttoned shirt leaned in close.

"Won't do you no good. Gonna git ridda all you niggers ain't workin crops."

Buck was stunned, but he said nothing.

"We got a new Constitution, new laws against nigger vagrants. This whole land openin' up to a new wave o' white folks, thank ye Jesus!"

"What about my land?" Buck asked.

"The swamp you askin' 'bout was ceded to the Memphis and Vicksburg Railroad."

"What you say?"

"Yep. Bought out by the Yazoo and Mississippi Valley. Y'all want land from it?"

"Maybe?"

"Then you got to write the Illinois Central. They own the Yazoo and Mississippi Valley. But they ain't sellin' to the likes o' you."

Two days later, as the sun climbed toward noon, the new men sat outside Buck's house along with Cicero who'd insisted Rose come along.

"Didn't just invite you up to visit your grandson," Buck said. "I wanted to introduce my new men."

"What does that mean?"

"Daddy, it just mean, they new, and sometime they work for me. Art'n Lem gonna own they own land. That's what I wanted you to know."

"What do you want?"

"You know things I don't. We been up to Friars Point, and the man say the Railroad own everything west of the Sunflower?"

"Our swamp?"

"Best I can figure," Buck said.

"But they haven't sold it to anybody yet?" Cicero asked.

"Don't think so. The old white man in the land office probably would have mentioned it."

"Forgot to ask," Dick said, "such a tiny detail, did you?"

"Far as I know they ain't sold nothin'," Buck said. "Just over west, closer to the railroad. Like land in Mound Bayou, Cleveland, Aaron Shelby's farm—stuff like that. That's the only land folks been willing to buy 'cause they got the railroad to travel on. Now look, we need a plan."

"Who put you in charge?" Dick asked.

"Mr. Winchester man?"

"What, Momma Rose?"

"Listen to Buck. Sounds like he knows what he's talking about."

Dick flushed crimson.

"Me'n Jasper ain't set much store in Mr. Buck since he built this house without askin'. Now, he's got these new men in here without askin' me or anybody."

"Didn't nobody put us up to nothin', Mr. Dick," Lem said, rubbing his nose.

"Then what're you doin' here?"

"We was invited," Lem said. "Yessiree! Me'n ole Art there— we pleased to be invited to Mr. Buck's home. We won't never go inside the deep swamp if we ain't wanted."

"I 'preciate the thought," Dick said, "but let's be straight. Who told you where to settle?"

Lem swallowed, looked to Art Canada, then back at Dick.

"We just tryin' to find a home, Mr. Dick. Around this swamp is the only place where white folks leaves you alone."

"'Tis a fact, I'm partial to," Dick said.

"Now, let's hear from Buck," Cicero said. "Go on—talk about the land. Nobody wants a land promoter to come into this swamp with an army of men to clear it."

Buck smiled and cleared his throat.

"All we got to do is write the railroad, and they'll put us in touch with one of their land agents. Then we can buy as much land out here as we want to. Simple as that."

"Are you certain," Cicero asked, "that they'll sell to you? Planters around here might be interested."

"As of yet, there are not enough white folks to buy as much land as the railroad wants to sell. Not many white homesteaders will move over this way either."

"Well then, Cicero," Dick said, "I guess you ain't worried about folks knowin' you live out here." He stood up and shoved a finger into Buck's chest. "You let everybody know you livin' out here just by goin' to buy the land."

"You sell whiskey!" Buck screamed. "They know you from out here. What's the difference?"

Cicero pulled Dick's coattail to make him sit, and Dick stumbled all over Lem Huntwell.

"Just be still!" Cicero ordered. "Right now, it seems right to buy some land. Rose and I will live in the wilderness all our lives."

"I ain't decided," Dick said, "whether to buy land or not. I tell you when I decide."

Cicero stood up and offered a hand to Rose. As she moved toward the door with Cicero, Sara came out of the back of the house.

"Thank you for comin', Momma Rose. I'm sorry I didn't have time to show you the house."

"House ain't important. You bring your boy down to see us more."

Instead of answering Rose, Sara looked to Buck.

"We sort of figured," Buck said, "that Jasper wouldn't want me down in his swamp."

"That," Cicero thundered, "is a damnable excuse. You were too busy!"

"Hush, cherie . . . Buck, you can't ignore your neighbors when it suits you. My boy ain't happy with you, but he'd never shoot you. If he wanted to you'd be dead already. Bring Cicero's grandson down like you oughta."

After Rose and Cicero explained to Jasper what they'd heard about Buck's plan to acquire land title, for a month thereafter, Jasper stayed away from his parent's cabin. The whole of his ambition was to keep the curious, the avaricious, and the foolhardy at bay, and now, his mother and Cicero had as good as welcomed two newcomers and agreed for Buck to go buy up his swamp—his swamp, his space for life. To him, it began to seem as if Dick alone truly understood the truth of having to preserve the swamp for living apart.

Meanwhile, the cousins remained stubbornly righteous after their dispute. Neither sought the other out. Buck piled his timber as he cut it, having no one to haul it for him. On account of Dick attending Buck's meeting, Dick and Jasper were tight-lipped with each other for a few days, but Dick's simple nature and Jasper's simpler approach to life quickly healed what was never a bruise between them in the first place. Dick and Jasper were now again working the Black Bayou still across the Sunflower beyond Roundaway because they were doing so much whiskey business that Jasper decided it was foolhardy to make whiskey so close to home where the smell of mash fermenting and cooking might beckon local law enforcement.

Most evenings, while they were away from home tending the still, they were fed by Mabel Scroggins who worked as a cook in the logging settlement east of the Sunflower. Her three year-old toddler, Bud, began looking forward to the nocturnal visits of the men, and he followed the Winchester Man around like a little hound dog, as in the game they played,

Dick barking and howling, and the infant giggling, and sometimes trying to do a baby howl. Which suited Mabel and Jasper
fine. Jasper began spending more time with Mabel than in his
own cabin.

Meanwhile, Sara became concerned about the rupture be-
tween Buck and Dick, though she had her reasons to be happy.
She rode Buck's horse down into the swamp and consulted
Rose about what she sensed was more than a casual thing.

"Let the men work things out, cherie. More to this than
you see."

"But I started it, Momma Rose."

"Listen, cherie, you just followed your nature, done what a
woman makin' a fam'ly got to do. But this thing between the
men, it got more to do with how they look at life. You come
talk to Mr. Cicero sometime. He the only man 'round here
can kinda step back from what's happenin' and look at it.
Me—I haveta go on my hunches and feelin's."

"Tell me whatcha feelin', please."

"Non, non. This a fam'ly matter. I go messin' in, I change
things. Then the weight on me to be right."

"Who's at fault?"

"If I say one or the other, I 'spect I be wrong. Most things
our people fight about connected up to them devil white folks
one way or 'nother."

Sara spent two days in the swamp, and her son hardly ever
left Rose's arms. Together with Cicero, she would lie in the big
bed with the boy as Sara watched from a nearby rocking chair,
and Cicero would try to make Little Buck speak to him. When
he failed, he would cradle his grandson in his arms and explain how he was the first of a new generation, one that would
see more of the world than his father, Buck, ever had. Cicero
began to think about tutoring the boy. He would begin earlier
than he had with Dick because all he had was time.

Listening to Cicero talk on that visit and on subsequent

visits, Sara decided that the old people in the swamp really could be helpful caring for Little Buck as she traveled to Memphis to furnish her new house. By agreement with Buck, neither wanted hand-made anything, and going to the big city avoided local merchants in the Mississippi Valley who treated them like dirt.

Dirt, fulcrum of all that was happening. That December, Buck, Art and Lem gathered at the Bobo train stop. A railroad land agent had agreed to meet them, and when the agent got off the train, Buck knew him in a minute. He sported a dapper tan bowler hat and a very fashionable, brown and yellow striped suit. A man in a white suit and tie who would be introduced as Mr. Crumby was also present.

"My name is Samuel R. Grant. Call me Sam."

"Mr. Grant," Buck said, "Welcome, welcome."

"A pleasure to meet you, Mr. Morgan."

"How was your trip."

"Better than passable," Sam said. "We came down from Memphis after a most stimulating visit there. Mr. Booker T. Washington himself graced our small sales organization with his presence."

"Oh my! That is something. "I bet Uncle Isaiah—"

"Mr. Isaiah Montgomery?"

"Yes. Mr. Washington is one of his friends, and they correspond."

"There's a new conservative mood in the nation," Sam said. "We need men of discretion and business judgment. Welfare policies toward negroes have done little except to make the white man think we all want a handout."

"Uncle says the same thing. A few people speak badly of him because he let himself get elected to the Jim Crow Convention."

"Well, if not him, another. Got to go along with what you can't do nothing about. Progress is for those with the talent to exploit the world—like you, Mr. Morgan."

"We may wish to purchase a quarter section of land," Buck explained, "lying principally in Bolivar County, though I don't know if you can handle such matters."

"How so, Mr. Morgan?" Sam asked

Buck leaned close and whispered.

"Are you or Mister Crumby there, in charge?"

"Crumby is along to help me, Mr. Morgan."

"You represent the railroad?"

"Um hunh."

"And you one of us?" Buck asked.

"Yes, I'm the land agent. My say so goes."

Crumby was still poking along the track like a little boy.

"Well thank the Lord," Buck said. "Good for our people to be in charge."

"Right you are, Mr. Morgan—may I call you Buck?"

"Sure."

"Call me Sam, will you. Hate to stand on ceremony with my brothers."

"This is Mr. Lem Huntwell . . . and Mr. Art Canada. They are my associates."

"Pleased to meet each of you," Sam said, offering his hand first to Lem then Art, who was huddled in awed silence.

Lem rubbed his slicked-down hair nervously as he presented Sam Grant with a rough sketch of two plots along the Alligator Road.

"Everything measured from points along Harris Bayou," Lem said. "Best we could do."

"Surely adequate," Sam said.

"I know some folks might buy a little extra land," Buck said. "All depend on the price you offering."

"Now, now, Mr. Morgan, you know as I do that the price is fixed by the railroad. I can't give you any special deal. I'm a nigga like you, and these ain't the Sixties with all them crazy nigga notions about forty acre and changing the world. You unnerstand."

"Not sure I understand this time."

"I can't give you a deal just because you or yours was slaves. Racial favoritism is not the American way."

The three men from Africa glanced nervously toward Crumby. Sam Grant chuckled.

"There's lots of folks," Sam said, "who want to buy my land, so I can't undercut another agent. And being of your color, I can't push too hard. I like you, though. How much you willing to pay?"

"I can't say, Mr. Grant." Buck cleared his throat. "I'd have to check with Major McGinnis."

"McGinnis!"

"Yessir," Buck said. "My relation did some business with him years back."

Sam cleared his throat, glanced at Crumby, then stood and stretched.

"Major McGinnis isn't in charge of railroad land now," Sam explained. "Different white folks in charge of everything, and all sales are through me. They hired me in Chicago. Years ago you could buy as much land as you wanted, and the railroad would take your note, but now you got to have cash money."

"I guess," Buck said, "I may as well head on back home."

"No, Mr. Morgan, I said Major McGinnis is no longer in charge, but that doesn't mean we can't work something out. Course, land is costing twenty, twenty-five dollars—"

Buck interrupted with his hand.

"We may as well go home."

"Wait a minute, Buck," Lem said.

"Goddamnit, Lem! Man said he couldn't gives us no special price. You know we cain't pay for no land that expensive. We got to move on off an' find somethin' cost less."

"Mr. Morgan—gentlemen," Sam Grant said. "Don't lose hope . . . I can't guarantee anything, but if you willing to pay eighteen dollars an acre . . . They'll accuse me of favorin' you 'cause you my people, but I will at least submit your proposal to my boss."

"Mr. Grant, let me put my cards on the table. I came up to the Mississippi River Bottoms with Mr. Isaiah Montgomery, and you know him."

"Fine gentleman you mentioned before. Down in Mound Bayou."

"Yeah, well, Mr. Montgomery is my uncle."

Sam began wandering about.

"I heard you say "uncle", but I took it for a figure of speech."

"Knowin' what I do is why I figured on paying twelve to fifteen dollars an acre tops, and the top is for partially cleared and well-drained land."

"Um hunh! I quit playing games with you, Mr. Morgan. You know what's what. For twelve dollars an acre, I can go get approval to do a little business. Forty . . . maybe eighty acres. So you'll need to let me know exactly where all of your homes are located. Very precisely measured out, yes indeed."

The apparent turnabout brought smiles. Crumby was openly sulking, off to the side shaking his head.

"Lose your job thatta way, Sam," he said. "Man of your complexion cain't keep makin' low-bid on land."

Sam Grant ignored Crumby while shaking hands with each of the men from Africa.

"Fine meeting, gentlemen" Sam said. "You should inquire in Alligator about this time next month. No sense putting anything in the mail. Can't be delivered out where you live, anyway, but I'll be back through in a month, and I'm a race man. I ask you gentlemen to pray to the One on high that he'll touch the folks I work for, let me help you good men become freeholders." He turned an angry face toward Crumby nearby. "You let me worry about my complexion, mister!"

Sam straightened his collar and walked away. Crumby followed, still complaining about the low price. Lem was straining to hear what they were saying.

"Straighten up!" Buck said. "Don't look so damn interested."

"Cain't help it," Lem said, rubbing his nose. "Man takin' a chance for his brothers."

The land agent turned an embarrassed glance as if he'd overheard Lem. Behind Crumby's back, Grant placed his finger against his lips, then pulled Crumby to a halt.

"Listen, Mr. Crumby, give me a chance to do something for my people."

"Dunno, Sam. I sleep on it."

"I've made sleeping arrangements in this hamlet," Sam said, "and I think I can convince you before the evening train that these are fine men we represent."

"Just shut up, Sam. I crave a drink so bring your tail on."

By now out of hearing of the men from Africa, Crumby leaned close.

"Are we going back to the Social Club?" he asked.

"Yep. Got a yen for more conversation with the proprietor, what's her name?"

"Matilda."

Sam glanced back to make sure he wouldn't be overheard.

"Yeah, and if I know women, me'n you won't pay for no room tonight."

The cold persisted through March. Nor was there any warming between the cousins. Buck continued to cut timber and to let it lie. Dick worked the still and made whiskey deliveries. With the county going dry, people were stocking up on whiskey, and having too much work began to dry up Dick's eagerness. He had more money than he could spend. A crisis of purpose had him holed up doing nothing for several days, lying in bed all morning waiting for the sun to take the chill off when he heard men laughing in the distance.

Dick poked his head outside to listen, but he couldn't hear much before he shivered and retreated back inside. The chill encouraged him to dismiss the unintelligible voices as coming from Buck's house, probably Sara's kinfolk. He was sitting on a stool wrapped in a blanket debating whether to kindle a fire when Jasper kicked open the door.

"Get up!"

"What for?"

"You hear that?"

"It's Sara's folks havin' a hoorah about somethin'."

"They's white, Dick. Get dressed and bring your gun."

As soon as Dick got dressed, the two raced toward the sound. Jasper stopped in the well-worn trail Dick and his mules had made.

"I don't want to see another trail like this anywhere."

Dick nodded assent, and they eased into the undergrowth off-trail and snaked their way closer toward Buck's house. What they saw were three white men strung out over the continuation of the path Dick and Jasper had move off of, as it turned north past Buck's house toward the Alligator Road. The men were signaling each other while surveying the land. The man in the middle was passing messages from an almost invisible man to the north. In front of Buck's house, a stoop shouldered man wearing jodhpurs many sizes too large held a tall brightly colored pole. At his feet, an iron stake marked a sighting already made. No sign of Buck or of Sara from the house.

"I wonder if I'm gettin' old, Dick."

"Say again, Jasper?"

"There was a time I wouldda run these men out without thinking twice."

"So, whatta you thinkin'?" Dick asked.

"Hates to see white folks so close, but they measurin' to put the land on a piece o' paper for Buck, and he even got my momma behind that."

"That was your choice, not mine."

"What I'm gonna do, fight my own momma?"

Jasper turned away. Dick hurried behind him.

"You leavin' 'em be?"

"They got to measure, so we leave 'em alone—you hear me!"

Jasper headed deeper into the swamp.

"I keep the eye on 'em," Dick said. "Got nothin' planned 'till afternoon."

"Do that."

Dick wandered back to hide within sight of the men working. All morning, they inched their way south toward the end man with the striped pole. He would put it aside every half hour or so to drive a metal marker into the ground. The surveyor carried his tripod closer with each sighting.

"Got to stop rat heah." The man closest to Dick hitched up his jodhpurs. "Ain't no trail down into that swamp."

"Hold on, I run up an' tell the surveyor."

"Don't git that surveyor's dander up. He ain't from heah'n don't know 'bout Africa."

The middle man ran off. A few moments later, the surveyor arrived accompanied by the man who'd worked the middle.

"All right, boys," the surveyor said. "I got the section line between counties pegged off. Enough for one day. Tomorrow we mark straight on down through that forest."

"That theah's a swamp, mistuh, and you has better bring some wood choppers'n men wit guns," the end man still grabbing at his trousers said.

"You fellas can hire some axemen, can't you?" the surveyor said.

"We ain't goin' in theah, is we, Otha?"

"Nossir! Mr. Shapiro, we ain't signed on to go into no swamp."

"Well, I'll be damned."

As Dick listened, an itch grew in his nose. He fought it and rubbed but to no avail. He held his hand tightly over his face, and that seemed to work, until an image of Lem Huntwell's big nose made him want to laugh, and he sneezed.

"Goddamn, Otha—come on!"

The two hired men ran away under the surveyor's hostile glare. He did not follow immediately, and Dick listened to him cursing the railroad for making him put up with fools. The man named Otha paused a hundred feet away and yelled back.

"You best git! There's niggers in them woods crazier'n you ever seen. That sneeze on purpose. They tellin you to git!"

AFTER THE SURVEYORS TRUDGED away, Dick moved into the sun before returning to his cabin. Warmth on the left side of his face told him it was afternoon, and he had a date with Matilda.

The Social Club sat on the edge of a collection of shacks a quarter mile west of the Bobo railroad stop. As Dick rode up, he turned cautious. A straw fan in the window, Matilda's all-clear signal for Dick, was missing. He dismounted and circled to the back door. The only noise came from the Social Club next door. So, he tethered his mount to the back porch and walked in. The house was deserted. He went back outside and led his horse to the nearby corral he used in return for whiskey.

Later, in the front parlor reserved for Matilda's private use, he tried to relax. A half-hour passed before Matilda emerged from the Social Club her arms link in the arms of two well-dressed men, one black and one white-skinned, though Dick began to doubt the fair man considered himself white because the black man treated him too familiarly.

"We sorry you can't entertain tonight, Miz Matilda," the darker skinned man said. "Mr. Crumby and I were looking forward to your company."

"Sam's right," the light skinned man said.

"Ah, would you mind if we had a few more drinks with you, gracious lady—just until your guest arrives? I meet few extraordinary women in my work."

Sam Grant kissed her hand.

"Now, boys," Matilda said, looking up at that moment to glimpse Dick inside her door. "I am sorry, but I have other engagements. Go on back inside'n have a drink on me. You distinguished colored gentlemen always welcome when you in this area. Please, do come again."

After the two men re-entered the Social Club, Matilda rushed up to her door, but Dick blocked her way.

"Who the hell was they?"

"Customers."

"Shouldn't have left me waitin', woman."

"Oh, is that so?"

"Been in the bushes all mornin'. My nature's up."

Dick moved aside to admit Matilda, and the screen door pressed her into him.

"Meoooooow!"

Matilda started laughing as Dick grabbed her, but after a moment of feverish embrace she pulled away to hide behind the window curtain and peer out.

"What's wrong, little pussy?"

"Be quiet, pretty man."

Still holding the curtain as Dick joined her, Matilda raised her face to be kissed. Instead, Dick snatched her from the window, and crushed her in his arms from behind. His nails dug into her hips.

"Owww! Wait a minute!"

Matilda look outside again, but she reached behind herself to fondle Dick.

"My, my . . . baby got lots o' nature."

"Say 'meoooow', my little pussy."

Dick tried to wrestle Matilda to her knees, but again she resisted.

"What's wrong, woman?"

"Listen to me, mister 'meooow man'. I heard somethin' months back, but I didn't know what to make of it. Them niggas in there—"

"Ones you was talkin' to?"

"They with the railroad. Got plenty money, and they ride the train up and down the line free."

Dick cupped Matilda's breast and purred, but she pulled away again.

"Goddamnit! You must be givin it to them mangy strays."

"No, no! Listen, baby, I got things to say."

"Why is it you're talkin' 'bout *them?* It's me come for your good stuff. Say, meooooow."

Dick panted and screwed up his face like a cat.

"Be serious, sweet baby. They tryin' to take away your friend's new house, and maybe yours, too."

Dick froze, allowed himself to be pushed away.

"What d'you mean?"

"Your friend been trying to buy railroad land. Well, them snakes next door is land agents. One of 'em masquerades as white so they kin pull the wool over niggas' eyes more easy. They find out where somebody livin' who wants to buy land, but before you know it, they go and buy up the land. Man already livin' on it got to buy it back from them, at their price."

"I don't know nothin' about land schemes. My cousin is handlin' all that."

"You better learn quick."

An unfamiliar fear made Dick's heart race, drumming up its equal share of anger toward the land agents. A breeze from the door carried Matilda's perfume to his nose. Dick growled and pounced, his anger become passion. He swept Matilda off her feet and onto a woven oval rug.

"Ooooo," she said, clutching her knees together in mock modesty. "What about your friend?"

"Forget about it, dammit!" Dick said, rubbing the cream of her thigh above peach colored stockings. "Say meooowwww."

Dick rubbed himself against Matilda, then fingered the rolled silk to free her legs. Her tongue emerged through scarlet lips, along with a purring deep in her throat as she warmed to the game. Her eyes fluttered as his fingers probed. When her legs loosened, he stopped. She sat up and began to undress as he snatched at his boots and trousers.

"Rrrrrrr."

He flipped her to her knees and climbed over.

"No, no, baby! My wittle knees on de hard flo.'"

Matilda slipped onto her back and began to giggle as Dick pressed into her, stroking hot and hard. A scream leapt out of his throat almost immediately, embarrassing him enough to grab his mouth because the front door was open. Then he collapsed on top, spent. Even so, Matilda seemed to keep writhing, and her nails gripped Dick's arms every little move he made, finally spurring him on. But the gallop was awkward.

"Stop, baby! Goddamn rug is takin' the skin off my back."

Dick doubled over laughing as things came clear—muscles clenching, nails along his arm, symptoms of pain and so far from passion as to leave them both only laughter. Matilda got up and took Dick's hand.

"Meooowww," she said.

"Pffffft!"

She led him into the bedroom. This time, she began the soft sounds and ritual motion. No resistance, recent error out of mind, he firmed in the right place. Then, as only she could do, she began to describe just how right he was making her feel.

A train whistle etched the afternoon quiet, the southbound train approaching. It would slow as Mr. Bobo had insisted, stopping only if passengers were waiting along the track. Alligator was the main stop for passengers, Clarksdale for water and fuel. When the door of the Social Club slammed, Dick jumped from bed to run watch as the two land agents dashed for the tracks. To Matilda's laughter, he thrust his only possession vaguely resembling a weapon toward them.

Miles away, Buck was driving home when he heard the same train whistle. He'd been tight-lipped since leaving Alligator and hearing the whistle made him mutter to himself.

"Calm down, baby," Sara said from the buggy seat beside him.

Buck growled unintelligibly and stung the back of the little mare with his whip. Sara grimaced out of feeling for her pet, who lurched forward and cantered wildly against the weight of the buggy, which further aggravated Buck who lashed her again.

"Don't take it out on Buttercup. She can't help you bein' mad."

"Ain't mad."

"You are, too."

Buck turned to argue, but Sara looked away.

"You know I ain't mad at you."

Sara rubbed his arm.

"Don't pay that white man no mind, Buck. Everything will work out right."

"How'd I know that survey party was trouble?"

"You didn't. You couldn't. It's that Sam Grant fella you talk about. Good thing you drove me into Alligator to do some shopping."

"Damn your shopping, I am truly worried."

Earlier, shortly after arriving in town, Buck had walked out of the Dolan store with a pouch of pipe tobacco only to see the crotchety old Alligator railroad agent waving him over.

"Hey, old Buck. How's the niggers treatin' you?"

"Tol'able fair, Mr. Shelley. Tol'able fair."

"You know," the old white man said, leaning forward out of a cane bottomed chair propped against a tiny sun shelter along the track, "I hates to see them railroad people hirin' nigger agents."

Buck said nothing.

"Ole Sam Grant holdin' a job what belong to some white man."

"Never thought about that, Mr. Shelley."

"Cain't have niggers workin' jobs like that and still keep 'em on the land."

"Whatta you know about Mr. Grant?"

"That bastard been up'n down long heah last two, three months, Buck. You a hard workin' boy few years I knowed you. Hate to see you git mixed up with the likes o' that nigger. He talkin' up cheap land to all the niggers what seem to have money. Him an' that Crumby took option on two whole sections east o' heah . . . Say, that over by you, ain't it?"

Buck could barely nod for swallowing.

"Oh, lordy! You ain't signed up to buy nothin' from him, is you, Buck?"

"Nawsuh, nawsuh! I come heah to you for anything 'bout the railroad, you know that, suh."

"That's good 'cause niggers ole Sam been makin' deals with gonna be mighty mad when they find the boy done formed the Afriky Lan Comp'ny an' took option under 'em so's he kin make a killin' on the resale."

Thinking of Grant's Africa Land Company made Buck sting the mare's rump again, even as he turned her into Art Canada's yard.

"Quit it, Buck!"

The buggy was coming to a halt. Sara jumped down before Buck could come around and assist her. She was greeting Mrs. Canada when he arrived at the porch. In the distance, the train whistle sounded a second time as it approached Alligator.

Back at the Quarters, Matilda shook Dick awake when she heard the second whistle.

"Come on, sweet baby."

"Hummmm?"

"Thought you was gonna search out your friend?"

"Yeah, guess it's time for serious business."

Dick got up marveling at how dispassionately he watched Matilda rise naked and draw a robe around herself. Thighs recently so alluring with a fine down of feline hair now conjured up the legs of a fat little boy.

"You take care," he said, reaching for his gun in the dim light of the unlit front room.

"Wait a minute, baby!"

He walked through the screen door before turning to see her lighting a lamp.

"Hurry up. Got to be on my way."

He watched her hips undulating beneath her gaping robe as she walked down hiding something behind her.

"Here, Mr. Winchester Man!"

It was a new, wide-brimmed gray hat, a Stetson.

"Know you gonna look good in it," she said, and kissed him lightly before running back inside out of the chill. "Always remember, baby, that Miz Matilda said you was the prettiest cat, she ever petted."

Dick was happy as a child after Christmas as he rode home. To brag about his new hat as much as anything, he decided to gather the new men living on the Alligator Road before visiting Buck. He bowed to every person along the way and grandly removed his hat in the process.

By the time Dick reached the Alligator Road and turned toward the east, the sun behind him had dipped below the tree line and his enthusiasm for his new hat vanished. He cursed the coming dark because a wagon rut might cripple his horse. Being in such a rush of passion earlier, Dick had left his saddle lantern home. With or without the lantern, it was too dark to ride into the swamp and tell Jasper what he'd just heard from Matilda. There was no rush, he told himself.

Whatever devilment the railroad land agents had up their sleeves would probably take more than a few days to bring off. What frightened Dick was that he was no lawyer. Cicero had never even been able to make him see the need to understand bookkeeping, much less how the law worked. Bright and early tomorrow, he'd personally go tell Jasper that Buck had stirred up a bunch of vultures scavenging for morsels of land.

Art Canada's house had been built along the Road at the end of Harris Bayou where its muddy flare curved north. Art was not intending to grow much crop because he had a handyman job in Alligator, and he had located where he did to make sure his family and livestock had easy access to water. Not a single pump had yet been sunk in the area so that having to hand-carry water when the rain barrel went empty was common.

It was a pleasant surprise for Dick to see Buck's buggy along with Lem Huntwell's horse parked together in Art's yard.

"Come on in, Dick," Sara said. "Miz Canada would be answerin' the door, but she busy with her young un'. How you doin'?"

"Just fine, Sara."

Dick walked inside and nodded to the three men seated in a tight little knot. He belatedly offered his new hat to Sara.

"Hope it don't burden you to take care of my new hat?"

"My, what a wonderful hat. Look, Buck."

"Matilda give it to me."

Sara tossed the hat into a corner.

"Haven't," she said, "seen much of you, Dick."

"No, but your friend, Matilda, sends her regards."

Buck was up and pulling on Dick.

"C'mon, talk. We got problems."

"Is that right?"

"I know you're going to crow, but it wasn't my fault."

"What's not your fault, Buck?"

"About the Africa Land Company."

"Africa Land Company," Dick repeated slowly. "Is that somethin' you set up, Buck?"

Buck and the other two men looked at each other. Art whispered to Buck. Lem stared straight ahead, double-sized nose twitching.

"Just thought I'd ask," Dick said. "You the land expert. Is there something I'm supposed to know?"

"How'd you hear about that?" Buck asked.

"We all just heard," Lem said.

Dick sat down and crossed his legs.

"Belay your questions, you just told me somethin' about a Africa Land Company, and now you act like I'm supposed to know something."

Gloria Canada emerged from the back room to stand alongside Sara.

"Let's go behind the house," Buck said. "No sense botherin' the women folk."

"Quit actin' like little boys," Sara said. "We hear anyhow."

The four men filed outside. Dick dawdled behind, and when he finally reached the others, a silent fear was mingled with the dusk.

"See here, Dick."

"Yeah, I'm listenin'."

"We got a problem."

"Dammit, Buck! You said that already. This some kinda secret you don't want me knowin'?"

"I offered," Buck said, "to buy land from a railroad land agent, and I was just told that this agent is using information I give him against us."

"Damn!"

"Yeah," Buck said, "it's serious. So, that's why we here tonight meetin'."

"Ah would you be more precise? Did this agent take your money?"

"No, Dick. Ain't that simple. He went and bought up title to my house and maybe the land under this house'n Lem's too. Couldda bought up some of the swamp below here, on top o' that."

"Have you talked to Jasper?"

"Dick, I ain't in no mood to play."

"Well, I'm damned to hell if I come here for more o' your attitude. Seem's like you the one messed up. Wasn't me, and now you act like your mess-up mean I'm the one got to bite my tongue. I say again, you go see Jasper. First off, in the mornin'."

"Where you goin'?" Buck asked.

"To git my hat'n go home."

"But, Dick . . . Don't you have no ideas?"

"Oh, I got ideas, but I figure you got your own. I just told you to go talk to Jasper. Or you want me to help you without my partner bein' in it? I ain't doin' that."

Dick headed for the steps up to the back door of the house. Sara loomed inside the screened door.

"Why you can't talk to your cousin like you used to?" she asked.

Dick halted, ignored Sara and turned around to address Buck.

"If you scared to go see Jasper on account o' all you been doin', come git me tomorrow. I'll ride down with you." Dick raised his hand to silence Buck. "You come git me, I help you make peace."

Like the waters of far-off snow melt, momentum was gathering—Buck's commercial impulse, a growing communal reality, Jasper's guardian spirit, the concupiscece of all and in particular, Samuel Grant, common in human source but still dispersed, these currents. Whether and how the human grains of sand would remain at rest or tumble was yet to be seen, but a tide had begun to gather.

The following morning, Buck rounded up Art and Lem and headed over to Dick's cabin. Dick was already dressed, sitting on his porch turning his head back and forth as if talking to his mule.

"Mornin', cousin," Buck said.

"Mornin'. Let's git at it . . . Boys, ride slow. There ain't no trail to Jasper's cabin."

"I thought maybe we go see my daddy first," Buck said.

"Fair thought, but, you need to talk to Jasper, and you know it."

There was a dark buildup of clouds that morning, and Lem was concerned a big early rain might strand them without a boat. Dick had just about calmed him down when a snake frightened Lem's horse, and it threw him.

"Ain't make no sense come ridin' into this swamp," Lem said, rubbing his back. "I'm walkin' rest of the way. This ain't no path atall."

"Got to be that way," Dick said. "It ain't a highway."

Buck finally explained what the Alligator station agent had told him. Dick had to bite his tongue to keep from gushing out that he already knew. When Buck quit talking, Dick turned to Lem.

"You look like a man knows a few ladies," Dick said.

"Used to, but now I ain't got the time for nobody ain't out in the field with me."

"'Tis a pity." Dick spoke a little louder so Buck would hear. "I used to have a cousin o' mine to run with. Now he's married."

"Well, Mr. Dick," Lem said, "I ain't got no money, and I'm bound to work my land an' stuff for Mr. Buck 'till I pay him back for my land."

"For your land? Ain't you buying it straight out?"

"Oh, yessuh! But Buck chargin' us for the loan o' his money'n all."

Jasper's cabin was empty when they arrived, and they continued on across to find Rose and Cicero. Buck explained what had happened, and that they had come for Jasper but that Jasper was away. Rose silenced her gristmill.

"He oughtta bring that widow lady up here to live with him."

Cicero went and fetched his rainslicker out of the cabin.

"I'm going," he said, "to get Jasper."

"Who is this Crumby?" Dick asked after Cicero turned to leave.

"Don't know," Buck said, "But his white suit is always near Sam."

"Aye, 'til I put some bullets in it," Dick said, cocking his rifle.

"Don't do anything until I return," Cicero yelled back. "Hotheaded and right-headed are not cousins."

"Aye, we'll wait."

"I hate guns," Art said.

"Git hold of yourself, Art," Dick said.

"Let me tell you all a story."

They all looked up. Cicero had returned.

"Remember back when I brought you cousins into this swamp—and Buck, think back to when you and I were re-united—what did I say about the world?"

Buck looked to Dick, but neither spoke.

"Buck claimed," Cicero said, "that white people were always in control. Now, it's come to a fight on account of this land. Well, sir, there's the white folks tribe and here's our own."

"Daddy! Don't be so, so—"

"Cold-blooded? . . . Truly I cannot change the way the world works. We have to sharpen our claws. Think of your children, Art. Do I make myself clear?"

"Like good whiskey, cherie," Rose said.

"Aye," Dick said. "You men best all head back up and keep watch on the edge of the swamp while Cicero fetches Jasper."

"Why not wait here?" Lem said. "I don't want to go back through no swamp tonight."

"Shush, Lem," Buck said. "We go up to my house. Won't be no trouble before the beginning of the work week, so ain't no sense in camping out."

"Buck ain't tried to be a gun-totin' cowboy in a long time," Dick said to the new men. "But listen to what he tells you."

"What you gonna be doin', Mr. Winchester Man?" Lem asked.

"Be needin' supplies for four or five days. We'll have to light out'n hide if they bring too many men in against us. You'll see me maybe tomorrow mornin'."

As the warning sank in, Lem got the sniffles and his nose started moving all over his face in the firelight. Buck and Art had started away, and Lem ran behind them.

"Wait up! I ain't ridin' alone."

Which led Art to pause and yell back to Dick.

"Bring some whiskey, if you please, I got nerve problems, too."

As the others left, Rose walked over to Dick.

"Mr. Winchesta Man."

"Yes'm?"

"Don't worry 'bout supplies, I come up to your place and get you boys fed every day."

"That's a wee too close, Momma Rose. Even if we run these folks off, they could return with a posse."

"Son, I been in danger all my life. No difference 'tween me'n you 'cept age. You faster, but I can shoot, and I'll bring my gun."

"Whatta you know, Rose? Tell me?"

"I ain't seen nothin' you ain't considered. Keep your head level. I'd say you ought try lure the enemy further into the swamp before you trap 'em. That way, you know the terrain. They don't."

Pondering such matters on his way home, Dick heard the wind whistling off in the swamp. The sky was dark with clouds that had held since morning. By that time, he had caught up with the others, and they rode together. As Dick neared his cabin, a flock of birds perching for the evening took wing and beat the air overhead, their screams slowly blending with the other noises of the swamp. It wasn't exactly comforting. Neither was the gray sunset that opened in front of Dick as he rode out of the swamp proper, and the rest turned toward Buck's house.

"Ain't so simple killin' a white man," Dick yelled to Buck. "You remember Mound Bayou?"

"Yeah, but so what?"

"I ain't no murderer, Mr. Dick," Art said. "I do declare."

Lem's nose was doing the talking. He said nothing.

"We got to plan, Mr. Winchester Man," Buck said. "We got to plan—if you willin' to keep talkin' to us?"

"All right, all right. No more fightin' between us. We siddown with Jasper soon's we can. We got serious business."

The following day was Saturday, another day empty of events but full of apprehension. By afternoon, everyone—with the exception of the wives, Sara and Gloria Canada—gathered again inside the swamp. When the outsiders arrived, Jasper was seated at the outdoor table with his mother and step-father, along with Mabel. Jasper said nothing about Buck's land, nothing about the new men standing in front of him. None of them took a seat or opened their mouths. Then Mabel reached over and rubbed Jasper's hand and he smiled. Mabel embraced him then, and Jasper kissed her in public, then bounced to his feet and went around clapping Buck and Dick on the back in an unprecedented display of affection. He acknowledged the new men with a nod as he picked up a whiskey jug and began choking down whiskey as if he could drink it fast enough.

"I've explained to Jasper what the problem is," Cicero said to Buck. "I think, though, that you should tell him all you know about Mr. Sam Grant."

Dick picked up Mabel's infant and tossed the toddler astride his shoulders as Buck began to talk.

"I apologize, Jasper—"

"Hush!" Jasper said. "Momma say 'fore you got married, your wife's poppa told you quit apologizin'."

Buck froze, as did Dick, the screaming infant astride his shoulders.

"But," Jasper continued, "I ain't got time to teach you no manners. I'm happy today—real happy, and that is your good luck. I got a notion them men me'n Dick seen up at your house is the ones got to come do their work before anybody else show up. I don't give a damn about no land title, but I do not intend for nobody to take what's mine. So, Mr. Buck, I say you lucky you got me in the fam'ly."

Out of the blue, Jasper reached and began tickling Mabel's bosom.

"Oh, mister! Oh Jesus!"

Whiskey had Jasper beyond appreciating the comparison as Mabel wrestled herself away from him and ran inside the cabin screaming for Rose to call off her son. When Jasper ran after her, Dick walked up to the door and yelled in.

"Hey, boss man! We got business."

Jasper poked his face out and grinned.

"Ain't you supposed to be the Winchesta Man? You handle business. You know what's what."

Jasper then withdrew back inside. When Dick raised his finger and moved to follow with a question, Cicero grabbed Dick's arm and motioned him to sit.

"Matters of great signification," Cicero said. "are underway."

Cicero then walked inside himself, leaving the rest perplexed.

"He asked me, Rose," Mabel's voice inside the cabin was saying. "I ain't push him or nothin'. He come right up to my door and before I could say 'wipe your feet,' he asked me."

Jasper clapped his hands when Rose and Mabel embraced, and when they started dancing up and down together, he belched forth the most god-awful noise intended for singing.

"Made two women feel good," Cicero said.

Jasper led Mabel outside followed by Rose, who emerged with her hands held toward the sky.

"Mr. Jasper is getting married!"

By the time Jasper took in the various looks of amazement, he became embarrassed. His playfulness evaporated. As if he could think of nothing to say, he pulled Mabel off into the swamp toward his cabin without saying a word.

"Be keepin' your boy, Miz Mabel," Dick yelled behind them. "He'll make a damn fine field hand . . . What say? You don't give a damn, eh?"

Rose started jumping up and down inside Cicero's arms.

"She finally pulled him in. Let him go easy like, but she pulled him in. Glory be! I'm gonna have more grandchildren."

"Take me," Cicero said, "for a walk."

"Yes." Rose tickled his chin. "We go down to the pond and sit awhile."

That night, a celebration swept railroad men and land schemes out of mind. When Rose and Cicero returned from the pond, she started dancing with the men to a tune Art Canada was playing around with on his harmonica. Jasper reappeared with Mabel, both dressed in finery. No matter that it was only store-bought common clothes, it was new and never worn, which was dress-up for Jasper who seldom wore store-bought anything.

"C'mon," Rose said, running over and snatching Mabel from Jasper. "He cain't dance."

"I do anything I want today," Jasper said, holding his arms to the sky and shuffling his feet through the leaves.

"Then go on, do it!" Rose shouted, clapping faster than the music. "Show you happy, cherie!"

"Have a drink, Art," Dick said. "Don't let the music get tired."

Art stayed in form, but he started dancing to his own music, and Rose hooked an arm in his, and hung on. Cicero began reciting lines of something, though no one knew what it was until he began yelling, holding his light up high with the rest, and his face and words were shining so they all danced around him.

"Come together," he was chanting, "in the old way, to celebrate the ancient ritual of dragonflies."

"Dragon what?" Rose said.

"Dragonflies!"

"Give him some more whiskey, momma," Jasper said. "Howdy-do!"

"A community of two, coming together without leave of law," Cicero shouted, "and nary a piece of dirt to land on. Sweet part to sweet part, ain't it good."

Cicero rushed over to repeat himself close to Rose, but when he kept repeating a phrase, she pushed him away and pulled Art Canada off into a reel of some sort.

"Ignore that man," she said. "Play on, Art!"

"We are Africans!" Cicero continued. "Don't any of you forget that." A sniffle overcame him. "And we will not forget you, Bill Williams. You were the first to speak of a real community with wives and children, a binding up of being torn apart. And here's to my son, Jasper!"

"Stop playing, Art," Rose said.

"Old Bill," Cicero continued, "taught us the importance of our past to our present. He opened my eyes . . . A tribute to Old Bill, the very first of us to come into our own new Africa."

Everyone raised a cup.

"May he never be forgot," Rose said.

"May his spirit," a drunken Jasper could barely hold a cup steady, "marry my momma like he always wanted. He, hee!"

"Play on, Art," Rose said. "Some of us more in the spirit than others."

Because the two new men knew neither Mabel nor Jasper very well, they were careful to show only polite interest toward his lady. Equally reticent, for some unknown reason, Buck remained the quietest of all. So, the two women often danced together if Dick or Cicero weren't dancing with one or the other.

The party had started out on common whiskey, and then Jasper stumbled away to return with a jug of corn liquor so smooth you could taste the water mixed into it, which would have been a crime. Everybody was dancing with everybody by then, and to those who knew Jasper, he proved himself human for the second time in a single day. He passed out. As it got late, Lem Huntwell and Dick commenced bragging about their bachelor exploits. Buck was noticeably still quiet.

"I think we need one more jug," Rose said, excusing herself to pull more whiskey out of the cabin.

When she returned, Buck who'd provoked a big laugh in Rose's absence grew quiet again. She walked straight up to him.

"Have your fun, cherie. I don't tell no tales."

Mabel looked startled.

"What're you sayin', Momma Rose?"

"His wife ain't here. Men do what men do, so let him talk free."

"Well," Buck said. "I been wonderin' how it is we gonna protect our land?"

"Aw, Buck, drink up!" Dick shouted.

"No, I've had enough. I'm goin' home tonight 'cause I got work. We got to get the women away from where there could be shooting. Tomorrow, you all come on up to my house again."

Sunday came on, uneventful but for hangovers. Dick led the new men back up to Buck's house, and by late morning,

Sara and Mrs. Canada were decked out in finery and sitting in Sara's buggy. The youngest Canada boy, Hiram, was squeezed in between them. The older boy and girl, happy to wear their only shoes, rode one behind the other on a mule hitched to the tail of the buggy. Little Buck was screaming his head off because Sara had decided it was time to wean him of her bosom, and he was black in the face with rage.

"Y'all go on in to Alligator," Buck said. "Stop'n spend time there, then head for Mound Bayou. You reach it tonight."

"Gonna be dangerous," Sara said, "driving after dark."

"You both got guns. Keep 'em in open sight outside of town."

"We make better time," Mrs. Canada said, "if we drive straight to Mound Bayou from here?"

"Quit raisin' problems, Gloria," Art Canada said.

"We want," Buck explained, "Alligator white folks to know you wasn't home out here, come any trouble. See?"

"Naw, I don't," Gloria said, "not if it mean we got to drive along that dark road at night."

"It won't be so bad," Sara said. "I used to travel with Buck at night."

"But it's dangerous for women."

"Stop at Deacon Jones' place in Alligator," Buck said. "Talk to his wife casual like, and make sure you visit the Dolan store and that other new store."

"We supposed to be bound for a church supper in Mound Bayou, is that what we tell people?"

"Tell 'em that exactly, Gloria," Buck said. "And let 'em know that the negroes in the swamp been actin' crazy. You can say they stirred up about something."

"I'll say I hope them crazy niggas don't steal our stuff when our men join me and Gloria in Mound Bayou. How's that?"

"Perfect, Sara," Buck said.

"Simple, too," Art said. "Just keep sayin' you scared o' the crazy niggas. Say crazy nigga to everybody."

After the women departed, Dick walked up to Buck.

"Just so's you know, there's nary a doubt in my mind about the shootin' part. If those men need to come out here to scheme, they'll die. What I don't know about is the law. I got reason to think the sheriff ain't so dumb as to ride out here on a dare. But legal matters o' title, Buck . . . What you gonna do?"

"Rose said to come back down to her cabin. Jasper and my daddy'll be sober then. We'll make plans."

Monday came and went. Rose got up at dawn on Tuesday as was her habit, and she sat alone on the east side of the cabin until mid-morning sunlight was sparkling down through the trees. Lem bumped into her as she was visiting each of the sleeping blankets dotting the clearing.

"Sorry, Miz Rose . . . I just—tell me again wheah the toilet at?"

"Walk straight off away from the front door. Ain't much of a path. That's on purpose."

Moments later, Dick went after Lem and rapped on the outhouse.

"Aw, please, Dick, go find a place somewheah."

"'Tis a pity you got such a delicate constitution, Lem. I was hopin' you'd be the man to help with a few ladies. C'mon outta there."

"I ain't thinkin' 'bout no woman."

"If you hurtin' serious, come to the pond. Sun's up strong. It'll soothe you a mite."

Aside from Lem and Dick, no one else moved, and when they did move it was slowly. Afterwards, the men departed for Buck's house to keep watch again."

More than a family, a community had now come into being, and the tide of circumstance was not yet spent. Wednesday crept by as the land crisis was pushed aside. The weather turned unseasonably warm. There was still no report of strangers. Then the cold returned on Thursday, a gray misty morning. Cicero and Rose stayed in their cabin. Dick showed up saying that the men at Buck's house had decided to leave the women in Mound Bayou for a few more days.

"How's things," Dick asked, "in the honeymoon cabin?"

"We haven't," Rose said, "seen Jasper or Mabel in two days."

THE FATHER OF RIVERS TRICKLES down from Minnesota, Michigan, Ohio, the eastern slope of the Rockies, the western slope of the Appalachians. Water is water and fungible to irrigate the land, but it is different in what it brings from where it comes, the red, the brown, the gray, the black dirt with which it is infused. Once it reaches the Mississippi, its massed flow answers to laws of its own, great and small vortexes generating a turbulence that overwhelms the affairs of humans.

Unknown to anyone in Africa, the man known in the string of little rooming and whiskey houses along the railroad as Smooth Sam Grant had ordered the troublesome Alligator station agent to hire additional men after the surveyor's helpers quit. The old white man refused to do what he was told. Though a black man, Sam was from the North. He had some inkling of the cynical motives of those at Illinois Central Land Associates who had hired him to go South and sell, and he generally understood the emerging pattern of racial discriminations that was being called Jim Crow because of the popular minstrel show of that name. However, Sam was unused to the quality of bigot in Mississippi, so he never guessed what the Alligator Station agent would do.

Sam was a businessman, good Republican credentials, a young new breed colored man in the mold of Booker T. Washington's dream. He felt entitled to exploit whoever he could

338

in this land of opportunity. Under the stimulation of the finest whiskey, he would often address the matter.

"Got to show the white man some of us can do him one better. Colored leaders from Civil War days don't represent black folks no more. All they do is beg, more welfare for the people. The new thing called Jim Crow—hell, we don't have to live all up in the white man's bosom. Avoiding Jim Crow is becoming a new excuse for my colored brothers not taking responsibility for their own lives. I make my own way. I am a businessman, and *we* are the future."

His sales tactics bothered him no more than they did his white competitors in the shell-game of railroad land.

"I'm a new breed of black man," he would say, "engaged in an effort of the highest ethical order. I will put more black folks on their own land than Fred Douglass or B. Tailiaferro Washington put together."

Sam had written Buck a letter explaining the delay in procuring his land. In it he shared other thoughts:

> *What nonsense civil rights and mass uplift. Leadership is needed, and by men of commerce like yourself. You will be more powerful than all the laws and preachers for social change.*
>
> *Earning more in America is infinitely better than arguing more—and all about so little. Water must seek its own level.*

All of which was why Buck never shared with Dick or with any of the others why he had been so blind. Sam had charmed Buck with thoughts surfacing in Buck's own mind. In fact, Sam had a following of sorts, but not the white Alligator station agent, Mr. Shelly. Old Shelly detested "Nigger Sam," and predictably took no action on Sam's request to hire axe men, figuring it was time to find out who carried the weight with the company—him or Sam. Sam discovered the dereliction several days later, when he arrived on the Monday evening train, about the same time the men of Africa were leaving the swamp to go take up watch at Buck's house.

"Hello, Mr. Shelley. Any mail?"

The old man regarded Sam Grant balefully, lips working overtime grooming a mouthful of tobacco that he spit uncomfortably close to Sam's pant's leg. Crumby, a wiser soul in his white suit, had remained distant.

"Look, Mr. Shelly—"

"Watch your tone theah, boy! You ain't up Nawth."

"Just give me my mail. I got land business."

"Ain't took no orders from a nigger in my life, ain't startin' now."

"The mail is supposed to contain new instructions about selling land, Mr. Shelley. We both got to make a living."

The old man's brows knitted up, and he licked his brown-stained lips. Sam skipped backward, but he was mistaken—no spit, Shelley was only thinking hard.

"We raised hell back at your damn home office," Shelley said. "Ain't seemly them puttin' folks o' your complexion out-heah to make all the money. New rules s'posed to let us track-side agent make a little money sellin' land, too.

"I know all about that," Sam said. "Just gimme my mail!"

"That tone can gitcha hurt."

Shelly stood up, half stretched and then did a little skip when a back pain seized him.

"Follow me over to the County Agent's office. I want to see your mail myself 'cause I spect we git some new rules any day."

Midway between the track and the line of buildings fronting it, Sam remembered his need for axe men.

"How many did you hire to work with Mr. Shapiro?"

"Ain't had time," Shelly said without looking back. "'Sides, that Jew doin' the survey ain't happy workin' wit colored, an' they was all I couldda got for him sech short notice."

The Africa deal had been on-hold too long, Sam knew, and there were others eager to buy. All were newcomers who had no fear of what seemed a kind of idiotic lore about swamp niggers. Just the kind of lies, Sam figured, white folk liked to spread about the colored, that they were lazy, violent and immoral. Sam took the very next train on down to Cleveland where he located Shapiro at the Blue Goose Hotel. It was three in the morning, when Sam barged in.

"Morning, Shapiro. Open up."

"Morning, my ass, Sam. Why'dja get me up this godawful time?"

"I'll make it brief . . . I don't care who you hire for that Africa job—white or colored. Just finish my job."

"Sam, people around here won't work that swamp. Two boys ran off last Thursday. Thought they heard a sneeze, you beat that. Run off in broad daylight because of a sneeze."

"You can hire white or colored, I said. Don't matter none if that's holding you up. But move!"

"Listen, Mr. Smooth Sam, I work for Illinois Central Land. Don't tell me who to hire. If your beloved station agent won't hire you extra men, you're outta luck. I can't spend company money on your authority."

"Why's that?"

"No budget for axe men. My work is supposed to be along the right-of-way or in sight of it. You got me skipping a whole section east of the railroad before I begin, which also means more sightings. Somebody got to find men willing to go in and hack out a path through that swamp."

"You must be pocketing your expense money."

"Hell you say."

"Well whatta you estimate it'll cost—two or three axemen?"

"I asked around last week, Sam. Nobody wants to work over there. Some kind of inbred people been causing trouble in the vicinity since who knows when. I don't know what to make of it, but one of my bosses told me not to push it. Could be dangerous."

"Just an excuse to hold us colored agents back. I won't stand for it."

"I'm going to sleep," Shapiro said.

Before the surveyor could push him out, Sam grabbed the door frame.

"Listen, Jew-boy, you come to Bobo tomorrow. I'll get you woodsmen, and I'll hire two, three who know how to shoot. Now, who's the constable in this silly little place?"

"Get out of here, Sam. I'll call you when I wake up."

"You come to Bobo—not Alligator. I don't want Shelly involved."

"Tomorrow, Sam. Tomorrow."

It was mid-afternoon when the two arrived at the Bobo Plantation. As usual, the area was deserted. After the train continued north, Shapiro sat on a rail, opened a pocket knife and drew a wood scrap from his pocket.

"So," Sam said, "whatta you do when you want to hire men?"

"Damned if I do anything."

"You don't like working with a black man, do you?"

"I don't mind black, but you are a son of a bitch. You have to make a killing."

"Oh, so the black man ain't good enough to make the kind of money the Illinois Central making?"

"You aren't that big, Sam. Take a little piece of cake. Be happy."

Sam Grant hurried to the Social Club to ask after a constable. Matilda laughed.

"Ain't none here, sugar. You got to go to Alligator."

Sam hired a horse and rode to Alligator, but he had no better luck. No one would enter the swamp along the Sunflower. Nor would the constable agree to take a ride out with a couple deputies for a few dollars under the table. At his wits end by evening, Sam returned to Matilda's for the night.

Next morning, Matilda provided a full breakfast, at least her cook did, Matilda herself having been somewhat more intimately occupied with her guest. Afterward, accompanied by Crumby and Shapiro, Sam wandered back out toward the track to await the morning train. A group of white men were at the train stop waiting.

"Wages and a half for up to four woodcutters," Sam announced, as he had been saying to practically everyone he met. "Double wages for two fully armed men to assist the surveyor here."

There were no immediate takers, but one stepped forward.

"I lives on the Mississippi up in Coahoma County. What's wrong with that swamp?"

"Not a thing," Sam said.

The stranger pointed to a local man standing nearby.

"You theah, darky, if I was to hire you on, would you lead us?"

"Nawsuh! Not for all the money."

"Well, then," the stranger said to Sam, "There you are."

"I'm a land agent for the railroad."

"Quit lyin' to me, nigger!"

"But he is," Shapiro said. "Paid and authorized by the Illinois Central."

"And why should I believe you?"

"Ask the agent in Alligator," Sam said. "He'll tell you I work for the Illinois Central."

The stranger ignored Sam, addressed Shapiro.

"I got a shotgun an' a rifle an' all the men you need from my friends standin' here. More comin' up on the train. We been huntin'. Long's they git paid like you promised and you find us some hosses, we handle anything you need. For me, I git double pay plus a extry ten dollars fuh my trouble."

The following morning was cool and misty, almost foggy when Sam Grant and Crumby rendezvoused with six disreputable looking white men and an old black man holding one Black and Tan and two mongrel hounds on leash. Two of the strangers were mounted, the rest were on a mule-drawn wagon. The stranger in charge wore a rainslicker and a floppy felt hat.

"Gots to be paid before every day's work," he said.

"Sounds reasonable to me," Sam said. "What say Mr. Shapiro?"

Shapiro nodded, as they had agreed, to encourage the hired men to think that the surveyor had charge of their pay. Shapiro pulled a roll of bills from his pocket and doled out the first day's pay. The men dallied for an hour while one searched out the operator of the Bobo plantation store, to sell them provisions, they said, though they purchased only liquor.

An hour later, as they turned onto the Alligator Road toward Africa, Crumby leaned close and whispered.

"Sam, them rednecks is wagerin' on who'll kill the first nigger."

The sun hid behind a thick haze, as if turning its back on the misbegotten expedition. Even the glow behind the overcast seemed ominous. The sudden turn colder had transformed the unseasonable warmth. Vagrant mists were moistening the bushes along the Alligator Road. In a clearing between some trees, blackbirds chattered hidden, until a gunshot set them aflight. Against the sound of beating wings and squawking, the smell of gunpowder was sinister.

When Sam Grant turned south onto the trail approaching what looked like an almost impenetrable expanse of swamp, he couldn't control his excitement. Buck Morgan's house materialized in a clearing, ample and well-built, white, trimmed in green with gables facing front and the side to the north. As the survey party rode closer, every eye was trained on the house.

"I'll own the land," Sam gushed to Shapiro, who glanced at the armed white men approaching. Sam giggled and spurred ahead to ride around the unexpected find in the middle of nowhere.

"Take note," Shapiro told the white men, "of those rods along the way. We put them in a week ago."

"Ain't no big thing, mistuh," the leader of the hired men said. "Don't talk so loud in fronta the nigger. He payin' fuh nothin' so let 'em . . . An' if he ain't, we git in some shootin'."

"Just do what you're paid to do. Clear a way to extend those sightings down into that swamp."

Shapiro chucked his horse toward Crumby and Sam Grant in front of the house while the others rode ahead toward the wall of swamp that had never been cut. In a few places along its edge, the mist had climbed up into the cypress trees, and the reddish wintered leaves were shivering with a sporadic breeze.

"What now?" Crumby asked. "We ain't got all the time in the world, an' frankly those gentlemen over there scare me to death."

The ringleader rode up to Grant and Shapiro.

"Tell us what to do. Your money."

"A straight line of sight into that swamp," Shapiro said. "That's what I need. Cut only the trees you have to."

"You heard the boss! Git to it!"

The men tethered their horses and wagon at the tree wall. Shapiro joined them and dismounted.

"Remember, don't cut more'n you got to, fellas."

"Money ain't yours," the ringleader said. "So shet up!"

Earlier that morning, as the Winchester Man headed out of the swamp to reconnoiter, he spotted the armed band on the Alligator Road and galloped back with a warning. The new men already gathered at Buck's house followed him down into the swamp. It was slow going along the ridge trail that day because the mist forced everyone to walk. The mist thinned the deeper into the wilderness they moved, and just before the men reached Jasper's cabin the first axe strokes rang out behind them.

Within the hour, six men along with Rose, armed with all the weapons they could carry, were returning toward the edge of the swamp. Rose split off from them with a wink toward Jasper. When the rest reached Dick's cabin, they herded their horses into his corral. The gray afternoon seemed to hold more chill than the morning had as they began walking toward the sound of axes.

"You take one group, me another, Mr. Winchester Man," Jasper said.

Art was shivering.

"Say, Art," Dick said, "I got a extra coat back inside."

"Y'all ain't got to stop for me."

"Be quiet," Jasper said. "No funnin'."

"No harm, Jasper," Dick said walking out in front of the men. "Why don't you take Buck'n Mr. Cicero, circle to the southwest. The rest of us'll inch up close as we can on this side."

Jasper nodded.

"When you get in place," Dick said, "start blastin'. We let 'em have it soon as we hear you start up."

"Damned," Lem said, "if you ain't cold-blooded."

A smile struggled to show on Jasper's face, but his dour self won out. Buck and Cicero joined him to one side as Dick turned to lecture Lem and Art.

"Like Jasper say, this ain't no play game. You remember that nigga got hung out for the buzzards a few months back? Keep that in your head, how they whipped him and cut him up before they burned him. Remember that and you won't have no problem shootin' these white folks. They ain't loved by nobody our color."

"Y'all don't know," Jasper said, "how hard it is to kill a man first time. You got to have a reason, if you ain't a mad dog. This land is yours—ours. You need a place ain't no trouble-bent white man gonna set his foot again, you hear me! That's the only way you got a home. Anything else is sharefarmin', you be givin' up the rump end of your life, leaving your children to pick over gristle and bone. That is, if you got any juice left in you."

"Um hunh, yes, Lord!" Lem said.

Rose appeared out of the thicket, and the men walked to meet her.

"Just a handful of men with dogs. Dick, you should always wait until you know what you're facing before you fight. That goes for you, too, Jasper."

"So, where are our supplies?" Dick asked.

"At the pond, Dick. Your cabin is too close to the outside. If more men show up than the ones I've seen, and you have to run, you all head back down to the pond. I'm going there now. If you're on the run, I'll have ammunition and food waiting. If I hear shooting coming near, I'll sneak around behind you and ambush your attackers to give you time to re-supply. Jasper and Dick can lead you further in to hide."

As the men from Africa moved out, the wind did nothing to dispel the dampness coating the bare branches. It was the strangest weather. Errant breaths of wind continued to whip the mist smell up from the ground until the men entered the fastness of the trees. All the anger of the past few days seemed to ease into their limbs. On top of that, a little cold and something like anticipation of the evening-up about to come. It set legs to trembling as each watched the others watching and sharing silent understanding. Each person had his own tally sheet of wrongs about to be righted. It didn't matter not to know the intruders personally. Bill Williams had called them members of the white tribe, which made them all invaders. As for the railroad men, deception had delivered them to their fate.

Not since Mound Bayou had Dick felt the score about to come even, at least for a while. A man being forced to mock his manhood, head bowed, smiling at defilement to reassure every white man he couldn't possibly be a threat. Each woman walking a garden path subject to some white man claiming her womanhood as a trophy. Human beings had not been created to serve white lords and ladies in a make-believe world of stereotyped lazy and worshipful lesser beings.

"Come on, Dick," Lem said. "We got to move."

"Settle your nose down, Lem. We have to go slow to give the others time to get in place."

There was a sudden bugling of hounds, and the axes went silent.

"What the hell happenin'?" Art asked.

"They got daaawgs! " Lem said, his nose working overtime. "And ain't but three of us."

"Shut up, Lem, an' follow me," Dick said. "Them dogs smell the others on the wind. Damned to hell if I'll let 'em be caught by theyself."

All hurried forward now, their own noise masked by three dogs barking. A short distance further, Dick froze and slammed his arm into Art's stomach. Ahead was a blur of motion. Dick pointed and crouched.

"Ease off to the south a bit," he said. "So's we don't shoot toward our own. Jasper must be near. Be ready to shoot."

"Dogs first!" Art said, and Dick gave him a friendly clap on the back of the head.

A gunshot deafened them all, and the dogs went wild. One of the closer-by white men had shot at something. Through the thick undergrowth separating them from Dick's group, six armed men were crouching with backs exposed, one unleashing the last dog toward Jasper's group. As Dick moved forward, a bullet tore through the Black-and-Tan hunting dog. It somersaulted in the air. Another dog crumpled before Dick could aim, and the third disappeared into the trees. Dick lowered himself to one knee and caressed his hair-spring trigger. His bullet drove a head above a rainslicker into a tree.

Then Lem and Art began firing. Two white men were already lying on the ground, and the old man who'd held the dogs was down on his haunches screaming. The other surviving white men had scurried off into little pockets of bush and cypress burl that extended down into a nearby soggy expanse. The land agents were on the ground, too, the white-looking one either cradling Sam Grant in his arms or hiding behind him. Crumby was screaming and shaking his head in air, eyes closed tight.

"Lordy, lordy! I'm a nigga! I'm a niggaaaa!"

"You sons o' bitches," Dick yelled from cover, "stand up wheah I can see you!"

One man, lying on his back continued firing, walking himself around in a circle like a crab, first one direction, then another. Dick pulled aside Lem's gun, aimed and shattered the man's leg.

"Stand up where I can see you!" Dick repeated.

None of the white men moved.

"Every body down will be dead!" Dick said. "Cover me, Lem!"

No one except Dick moved until the surviving intruders gave up their cover. Even the wounded tried to stand. Dick was completely out in the open then, and he walked among the white men with a fierceness on his face.

"Jasper!" he yelled.

"Yeah!"

"Me'n you! Come on out! . . . Rest of you, stay put."

The acrid smell of gunpowder was on the mist. In a solemn quiet marked only by the whimpering of a dog and the crunch of leaves as Jasper walked, something screeched on the wind overhead. Jasper halted apart, still wary of an ambush, but Dick walked around each of the intruders, poking their hands away from their sides with his rifle. Three lay unmoving, including the corpse embracing the tree. The old man remained on his knees, head bowed and unmoving but for a heaving chest.

"Git up grandpa!" Dick ordered.

"Yassuh."

The man stood on trembling legs.

"We will leave, if you let us," Crumby said. "Look heah, he hurt bad!" He nodded toward Sam who was cradling a bloodied arm.

"Be quiet!" Jasper said.

The man whose leg was shattered moaned.

"Where you from?" Dick asked him, quickly surveying two other men nursing superficial wounds and one gasping for breath through bloodstained lips.

"Beyond Friar's Point," came the answer. "We ain't know'd. We ain't know'd, lordy we ain't."

"Know'd what?" Jasper asked.

"We ain't know'd. We sorry we come," the man said, his jaw beginning to quiver.

"Bury 'em," Dick said, walking away.

"Please, please don't—not me!"

"Shut up, fool," Jasper said. "He ain't meant to bury you."

The sky began to darken as the dead men and dogs were buried by the survivors in a series of shallow holes scraped out of the soft earth of the nearby depression. Before all was done, the fourth man stopped breathing. His body was buried on top of another. The railroad crew saw only two faces: a strange, bloodless young white man—they thought—and a giant black man wearin' a bearskin who was somewhat rougher looking.

"Got local kin?" Jasper asked.

"Why you askin' about kin?" Dick whispered to Jasper.

"No kin, white folks be easier to deal with when they move on, non?"

Jasper ordered the survivors onto their horse and wagon, and Dick led them back almost to Buck's house from the edge of the swamp.

"Don't even think on returning," he said, "or you'll die."

Back inside the swamp, Jasper was whistling to himself as he collected all the weapons and tools that he could find. He then tied them inside the rain slickers of the men. Only then, after the white men were far enough away not to recognize a face, did everyone in concealment come together. There were no congratulations, no small talk. As Jasper finished his chore, everyone followed Lem's lead and sat on the ground, bone tired. They watched the tiny figures departing on Buck's path turn onto the Alligator Road.

"Ain't no tellin' what come next," Jasper said. "We done what we had to. Don't nobody doubt it."

"He's right, too," Cicero said.

"I sure do hope he is, Mr. Cicero," Lem said, shaking Art Canada by the shoulder. "Perk up, Art."

"Yeah," Jasper said, "you became a Africa man, today."

"A what?" Art said.

"Means you like me now," Jasper said. "Niggas what kill a white man ain't got to take back seat to nobody. You, too, Lem—y'all welcome in the deep swamp for any reason. Come git me, you need my gun for any redneck give you hurt."

"Would be my pleasure you'd all come visit the house," Dick said, returned from escorting the white men away.

"Mine is closer," Buck said.

"We been at yours, Buck. Come on by mine. You got a wife'n good furniture. I got better whiskey, and I say we need a bellyfull."

"Drinkin' a little help keep ev'rything clear," Jasper said. "Old Bill useta say memories like this what keep a tribe alive. Whatcha had in mind talkin' 'bout, Dick?"

"Nothin', wasn't nothin' special, I just feel like telling some of Bill's stories about this land."

"Our land!" Jasper said.

Variously they stood up, shook hands and started toward the path.

"If somethin' don't happen by next week," Dick said, "Won't be no posse. Local folks know better than to come out here in a small group, and unless the sheriff form a posse, maybe it all just pass. I'm hopin' it will. Even the hotheads know it won't be a turkey shoot. They only hoorah niggas who run and scream."

"Where you off to, daddy?"

"To be with Rose. You young people do too much drinking."

The day would not be celebrated in the history books, as Rose so well had understood the night Bill Williams died. Tribes celebrate neither defeats nor sins. Buck and Art went out the back door of the swamp along the Hushpuckena and surfaced in Mound Bayou where they remained with their wives until the agreed signal from Dick, who made daily trips up along the Alligator Road to nose out trouble, avoiding the open trail the first several days. Within the week, he sneaked over to visit Matilda, and hearing two men say she'd been away for almost a week, he hung around waiting for her to reappear. When people got off work, laughter in a nearby house caught Dick's ear.

"She gone, fool!" a woman said. "I'm all you got left."

A man was replying angrily as Dick moved closer.

"Miz Matilda gone, child," the woman said. "Got her a railroad man and gone to the big city."

"I didn't like her, baby, I just did my drinkin' over theah."

Dick rapped on the window frame, bowed when the couple turned.

"Would you be knowin' why Miz Matilda left?"

"Sure would," the woman said. "See, these railroad folk stumbled into some trouble. Claim they was waylaid by outlaws in the swamp—niggas, at that, they said. Man sweet on Matilda, come askin' to marry her fancy ass. Ha haaaa!" She pointed to her husband. "Niggas' like this one been grievin' ever since." When Dick said nothing, the woman snorted . "If you here for her, she took the train to Memphis and gone!"

Dick pretended to walk away, but he sneaked back to eavesdrop around the closed Social Club. Word was, the railroad men had been waylaid by brigands. No one understood why the survivors had left without waiting to give details to the sheriff, who even then was riding the track from Cleveland all the way up to the Coahoma County line asking after a band of armed strangers. There was some debate between those who swore the old crowd living in the swamp had struck again and those younger and more vigorous who knew with equal certainty that no negro would ever attack a white man.

Spring was soon upon them again, and another promiscuous green smothered the swamp. The rain awakened sleeping bayous, and they moved across the land but well below the ridge trails because levees now enclosed the Mississippi, and there was only the rain. For a very short time, Africa became a place apart almost like in the old days. All of its inhabitants, like waters withdrawing into their separate streams used that time to themselves, though in very different fashion.

Every time recent events surged into Buck's mind, he was both embarrassed by his own short-sightedness and by a lingering fear that the shooting in Africa still might prompt the authorities to take further action, at least call him in for questioning. Sam Grant had been dispatched back up North, but Buck made no immediate move to locate another railroad land agent even as he listened to white folks make small talk about new white settlers bringing a Renaissance to what many had begun calling "the Mississippi Valley".

In part because Dick had completely taken over the retail part of selling Jasper's whiskey—but also because of the trouble, and an injured hip that made if impossible for him to run—Jasper afterwards rarely left Africa and then only down the county to the wilderness east of Cleveland where Vern lived in what was no longer uncut swamp. Settling in with Mabel was perhaps an even bigger reason for ignoring the outside. Jasper took her to Vern's wedding shortly after Buck and Dick declared an all-clear behind the trouble. When Mabel returned with Jasper, she was all talk.

"Jasper treated me like he was a boy in love, Rose. He took me to three different camps and told everybody how much I been doin to help build his house bigger and keep his business straight. He even—and I don't think he knew I figured it out—introduced me to some woman he's been seeing right along."

"One was wanting to come up and marry him years ago," Rose said. "I was hoping for it until you came along."

"Thank you, Momma Rose. I had no reason to git mad, but the woman act like she still got a chance at somethin', come makin' him promise to visit next time he down there. He he . . . I oughtta said somethin', but I know Jasper don't like her much. Figure I act calm and maybe he feel guilty one day I point out what I know."

"What life you got in mind for my son?"

"Beg pardon?" Mabel asked.

"Why y'all git hitched, cherie? Had to be somethin' beyond bein' man'n woman together. You older'n most folks in that situation, an' I assume you was doin' it already."

"I'm a woman of God, Rose. The Lord brought me'n your son together."

"To do what, child? What you two gonna do together that you wouldn't have done apart?"

"For one," Mabel said, "I'm gonna build me a church."

"What you say?"

"A church family—a congregation, Rose. It's the only thing we women got where we have as much say so as the men, and we can show our children how to grow up."

"You want to build a church?" Rose repeated what she had heard as if not able to believe it.

"What I want is to get to know the folks hearabouts and kinda get 'em to understand what all a church can do for us. A church for Africa be a place where the best inside us kin come out and mix together. That's what I believe."

"Mabel?"

"Yes'm."

"I ain't a church lady in the same way, but I do believe in gettin' together, which is the part of church that make so much sense to me."

"What Jasper think, Momma Rose?"

"Ask him. Don't put me in between. But if you help me catch up on my work these next two days, I take you around the swamp nearby and introduce you to the folks I know."

"There's others nearby?"

"Sure, there is—mainly our people, too. They settlin' in the edge of the swamp this side of the railroad."

Mabel and Rose became a twosome, roaming. First, a little more than an hour's trek up to visit Sara. Mabel convinced Sara to hold scripture readings at home every other week for those interested, including a handful of new people now settling on the Alligator Road a short distance from where it crossed the main county road near Alligator. There was never a soul who didn't like Mabel, and she and Rose walked along the whole western edge of the swamp, Rose introducing Mabel to squatters clinging to survival like the smoke of a passing train. However, the first time Mabel invited some of them to come visit her house and hear scripture read, Jasper got angry. Rose happened to be around, and when he opened his mouth to complain, she gave him the evil eye. Jasper walked out of his house. After all the guests but Rose had departed, Jasper returned and pulled Mabel aside.

"Ain't havin' strangers in my house," Jasper said. "What you take me for?"

"This is the Lord's work, sugar," Mabel said. "I know you ain't a believer, but you ain't agin it."

"I'm tryin' to git by in this raggedy-assed world, and I ain't havin' the way to my home open to everybody."

"Marriage is for two," Rose said.

"This ain't concern you, momma."

"Alright, I keep quiet," Rose said.

"Now, Mabel, if you got to worship, do it yourself."

"It's all part of havin' neighbors and bein' civilized, Jasper. Look at your poor momma . . . You know how long she been waitin' to have folks mingle around here?"

"You in on this, momma?"

"Yes and no," Rose said.

"Well, what is it?"

"I introduced Mabel to the people, but the church is her idea."

"A house for the Lord—" Mabel began.

"Damn that!" Jasper said, taking his gun outside. "I'm goin' off for a few days. When I come back, you kin live in *my* house or in the lord's house—I'll even help build him one—but he ain't holdin' forth in mine."

"You full of anger, ain'tcha, sugar?" Mabel said.

"Quit talkin' like you ain't heard me."

Jasper walked away then, but Mabel ran after him.

"I pray for you, husband. I ain't forcin' nothin' on you."

"Ain't no heaven or you'da walked to it by now," Jasper yelled from a distance.

"You handled that pretty good," Rose said.

"Aw shucks, I been lonely too much not to see the good in a man want to live with me."

"You of a mind to fight him?"

"Heaven's no! I know he care for me, so I can take some yellin'. I just go along do like I want, make a little compromise when I have to."

"Where you from?" Rose asked.

"Born down below Cleveland, way down almost to Greenwood where they got a whole bunch o' lumber camps on the Yazoo River. My pa used to beat us every day almost. When he caught hell, he brought in home to us, which was why I run off awful young to git married the first time. Had a baby quick, and my husband got a job helpin cook and do odd work for some loggers come up to build a new camp over 'cross the Sunflower."

"Wondered how you got over there," Rose said.

"But the Lord had other plans. My husband died almost as quick as I got with child—tree fell on him—and all I had was a job cooking for those white men"

"I heard Jasper tell o' that."

"Hadn't been for me bein' with child, I don't know what them men mighta done to me, but I was big. Then Jasper come along, and even when he wasn't there, them white men knew I had somebody to turn to . . . That's when I got born again in the Lord, and if I have my way, Mr. Jasper will be, too."

SO IT WAS THAT SWAMP ONCE considered unhealthy for white people became a lure. The railroad extended its line southeast from Clarksdale down to Minter City, a settlement east of the Sunflower and miles beyond the logging community where Jasper had met Mabel. The new line turned a lot of landlocked timber into money as white railroad gangs began clearing that right of way and hauling out the timber to pay for more rails to extend the line through further stretches of the no longer so great swamp. Within a year, the railroad extended a spur from the Minter City line west toward Roundaway itself. New immigrants began pouring into the Mississippi Valley.

Forewarned by what had happened the year before, Buck cautiously approached another land salesman. Taking a page from Sam Grant's book, Buck told the man that he represented a syndicate of black businessmen who had adopted the name Africa Land Company. Like Sam Grant, the railroad man seemed eager to do business, but he told Buck that land that had never been surveyed couldn't be sold.

"Daddy," Buck explained to Cicero, "the railroad ain't willin' to survey over this far."

"Why?"

"Because the sheriff won't guarantee protection for the survey."

Little Buck had been down in the swamp for almost a week. He was growing and had become a bundle of energy. He began kicking to reach the floor, and Cicero handed him to Rose.

"Who told you this, Buck?"

"Mr. Shelley in Alligator told me. Families along the Alligator Road got the worse problem because folks we don't know are starting to use that trail, and they can see all the work been done on the land."

"Have you figured out who's behind the problem?"

"Not the plantations. So far as I know, they're not ready to buy over this way yet. I don't really know what's going on. Just so many new white folks coming, we got to do something. I figure if you convince Jasper and Dick to put together their whiskey money with what I've saved, we'd maybe have enough cash money to buy a whole section of land. In which case, the railroad wouldn't worry about a little survey expense. That could solve part of the problem."

"What's the rest?"

"The insurance companies won't talk to me about mortgages. They say Africa's reputation impairs security, but somehow I get the feeling the local agents don't want black folks on their own land."

"Well, don't talk to Dick or Jasper. You still haven't made up for going off and bringing new people in on your own."

"Daddy, I swear!"

"Just wait . . . You are more Isaiah's son than mine, and now I accept that. But, you need to think more like us. We don't do things without general agreement. Otherwise, you have to split up a camp and separate. Lose your power that way. Now, here's what I'd suggest. Rose and I have money stuck away with Jasper and Dick's money."

"Great!"

"For who, Buck? . . . I'm doing this in part because I've grown quite fond of your big-headed little son over there. He, he's giving me a chance for family I never enjoyed. So, I will deliver this money, and all I want is one promise."

"What's that, daddy?"

"We will never put people on this land and work them like mules. I do not hold with sharecropping. You understand?"

"Aw, daddy, there you go again. This a new day for the black man."

"Maybe, but answer my question—you agree to no sharecropping?"

"Okay, okay. Now, with a little credit we could buy two whole sections of land, and that would discourage anybody from trying to form a big plantation out of Africa."

"Wouldn't the railroad make you sign notes they could speed up and squeeze you?"

"Listen, daddy, since you helpin' me out, listen to this . . . What if we turn around and sell part of the land to folks willing to live out here where white folks don't mess around. Their money would pay off the note to the railroad."

"One more thing . . . Say nothing to anyone about where your money is coming from, not even to your wife, nor Dick."

"I understand."

Seeking to bypass Shelly through making a second railroad contact led Buck to Mound Bayou. Isaiah Montgomery gave Buck the name of a white man described as a sales manager. His office was in Memphis, an address that Isaiah cautioned Buck was not the same as dealing directly with the home office as Isaiah had done in his day. Buck posted a letter immediately, but sadly, he received no response from the new contact, and before writing a second letter that might result in word of his efforts leaking down to some local white man, Buck decided to go inform Shelly, the bigoted station agent, what he had been doing rather than to have Shelly discover it and think Buck was trying to cut him out of the deal.

"Cain't buy whole sections o' land," Shelley said. "We had too much experience with people o' your complexion buying up land they cain't pay for and tryin' to go hoodwink others they was tryin' to sell to. Now that land sales is bein' handled by us real railroad people, we ain't doin' no entrepreneur deals."

"No sir, I expect not. I don't want to buy options. I want to buy the title."

"Heh, heh, and where the money come from? I hear the mortgage man done turnt you down, and we ain't sellin' on credit."

"Then I have to pay cash."

Shelley's parched skin turned red. His eyes fluttered.

"Buck, let's get this straight. I ain't sellin' whole sections of land to no niggers. 'Sides there's white folks got interest."

Shelley spat tobacco juice. As he wiped his mouth and turned back toward the depot, Buck turned away. The man's flat-out refusal to take Buck's large order made the silence of the railroad Memphis office more ominous. Buck's response, still unwilling to chance bringing Dick or Jasper into his confidence, was to ease off, to buy small parcels at a time—enough to equal a half section at first, but in different names: his own, Lem, Art, even Dick and Jasper, though Buck never told them at the time.

A few weeks later, Buck paid cash for the final parcel of the first half section and took title in his own name. He heard no more from Shelley about another purchaser interested in the land, and he held off raising the issue. His anxiety remained higher than that of anyone in Africa. At least three more purchases needed to be made, and he was afraid to ask what was going on behind the scenes.

Meanwhile, Jasper was having a throwback to his younger self. Mabel reported to Rose that he just wouldn't stay home. She'd see him for a day or two, and he'd be gone again. Rose's sharing that Jasper had always been one to take off on forays through the swamp was comforting, and Mabel made no further complaint to Jasper.

Jasper's whole view of the world was in turmoil. He was not blind to what Buck was doing—not that he knew of Buck putting his name on deeds—but he could count and the new houses going up along the Alligator Road were a kind of dull ache reminding Jasper of all that was changing—the new river levees, the immigrants rushing out of the trains in Clarksdale and down the line. He heard for the first time about the new rail line over east of the Sunflower and decided to go take a look.

It had been years since wandering was so in his blood. Years before, he'd carry a few skins of whisky and just wander. Selling part of his whiskey would allow him to buy food if he chose to. When he sold out, he'd return home. But now he was older, married, no longer in need of money and chary concerning his own stamina compared to the man he had been as a youth. So, while he did not plan on leaving the swamp as such, he left home feeling guilty for having allowed the land around him to go un-scouted for so long.

In such mind, he walked over east of the Sunflower River and ran smack into work on the new rail line. Instead of lingering, he turned right around and marched back home. Dick, Buck and Cicero followed him back over to see for themselves, and Cicero prevailed upon Jasper to pose for a photograph, for his mother, Rose. A railroad man charged Cicero dollar apiece to take a picture of each of them.

Back home, Rose looked at the four photographs and stood shaking them as if they were wet.

"This pleases me," she said.

"Why are you fanning them around?" Cicero asked.

"I have no idea. Soon as I touched these pictures, I was happy like a few times when I was a girl. There's somethin' to be learned from all this. It's happy, but it's dangerous, too— like when I know a flood on the way that'll change everything. Caint' nothin' stop it, and I wouldn't try. So I try to see that water rushin' in on me like it was a friend."

"Other folks are interested in buying this swamp. That station agent is a crook and a Klansman."

"Relax, cherie, what can you do about a flood?"

"Aww, Rose, I know I can't do a damn thing."

"Then ease up inside. Come, I want to take Little Buck for a walk."

"How's he been?"

"Sick again, cherie, and I think it could be tired blood."

"What is it you think?"

"I don't know why he's so weak sometimes. He won't stop running around most times, then it's like he runs out of fire. End of last summer same thing."

"Mosquitoes, you figure?"

"It's what your newspapers say, and it squares with what I see. If he keeps having these spells, one might take him on away from us."

Rose walked over and cradled the sleeping little boy in her arms. He was now four years old but still under-sized. He awakened as Rose picked him up.

"Hey, cherie. Let's go get some air."

"Framma, frampa . . ."

"My own little grandson," Cicero said.

When they stepped outside the cabin, the child pointed and screamed in delight. Cicero stopped and watched the child's nostrils flare to the green smell, big eyes climb to the weave of branches from massive oak limbs overhead.

"Tell me what you see?" Rose asked him.

"Trees," Little Buck said. "Sky trees."

"Yes, indeed, cherie," Rose said, "little branches waving friendly over our own little piece of dirt. You hungry?"

Little Buck grinned and kicked Rose in his enthusiasm as he put both arms around her neck. Moments later, as the three of them wandered toward the pond, Little Buck was chewing on his thumb and still kicking against a tolerant Rose. Cicero wiped at a tear.

"What's wrong, cherie?"

"Life will have its own counsel, but I'm hoping we can make enough difference for this little one so he'll have a long, long life."

Trainloads of the immigrants flocking into Mississippi to harvest timber left Clarksdale each morning along one of the two iron roads now poised like scissor blades on either side of Africa. Along the existing rail line west of Africa, the railroad basically contracted to clear land for owners fronting its right of way in return for the timber. No longer Irish, the new men hailed from central Europe and many couldn't speak English. The new foreigners were called Slavonians. They lived in company barracks and worked for day wages, often giving up barracks for cheaper-yet rooming houses, many no more than barns with bunks in cubicles partitioned off by sheets. Dreaming of buying land if their wages kept steady, they extended a hand to others struggling like themselves. Black people, as well as white, advertised rooms for rent and took them into their homes.

Toward the end of 1894, twenty Slavonians came to live in what had been Matilda's Social Club, which had been renamed "Miz Matilda's Rooming House" to cater to the immigrants. Much to Dick's regret, she never moved back, though her neighbor informed Dick that she reappeared for a scant two days to sell her belongings, bragging to everyone of being married. She sold the house and Social Club to a Memphis businessman convinced the booming Mississippi Valley would make him rich. Mississippi Valley was the new name being bandied about—no more swamp, no more bottoms.

The businessman was Henry Potts, a short, wiry, coal-black man with the lumpy face of a gnome. Like Jack Sprat, little Henry was married to a big, friendly-faced woman who might have passed for white but for auburn hair that was cottony. They moved with two teenage daughters into the parlor section and downstairs bedroom formerly occupied by Matilda.

Mother and daughters cooked and served the Slavonians rooming upstairs and next door beside them.

"He a Jew, he is," Matilda's former neighbor said of Henry to Dick. "Make a quarter for every meal he sell'n a quarter more for every man sleep in his place. He don't pay me nothin' but always got some white man comin' to use my corral. I cain't say 'no' to no white man, kin I? . . . But his wife sell us leftover supper for half-price. She cook good, too. Mr. Buck Morgan told Henry Potts there ain't no safer place for folks our color to build a house than out near him. Mr. Buck say that's because white folks stays away from out theah."

That Christmas, it was pure sentiment toward Matilda that led him to go sample a meal at Matilda's old place. Instead of entering the Social Club—now a cafe where only food was served—he walked absentmindedly into the open house at dusk. A shadowy figure was dressing behind a curtain.

"Git outta here, you son of a bitch!"

Dick hesitated. For his trouble, a hot smoothing iron struck him in the chest. Swatting it away seared the flesh of his hand. Howling in pain, he backed outside and waited to confront his attacker, but no one emerged. He then stormed next door into the former Social Club.

"Who in hell is in charge?"

A tall, broad-chested, raw-boned woman in her middle years with woolly brown hair rushed forward.

"C'mon in, sit down, mister. We glad to see you."

The woman's ruddy-cheeked smile was compelling as she pointed out a seat on one of several rough benches that had replaced Matilda's upholstered couches. Dick wavered about mentioning the encounter next door as he reflected that he had barged in without knocking. Making his mouth water was the smell of onions and meat and something like gingerbread. The woman was cooking behind a new waist-high counter. Instead of Matilda's stained wall paper, new white paint glistened underneath fir tree boughs tied with red ribbon in celebration of the season. Footsteps drew Dick's attention to the woman bringing him a steaming bowl of coffee.

"Twenty-five cents for dinner. That include all the coffee you want."

She smiled and returned to dipping and portioning something onto plates. His hand began throbbing from the hot iron.

"S'cuse me, ma'am."

He walked back to the partition.

"Somebody in your house threw a smoothin' iron at me."

He held out his hand to show the blistering skin.

"Oh my! Here, let me put somethin' on that."

The woman led him back into a storeroom and reached a dipper from a water barrel. After wetting his hand, she packed on cooking soda.

"That was my gal, Fannie. She ain't mean harm, jes sort o' scared like—high strung'n jumpy. Runnin' a roomin' house with all these strange men do keep a young gal nervous."

Dick nodded, more than a little amused because the woman was talking to him in that peculiar combination of fear and humor used to calm an angry white man. He said no more, and when the woman motioned him back out front, he followed and settled down to watch her prepare his plate.

"Wouldn't you like a dessert before dinner? No charge, mister because you a real fine gentleman. I can tell you got some real fine manners, like rich folks has."

"Thank you, ma'am."

Dick felt a trifle flabbergasted because the one thing that he knew was that his rough upbringing had left him short on manners.

"My name Nan . . . Nan Potts."

The woman placed down a saucer of hot gingerbread overflowing with lemon sauce, just as the door scraped open. A younger, bronze-colored version of Nan appeared. She was taller than Dick, with dark coarse hair well brushed and heavily oiled but not hot combed, and it covered her head like a lion's mane, making Dick think of Rose. The face was chiseled in planes and angles where her mother's flowed in soft curves. Nor was she as ample-chested as her mother, but the swell and detail of her young body was a sweet challenge as she rushed to the counter and grabbed a butcher knife.

"Momma! This man walk in our house while I was undressed."

"You put that down! This a customer, an' he ain't done nothin' but git the front door confused."

"He watchin' me momma, I know."

"Shush up!"

Nan shoved Fannie behind the counter, then raised her beefy arm threateningly when Fannie balked.

"Git at them plates. Men be here soon." Then Nan spoke to Dick. "I apologize again, mister."

A group of Slavonians gathered in the doorway, and the babble of a foreign language overwhelmed the small room. Nan smiled and bowed.

"You gentlemens know there's water . . . water," she said, rubbing her hands together and over her face.

Two of the men returned outside, and turned in beside the building to a rusted pump and water trough. An older man remained inside. He flopped down heavily and snatched a sawdust encrusted handkerchief from his head.

"Nan . . . food!"

"Sure is, you wash . . . washey," Nan answered, snatching up the soiled headrag for emphasis.

A torrent of foreign words erupted as the man started outside.

"Git on with that servin', Fannie," Nan said. " You late."

"No such. Sister Babe ain't here yet."

"I got a word for her, too," Nan said.

Fannie was still holding her knife as she refocused on Dick.

"You want trouble, I give it to you," she said, snatching up an apron to begin work.

Dick watched her through his meal. More men entered, and Nan repeated her "washey, washey" each time. The fried pork chops with lots of rice and a brown gravy with onions were excellent. There were biscuits, too, and good buttermilk with ice in sweating tin pitchers.

The other sister finally arrived, and Nan began hissing inaudible commands to her tardy daughter, Babe. Like Fannie, the other sister was tawny colored and tall, though slimmer than Fannie. Fannie stared boldly when Dick walked toward them wiping his mouth. He tossed a quarter on the counter and headed for the door. Nan ran after him.

"'Preciates your business, mister. Come back an' bring your friends."

Sara Morgan usually made it a practice to withdraw whenever Dick started talking to Buck about women. This time, after a drink of whiskey herself, she hung around when Dick began describing a gal named Fannie who'd mistaken him for a white man and tried to brain him with a smoothing iron.

"Old man is evil, too," Buck said. "Other day, he chunked a stick of stove wood at that other daughter o' his. Said she was lazy."

"You're lyin'," Dick said.

"No siree, I ain't. Henry say 'Evuh crawlin' ant got to carry his load, gal.' Then—whap! He chunked that sticka wood right at the big gal's chest. If I was you, Dick, I leave Fannie alone. She even bigger than Babe, and that Babe just reach out and—Snatch! *One hand* grab that piece of wood. Caught it in mid air and chunked it away like a toothpick."

"You lyin', Buck Morgan!"

"May I never drink whiskey if I'm lyin'. I seen it!"

Little Buck had just had pneumonia and was no longer being cared for by Rose because Sara had insisted that Buck take their son to the white doctor in Alligator. Sara was tired from nights up tending her child. She refused another drink, however, because she believed no lady should touch more than one. Her going to bed left the cousins to drink and talk, louder and louder. The next morning, Buck and Dick were snoring where they sat.

The following afternoon, Dick walked behind Buck to where the trail in front of his house intersected the Alligator Road. There, a gnarled old man gleaming ashy-black in the winter sun bent over a building plan with Lem Huntwell. Art Canada and Art's oldest boy were hammering on a new wall frame while a third man issued directions.

"Good day to you, Henry," Buck said, as Henry looked up.

"Got my ca'pentuh workin'. Ain't got time fuh talk 'cause he got work to finish heah 'fore he git on back to Alligator."

"CC will give you extra time to talk to me. He drew the plans for my house, too."

"Yessir, Mr. Buck," Charles Caruthers said. "Anything you say, that's the way it be."

As Henry left his plans and ambled closer to Buck and Dick, the sound of timber hitting the ground startled everyone. Art Canada—whose humpback made walking and riding awkward—had knocked over a timber frame delicately balanced in place.

"Goddamnit, old man!" Henry said. "Cain't you watch what you doin'? You jes' loss yoursef a half day pay."

"C'mon home, boy," Art said to his son. "We ain't got to work for nobody."

"Wait a minute, Art!," Buck said, turning then to Henry. "This kinda like a fam'ly place, Henry, and we don't treat folks like they ain't due respect. I invited you to buy land here so you could be part of that."

Henry's brown eyes glowed in the sun as he shook his finger toward Buck.

"'Til you start payin fuh dey time, Buck Morgan, let me run things my way . . . Y'all git on home, you want to go."

Lem and CC returned to work while Buck shook his head, but Henry put his fists on his hips and faced off Art Canada.

"You leavin? Don't take all day. I got a house to build."

Henry spoke slowly, licking and sometimes flaring his wide and supple lips, as if he could feel and taste words in his mouth. Heavy eyebrows, high cheekbones and a massive nose made Henry look brutal. On Fannie, it was all blended with her mother's size and softness. But Fannie's eyes were all Henry's, orange brown and burning, almost wet with intensity.

As Art and his son walked away, the boy smiled up at Dick who saluted him. Henry turned to stare.

"Ain't made your acquaintance, mistuh. Seen no white gentlemens this fuh out before."

"He's my cousin," Buck said. "You hear tell of the Winchester Man?"

"Ain't had the pleasure."

"Anyway, this him. He live further in the swamp."

"Don't say? Evuh work fuh a livin', boy?"

"Dick kinda got his own business, Henry."

"I doesn't care. Let 'im speak fuh hisself."

"I work when I need to," Dick said. "Seems to me you're the one in need."

"Humph!" the old man said, clearing his throat before letting fly a stream of tobacco toward a pile of ants on the edge of the fire-cleared area set aside for the house.

"What do you say, Mr. Potts? Need me to work for you?"

"I say, you got muscle you kin use it. I pay good money you prove yourself. Meanwhile, till I see what kinda grit you got, I pays fifty cents a day plus supper at my place up in Bobo you wants to ride that fuh. Take more in oats fuh your hoss, I 'spect, but theah it is."

"Don't be a fool!" Buck said. "Haulin' my timber pay you more."

"I'll take your job, Mr. Potts, supper'n all."

"For fifty cents a day?" Buck snatched his hat off.

"'Tis fair, to let him see my work."

"Slave pay!"

Two days of house building passed uneventfully, Dick working faster than Lem Huntwell thought reasonable until Dick told him to shut up and quit complaining. Toward the end of that second day, though, Dick laid his hammer aside and walked to join Henry who was sitting on a stump.

"You ought to cut more timber along your lot edge. Better work room."

"Who say so?"

"Me, for one. Space between your walls and the trees is cramped. Why you think Art bumped your frame over?"

"Ain't wastin' good money to make it easy fuh careless work."

The first Sunday after Dick hired on, there was no work planned, but he persuaded Lem to help fell three good sized trees along one side of the new house. Dick then hauled them away with his mules. On Monday, Henry looked at the newly cleared space and grunted.

"Like's a man with a mind of his own."

And that was that, no thanks, and no pay for the overtime. Though confessing his aggravation to Lem, Dick meekly returned to work. On the following Sunday, he rode to the cafe. Fannie was alone.

"Go back outside. We doesn't serve colored where white men eat."

Dick did not return to the cafe all that week. On Friday, Henry approached Dick at the end of work and offered a plug of tobacco.

"Doesn't chaw, huh?"

"No sir."

Henry pocketed his wad and kicked through a pile of wood shavings at his feet.

"Be wrapped up heah in a few weeks, nearest I kin figure. You gonna work that long?"

"I ain't sure."

"Listen heah . . ." While motioning Dick to sit, Henry pulled a knife. ". . . You been takin' note o' one of my gals."

Dick stood up, backed away. Henry bent to scrape clay from a boot heel.

"Hit's only natchur'l, boy. She big, fine lookin', but she mean like me. Young, too. Ain't but sebenteen, an' used to gittin' her way. She fights wit the boys—leastways useta 'till I threaten to bust her head in. Caught her down on the groun' tryin' to choke this po little man to death what musta said somethin' personal to her. I had to put a end to that. Gal grown so her titty hangin' out, an' she rollin' roun' wit the fella. You know how folks talks."

Dick said nothing. Henry shrugged, turned back to cleaning his boots.

"You come eat suppuh any time you wants. Use the house. You understands 'bout dat cafe, don'tcha?"

"Yessir."

"Then, you got my p'mission . . . that is, if you man 'nough to handle Fannie."

When Dick visited the cafe, all he got was Fannie's bad-mouth. Only at her mother's insistence did Fannie ever serve him—once. He took to riding by from time to time, but Nan was the only person who ever came out to greet him. With Dick moping about and doing odd jobs for Henry, Jasper hired Lem Huntwell to help deliver whiskey.

"Why the boy so took with the girl?" Jasper asked Lem.

"'Cause he is."

"Why work for the old man? Dick cain't git nothin' outta him."

"You better ask Dick?"

Lem accompanied Jasper to Rose's cabin on the way to the still.

"Every time I see the fella," Lem said of Dick, "he ain't got no life, no jokin', no nothin'."

"Workin' too hard for too little money," Jasper said.

"Maybe it's love," Rose said. "Like you once felt for that young Maidy gal.

"Maybe they drugged his food," Jasper said.

"Nothin' to do with his mouth," Rose said.

Jasper began to brood on his young partner's plight. He told Mabel he was going to have a talk with the old man.

"Don't do no such. If you make him mad, he hold it against our Dick."

"Well, that's your opinion."

A few days later, Jasper appeared out of the trees at Henry's side. Henry walked away, until Jasper leveled his rifle.

"Don't even think of reachin' for your gun. My name, Jasper, and I already know yours."

"Folks know my name ain't usually drawin' on me."

"I killed more niggas and white folks'n I can remember. That mean I ain't a usual kinda nigga."

"Why you sneakin' like a rat?"

"'Cause of my young friends—you know Buck Morgan and his cousin, Dick?"

"I knows the gen'lmen."

"They tell you anything about my swamp?"

"Your swamp?"

"That's what I said. My gun keep this place what it is."

"Okay wit me, I see yo point."

"Now, set'n listen!"

"Always willin'."

"Why you workin Dick like a slave?"

"He freer'n me, wit his bright-skinned self."

"I ain't laughin'."

"Wasn't no joke, Mistuh Jasper. I ain't holdin' no gun on him."

"Stop takin' advantage of him."

"Got to be frank, suh. I ain't gone seekin' this young man. He come to me. This heah wheah I'm gonna live—less'n you

got some objection. The man ast me fuh work, he want somethin' I got. I ain't ast him for nothin' . . . Now, me'n you kin be
frank 'bout what he want."

"Talkin' 'bout your daughter?"

"Be happy to marry that gal off, yessuh! . . . Come ovuh
heah close. Cain't yell talk like this."

Jasper stepped closer and hunkered down.

"Girl chil'ren got to leave home sometime, but if it ain't a
good situation, dey come on back, an' then dey bringin' another mouth to feed. Know what I mean?"

Jasper nodded agreement.

"Fannie a problem 'cause I ain't met the man could handle
her, an' that's wheah your young friend come in. See, he ain't
scared of her, he jes' don't know what to do. But he aftuh her
like a good young bull. Gal high strung as Fannie ain't gonna
take up wit no boy ain't hangin' round long 'nough for her to
git over her fright. Now, that may surprise you, but it's the
truth. She big an' strong, but she sorta scared of bein' a
woman."

"If you say so."

"Oh, I do, an' I ain't wantin' her to try an' kill her husband
about somethin' neither. My girls took my ways—they fights.
Raised 'em that way cause they had to work the business."

"You made men outta them women?"

"Nawsuh, taught 'em how to keep men offa 'em. Fannie
don't need no knife or gun, she damn near kill a man wit a
pieca wood."

*"**H**elp! . . . Oh, please."*

Her wheelchair tipped over in the surf, and she struggled to hold her face above the surging waters. Her floppy hat, the afternoon sun glinting off its big white bow, was already floating out beyond the rocks that broke the wild surge of the ocean toward the beach. A wave washed over her head, and she choked, but he was there, wrapping his strong arms around her tiny, crippled body.

Sara Morgan put down her *Ladies Home Journal.* "Aileen: The Story Of A Winsome New York Girl" was into its third chapter, and Sara had read them all. But the words about the frail and crippled young woman might as well have been about her own undersized son. She got up and went to the middle bedroom and gazed down at the sleeping child who still seemed to be in recovery from his pneumonia. She blew on his long curling eyebrows and smiled as his little fist struck out against an imagined foe.

It was August, and the gauzy white lounging gown Sara had sewn was clinging and too warm, but she had it on because Buck adored it and he was due home any time. She had made it from a pattern in *Saturday Evening Post* whose clothes she preferred. But it was the *Journal* and its saga of crippled Aileen that kept her heart aflutter.

Sara walked back into the front and continued thumbing without purpose through her magazine. New people were

376

moving in closer. Those who had begun to settle along the Alligator Road a half mile or so to the north would soon create a community of their own to drop in and visit, and Sara looked forward to it because living on the edge of the swamp was lonely. Her parents lived all the way down in Mound Bayou now.

Unfortunately, Henry Potts' wife Nan—as friendly and unpretentious as she was—made Sara feel not quite up to the mark, that of becoming a gracious lady. It was as easy with family as owning a big house and store-bought clothes. Sara's kitchen was as big as her dining room, and she had a cooling pantry the width of the house. But when visiting Nan, whom Sara considered one of the better class of colored women— those who had lived in a real city—she plastered a constant smile over her yawning insecurity and kept her mouth closed to hide her ignorance of all the things she feared she should but did not know.

Slow hoofbeats in the distance announced Buck returning. At that moment, Little Buck screamed, and Sara tossed her magazine to the floor and ran. Out of the little bed with side rails almost still like a crib, she snatched him up still screaming and writhing to get out of her arms.

"Oh, my sweet l'il thing. What the matter?"

But the child screamed even louder, and he was so hot to the touch Sara panicked. When Buck finally walked inside, Sara was screaming along with the child.

"Calm down, Queen Lady, I'm here."

"Buck, Buck . . . the baby. I was sittin' like a pure fool with my magazine and ain't payin no attention to my baby. I shoulda known he was ailin' before he start screamin' his lungs out. Oh, Buck! He dyin' this time."

"Hush, Sara, ain't no thing like that gone happen. Gi'm to me."

"Momma Rose say keep him wet when he hot."

Sara shoved the angry, screaming child into Buck's arms

"Got git some water then, and some towels. This dog-day weather got him goin'."

Sara ran into her nearby bedroom and returned with the pitcher and the nightstand basin. Buck lowered the child, short pants and all into the basin.

"This cool him off right quick."

"Maybe we ought to take him back to the doctor."

"You want me to drive him into Alligator?"

"That Alligator doctor didn't do no good before."

Buck was busy ladling hands full of water over his son, whose bawling had ceased, and his big feverish eyes reflected his shock every time a handful of cold water broke over his tiny body. Buck finally looked to Sara, shook his head.

"I'm thinkin' Rose again, Sara. That white doctor in Clarksdale don't like treatin' our people, and I know folks say havin' him is worse than not having a doctor."

"But long as Momma Rose been givin' him stuff, he ain't got no better."

"Hell, she'n my daddy love this child. That bastard in Clarksdale ain't gonna put his hands on my son. I'm goin' down into the swamp."

"What about his medicine, Buck? You gonna take that with you or you gonna ask Rose to do her roots."

"Sara, doctor say give him quinine anytime he start with fevers an' chills. So I'm takin' it with me. Now, relax. I don't believe in magic no more than you. Rose know roots to make a person stronger, and that is what I believe in."

"Humph! Why you don't believe your own father."

Buck lifted the dripping child and handed him to his wife

"Wrap him up in some dry stuff, but leave him wet. I'll git a mule saddled."

Buck walked straight through to the back. Sara followed Buck and watched him run out behind the house to the barn. Within minutes, Buck rode up to the back steps and reached.

As he accepted the child, he circled his free fist with the reins of the mule.

"Don't look for me back tonight. I'll stay with Cicero and Rose."

"Be careful in that god-forsaken swamp, sugar. That's our only son in your arms. You know I cain't have no more."

Down into the swamp Buck rode, caring little where his mule stepped. Cicero was off fishing when Buck arrived. As soon as Rose looked at Little Buck, she walked over and snatched a ball of clean smelling tree gum from a saucer.

"He likes it," Rose said. "Give 'im a reason to smile."

And so the child did as Rose eased the fragrant ball into his mouth. In fact, he bounced from his back and began trampolining up and down in the bed on his knees, his fever suddenly a bouncing frenzy.

"Git you somethin' to eat if you hungry, Buck. I expect you want to stay the night."

"If you don't mind."

"Now, why would I mind? Your poppa would like to see you more often—I know, you're busy. Did you give the little one his quinine?"

"Oh, yeah, it's about time."

"Cicero says you have to be regular."

"He get it regular enough. Maybe hour off here'n there."

Rose pulled a cup off the wall rack and poured a dollop of syrup into it. Buck opened a vial of white powder and dusted out enough to cover the nail of his index finger. The first measured was wasted when Little Buck jumped into his approaching father's hands. So, the father measured again. Rose sat beside the child and calmly snuggled him as if for a kiss, and he quieted enough for Buck to approach with a spoon. After the little mouth opened, Rose rubbed the child's head and stood up.

"You keep an eye on the little fella. I need to go find something."

"It's late, Momma Rose. Where you goin'?"

"Not far, I hope. "

When Rose exited the cabin, she took a deep breath. Young parents that they were, Buck and Sara easily persuaded themselves that something they wanted to do was more important than full and nourishing meals for Little Buck. Sara didn't like to cook anyway. As Rose walked around behind her cabin, she shook her head to rid it of her judgmental thought. She moved a few hundred yards toward the Sunflower and then south into the least traveled of what remained of their swamp to find a calico tree, Rose's own name for its mottled bark. Cicero had explained about quinine from bark, but this was different. Nothing related to malaria. Rose had decided that Little Buck was what in another century would be called over-active. A sedative would allow him to rest more deeply.

As Rose searched for her calico tree, she began to smell the dissolution of life that arose inside the swamp late every summer, a funk that lay harsh in the low trail below the Sunflower River ridge, but then a breeze stirred and pushed away the dissolution of plant and animal parts becoming mud. Seeds of the future tumbling free rode the wind into her face subject, she mused, to whatever currents were imposed by existing hearts, minds, tribes, and gods. Human kinship, more than any of the principles Cicero affirmed, seemed to lie behind how people and their cultures were remembered. The past was a kinship place, where Rose's broken lines to Africa gathered in her person, or in what Songhai had known, as they did in common habits she and Cicero shared, their conscious choices repeated. Yes, especially those choices, for she and all displaced Africans were a tribe newly defining themselves in a hostile land.

The soar of her thoughts took Rose away from her preoccupation with Buck and his son. Her heightened awareness of her surroundings brought her tired heart out to feel the late afternoon glow coming down through the trees, and sud-

denly, Rose was in total awe of one spreading lordly oak atop
the high ground to her left, a small nation of limbs the size of
a man's waist intertwining and reaching upward. Surrounded,
it was, by cottonwood and willows. There was an order to living, and Rose knew that all she could do was to administer a
few ordering substances to nurture Little Buck's small life.
Sara was a decent mother. Little Buck just needed more than
she could deliver. Rose chuckled at how much in love with the
child she was.

A greater whimsy now came over Rose, and each of the
trees she approached greeted her upon passing—an oozing
red gum tree, an acorn-spitting overcup, and a rustling water
oak community growing down the incline. Below them, a
silent spotted sycamore lurked, two upright and very proper
ash trees and a delicate-branched elm let a flock of birds do
their talking. Further down in the places that would actually
hold water in the spring, thuggish hordes of black willow
clamored for the attention of ever sentinel cypress that
bragged of being older than time itself.

But no calico tree, and few could be found. In fact, since
leaving the Gulf Coast, Rose had seen only two. One was a
ways ahead, it's bark mottled like that of a sycamore tree, but
calico bark contained the sedative she was seeking. As Rose
approached a narrow depression that had flowed into the
Sunflower three or four years back but now simply gathered
water for a couple of months, she walked up over its ridge and
paused to scrape into a pouch a goodly amount of the green-
est of the hearty algae sprouting atop the few places of watery
mud. Algae was nourishing and the simplest of foods, something Yellow Woman had always harvested and sneaked unknown into soups and breads to disguise it from the finicky
disdain of the men of the family.

She recalled something then that Abyssinia had said of
Mrs. John Clark, that she had been sent as a sickly white girl to
live in the hills during the hot season. As subject to illness as

Little Buck was, not up in the white hill country, but perhaps up to Memphis. A summer or two in Memphis was certainly a possibility. Sara might herself enjoy the diversion.

With so much about Little Buck on her mind, Rose almost did not notice the suspended cache of deer meat, some of which dated from the year Cicero got so busy early in the season in his orgy of guilt about being away. Dry and tasteless, the critter had been because he'd been killed at the end of winter, but the dark meat, cut in strips and salted and dried before being rolled inside a skin was still there hanging in place. Rose walked over and climbed up to the rope securing the bundle above harms way. For no reason, she cut the rope and watched its burden tumble to the leaf-covered ground. Because of recent heat, the meat inside had sweated, and Rose's face reflected her disdain for the smell. Its taste would be off and not very attractive to anyone having her pick of a fresh kill. While thinking on changes within the meat, it occurred to Rose to force young Buck through a good sweat. Whatever else, a cleansing from poisons leaking out of his sick blood should help.

Then Rose saw her calico tree, healthy and surrounded by suckers growing from its roots, themselves circled by a ring of three-foot high gnarl from a massive cathedral of cypress trees. Their knobby knees would not grow up an incline, a dry one at that on which the calico grew, but those cypress knees made a tight fence at the base of the incline. No other trees had made it through, not even the ever-present cane.

When Rose returned home, she set about preparing her special feeding for Little Buck. He was all eyes as Rose began the first stage of concocting her remedy. She had gathered a bag of scuppernong grapes on the way home and began boiling them down with added sugar because they were not fully ripe. The sweet smell caused a tantrum because Little Buck didn't want to wait. After he quieted, Rose crushed her bark and steeped it directly in the fruit compote. Once cooled, she would strain it and mix in the algae. Buck, Sr., also watched carefully. Rose explained that all she was preparing was a country remedy.

"But I was born in the country, too."

"No, cherie," Rose said. "You was born in Vicksburg."

"Naw, naw—it was on the old plantation south of Vicksburg. That's where momma was living."

"Buck, I never met your momma, but Davis Bend was the closest thing to a town. Then Vicksburg and Isaiah Montgomery's new town, places folks had the best there was. My remedies come from where people don't have nothin'."

"Well, maybe so."

"No maybe about it." Rose put down her spoon, ignoring a reprise of Little Buck's squeal of disappointment.

"You don't have a country person's sense of the little things —how to enjoy what you got. The future ain't guaranteed."

The next morning, Cicero had not yet returned. Rose was up and mixing the cooled mixture, adding in her algae, when Buck headed for the door.

"Don't have to go, son."

"Got to."

"Your poppa," Rose said, "would like to see more of you."

"I got work waitin'. Tell him I wish him my best."

"Cicero want you to tell him the latest about the land."

"Nothin' yet to say. I'm tryin'."

As Buck turned and stepped outside, he walked into Cicero.

"How's my Bucko?"

"Oh, daddy! I wanted to wait, but I couldn't."

From inside the cabin, Rose's voice.

"Little Buck had a fever that turned into a chill last night."

Cicero rushed past Buck and inside.

"How is he now?"

"Look for yourself," Rose said.

Little Buck was sitting up between two pillows waving his fists. Grape colored jam surrounded his mouth.

"Frampa!"

"Hey, my little son!"

"You mean, grandson, don't you?" Buck asked.

"Time with him is like time I didn't have with you."

Cicero was still holding a sack of fish in his hand. Rose took them from him and walked outside. Cicero sat on his bed and lifted the tiny boy who for some unknown reason started trying to kick his grandfather.

"Here inside the swamp . . ." Cicero paused to corral the boy's legs with his arms. ". . . my life was reading, hunting, helping my wife and making notes for memoirs—until you presented me with new family. He is more important than everything else, now."

"Aw, daddy."

"Don't let this little one pass you by."

"Yeah, I know."

"I wouldn't say this to Dick or to Jasper . . ."

Little Buck broke free, climbed down from the bed and ran outside. They all watched him leaping up trying to get at a scolding rooster in the suspended chicken cook.

". . . and I don't disrespect who they are, but *you*, Buck, are likely to become the future of this land. Dick and Jasper are good, strong and fearless. But life is about the peace time, and you understand some of the things of peace—trade and what not. I wish this swamp would last forever, but . . ."

"Why ain't you never said—"

"Hear me out . . . End of Reconstruction, our most forward thinking people got lynched. Freedom and voting had made us grin only to have Reconstruction kick us in the teeth. Meanwhile, our handful of so-called success stories like Isaiah went about becoming Big Negroes . . . So, I'm thinking now, maybe you begin to set an example for forward-thinking Big Negroes."

"Look," Buck said. "Weren't for Mr. Booker T. Washington, no tellin' what shit we be in. White folks got no use to pretend no more."

"Who helps you on the outside? Old Senator Bruce over in Rosedale—even Booker Washington—your Uncle Isaiah knows them, but who do you know?"

"Uncle know 'em is enough."

"Hell!" Cicero laughed. "They're black like us, but they're walking in shadows. Blanche Bruce got his pride hurt when he tried to get a law passed to protect us from the Klan. All he has left from all his politics is patronage, a tax collector job. Same for John Lynch and the other Nigga-publicans who didn't fight their way out of that trap."

"Uncle Isaiah say, take as much as you can get. Otherwise the other fella—or the other race—take everything. Been that way since the world started." The wrinkled brown of Buck's face relaxed, and he smiled. "So long as the white man can run things, both the Northerners and the old mastas are happy. As long as they happy, people like me can do some business."

"But what are you doing for the people?"

"Me!?"

"That's what I asked."

"I'm a town builder."

"So you will never challenge the system that makes everybody but you town builders stand in misery?"

"No, daddy. That ain't what I said."

"It's what I tell you will happen, if you don't make the decision not to let it."

"But, daddy, it was when folks like you tried to make us vote for our own people that things got nasty. Me'n Mr. Booker Washington agree. We let the white man have politics. Black folks should be worried about makin' a livin'—or makin' they fortune, leastwise us who got it inside to do that. That's why it's taking so long with the land title. No sense in me yellin' and screamin'. I got plans for after I get the land."

That afternoon, after the sound of Buck's mule had faded, Cicero walked out to join Rose who was scaling fish.

"I'm walking over to Jasper's so I can bring young Bud back and let the boys play with each other."

"Good idea."

"Mabel can use the time. Bud must be at least six years old, and while I wouldn't live on the outside and do it, I'm thinkin' of a school right here."

The idea had a long history. Teaching was Cicero's initial profession, the way he had first earned a living at Davis Bend, studied in college. That very week, Cicero arranged to have Bud and Little Buck, along with Art Canada's oldest son down at his and Rose's cabin. Rose was as pleased as was Cicero, and they boarded the children like an army of charming brigands. Not even to Rose, did Cicero admit what was really on his mind, that if he had lost Buck to the world of exploitation, he would pour out all that he had into this next generation so that perhaps one of them might grow up different and become the center of a new ferment toward justice in the world.

Each day, the three boys became Rose and Cicero's own tiny community. She would get them up in the morning and teach them sharing and respect. Rose took her time to intercede in each and every little squabble that broke out. Cicero easily taught Bud and Art, Jr. the rudiments of verbally repeating the alphabet. Little Buck just wouldn't sit still for it. About two weeks into his effort, still a warm Indian Summer day, Cicero took his three charges to visit the pond he and Rose used for bathing. It was the end of a trident-shaped fork of waters the northern-most prong being Dry Bayou along which Dick's cabin stood. This was the western end of the southern prong, connected by the back of the trident. It was not a flow of water, just a year-round pool thanks to some soil condition that did not allow for seepage away.

Cicero's mind was less on the children than the coming opportunity to soak his aching back. Little Buck led the charge of the children, and Cicero heard the screaming bravado, the doubting taunts, the dare, the sudden silence. Only when he came in sight of the water did his heart lurch and he begin to run. Little Buck had leapt into the pond and was thrashing about unable to swim.

"Throw him a stick, Bud!" Cicero yelled.

Bud calmly kicked off his shoes and waded in. The water never came above his shoulders. Little Buck had been floundering in water he could have stood in, but for his panic.

"Come on out of that water!" Cicero yelled as he paused on the edge. Little Buck was still gasping in the grasp of Bud's arms, and he was clutching Bud like a lover. Art, Jr., also older than Little Buck, waded out beside the other two. But every step Bud took to exit, water sloshed over Little Buck's face, and he screamed. Cicero growled, walked in with his shoes and picked up both boys. Art, Jr. followed them out.

"You are one crazy child," Cicero said to his grandson.

"I want to swim!"

"No, you cannot."

"But, frampa, I can swim!"

"Don't say you can when you can't."

"He always act crazy," Bud said.

"I do not!"

"Yes, he do, Mr. Cicero," Bud said. "When you go inside, he be climbin' on the wood pile trying to get on your roof, and he jump off like a fool."

Cicero's mouth opened, but nothing came out. He, himself, had not been a particularly physical child, except for sneaking down the bluffs of Vicksburg when his father, Morgan, was away. Cicero usually never even played out of Morgan's sight. Recalling this made Cicero laugh, and so did Little Buck. Then the tiny but irrepressible big-eyed child started turning hand-springs, and the older children followed him away. Leaving Cicero to purse his lips, until he gave up trying to fathom the mystery of life inside his grandson.

Bud returned unnoticed, and his little hand grasped Cicero's pants.

"Momma say he got the heart of a dead man."

"What?!"

"Say if he didn't near die as a baby, he be scared to do crazy stuff. Praise the Lord, Jesus."

Later that afternoon, after Sara had ridden into the swamp and picked up Little Buck and Art, Jr., Cicero walked Bud home They were walking single file. Bud seemed to know the way.

"So you believe what your mother believes?" Cicero asked ahead.

"Yes."

"What is that?'

"We got to praise the Lord," Bud said.

"Do you know what that means?"

"No."

"Then why do you say you believe in that?"

"What does 'believe in' mean to grown people?"

Next day was Cicero's planned day off. Rose had left on an errand, and Cicero had eaten but could find no reason to dress. He heard the slowly emerging noise of feet through the leaves walking closer. When the noise stopped Cicero looked up. The cabin door opened, and Bud stepped inside.

"Mr. Cicero?"

"Come on in, Bud."

Cicero hurried out of bed and into his trousers as the child stepped inside.

"Mr. Cicero, I brought you this."

He held out a jug of whiskey.

"Who sent it?"

"My daddy."

"Your daddy should know," Cicero said, "that we have whiskey older than you."

"He wanted me," Bud said, "to see how long it took coming over here."

"What!?"

"He want me outta the house more. Momma didn't say nothing because Mr. Buck was there."

"Buck was at your house?"

"Momma want Mr. Buck to teach me about white folks. Daddy say I don't know enough about the swamp, and momma and him was yellin' when Mr. Buck left."

"So what happened?"

"Daddy told momma he wanted me to come over here."

"And your momma didn't say a word?"

"Daddy think I'm learnin' about the swamp, but it ain't nothin' to learn walkin' over here."

"Your poppa," Cicero said, chuckling, "never did understand that other people are hard critters to handle."

And then Cicero recalled Little Buck's refusal to sit still for alphabet drill, remembered years further back when he was tutoring Dick, how only by teaching Dick to teach his mule had Dick learned to read.

Next time the children gathered, Cicero put aside his alphabet. Instead he told stories, stories about white masters bamboozled by their slaves, stories of the swamp, of the giant bear with the head of a man, of garfish longer than a boat, of tiny little minnows that could swim up your nose. And as he tired, and took liquid refreshment, he began talking about the war to free black people and of the great struggle to remain free and to keep the vote.

"Yes, Bud?"

"Mr. Buck say, only thing worth worrin' about is this land."

Buck advised Shelley, the railroad station agent, that he was ready to buy more land, but the station agent turned away, and otherwise ignored him. Unwilling to push, Buck went to purchase home supplies in town, but before Buck left Alligator he heard Shelley talking with a passer-by about a nigger from the swamp throwing his money around. Within a week, Isaiah Montgomery had heard the grousing repeated all the way down in Mound Bayou, and he sent word for Buck to come visit.

"You makin' big time moves up your way."

"Nothin' more than you taught me."

"No, I'd say you doin' me one better. First off, you didn't start out with nothin', and here you already bought near a whole section o' land."

"Me'n some others."

"I know, but you got the 'tention of the big white folks in the north county. Understand the tight you in, young nephew. The white folks crave what you buyin', but they ain't willin' to give cash money."

"How you know, uncle?"

"Mr. Boudreaux. Some of my people still makin' time payment to him. He ain't from around here, though he a Southerner. What he don't know is my connection to you. He told me railroad want to go ahead and wrap up its land sellin'.

Said, too, that some plantation people cross river from you
tryin' to block your deal . . . And, there's Klan people making
common cause with that red-neck station agent. He so jealous
o' how much money you kin raise, he got his Klan buddies up
in arms."

"What are telling me to do?"

"If you lucky, Boudreaux and his white folks will tell that
redneck station agent to back off. You be real careful, though,
'cause once a po peckawood hear you gone over his head,
look out."

"Yes sir."

"By the way."

"What?"

"The County Road Supervisor want to meet you. He the
most important white man you got to deal with in breakin' up
your land for sale. Keep your community a fam'ly place. No
disreputable types whether they got money or no. Whatever
folks livin' around you do, it will be blamed on you personally
'cause you the town-builder."

That last piece of advice stuck in Buck's mind because he
had been raised to prove himself to the world. He began keeping track of who moved close to Africa, squatter or otherwise.
Some of Sam Grant's prospects began clearing plots along the
Alligator Road as others already had on the western fringe of
the swamp along the railroad. People learned to go seek
Buck's permission, acknowledging that there were those in
the swamp who might have to be placated

Never before had the Fourth of July been celebrated, for it
was no holiday in Africa. Every day was for work, even Sundays, especially as the new people understood the need to save
every penny toward buying up the land they were living on.
But by the middle of 1895, the population on what people
were calling "the Road" had grown to where they—being
newly from the outside—made plans to celebrate having
found a place of sorts in the world. There was no awareness of

any irony in Africans celebrating American independence in the middle of the Mississippi Valley.

All along the edge of Africa, black people considered themselves fortunate to be living near a place mischief-minded rednecks avoided. Some along the railroad right of way west of Africa had bought land directly from the railroad, but even those along the northern edge of Africa for whom the future was still uncertain felt happy and proud to be in place. Henry's house had been finished on schedule. The Canada family, the Potts, Lem Huntwell, "CC" Caruthers, the carpenter who'd planned Buck's house and now come join the group—all now lived along the dirt track heading west toward Alligator at or west of where the trail to Buck's house joined it.

Sara was delighted to be asked to help organize what she and Buck proudly called their Fourth of July town picnic. Some called Sara the most elegant woman out in the country, and Nan Potts, though a newcomer, was selected to help because she was so friendly. There was no organized sentiment to exclude those living in the deep swamp. Lem and Art knew them well enough, but not so the group who lived to the west where cleared railroad land abutted what remained swamp. Henry and Nan Potts, CC the carpenter, were apprehensive about those upon whose reputation with guns they all relied. A certain inconsistency, of course, but these were family folk, understandably cautious about being in the presence of the very people upon whom the tranquility in their community depended.

Most called Jasper and the others "swamp people" or "them old heads live back up in the woods." Mabel had met most of the new people on her bible Sundays, but they really didn't know how many, nor who her people were. Everyone had heard of the Winchester Man, whose reputation selling whiskey outside the swamp was mixed with old rumors about the swamp itself. Cicero was considered eccentric, and what he'd often thought meticulous dressing was by now old fashioned. Neither Jasper nor Rose—nor the numberless others by which imagination began to multiply the clan—were known personally.

Some twenty men, women and children lived on the Alligator Road at or west of where the trail up from Buck's house joined it. Not quite another hundred—a few of them sharecroppers for white farmers who'd begun buying up partially cleared acreage—were settled just beyond the western fringe of the swamp. Jasper had never visited the little farmers, and their axe strokes made him cringe as they little by little cleared their 20 and 40 acre plots.

"Why," Mabel asked Jasper, "you so against them little people?"

"'Cause, Mabel Scroggins, them corn'n hog people cuttin' back my home."

"It ain't even close-by," Mabel said.

"Go walk around you run smack into 'em."

"Oh, Jasper, ain't you happy since we been together?"

Before Jasper answered, seven-year old Bud ran to the window and watched as a rider rode closer.

"Finally heard that animal, did you?"

"I heard him," the tyke said to Jasper, "but I didn't want to disturb you'n momma talkin'."

Bud ran outside because Little Buck was standing on the rear of his daddy's mule holding onto Buck's shoulders. Bud ran down the trail to walk along beside Little Buck as he and his father continued on in.

"Hey there, Li'l Fella!" Jasper shouted.

Little Buck grinned and waved.

"Watch this!"

As Buck's mule passed under a tree growing over the trail, the child leaped off of the mule to grab an overhanging limb. Bud clapped his little hands, Mabel screamed and Jasper slapped his thigh in mirth.

"Hang on there, Li'l Fella. You shouldda been my boy."

"Hello, Jasper," Buck said, dismounting. "I wanted to be sure you heard me coming. Afternoon, Miz Mabel."

"Afternoon, Mr. Buck," Mabel said, coming forward to kiss Buck on the cheek.

"What you come for?" Jasper asked, watching Little Buck swing his leg up and over the limb to pull himself up and sit on it.

"Let him come inside," Mabel said. "It's cooler . . . Jasper piled dirt up against the south wall, Buck, so we don't git no hot sun."

"That boy o' mine . . ." Jasper pointed at Bud now climbing up into the tree to sit alongside Little Buck. ". . . ain't know enough to tell me somebody riding a damn mule down *my* trail in broad daylight."

"Mr. Cicero," Bud yelled from his perch, "say I can read good."

"Books," Jasper said, "ain't nothin' when you runnin' from the law."

Buck and Mabel had started into the house.

"Come on in the house, Jasper," Mabel said. "Mr. Cicero give him books 'cause he know my Bud smart."

"Ain't what bother me," Jasper said to Buck. " Tell that boy how you'n Dick had to kill them white men tryin' to hurrah Mound Bayou."

"Well," Buck said, "that was . . . seven, eight years ago."

"Jasper!" Mabel said. "Times has changed."

"No such!" Jasper said, passing a small jug of whiskey from his newly constructed front porch to Buck.

"Got a glass?"

"You kin drink from my jug or ask Miz Mabel for a glass."

"Oh, Jasper, you so ornery these days—he is, Buck, and I think it's 'cause he know he got to change with the times, quit his old evil ways."

"What you come down here for, Buck Morgan?"

"Sara asked me to come and make sure you and everybody down here is coming to the picnic on Saturday."

"What picnic?"

"Don't be mean," Mabel said. "You know what picnic 'cause I told you."

"Mabel be there, but there's swamp folk an' there's the other kind. I ain't changed so much I take pleasure from being around that other kind."

Mabel had been pestering Jasper for some time about his whiskey money. She was eager to confirm that they had enough to send Bud to board in a proper school, which had been Buck's suggestion to Mabel, to find a boarding school in which her son could slough of the roughness of growing up in a swamp. To get Mabel off his back, Buck's visit prompted Jasper to use the time.

"You visit with Miz Mabel, Buck. I got a errand."

"Things to do myself. I just brought word about the picnic."

As Buck waved farewell to Mabel and walked to pull Little Buck out of the tree before re-mounting his mule, Jasper headed off.

Not yet half-way to his mother's cabin, he approached a tree with a broken trunk green with well-watered lichens and hollowed out by rot. It stuck up like a dark chimney above a burl of brush and dead wood piled against the lower reaches of the trunk. As soon as Jasper climbed up onto the burl and looked inside, he was apprehensive. He moved aside the rotten wood covering his money box and pulled it out.

The money was gone, most of it. From panic, Jasper's emotion leapt quickly over into anger when he realized that there were no signs of his hiding place being broken into. The wet rotten wood covered with still growing lichen from on top of the money box had been carefully replaced. There were no gouges or other signs of recent intrusion.

Jasper walked as fast as he could over to Rose and Cicero's because part of the money belonged to them. No one living in the swamp had spent much money, and what they did spend was often taken straight out of new whiskey money which meant no one touched the stash more than once or twice a year to add to it. Jasper arrived close to dark, and he flopped down at the yard table to join his stepfather and mother.

"I don't know what to say," he began, running his hand over his face. "I don't even know what to ask you but . . . our money gone!"

Rose looked to Cicero, and when he attempted to stand, she placed her hand on his shoulder.

"So, what's the problem, cherie?"

"Momma?! You got something to do with this?"

"Yes."

"So, where our money?"

"I talked to Rose," Cicero said, "and back when you and Buck and Dick weren't always speaking to each other, I made a decision."

"What we done," Rose said, "was to take that money and use it to help buy as much of this swamp as we could manage."

"You what!?"

"We bought our land to keep others away."

"You ain't the president o' no bank!"

"You don't always see what's in front of your nose. You had no use for the money. Now it's out there workin' for us. That's what Cicero and I decided."

"Well, as Dick say, damn me to hell, 'cause that's the craziest thing I ever heard. Buck come in here an' just take over, shit in my face—and you, Cicero . . . I thought I could trust you."

"Mind your manners now, Jasper."

"Mind, my ass! Goddammit, I want my money back, and I'm goin' see Buck."

Rose stood up before Jasper came to his feet.

"Remember us raiding that outlaw cache in Louisiana? They'd captured you, and me'n Brother helped you escape?"

"Yeah, I remember, so what?"

"Part of that money was Confederate. It looked real so you took it. But you couldn't spend it."

"*My* money was good!"

"Not sittin' out there in that tree. Wasn't doin' nothing . . . I'm sorry son, but you don't know everything. I was sick to death that Cicero didn't join us until a few years after we left Davis Bend, but now, I understand what his reason was. I didn't understand at the time. We don't always understand what others in the fam'ly do . . . Verlean had disappointed you and sold her land after you'n Bill spent years keeping this swamp clear o' outsiders—how was you to understand what Buck learned about land title, what Cicero and me come to accept?"

"I do apologize, Jasper. It wasn't a straight-up thing I did."

"Keep it to yo'self, Cicero. I'm so mad I don't want to talk."

"Listen, cherie . . . Don't go screamin' at your wife. It surely ain't her fault. Tell her, I see her at the Fourth of July meal the outsiders havin'."

The great day of celebration arrived partly cloudy and gray. Those outside the swamp had no inkling of what Jasper had just discovered. By the time the people of Buck's circle had gathered in an open space on the north side of the Road near the intersection with Buck's trail, clouds were boiling overhead like dingy clothes in a cauldron. None of the "old heads" were among them.

The men there sat off to themselves and drank, not heeding the threatening sky. Some complained about how the women clustered together in a bunch and ignored them. Then there was a commotion among the people closest to the rise in the land that was the tallest part of the ridge along Harris Bayou. From up out of the bayou, stepped Rose and Cicero, followed by Jasper and Mabel. She led the way smiling. Rose and Cicero came next, somber faced. Jasper was last by some distance. When Buck ran up to Jasper, Jasper's face stopped him in his tracks.

"Keep away from me, little nigga! Got your hands on my money, and until I say different, you best figure out how I kin git it back."

"Now, Jasper," Cicero said.

"You keep outta this. You ain't exactly been on my side."

"Look here . . ." Buck pulled out a wrapped pouch of documents. ". . . I know you don't read so good, but these two here, it's a half section o' land all in your name. I got some for daddy, some for Dick too."

Jasper snarled and slapped the documents from Buck's hand. When it appeared he might attack Buck, Dick appeared, a jug of whiskey in his hand.

"I ain't knowed I had land in my name neither. Years ago, I ain't knowed I was a nigga, ain't knowed my momma was Cicero's sister—a lot I ain't knowed, and I been drinkin all mornin'. You git the hawk outta your eye—that's what Bill wouldda said. C'mon over here and show these boys how a real swamp man kin shoot."

It was as if Dick's words held magic. Jasper snarled but allowed Dick to lead him away. Nearby, stood a group of men and youngsters. One held out a rifle to Jasper. He snatched it yelling, "What I gotta hit!" From a distance, Cicero yelled, "Goddam dragonflies! . . . Look at them everywhere. Hells bells! Shoot the dragonflies!"

Jasper yelled so loud those closest fell back. He emptied the rifle handed him, each shot obliterating a two-inch winged insect, the rifle's report an expression of everyone's aggravation with the locust-like plague riding the warm up-winds above the bayou ridges only to slide down on picnicking folk in the marginally cooler air below. Half an hour later, Jasper had become popular among the younger men because none of them could duplicate Jasper's feat. A few sips of whiskey loosened his tongue, and when he paused in the drinking and shooting and asked after Dick, all pointed toward the young woman, Fannie, sitting apart with Dick at her side.

"Git down the road," Sara yelled to Buck, "with your shootin'."

"Ain't me shootin'," he said.

"Well, tell them who are. All that noise makin' some of us jumpy."

Jasper led the men away toward the west, leaving the cleared field free for the women and children.

"We been home-bound," Gloria Canada said.

"Is a fact," Nan said. "We got to share more—our time, too."

"You're so right, Nan," Sara said. "I been tellin' Buck it's time we women did something to uplift our community."

"Is this your first social with everybody, Mabel?" Nan asked. "I been too busy to attend your bible sessions."

"Naw it ain't," Mabel said. "I been visitin' most folks in the name o' the Lord, but this the first time we all together, which is lots better than borrowing and sharing with one or two."

Lounging on quilts spread over the rough stubble and ignoring requests for food from the men and children, the women took the social measure of each other. They discussed their burdens, loneliness and isolation, especially that of the few older children.

Now, by this occasion, Fannie was volunteering a little time with Dick, but nothing else. Mainly, he escorted her to or from the cafe. The escorting commenced after Nan ordered her daughter to be polite. Fannie's politeness on picnic day was still forced, and everybody but Dick knew so.

"Cousin ain't got his usual sense," Buck said. "Pass the whiskey."

"Wait your turn, little nigga!" Jasper said, drinking before passing.

"That gal," Art Canada said, "got your cousin actin' like a pet rat."

"That's right rough, Art," Lem said. "Dick jes tryin' to be friendly."

"Well, there's friendly," Art said, "and there's female foolish. I know which my money say it is."

"Naw, you old married men ain't got no fi-ness," Lem said, scrunching up his nose. "Dick' know you got to go real slow, talk sweet. My man ain't nobody's fool."

"Mr. Lem," Art said, "you know I ain't usually a bettin' man, but my money say that boy ain't gonna leave Fannie's side once this whole day."

"Git serious! How much you bettin'?"

Jasper held up his hand before Art could speak.

"Ten whole dollar, Lem."

"Damn!" CC said.

"Couple gallons o' whiskey is all that is to me," Jasper said. "You bettin' or just big-mouthin'?"

A fever of wagering arose, side bets popping up between others apart from Lem and Jasper. With the shooting competition over, the men who'd made wagers joined the women. Several walked over as if casually to shake Dick or Fannie's hands, and all of the men in on the joke would laugh. Out of hearing, a couple of young men who'd bet on Lem's side, that Dick would not remain at Fannie's side, made rude remarks hoping that Fannie might become offended and take herself away.

By mid afternoon, there was no sign of those betting that Dick would leave Fannie having a prayer. Ten dollars was a lot to lose, so Lem left the men to go have a talk with Dick as a swath of charcoal clouds boiled from out of the south laden with rain.

"You need a drink, pod'ner," Lem said.

"I don't care for drinking," Fannie said.

"Me neither, today," Dick said.

"Jes thought I'd ask. So, if I was to say we needed more of your good whiskey, would you go home and grab it for me?"

"'Tis a social for the ladies like Fannie here, not a git-drunk thing."

A rebuffed Lem fretted until the rains began. Women grabbed quilts off the ground and dashed across the Road to Nan and Henry's new porch. The children shrieked happily and pretended to dance between the raindrops. Grudgingly carrying out instructions shouted to them, the men lugged the food and two tables out of the downpour. When only a few wood chairs remained on the field and the downpour slackened, someone suggested running down to Buck's house, which was close to large enough to hold everybody inside.

Already wet and full of whiskey, half the group started running. Meanwhile, Art Canada pulled his wagon up to the porch and piled on as many of the rest as could fit. The wagon was so overloaded, mud bogged it down after rolling a few feet. While the revelers piled off to lighten the wagon, Fannie remained standing on the porch. Dick stood on the ground and leaned against a post beside her. As if in another world, he wore his shirttail turned over his head against the rain. When Fannie stepped into the yard, Dick whipped off his shirt and draped it over her head. She pushed it aside and walked on.

Lem watched Dick fish his shirt out of the mud. Jasper pulled his shirt over his head and danced up to Lem.

"Love, love!" he whispered. "You be sellin' whisky for a month to pay me off."

Jasper moved off cackling toward Buck's house. Dick and Fannie lagged behind, which gave Lem another opportunity to help his cause. He trotted back and threw his arm around Dick. Fannie glanced at the two when Lem blew out his nose, and she walked ahead.

"Hey, man. Whyn't you take Fannie away from these fools, encourage a little romance."

"Fannie might not want that."

"Dick, what's happened to you?"

"Nothin', Lem. Just that Fannie—"

Fannie turned to wait for Dick. Lem lowered his voice even more.

"You the Winchesta Man! Got more stuff from more women than any nigga I know. Look heah—go on down to my house. We all know Fannie a lady, but it be quiet an' romantic-like there, away from all these noisy fools ahead of us. Be bold an' don't worry 'bout me comin' home."

Dick ran ahead and held Fannie in a brief conversation before the twosome turned around and, to Lem's utter amazement that Fannie hadn't slapped Dick's face, headed north back toward the Road and Lem's cabin.

An hour passed before either the sun or the would-be-lovers reappeared. Sara saw Fannie approaching her porch, and ran out to join her in the trail. When Fannie paused to acknowledge Sara, the children playing nearby gathered around the two. Canada's oldest boy, who had been playing good-naturedly with his infant brother, Hiram, snickered. Angrily, Fannie stuck out her tongue and ran inside. Sara followed. As Dick approached the yard, Lem stood in Buck's front door grinning.

"What's the matter, pod'ner? You'n the lady didn't see eye to eye?"

"Leave me be," Dick said.

Continuing on past Lem and inside, Dick walked into Buck's dining room and sat on the floor. Somewhere Dick found a whiskey jug and seemed content to sit alone drinking. Lem danced through the kitchen and out to the men on Buck's back porch. He held out his hand.

"Come first o' the week," Jasper said, "you git your money."

Dick passed out before the party broke up. Jasper hauled him into a bedroom. Fannie looked in on Dick once, but when she bumped into Jasper, she ran away.

Jasper paddled home alongside the boat bearing Cicero and Rose.

"Why you think," Jasper asked, "Fannie give Dick so much trouble?"

"They had a way of marryin'," Rose said. "A friend each one trusted put they heads together. Each person got things they partic'lar about, and we used to say a man or woman in love never pay attention to things that allow people to live in peace."

She paused to catch her breath and ceased paddling.

"Talk slow, Rose," Cicero said. "Age is slowing you down."

Jasper laughed along with Cicero.

"Why you laughing, Mr. Jasper," Mabel said. "There's other slowdowns I been noticin'"

"Man an' woman," Rose said, "both sometime done it."

"Work things out you mean?" Cicero said.

"Most always the man picked somebody to do it 'cause most often the man was afraid a woman was gonna get on his drinkin' or cussin'. One of you need to talk to our Dick 'cause that Fannie a tough customer. I can tell she ain't like Sara. Sara soft enough to let Buck have some slack until they sort things out. Non, non, cherie, Fannie ain't like that."

"You sayin' she like you?" Mabel said.

"I'm sayin' she got one mind, her own."

Thᴀᴛ sᴘʀɪɴɢ ᴏғ 1896 ᴏɴ ᴛʜᴇ outskirts of Africa, planting crops took more attention than timber. Dick's mules weren't needed so often because logging slowed. The whiskey business eased, too, and Lem could always help out when needed. Fannie was working the rooming house, and Dick visited almost every day. Nan always made him feel welcome even when Fannie was nowhere around. He was so grateful that he struggled to act polite after Nan used the word, something he was sensitive about because of Sara's haughty dismissal of him as being a no-count when Buck first introduced them. Dick's roughneck life had taught him none of what Nan called the social graces. Nan, on her part, delighted in spending time with the young man. He may have reminded her of a suitor she'd had or perhaps only imagined.

By fall, Mabel convinced the women that, fretting about the land aside, it was time to build a church. Time was passing, children growing. Cicero was now tutoring—or babysitting along with Rose as some looked upon it—five children. A beautiful new church was confirmed as the best way of marking going from squatters to legal owners whenever it happened. The men agreed that something should be done to mark the emergence of a real community. With the women prodding them, the men cleared a one hundred by one hundred foot square up where the picnic had been held on the

Road. The clearing of trees and brush was done right away, but then the men seemed to disappear. Nor was there further work that winter or even the following spring when church building was put aside to concentrate on plowing and planting.

Again, it was high water time, but light seasonal rains did little to fill the sluggish Hushpuckena or Harris Bayou, and for the first time in memory they remained stagnant. Even the Sunflower remained well within its winter channel, and its wild sunflowers sprouted below what normally would have been the water line. Jasper told anyone who would listen that Old Bill had predicted everything. The new levees had pinned up the Father River like a fat snake. One day, his swamp would go dry. For most, though, the drying-out was a good thing because it allowed them to claim more food producing land along drainage channels.

Fannie agreed to go visit Mound Bayou, and Dick borrowed a buggy. Along the way, there was little talk, but as they neared town, Dick became animated and pointed out where he and Buck had ambushed the Klan years back. Fannie took his arm, which prompted him to pull off the road and park in a grassy field. An hour later, with a breeze wafting over them, they were lying on the grass, and Dick was explaining about his mother and father. He grew hesitant describing James Aloysius raising him, which led Fannie to scoot close.

"Folks you's given, I was told. No fault, no favor if they was one white an' one black. Where your momma from?"

"Mr. Cicero's sister."

"Where they from?"

"Below Vicksburg. When this Navy man got violent. I think she had to sneak away and go off by herself. That was when they was slaves . . . I read a book about a slave."

"What was it like?"

"Was a man named Douglas, and a couple different people owned him, you know. One thought Douglas was smart and all, the other was quick with a whip."

"You still got the book?"

"Do you read?"

"Sure, I read."

Fannie closed her eyes then, and Dick moved closer.

"Dick?"

"Aye?"

"Lets go meet Miz Abyssinia. She sound a lot like me."

Abyssinia was sitting on her porch when the buggy arrived. Masses of daffodils were sprouting brilliant yellow and green around the edge of the house. Abyssinia had aged. Her complexion was muddied and dotted with tiny moles. Gray streaked the hair shoved up under the wide straw hat. As Dick and Fannie stepped to the ground, Abyssinia pulled off her glasses and touched around her ears to make sure her hair was neatly tucked away. Dick had never mentioned Fannie, but others had.

"Are you Fannie?"

"Yes'm!"

Abyssinia giggled and hurried down the front steps.

"Child! Let's get friendly, 'cause I don't want you mad at me."

"What're you sayin', ma?"

"Aw hush up, Dick," Abby said, moving past him toward Fannie. "I got no practice being a mother-in-law."

Fannie grinned broadly.

"Dick, I'm just tellin' this big child that I won't cause her no problems."

"We ain't engaged," Fannie said.

"But it'll happen when you say, now won't it?"

"I guess," Fannie agreed.

"Well, you are good looking. Ugly grandchildren woulddda been a burden."

Dick came around the buggy to stand beside the two women.

"Well . . . well!" Abyssinia said, raising her arms wide to make a salute of her embrace of the two.

"Ma, I want you to meet Fannie Potts. Fannie—my ma."

"Pleased to meetcha Miz . . ."

"Miz Morgan. It's Morgan—Abyssinia Morgan."

"I'm sorry," Fannie said.

"Noooo, I never married Dick's father." Abyssinia pulled Fannie away from Dick. "Lets me an' you have a little talk while this one go get him something to eat. I want to be sure you like boys."

The next morning, though noise awakened Dick early, he kept to his pallet in the parlor. His mother and Fannie were cooking, and he fell asleep again. When he awakened the second time, the house was quiet, the women gone. No breakfast for him, either. Two dirty plates littered the kitchen table. He made the best of being alone in the well-appointed house and heated buckets of bath water before propping himself into a corner in a tub. Then he fell asleep. When he awakened, he found bay rum and a razor hidden away in a drawer in his mother's room. Abyssinia and Fannie were visiting Isaiah Montgomery's house where a number of townspeople had dropped in to take a gander at the Winchester Man's fiancee.

It was mid-afternoon before Dick and Fannie got underway, leaving Abyssinia in tears. They drove hard to reach Africa. Dick was preoccupied with not overtaxing his horses, and he paid less attention than he might have to Fannie's head occasionally on his shoulder. As was their way, neither made small talk. Toward dusk, waves of orange, red and purple colored the sky, and Fannie squeezed close on the buggy seat, which gave Dick his first hope that their feelings were finally flowing together. Dick slipped his arm around her waist and drove with one arm for more than an hour. As he turned onto the Alligator Road, that arm was aching, and his passion was smoldering like the sunset of a few hours before.

"Fannie?"

"Don't talk now."

"Thought you was sleep."

"No. I'm trying to keep the colors in my mind."

Ignoring all they passed who called out greetings from porches, the two clung to each other until they approached Fannie's home. Then, Dick pulled away from Fannie and reined in his horses.

"What you got in mind?" Fannie said.

"You're home."

"Take me to your house. I don't want to talk to nobody about it."

That night, their courtship roles dropped away. Her wariness grown weary, Fannie sat on Dick's front porch in a homemade swing and pulled him down to kiss her. Dick barely moved, and Fannie kissed him again and again, her breath coming sweet and fast. At some point while kissing, Dick began massaging her shoulders, as Matilda had done for him, and the touch made Fannie smile and close her eyes. When he stopped and her eyes opened, he stood up and offered her his hand. He pressed into her standing, but he continued to dig his fingers into her back muscles in the way that usually ran shivers up and down his own. At some point, Fannie sighed deeply and walked inside the cabin. Dick had his shoes and shirt off when Fannie turned around. She lowered her eyes and began unbuttoning her dress.

"Let me."

Her breath came more heavily as his hands brushed her breasts, but then he paused to caress her shoulders, to kiss them in the kind of slow preamble that had made him want to scream. He pealed her dress off, but she stopped him, moved back and raised her petticoats to wriggle out of her undergarments. When she saw Dick staring open-mouthed, she threw them at him. And then he grabbed her, and she laughed and resisted him wrestling her onto his bed, until he finally tripped her. They fell together, lay apart.

"Oh, Dick, I think I like you more than I know how to say. I ain't never had the urge like now."

"You my princess, my Zulu princess."

"What that?"

"It's a people in Africa. I seen the name on something my ma was readin'."

Fannie closed her eyes then, and two lovers gave themselves in an ancient game of make-believe. The dream forces of a ripe and rounded sunset engaged a full-moon magic striking through the window. Their delight and fantasy overwhelmed all fatigue.

"I'm just restin', Dick. Tell me my name again."

"You're my Zulu princess, and I'm your Africa man."

"Crazy fool!"

"Aye, crazy for you."

"Well, gimme some more whiskey. I declare I never thought I be feelin' this good."

To compensate old Henry for losing his daughter, Dick asked Buck and Jasper for suggestions, insisting that it be a gift Nan would enjoy. The week following his discussions, Dick drove into the outskirts of Clarksdale and waited while Buck ordered Nan and Henry's gift, though it wouldn't arrive until the end of the summer. When it did, in front of his in-laws' house, Dick parked a brand new buggy from the Clarksdale Machinery Company.

Fannie blossomed in the months after taking up with Dick. A quickly more mature and friendly soul replaced the anxiety-ridden girl who'd rejected life for so long. She interacted with her mother and father with warmth, and her taking left-over food from the rooming house to a certain sharecrop family on the edge of Africa made everyone take note of her generosity.

Sara confided to Buck the opinion that Fannie and Dick were civilizing each other.

Unfortunately, Fannie had an ancient, awesome temper and only 18 year old control. She was taller than Dick and built like a bronze colossus. Though they seldom had more than one or two harsh words, when that temper did assert itself, they fought like two men if neither one gave in. Having a potential battle awaiting him at home turned Dick keen on keeping deadlines for supper and things like that.

Not long after, James Aloysius Dolan had a stroke. Fannie insisted Dick not hide his feelings, that he go visit, which triggered an outpouring of feelings about his father and life that left Dick crying. News of his father's deteriorating health continued to claim his attention. In November, after the stroke, he visited the old plantation and discovered that Pamela Sue—married now with children of her own—still lived there. When they met, they embraced and held hands. The husband was away working that afternoon, and there was no need explaining themselves to anyone. After Pamela Sue learned in general terms where Dick lived, she undertook to send him messages by one of the Dolan sharecroppers whenever something happened to the old man. A black man named Frank Reid and his wife were recent settlers on the Alligator Road just on the south fork of Harris Bayo, and they lived in Art Canada's old house now owned by CC the carpenter and the Reid family. Frank became the one with whom Pamela Sue's messenger always left word. Mr. Reid then would carry the message on in to Buck's house. Which was how Dick came to know the Reid family better than some others.

The first stroke left JD incapacitated, unable with his own hand to obtain even a drink of liquor. From then on, he spent his days propped into a rocking chair beside his front door, looking through tiny glass windows along side that became his sole connection to the outside world. When anyone visited, the old man would shout slurred words to be noticed, and from every woman he demanded a kiss before falling back into his chair like a grinning rag doll. Dutifully, his new wife and young daughter provided both the nursing and the silence about his antics that he had married for. He died in January of 1898.

Fannie watched Dick turn away when Buck brought the news, and she followed Dick to his mules in their corral where he often retreated in moments of stress.

"I ain't scared to go with you, Dick, if you of a mind to attend the service. You know there's gonna be them try to keep you away."

Dick made no answer right away. Fannie stood there until he turned to her.

"Couldn't have you with me. If anyone got ugly, I'd kill somebody."

The next day, careful to avoid telling even Buck his plan, Dick dressed in crisply starched clothes. He owned no suit of flannel or wool like Buck. It was simply a jacket and trousers Fannie had bought out of Memphis for him. He rode off by himself that morning, circling Alligator to come at the funeral from the west, settling into a cluster of cedars and white oak near the little church west of town.

Amazing grace
How sweet the sound . . .

The strains of the hymn floated mournfully outside as Dick sat alone on that crisp January afternoon. He felt a self-pitying sorrow as the Alligator Bible Church choir sang. Then it was over, and anger began to edge Dick's sadness as he watched his half-sister dressed in black look his way and point. A woman squinted in Dick's direction before hustling the child back inside the church. The impulse to flee came as suddenly as water to Dick's eyes. He wanted no one to see his emotion and hopped into the saddle to gallop back through town almost hoping someone gave him an excuse to draw his pistol.

SHORTLY AFTER JD'S DEATH, Sara drove Buck into Alligator
to do some shopping. Alligator was a small line of stores along
a single street parallel to the railroad tracks. As Buck helped
Sara back into her buggy to leave town, the train depot agent
hailed them.

"Buck Morgan!"

Sara pulled her mare, Buttercup, to a halt when she saw the
white man waving. Buck stepped from the carriage and
walked over to talk.

"This letter come fer you."

"Thank you, Mr. Shelly."

The envelope bore a crest and the name Illinois Central
Land Associates. When Buck looked back up, the station
agent was walking away.

"What is this about, sir?"

Shelly shrugged and continued across the road. Buck
stepped down and ran after him.

"Sir, I do all the business through you that I can. You know
that."

"I ain't mad at you, Buck. It's them blasted railroad people.
Soon's them Northerners let us station agents sell land, I hear
they goin' outta the business."

"Whatta you mean?"

"Ain't hardly no more land to be sold."

"But that surprises me."

"Me, too, old Buck, but hell, that's the way it is. Guess somebody over your way must have done pretty good for hisself."

Buck was too panicked to ask more. As he returned to the buggy, his stomach felt hollow, the letter clutched tightly in his hand felt cold and ominous as a coiled snake. Sara held off asking what was wrong. Buck further delayed opening the letter until he was moving along the trail back into Africa. He tore a strip off the envelope with his teeth. Inside was a letter with the same crest and Illinois Central Land Associates name.

"What is that, Buck?"

"Sara. Just be still."

"Oh Lordy, must be bad news 'cause you don't git mad at me unless you scared."

LEGAL NOTICE
Failure to Reply
May Result in Forfeiture

To: Buck Morgan and parties at interest.
From: Illinois Central Land Associates.

One of our former sales agent, Samuel Grant, held options on land that included what has been reported as your purchase interest. His employment was terminated under questionable circumstances, and his rights have expired.

With railroad station personnel now authorized to sell land, some confusion has developed because you are reported in some way to claim an interest in the Africa Land Company. Thus, I am writing to confirm whether, in fact, you claim interest in the land purchase originally optioned by Mr. Grant.

Please reply to the attention of M. Boudreaux.

The legally ominous legend panicked Buck. Was the document just another put down by one of the big white people beyond the reach of the small but growing reputation Buck had been carefully building? Then there was the matter of the Africa Land Company. Bravado had led Buck to use the name in conversation with the second land agent. Now he wondered if he should consult a lawyer because, perhaps, he could claim rights under the Africa Land Company name. Full of anything but confidence, and not wishing to take his concern down to Mound Bayou where he would have to disclose to Isaiah Montgomery's de facto lawyer Ben Green the essentially slapdash way he had proceeded, Buck decided to go back into town and pump the Alligator Station agent for information.

"I ain't authorized to help you buy more land, Buck. Guess you lost out."

"That's what I thought, too, Mr. Shelly, but then I got a letter telling me to contact somebody named Boudreaux."

"Mr. Boudreaux don't sell to nobody but plantation owners. Think you in they league?"

"'Course not, sir. I just figured you ought to make the commission on anything I do, so I come to you. Truth is, my folks want to buy all that land over where I live."

"Buck, you raisin' that much money 'bout as likely as me marryin' your wife."

"Whatever you say, sir."

The old white man waited, but Buck said no more. Shelley's eyes fluttered.

"What's in yo' head, Buck? . . . You come in heah'n proposition me after you been told ain't no possibility. What you know I don't?"

"Don't know nothin' aside from Mr. Boudreaux trying to quick-sell all the railroad land left. Mr. Isaiah Montgomery told me so. Say Mr. Boudreaux told him there was white folks interested—just like you told me—but they ain't gonna buy."

"How he figure?"

"The big white folks won't pay cash money."

"How a nigger hear shit like that?"

"Sir, all I ask is for you to check again to see if maybe you could handle sellin' me some land?"

Buck shared neither the notice from Illinois Central Land Associates nor the conversation with the Alligator station agent with anyone. A few days later, five armed white men rode along the Alligator Road. Lucille Reid, who lived with her husband toward the end of the Road nearest Alligator, was working in her garden and saw them coming, but they were too close when she saw that they were white for her to do anything. The men continued on past the place where the trail to Buck Morgan's house branched off south, on to the eastern end of the Road, where a dirt track continued northerly parallel to the Sunflower River toward Clarksdale. Lucille had been so startled by the men appearing that she followed them at a distance until they continued on toward Clarksdale, and then she roused other residents of the Road who decided to go bring Buck up to see what was happening. By the time he joined his neighbors, the armed white men had long before ridden out of sight.

Word passed from Buck to Dick. Later that night, Jasper was livid when he heard that white men had dared ride so close to Africa, and it was to placate him that Dick promised to nose around seeking some information about what was going on. Next morning, he rode his horse behind the path of the wagons up toward Clarksdale, and the first thing he noticed just outside of Clarksdale was a group of road men with shovels and a heavy, mule-drawn rolling drum filled with water carving an intersection into the main county road that entered Clarksdale across a Sunflower River bridge. Under the influence of a proffered drink of whiskey, one of the men, who had no idea Dick was other than another white person, said the road work was to make it possible for one of the local plantations being assembled just south of Clarksdale to have access to the main county road near Alligator.

No sooner than Dick reported back, Buck headed in to Alligator to post a letter to the Memphis railroad office claiming interest in all of the land formerly optioned to the Africa Land Company. He was blaming himself for waiting so long, for pehaps allowing some local landowners to make a move. He was startled when the station agent pulled him aside.

"Buck, Mr. Alex Chicoupapoulis wants to see you,

"Mr. Chicoupapoulis?"

"That's right. You tryin' to do somethin ain't seemly for no nigger. Mr. Chicoupapoulis said he take it hard if you wasn't to heed his request."

As Buck drove away, he was in turmoil. It didn't figure that he'd been invited to a lynching, though anything certainly could happen. He also hesitated to go seek Dick or Jasper's help because if they threatened anybody, appropriate as that might be as a matter of logic, it would harm Buck's mild-mannered pose with the white folks. And yet, resolving the question of title to the land could no longer wait.

When he arrived at home that evening, he said nothing to Sara. Instead, the following morning, he pleaded one excuse after another to avoid all chores and disappeared after directing CC, the carpenter, to take over all decisions at the sawmill. Dick was mystified when he came away from a weeping Sara who said that Buck had never before simply vanished. All she could tell Dick was that Buck had confessed to a confrontation with the Alligator station agent.

When Buck did resurface, his clothes were wrinkled and awry from sleeping in them, though no one took note other than his wife. Dick hauled Buck down into the swamp for an all-night session with Jasper.

End of that week, in Alligator, three horses were tied to the hitching post outside the office of the County Road Supervisor when Buck drove up. Sitting inside the office, attended by the railroad station agent, was Alex Chicoupapoulis, who

Buck knew to brag of being local spokesperson of the Ku Klux Klan.

"C'mon en, Buck. We ain't dressed for lynchin'."

The other white men chuckled. Alex Chicoupapoulis was wearing his trademark white suit. Tall and grossly overweight, his nose and cheeks were pink with sun-ruined skin.

"Come en here'n sit down, boy."

"Yessir, Mr. Chicoupapoulis."

"My colleague," Alex pointed to Shelley, "tells me you got your hands on the money to buy a whole section of land. Is that true?"

Buck nodded.

"Say you already took title for more'n a section in other names."

Taking their cue from Chicoupapoulis, one of the other men circled behind Buck and slammed shut the door.

"Mr. Chicoupapoulis, that closed door makes me more than a little nervous."

"How es so? We god-fearin' white men. You the one got nerve to be a land speculator. We cain't be havin' no more negger towns built."

Buck cleared his throat and walked over to lean against the window that faced onto the sidewalk.

"All I'm doin', sir, is buying swamp land that some people been livin' in for years. They not like people on the outside, and I do little things for 'em so they leave me alone. I'll wager you know the people I'm talkin' about."

"I know some deviate neggers call that godforsaken swamp home. Jim Dolan's bastard live out there, too. What bother me is you, Buck—Why you workin' for them?"

"Me? Oh, I ain't proud, suh. I do what I'm told, by some of the black ones too. If I didn't, I could git burnt out."

"Well, that's why you here this evenin'. My railroad colleague say you know your place else thees wouldn't be a talkin' visit. You go on back and tell whoever sent you that you ain't buyin no more land. Tell 'em I said so."

"Yessir."

"Don't sound convinced. We mean business."

A man struck Buck in the back, and he let out a wail. Before he'd closed his mouth, the door exploded open, and everyone looked toward the man stepping inside. Dick Dolan had kicked the door open. His pistol was trained on Alex Chicoupapoulis.

"Evenin', Alex."

"Well, if it ain't Jim Dolan's bastard."

"Don't nobody reach. You could die."

With a flick of his wrist Dick motioned the white men together. Alex took a moment to lift his bulk to his feet. He stood almost breathless for a moment, and then walked his belly over to crowd Dick.

"How es it livin' with a passle of coon dogs? Wouldn't do no good me ask Buck. He got a house. How you'n them wild neggers live?"

Dick rammed his pistol into Alex's stomach, and the man gave ground.

"Like men, Alex. Leave off the nigger talk."

"Your momma was negger, you a negger!"

A flash of red surged into Dick's face, and he headed toward Alex Chicoupapoulis. One of the white men grabbed his arm, another charged into him. Dick fell into a table snarling with a white man's arms around him. Buck watched in silence as Shelley and another piled onto Dick. None of them noticed Jasper ease inside, until Jasper pounded the stock of his rifle on the floor.

"Git up!"

"Who you?" Shelley asked.

"Your undertaker."

Dick freed himself and retrieved his gun.

"Your timin' was excellent," Dick said.

"Kill 'em, get it over with."

"No, No!" Buck screamed."

Ignoring Buck's protest, Jasper walked up to Alex and shoved the muzzle of his rifle under the white man's chin. Alex began choking, but Jasper's strength was more than enough to resist the effort to move it away. Dick turned to Buck.

"Told you not to visit these bastards. Now, go on home! Me'n Jasper got business you ain't part of."

Buck put his hat on and looked to Alex for permission. Jasper snatched his rifle barrel from Alex's throat and raised his gun as if to strike him with it.

"Tell him, old white man," Jasper growled, "to get outta here."

"No, wait, boy!" Alex screeched at Buck. "Bring the deputy heah!"

Jasper pulled a knife from his boot as Dick slammed the door behind Buck

"Say that again, white man," Jasper said, "I'm gonna cut your throat."

Alex raised his hands to ward off the blow.

"We gonna send a bloody message to your Klan people."

"Hold on a minute, you!"

"My name is Jasper."

"You, Jasper—"

"Mister, Jasper."

"Mr. Jasper, you'n that boy beside you, y'all cain't just commit cold-blooded murder."

"Nobody give a damn about you," Jasper said. "If they do, they got to come git me outta that swamp, and I don't rightly figure they'll catch me. I figure on cuttin' your evil tongue out 'fore I kill you."

Just as Alex opened his mouth again, Jasper feinted with his knife but swung the butt of his rifle to strike Alex Chicoupapoulis in the face. Before the man recovered, Jasper circled his rifle arm around the man's neck and straightened him up. When Jasper raised his knife, a guttural screech punctuated by choked-out foreign words filled the room. The station agent broke for the closed door only to be stuck on the head by Dick. The big man Jasper still held in a choke hold began weeping. Jasper snarled and pushed the white man away.

"Goddamn nasty bastard! . . . You got snot all over my arm."

Angrily, Jasper raised his knife arm.

"Hold on, Jasper," Dick said. "Maybe old weepy Alex there's of a mind to save his mangy neck. Are you, Alex?"

"If all thees es about the land . . . Es a railroad matter."

Other than Alex's sniffling, no one said anything, and the silence stretched out. All of the white men seemed to be waiting for some word to end their discomfort. In the silence, Dick moved to stand in front of Jasper.

"Alex, despite the grudges I hold against you, shootin' you in the head won't make my aim no better."

"What're you sayin'?" Jasper asked.

"If we kill these dogs, Buck will probably get blamed."

"That's Buck's problem."

"Aye, and you'd be right . . . Listen up, Alex."

"I'm listening."

"People farming near Buck Morgan, they are my neighbors, and that redneck station agent over there holdin' his head is causing me worry. You be sure and spread the word to leave Buck alone. If I hear of anybody meddling my neighbors, I will kill you, Alex. I don't care if you hide, I will get you. And if I can't, I'll pay a bounty to whoever does. I got more'n enough whiskey money for that or do you doubt me?"

"No sir, Mr. Dick," Shelley said.

"Speak up, Alex!"

"Yeah, we hear you."

"Say again, fat man?"

"I mean . . . yes."

"How about you, Jasper?"

"I just as soon not have this weepy pig's blood all over my clothes."

"Then, head out. I'll follow."

Few of those living on the edges of Africa ventured away from home right after word was passed. Only Henry Potts insisted on driving back and forth to his rooming house, but his wife did not accompany him on the drive. She spent her nights in the Bobo community where the black people around the business could provide protection should the Klan gather. Art Canada, who worked as a handyman near Alligator, went to work as usual, but just in case, he forbade his oldest son, Art, Jr., to accompany him. Buck tried to convince him to take a week off, but Art pleaded that his family needed every penny he could earn, and no way could he afford to lose his job.

When Art arrived back home after the first day of work, he was all smiles. He had stayed put and not traveled away from the farm where he worked, but everything appeared normal. He did report that when he rode home along the road thru the Alligator settlement that evening, the station agent, Shelly, was perched tight-lipped and alone on a cane-backed chair against the sign along the track announcing Alligator Lake. Extraordinarily, not a single one of his usual redneck entourage was present.

Toward the end of the week. Henry Potts reported that two land agents had spent the night at his rooming house and got drunk together to mark their last night in the Mississippi

Valley. According to Henry's wife, Nan, who waited on them, Illinois Central Land Associates, was being reorganized or somehow re-absorbed back into the main railroad company. Or so she understood. Ever alert, Nan had asked what the men planned to do in the future. Put the raggedy-assed company behind them, was the reply. Neither had earned more than they had spent in the short time they had been with the company. Seems a number of land agents had resigned back after one of their own had been waylaid over in the old swamp. Neither of the new men had known how little opportunity remained when they jumped at going to work for the land company.

The rains that year began in February, days of drizzle and days of downpour separated by a couple dry days. Soon most—aside from Dick and the others living deeper inside the swamp—prayed for rain to end. All except Little Buck. He had learned how to swim and had his mother's nerves in shambles. Little ponds of water collecting in Dry Bayou cried out for him to come jump in. Telling him not to, was futile, and Sara finally latched her front door and made every effort to keep her son in view. Only to have him dart through the back porch and down the steps to dance in the rain chanting "wet, wet" and skipping about, hands raised to catch raindrops.

Otherwise, too, it seemed an odd-omened time. People were eager to get on with farming that for the first time would take up as much effort as clearing homesteads, but the rains said, no. The influx of new families slowed, too; not only the mud, but those already in place consolidated their hold on the land, added acreage here and there and spoke against bringing in too many unworthy new people. Some like Buck began looking around for land to buy in years to come. As the weather ripened, the newcomers rushed to plant cotton, corn and a little rice along the sloughs looking toward a cash dividend come harvest time. Even Fannie Dolan planted a home garden. A prosperity of sorts beckoned to them all, and as its symbol, the new church begun that winter was nearing completion. Rose and Cicero had agreed to organize a school there for children of all ages.

On a Tuesday evening in early April, Dick was returning home along the Road after a whiskey delivery. It was a blustery, gray day, and he was riding in a scattered frame of mind, ignoring repeated greetings from a man walking along the Road in the same direction. When the indignant traveler yelled, Dick startled and finally muttered an apology. But he chose not to dally with the newcomer, one of the first to move east of Henry Potts along the Road. Instead, he abruptly heel-chucked his horse and returned to brooding.

A breeze brought the smell of rain, and Dick stared off north. A conductor on a train stopped in Alligator had reported a break along the new Mississippi River levee in Tunica County. Word was the track to Memphis might soon be flooded and closed to traffic. Ahead of Dick loomed a bridge of logs spanning the south branch of Harris Bayou on top of which four-by-fours had been spiked and then covered with planks. Water flowing underneath would continue into Howden Lake. A cascading muddy flow was carrying along limbs and small trees, which shocked Dick because there had been no significant flow under that bridge—apart from during and after rainstorms—since levees closed around the Mississippi about five years before. And muddy water meant flood water.

Certain that a flood was coming, he halted and debated whether to raise an alarm. Floods had been common-place a few years before, but the new people certainly wouldn't read the signs and might not be prepared. Still undecided, he drove his heels into Lightning's flanks and rode onto the bridge, just as a woman's voice reached him.

"Mr. Dolan! . . . Yooo hooo, Richard!"

A woman was running toward the Road from a cabin just west of the water. It was Lucille Reid whose husband, Frank, had carried Pamela Sue's messages about Dick's father's health. Quite beautiful, she was, Dick noticed, pushing out top and rear under a shrunken housedress. Rather comically, she was clasping a tiny scarf to her unruly hair in the rising wind, and she was barefooted. She and her husband, in partnership with CC the carpenter, were trying to clear the least desirable acreage along the Road, difficult land because it straddled the southern spur of Harris Bayou itself. That channel wouldn't be useful for farming unless the bayou itself dried up and was filled in.

"Yes ma'am?"

Dick's stallion followed his lead and turned toward the woman.

"I'm heah alone, Richard, and I want you to tell me somethin'."

"As you please, Miz Reid," Dick said, exploring a glowing brown expanse of bosom inside the gaping shirtwaist dress while the woman raised her arms to tie her head rag.

"That crick over theah been runnin' like that for a couple hours. It ain't suppose to, you know."

"No'm it ain't. Was watchin it myself, but never been a flood reach over here. One time the Sunflower inched over into Dry Bayou, but it didn't go nowhere—just drained into the ground."

"Well, I saw you pass by and I waived, but you was lookin' off. When I seen you was watchin' that water, I say to myself, nigga, git yoself on out there an' ast the man what's happenin'. You know what I mean?"

"Yes ma'am, I do."

With the slightest flutter, her eyes dropped to her bosom.

"I must look a sight."

"Pleasant sight, ma'am."

He let his eyes linger on the tops of her bare breasts. No binding cloth held them down.

"You wouldn't like a toddy, would you?"

Yes, indeed, Dick thought, easing up off his saddle to relieve the pressure. Then he remembered that Fannie was expecting him for supper.

"No'm. Don't think that's possible."

"Oh, foots, why not? You could say you was protectin' me from this flood we got comin'."

"Miz Reid, there is a levee break up north. Some loggers blew the levee to git water into Yazoo Pass so's they could float some logs toward the railroad steadda havin' to pay mule drivers. Leastways 'tis the gossip." He glanced toward the open cabin door. "Might be better you stay with somebody . . . ah, your Mr. Reid and CC—where they at?"

"Gone! They in Moun' Ba'ou with Mr. Morgan. CC gonna sell his interest in this land to me'n Frank, and CC buyin' some land from Buck. They got to take papers to Rosedale, and CC's wife in Alligator where she still live most time."

"I see."

"I'm all alone."

"How come both of the men left you alone? Don't take but one to file papers."

"Ain't it the truth . . . Well, CC excited 'cause Buck got Jasper's permission to sell him land in toward the old swamp, and Frank jes went along."

"Tell you what. I'll stop by tomorrow mornin' when I head out. Ain't much to worry 'bout. Worse happen, I figure you git a muddy yard a couple days."

Dick bowed from the saddle, and the woman curtsied, not so accidentally pulling the bottom of her dress away from her legs. As he headed home, he glanced over his shoulder at her standing beside the road waving.

By morning, the sky over Africa looked just as bad as the day before. As Dick came to the breakfast table, he was shaking his head.

"I got a delivery, Fannie."

"Deliver whiskey in this weather?"

"Ain't so much whiskey as goin' out to hear the flood talk. Takin' a delivery along to make use of my time."

"What flood?"

"Heard talk of it yestiddy, and I need to snoop around see how much high water we got comin'."

"Should I do anything?"

"You ride down and warn the old people. They closer to the Sunflower than us. If that river go crazy, it could give 'em problems."

"Poor, Momma Rose."

"Naw, they know about floods. Just gittin' old'n could prob'ly use help."

Fannie nodded, and before Dick left the house, she was dressing to travel. Dick left home at the same time, and when he reached Buck's house he could smell the new rain. Off in the distance, tell-tale dark patches spotted the rain already falling as Sara came out onto her porch.

"Howdy Sara. Where's Buck?"

"He still gone, Dick. You know they went to Cleveland—or maybe it was Rosedale?"

"Well, be on the watch for high water. Put up your chicken's and such."

"I already did that. Used to flood terrible over at the Quarters, so I know what to do."

In that way in which insignificant things take on significance from proximity to things in the mind, Dick's guilt about his inclinations toward Lucille Reid turned him testy as Little Buck streaked out from behind his mother and charged yelling in a childish effort to spook his Uncle Dick's horse. Dick allowed the animal to move on off to get away from the child, and he yelled back to Sara.

"Put a switch on that one, or send him down to his grandpa. He'll tame him!"

It began raining in earnest then as Sara ran from her porch to grab her son, but the child dodged and ran off. Dick had no idea of the child's penchant for swimming or for playing in the wet. Now, suddenly, the child ran back toward the house screaming in glee and climbed up into a tree at the corner of the house. Sara was on the ground stamping her foot and screaming as Dick rode off.

Some time later, when the bayou forking across the Alligator Road came into view, the surging brown water was above the floor of the bridge. Only the hand rail rose above the torrent, and there was so much dirt in the water, Dick knew that a big flood was coming. Lightning hesitated, then balked a distance from the forty foot wide mass of foaming water. Far off bursts of thunder erupted in the dirty gray sky. Dick mused over the safety of the old people in the swamp, but he reminded himself that they'd be prepared. The outsiders, on the other hand, would just have to catch as catch can. They didn't worry about his business, he'd leave them to theirs. He was grinning to himself as he imagined haughty Sara having to deal with a houseful of mud when, all of a sudden right in front of Dick, the two-by-four bridge railings suddenly collapsed and were swept away.

Sensing an omen, Dick was possessed by a strange fear of drowning. His heart pounded as he sat on his equally skittish horse and reminded himself the bayou wasn't deep even if he misjudged the edge of the bridge and fell in. In a bravado that he did not feel, Dick chucked Lightning ahead. The stallion whinnied and balked once more, angering Dick, who smacked the animal's flank until it galloped forward. The water almost reached the horse's knees, so far above the bridge had it risen.

As Dick cantered toward the lone cabin off the road, Lucille Reid emerged onto her porch holding her arms about herself against the damp wind. She yelled something, but her voice was lost in a clap of thunder. Dick hopped directly onto her porch and hurried inside to be out of the bluster and noise.

"This weather is chilly, ain't it, Dick?"

"Aye," he said, shaking water from his slicker, pulling it over his head.

"I'll go put on water to heat."

Lucille left him in the partially furnished front room. While he waited he watched the rain through the open door. When Lucille returned from the kitchen, Dick walked over to sit on a bed against the wall.

"Excuse that bed, but you know we got two families makin' home in here."

"Me'n old Buck used live in one room."

"You and Buck?"

"In a cabin before he married six, seven years back."

"Feel awful good havin' you here, Mr. Richard."

"Do whatever I can for good people, Miz Reid."

"Child, call me Lucille. Ain't no need to stand on ceremony."

"Well, Lucille, I be thinkin' Frank and yourself know a bit about me on account of them messages you handled a while back, but 'tis fair little I know."

"What you want to know?"

"Tell me about you'n Frank."

"Let's see . . . married Frank two years ago, while I was working as a maid down near Cleveland. Teeny-tiny little plantation, but it was work, and Frank come along talkin' 'bout buyin' him some land, so I kinda latched on."

"Latched on?"

"Well, we thought I was carryin' a baby." Lucille chuckled. "Frank had been wantin' to marry, and I let him."

"Then, it's kinda like he's your true love?"

"Said he had land waiting for him to clear, so I wasn't a fool."

Lucille ran to silence a whistling kettle . She prepared a tray of tea and cold biscuits before returning to the front room. Lucille seated her tray on a table in front of Dick and began pouring hot water and whiskey. Dick said nothing. When Lucille offered him a drink, he seized it eagerly.

A cloudburst dropped over the little house, and ended the exchange. The horse outside began whinnying.

"You got a horse shed, ain'tcha?"

"Naw, we ain't, Richard. You haveta tie him under them big trees out back. That's what we do when company come."

Dick ran outside and led Lightning behind the house to the shelter of two spreading oaks. Quickly, he unsaddled the horse. Lust and guilt competed as motive to get out of the open and back inside where it was warm and promising. Lucille was waiting in the back door, her dress unbuttoned halfway down.

"Lord, you must love that horse."

He dashed up the back stairs and peeled out of his wet jacket as he moved by Lucille. When he leaned forward to shake the water from his hair, she crept up and lay her arm around his back. A long and lingering kiss held them. They stepped back for her to pop open the last button holding her dress. Her right leg whipped out and locked around him.

"Maybe we play horsey," she said, dropping both her leg and open housedress. Dick followed her toward the bed along the wall. "You do love your horsey, don'tcha?"

In mid afternoon, the sound of wood tearing apart startled both of them as the bridge gave way. Rushing to the window, they watched the twisted timber thump into a stand of trees downstream. They also discovered the house standing in a lake, water from the overflow covering everything, even in the distance, which reinforced a cozy sense that no one was around to point a finger.

Afterward, the rain stopped, though the sky remained overcast and dyspeptic. Shadows of black crows passed forlorn and raucous as they moved to some more beckoning shelter during the pause in the storm. The wind was now gusting, occasionally spraying the tin roof with water. Otherwise, there came only a regular sound of water dripping. Soon, even that stopped.

"Oughtta be leavin'," Dick said. "It's the quiet at the height o' the flood. A old Indian I used to know called it 'the time o' the dead'."

"Ooo, why he say that?"

"You see dead people float by after the waters quiet."

Dick stood up and stretched.

"You gonna leave me alone?" Lucille asked.

"Surely, you ain't afraid of the dark," Dick said, fumbling with a box of matches to light a coal oil lamp. "This water will leave most of our folks in need. We'll need to help each other."

"I figure you could stay the night."

"Jesus, woman, would you have me grin up in your husband's face when he returns?"

"No call for that," Lucille said, lurching up and swinging out of bed. "Damn, suh! Now, look at this . . . " A splinter from the rough floorboard had pierced her bare foot. ". . . How'm I gonna git this out in lamplight?"

With a growl, Dick grabbed the lamp and brought it close to Lucille on the bedside. Carefully, even tenderly, he caressed her foot, seeking the protruding splinter. He yanked it out with his nails and sighed with small comfort for having performed his act of neighborliness.

"Stay with me, Richard. Frank won't be back for a day more, maybe longer with this flood."

Lucille draped her arms around Dick's naked back.

"Cain't you forward-lookin' men extend a little friendship?"

"What about supper?"

"I'll cook for you. Won't nobody be out in this weather."

A lingering anxiety sullied the air. Neither touched the other, not even after a hearty supper of biscuits, ham and gravy. Later that night, after beginning to make small talk,

Dick ate a second meal, and the festering discord subsided with Lucille parked on his lap.

Breakfast in the morning was so huge that it left Lucille and Dick fit only to cat-nap. When afternoon headed into a second evening, Dick silently searched out his clothes and dressed.

"I'm ridin' to Alligator. There'll be no big water to cross."

"Humph! You jes scared."

"Don't, Lucille. You ain't supposed to tempt fate."

Lucille said not another word after it was clear Dick would leave, and when he waded out back and re-saddled his horse, she stood defiantly in the doorway, until he waded back up and she sullenly moved aside to allow Dick inside to retrieve his jacket in the front room.

"Goodbye, Lucille."

Nothing but silence accompanied Dick as he walked the length of the house, out the back door to mount Lightning standing in water up to the horse's belly. Dick felt a momentary anxiety because he had never known flood water to be so deep. Suddenly, he realized, not one of the new houses had been built high enough to escape this water, and the thought was sobering. Then, Lightning whinnied and Dick knew it would be good to find him a dry stand for his hooves. He then navigated the water back around toward the front of the house. Before he gained the flooded road, he heard a splash. Turning in the saddle, he watched Lucille shaking out an empty chamber pot whose contents were floating mid-way between him and the porch. So much, he though, for neighborliness.

Water from the Mississippi surging through broken levees had flooded all the land between the big river and the Sunflower. With the ground already soaked by rain, very little run-off could be absorbed, which granted the water almost a week of dominion over the land, a little less each day. Trash-choked bayous that hadn't flowed since the big river was closed in breached all flood ridges. Life came to a stand-still for a couple of days before the water began to roll on off in earnest. In time it would return again and had come many times before, but this particular flood muddied a lot of dreams. Houses were undermined, and floors sagged. All the homes took on water. Not even Buck's big house, escaped. Clarksdale, Alligator and the nearby towns were flooded, too. Travel by boat was again suddenly common.

When Dick reached home on Friday, mud hardening on the floor greeted him, and water remained everywhere. Instead of riding into Alligator, guilt had led Dick to swim Lighting across the south fork of the bayou and to ride home to put the horse inside the cabin, to allow his hooves to dry and not become tender. The muddy floors didn't bother Dick because he and Fannie owned nothing in the house they couldn't do without. After putting his mules inside to join his horse, Dick took a boat into the swamp to join Fannie with Cicero and Rose. They'd hardly come close enough to touch before Dick was dropping bouquets of kisses and puppy dog manners everywhere.

"You was scared for me?"

"Aye . . . scared. Wouldda blamed myself for bein' apart."

Jasper and Mabel and her son, Bud, had joined Rose and Cicero during the flood, to help out. For the deep water days, they all stayed out on the roof as in former times. During the day, though, Jasper put on boots and moved about doing errands for those bordering on becoming elders perched on the roof. Trudging through so much water turned him light-hearted.

"No one couldda survived nothin' like this but the swamp," he told Mabel.

"Sacrilege, Jasper. It's a sin against the Lord's bounty to say that."

"Hell you say, it's true. All them new folks know about it now. They little houses turnt into boats. Wish they'd floated away."

"Forty days and night did it rain," Mabel said, "and Noah brung his people through with the Lord's help."

"Didn't need no help, he had built his house on high ground."

"He was in the ark, Jasper."

"Then that ark was on high ground."

"Don't be evil."

"I ain't no such."

"Then why you so down on the Lord?"

"That's you talkin'. I ain't never met him."

"You got a cussedness. I pray for your sins—all your whiskey, them nasty women you useta know—"

"Wait, now! Keep your mouth offa me."

Mabel was a diplomat. She smiled and turned away. Rose and Cicero took it all in joy, the flood and Jasper's whimsy. Cicero was fretting being cooped up inside or stuck on the roof, but Rose didn't want him traipsing through the water for fear of illness. Then, too, even before Jasper showed up in a boat with his family, Cicero had been with Fannie and Rose so much he was feeling the need for a little solitude. He was also eager to be about to hear what had happened. Mabel fired up the raised fireplace inside the cabin as soon as Jasper could provide some dry wood, and she fixed a big meal.

"Wind'n water runnin' free, like me'n you useta," Jasper said to his mother. "Flood just a footprint of somethin' bigger'n us all."

"Is that what you believe?" Rose asked Mabel.

"Yes, Rose."

"Your religion got hold of my boy."

"Well . . ."

"We ain't agreed on what I believe," Jasper said. "But I know what I know, and it ain't no forty days and nights story."

During those first two days after the flood, a kind of innocence prevailed up on the Alligator Road. Before the community began shoveling out, one family would paddle or slog through the water to visit another, share tales of loss and usually a meal. Then both would get up laughing and drop in on a third. The weather was gentle, and out of the act of god surged human caring. Innocence, though, is never proof against tragedy.

IN MEMORIAM

Buck Morgan, Jr.

Last week's Flood of the Century was deadly for those of us who loved young Master Buck Morgan, son of Buck Morgan, Sr. of Africa and Sara Wiggins Morgan, formerly of Bobo Plantation.

He was a boy of intense feeling and heart, if not always thoughtful action, much given to the affection and attention of one and all. Tragic, by all opinion, the accident that took him from us is little known as his mother remains sedated and under the loving watch of her neighbors and loving husband.

It was known that Little Buck, as he was know, loved swimming. He loved climbing trees and roofs and all of the things children do not fear. That he had no fear was his undoing. He was found floating in the high flood by his mother.

A memorial service has been scheduled for Saturday, week, at the home of the bereaved parents. Family and neighbors are invited.

Sara Morgan snapped coming face to face with the unthinkable. Back during the first day of flooding and rain, she
heard her son screaming and searched the house, but he was
not to be found. As she walked back into the front room, she
heard him scream again, just in time to go open the door and
watch her child jumping up and down on a limb in the tree
Sara and Buck had left growing at the corner of their porch
for shade. Before Sare could react, Little Buck turned his face
into the rain and dove head first into the swirling waters
around the porch for he never imagined water too shallow for
diving. Sara screamed and waded in. The child—face un-
bruised but no longer breathing—was floating in flood water
and wedged against a bush growing to screen the space beneath the Morgan house and the ground.

Sara collapsed into the water, grabbed up her inert child
and wept. No one was abroad during the worst of the rain and
flooding, and Sara screamed herself hoarse trying to revive the
child, but nothing worked. When she realized that Little Buck
was dead, the horror of it repulsed her, and she shoved her
son away. And she wept. Hours later, she pulled herself and
her son's body into the by now water stricken house where she
began to bathe the body, over and over again trying to wash
away all smudges of mud and the bruising now covering his

neck and face. But the water was so muddy, Sara finally gave up. She put her son in his bed and took to hers.

No one knew anything about the accident, or about Sara's condition. Hidden away inside the house, when she wasn't sleeping, or weeping, she just lay on a ruined bed inside a mud-floored house, until Buck came home almost two days later. When he opened the front door, Sara was standing in her lounging gown trailing mud, Little Buck in her raised arms like a gruesome present.

"Do something," was all the she would mumble, and she kept repeating herself as if Buck might do something about the tragedy. Buck gently disentangled Sara's arms from the little body and, giving way to his own tears, headed out behind the house to bury his son. Unhappily, the ground was still covered by a couple inches of water, and Buck knew better than to dig in the mud. So, he pulled a tarpaulin out of the barn and wrapped Little Buck securely inside. He put the bloated body on a shelf in the barn and closed the door to keep animals out.

Then he went back inside and led a mud-encrusted Sara out to the pump, and he began to pump a fresher water. Sara was covered in mud and half-deranged.

"Clean yourself up, Queen Lady. Think on your momma. Little Buck gone, and ain't nothin' we can do. You got to pull yourself together."

But Sara did not pull herself together. She just stood blank-eyed until Buck began to pull her near with one hand as he pumped water with the other. There was no one in the vicinity, so Buck snatched the soiled gown from his wife's body and lovingly ladled water over her shoulders, face, body. He left her standing there for the time it took him to run inside for a couple towels. Then he led Sara back inside.

Their bed was a mass of mud. Buck pulled everything off onto the floor and made it up from sheets in the cedar chest that had not taken on water. Sara crawled in and curled up in a fetal position. Buck knew that he had to go get help, but he knew nothing of what had killed his son.

"What happened, Queen Lady?"

"He drowned," came the whimpered answer. Sara did not that day or ever again speak of what she had seen her son do. All she would say to anyone who dared raise the subject was that her son was weak in constitution, that he had not been able to live. They buried him the next day in a grave dug by Lem Huntwell and Art Canada even before Dick and any of those in the swamp could learn of the tragedy.

Fannie and Rose rushed out of swamp to comfort Sara, and the two women slept in the Morgan house to help Sara calm down and to prepare for a commemoration Sara was insisting on for their son. By the time Lem Huntwell returned with them, Buck and Sara had offered to hire a couple of men to shovel mud out their home, but the newcomers from the Road refused the pay and passed the word. Neighbors gathered, sad old songs were sung in snatches, introductions accomplished. The volunteers sloshed buckets of water on the wood floors and swept the mud out. Rugs were hung out to dry, and Buck sent Lem into Alligator to purchase a new bed and some wood chairs. Buck then rode into Clarksdale to find a casket maker to rush a little casket. He also searched out the local photographer to make a large copy of a photo made some time before.

It would be more accurate to call what transpired, a memorial. There was no minister, no theological nicety. The made-up ceremony was like what Buck vaguely remembered from the death of Isaiah's father, Benjamin Montgomery, back at Davis Bend. Buck asked his neighbors to pass the word that there would be a remembrance for Little Buck the morning of the Saturday week after he returned home.

Mabel had waited behind in the swamp with Cicero and Jasper. Actually, she was not sure how much she wanted Bud exposed to what Lem had described most sadly and full of grisly detail about the condition of the child's body. Bud cried

over the death of his playmate, but it was Mabel who was taken
aback enough to question in her own mind how a loving god
could allow an innocent to come to such an end. On top of
the death of her husband before she could deliver Bud, it was
too much. Her answer was to become a Christian who never
looked to her Lord for what she could do herself.

Rose and Fannie helped Sara cut out almost one hundred
black arm bands from a bolt of black crepe that Buck bought.
It was Sara coming out of her fog who told Buck that it was
expected from a man of his stature to write up an obituary to
be inserted in the Clarksdale Newspaper. Cicero volunteered
to do it for him. A painted black box, empty of the already
buried little body, was set in the dining room atop a cedar
chest. Overhead, Sara draped her finest lace table cloth so
that it created an airy tent, one flap raised by a black satin
ribbon pulled to the side and nailed to the wall so that all
could come close and gaze upon the fine white satin pillow
Fannie had sewn to cover the top of the casket. On the pillow
was a huge copy of a portrait of the family, but with the images
of Buck and Sara alongside Little Buck masked in black
crepe.

The life-sized, silver and gray-brown daguerreotype of the
intense child's face, whose huge head seemed too heavy for
his slim neck, was softly lit by flickering candles. Those who
knew him could read the devilment hidden in the huge eyes
startled by the photo flash that had gone off an instant before
the shutter snapped, long lashes almost too pretty for a little
boy. Sara and Buck stood beside the casket ramrod stiff and
formal for almost an hour before a mutual glance sent then
reaching, and to the applause of Rose and others close, embracing. Sara wept for awhile, but afterwards, she began talking to her neighbors for the first time since her crisis began.

There was an impromptu church booster meeting during
the memorial. Several conversations merged, and afterwards
those who'd spoken together promised to pass the word.
Those who came to pay their respects later were told by those

still present of the sentiment. Jasper arrived just before dark. He walked into Buck's house for the first time ever, head bowed. Everyone moved aside and allowed him space. He walked straight up to Buck, Sr.

"I apologize . . . L'il Fella was alright wit me. He was a hellion."

One watching from a perch above the ceiling might have feared that mud clods littering the Morgan's newly cleaned floor from the shoes and boots of guests would turn instantly into mud, there were so many tears. And Jasper was not finished. Holding hands with Mabel, he told the men to finish building the church, that the Lord they, if not him, all worshipped deserved his own house. Rose was the one who demanded that a deadline be set for completion, and they all settled on the fourth Sunday in June.

With so much flood clean-up and rebuilding on top of crop planting and hoeing, the sadness of Little Buck's passing dissipated with the last of the flood. Both seemed harbingers of the uncertainty and of the willfulness of life. Never after, would Africa be quite the same again. No longer pure and introspective in its focus, a corner had been turned. Buck Morgan, Sr., and his outside people were in the ascendant, and yet the extended family was intact, all parts, all minds, all souls still part of Africa.

In the weeks that followed, the women pressed the men to keep them at rebuilding and finishing the church, with the exception of Henry Potts, who flatly refused to worry about a church until his business was running again. Mud was removed. Church floors were shored up where the supporting logs had washed away. Painting commenced, and new oak trees were planted alongside the building to mark the flood for years to come.

Mabel was asked to plan the service. The women who had benefited from Rose's advice and help: Sara, Fannie, and Gloria Canada convinced the other women that Rose should give a homily for the occasion. For the first time, relatives and friends from outside of Africa were invited into the settlement along the Road. People drove from Alligator and Clarksdale. From Mound Bayou, Abyssinia Morgan would drive Buck's mother, Suzy, and herself. Lucille Reid invited her sister up from Cleveland, sister being curious to lay eyes on the handsome admirer Lucille had written about.

The fourth Sunday dawned—the opening chapter in a new book—and it offered a glorious blue sky under which to worship. To those unable to squeeze inside the building, it was as if the music being sung inside resonated in the vault of the sky and brought back the blessing of the sun itself. The old and young, believers and doubters sang together because they felt of one family if not belief. It was a healing feeling, spreading cheer and forgiveness, soothing the wounds of the work week and binding those sitting on wagons outside the tiny church with those inside.

"Y'all stop singin' now," Mabel said.

The crowd quieted, though the women of Africa continued humming as rehearsed. Mabel was standing on a raised platform not yet adorned with a pulpit.

"Y'all free to git with the spirit if you feel it."

Some of the women were standing in place, dancing from the soul.

"I want to acknowledge," Mabel said, "Ms. Alonia Jones and CC's new wife, Phyllis Carruthers, both from Alligator Lake where all the people dance in church. I used to do that myself when we didn't even have no church. Praise the Lord!"

There were rousing "amens" from those in the spirit.

"I want to welcome all of you to this first celebration of our Lord Jesus Christ—now here goes . . . at Mistuh Pleasant—I mean *Mount* Pleasant Missionary Baptist Church."

A scattering of further applause greeted her words.

"Some o' you is Baptist, some Methodist, and some is Holiness, but forgive us peoples, Lord, for dividin' up your fam'ly .

This is a church for all you people out there no matter what you believe, and before we change that, you got to talk to me about it . . . Our most important announcement, we dedicate this service to the memory of all our departed loved ones and in particular, Buck Morgan, Jr. . . . Now, before we hear from Momma Rose, I got a few more announcements to make . . ."

The hypnotic humming turned more subdued. CC's new bride, Phyllis, and Alonia Jones both quit dancing. Mabel leaned over to begin reading again, but she stopped. Her head turned toward Lucille Reid who was singing louder than anybody.

"Got to acknowledge Sistuh Lucille . . ." Mabel waited for Lucille to pay attention. ". . . Lucille'n Frank Reid, from Cleveland—soon to be the parents of a new baby. Praise God!"

Lucille looked startled.

"Praise the Lord!" her husband shouted.

"Bless you, Mabel!"

Mabel craned her neck toward the back of the church. The one who'd shouted was a woman who'd taken Mabel in when the logging company evicted her briefly the week after her husband was slain. Mabel put her hand over her heart in joy, thrust her clenched fist toward the sky and closed her eyes.

"Praise his name, praise his ways!" she said, ending with a tiny wave toward her visitor. "Now, to announcements for today's service . . ."

Fannie had not practiced with the woman's choir—lack of interest on her part rather than a feud—and she didn't know the music. Neither Henry nor Nan Potts had been strong church people, and Fannie was for the first time ever in her life regretting that they hadn't been as she sat quietly with Dick in the second bench from the front, across from Buck and Sara who were singing along behind Mabel's announcements.

Rose was wedged into the front bench between Jasper and Cicero with her eyes closed. She was sweating from being surrounded by so many people in the packed building. In addition to the hot day, she was wrapped in a new long-sleeved white dress to match the other women of Africa. From sitting so long, the feeling was draining out of her arms and legs. Often now, when she would close her eyes and sit for a spell, she wasn't always sure whether she was going into a trance or merely losing feeling in her limbs. A natural consequence of aging, that numbness was, so she wasn't disturbed. More than once, she'd reminded absent-minded Cicero that old people, as they withdrew from the world of young people, had better learn to enjoy the memories they had. It was a truth that Old Bill had left with her. Now, she was pouring over hers, trying to select what to share with the young folks of Africa when she would stand to deliver her homily.

An indescribable joy overwhelmed Rose as she realized that she had not had the power to make what had happened in Africa come to be, but it had. Her gratitude radiated inside a blessed silence, like an opening of herself to all of the powers beyond her sight, especially to Old Bill's Great Spirit because he had been such a great and noble spirit. She began whispering "amen" to every word that was sung or said around her. Bless Cicero, she thought and tightened her grip on his fingers as she began to feel dizzy.

Humming from the congregation overwhelmed Rose. Light began growing and filling the space behind her closed eyelids. The humming focused her feelings, making them vibrate right in the center of her. She was reminded of sunlight in her eyes, of a happy time as a young girl tumbling on a grassy knoll. Little Buck was there, a young life that Rose had not known as a girl giving chase and wrestling with her until his big eyes gave way to a blaze of sun momentarily blocked by his head. She began to move forward toward the light, seeking the living blaze at the core . . . Light—neither warm nor cold—now enveloped her, leaving her just on the verge of an unrealized ecstasy. Shadows around her in the church were flickers on the horizon, each flicker drawing away some of her feeling for the light, and she decided to resist them and to strain instead toward the all-consuming light. At some point she willed herself into the radiance, and it gave birth to new shadows that hardened into form and came alive.

Feelings beyond thought flowed out of them and over her. Opening herself, she was overwhelmed. Her past arrayed itself at the edge of her consciousness like the flickering dark surrounding a torch held close before the eyes at night. And there was music, still, as in a place away where she knew her body awaited. Her momentary focus upon the music had made her less intent on the light, and in the shift of concentration the shadows began closing. Some she recognized, part of herself and yet separate, a corona of hot spurts and dark filaments in the flame of her own being. There was a form etched in brightness and darkness for everyone she had ever known.

Touching her heart first, a warm and unknowable presence that was her birth mother. Then Songhai, who had raised her, surrounded by the vacant unknown faces of the slave pens upon whom she had looked so briefly but with such feeling as to indelibly stamp a response in her own being. Her son, Jasper—no, her first Jasper—incandescing like oil dashed into her flame. She wavered on the verge of letting go of the others and flaring after him, into some realm beyond her own limits where stood the people of childhood, Jamaica Rex, and a white man talking about her weak mind for daring to run away. Others—a multitude of consciousnesses touching and seeking rediscovery—surrounded her like burning air, giving form to her own being and reminding her of when they had shared time and place. Those most familiar remained close, they of past and present, many the people of Africa. It was a realm more real than any she had ever imagined and everybody shared the same eternal being.

But the light dimmed, as when a cloud eclipses the sun, and the anguish of losing it made Rose cry out. She tried to hold all in mind, but the separations of memory had begun to blur. She called names, over and over, amazed that she could speak in a language that spoke to all at once. But she was struggling against the inevitable as the light diminished. Even the most familiar of recent memories lost their knife-edge, and some whom memory had sculpted the moment before now became dust blowing away. Like wind in the cypress trees, the sound of those fading seemed to ebb and to flow as they receded, and her words to them failed. She knew she was close to her body again, feeling the music, which brought a measure of relief and ease. Then she began to feel tired and she quit trying to remain open to the realm of multitude.

She was possessed by a sadness over so much memory being snatched away, and the feeling in her soul grew heavier as she reflected on the violence and suffering that littered her passage from and to her Africa, an ocean of sadness in between, a deep black cold and yet indomitable as the blues as it bore her back up out of the depths. Rage now dominated the music like an harmonic anger suddenly astride melody, twisting and moaning, conjuring pain that refused to fade. Rose felt empty as a moan at midnight, and then the pain lost its edge, anger shaded back into a remembered sadness, and the music made her its own. She was cradled into a place of rest. All of the hovering people of the church were there. Cicero was crying. He and Jasper were holding Rose's hands. Her locked fingers had to be pried from their own.

"Turn loose, Momma Rose," Mabel said.

Off to one side, as if not a part of what was happening, sat Lucille Reid, sobbing. It was she upon whom Rose's eyes came to rest.

"Lucille?"

Lucille covered her face.

"Momma Rose in the spirit," someone shouted.

Two women tried to lift and bring Lucille forward, but she planted her feet and refused to be moved. She began screaming, and they left her on the floor, weeping.

"You stop worrying child," Rose said. "God always provide in his own way. Your baby gonna be fine."

For some reason unknown to the people standing about, Rose's words seemed to calm Lucille. She allowed herself to be brought forward by the two white-garbed sisters, and Rose smoothed her hands over the young woman's face.

"These oughtta be tears of joy over life . . . Let 'em be, Lucille."

"You was speakin' in tongues, Momma Rose," Mabel said. "I ain't never seen that. Praise Jesus! An' you was callin' our names and names that musta been prophets—Lucille's name, too."

Off in the edge of the crowd, Sara Morgan was holding her arms as if clutching her son to her bosom and raising again her beautiful soprano voice in song.

In December, Lucille Reid delivered a beautiful baby girl. No one knows why she named the baby Catherine. At the time, no one asked or thought there was reason to ask because it was a matter between her and Frank. Catherine was colored like caramel at birth, and because many babies are lighter at birth than their parents, no one in the community thought anything of it. The sun would ripen the child to her natural color, nearer the hues of her parents. But came the spring, and the sun proved powerless to darken up little Catherine, not even close to her mother's rich brown, let alone Frank Reid's blue blackness.

In the middle of May, the people of Africa along the Alligator Road who happened to be outside were surprised to see Lucille walking so soon after being all bruised up, she said, from a fall off her front porch while bending over to watch the daffodils sprout. Lucille seemed strangely preoccupied on her walk and spoke to none of those who waved and nodded neighbor-like off their front porches as she passed with Catherine in her arms.

Extension of family is a common Africa love. Before Lucille's own confinement, for some reason none who took note understood, Lucille spent more time with Sara than did some of the women Sara had known longer. "God always provides for us sinners," was all that Lucille would share with those who questioned her, except that once when she got fed up with a neighbor's meddling, Lucille told the woman to go read her bible and that Momma Rose was a prophet in her own lifetime. Such opinion aside, Lucille and Frank Reid were still so very poor that it was not without precedent when Lucille appeared at Sara's house that day in May and gave Catherine to Sara to raise as her own.

Call 1 (866) 455-8209
if your bookstore does not stock *Africa, Love.*